The

Split

By Kyle J Schweihs

Widespread infection.

Ignorant people.

Miscommunication.

Desperate and feeble.

~ . ~

Corrupt government.

Civil war.

Sudden deployment.

No more.

To all of you cool people.

This is my first novel in what I hope to be a long career of writing. This story holds a special place in my heart, and it always will. What you are about to read is the product of several years of revision and devotion of time that should've been spent doing schoolwork. I'd say time well spent. This loops back to my teachers in school, the ones who told me to always keep writing. I owe them much gratitude, an immeasurable amount.

The same immeasurable gratitude I owe to my family. My Mom was always supportive and offered ideas that I hadn't previously thought of when I experienced writers block. My Dad isn't the most literarily engaged man, but nevertheless, he tried and that's what matters. Both my Mom and Dad are my biggest cheerleaders, and I don't know what I'd do without them or the unconditional love and support they provide. To Mom and Dad: thank you truly from the bottom of my heart. You guys are pretty neat.

I would also like to thank my Grandma Bonnie. She designed the cover of this novel with her unmatched artistic abilities. The breathtaking cover wouldn't be possible if it weren't for her tremendous efforts. Though we're separated by several states, she shows as much support as anyone else I've mentioned. Thank you, Grandma, I hope to see you soon.

I owe as much gratitude to all who helped this novel come to life. People suggesting ideas/helping with editing and friends along the way telling me that they can't wait to read it. Nothing means more to me than all the people in my life, people are impossibly valuable, and you cannot put a price on how much I truly value the relationships I've built in this town. Though a small town, one with flaws, I owe it to the people who live here. Much love to everyone I know, you guys are awesome.

Publishing this is the biggest thing I've ever done. I hope sincerely that you enjoy yourself while reading my work.

And now, my gratitude goes to you, the reader. Thank you.

Enjoy the book.

THE SPLIT

Division is rampant, the people are *split*. In the midst of a highly political civil war in the U.S, a virus begins to slowly infect the populous.

Things aren't getting better, they're getting worse. Things won't be good for a long time to come, the only thing that people can do is fight back or run away. The military was covering up what was already common knowledge. People weren't dumb, they knew what was coming.

But nobody knew how bad it was truly going to be.

Nobody was prepared, except the military of course.

Prologue

"Are you scared?"

Her voice was a light in the dim hopelessness that he felt conjuring deep in his gut. His mind was racing, but his mouth was silent. She knew he was scared, but somehow it seemed like she should ask him to confirm.

"I'll be back in no time."

He wouldn't.

"Yeah, but you don't have to be scared. Jade and I will be here waiting for you."

They wouldn't.

"I know, I know."

He didn't know anything.

Slouched over the kitchen counter with a light strung above him, poorly illuminating his body and casting a shadow beneath. He laced his fingers nervously. He was just hours away from having everything taken away. He didn't want to cry. He didn't want to go. All he wanted was more time.

The day before deployment was spent with his wife and daughter, his two favorite people. But time went so fast, so incredibly fast. It didn't seem fair.

"You're going to be okay over there, they'll like you."

"Yeah… maybe."

He wasn't too sure. Giving her a vague response seemed to prolong the inevitable, but she only had so much to say to him. He moved his hands to his head, wrapping them around and then moving them back down to the counter, lacing them once more.

"I just don't want to go."

"I know, but sometimes we just have to."

She also tried to comfort herself, crossing her arms around her body and giving the feeling that she was being held. She didn't want her husband on the front lines, certainly not out west. Someone had to do it and unfortunately it was the man she married.

"I want to be here, for her."

He sternly motioned upstairs to his daughter who was already in bed.

"She needs guidance, and I don't want you to deal with that alone."

She stopped for a second, thinking about what to say next. She put her hand to her mouth and chin, then relinquished the next line of dialogue.

"We'll be fine, I promise you. Don't worry about us."

She told him not to worry, although she knew he would regardless of anything she said.

He knew that they'd ultimately be fine and chose to put his faith in that.

"But will you?"

"Yeah, of course."

~ . ~

He left before anyone had woken up. He wanted to save the goodbyes for another time and simply leave it off on a happy note. The sun hadn't even started to glimmer beyond the horizon, he was on the road. The bumps in the buckled Minnesotan pavement rocked the car back and forth with each pothole. No music played through the speakers, not even the morning radio. One hand was on the steering wheel and the other was pressed sternly against his forehead.

The winding road led out of the Whitewater valley, presenting Evan with the same splendor he had laid his eyes on hundreds of times before.

He was filled with dread.

The silence that filled his car was so loud. The engine produced a shallow hum that was barely noticeable within the cab. He didn't blink. He didn't breathe. He didn't take his eyes off the road. He didn't admire the splendor, he simply lowered his foot on the acceleration. His speed increased steadily, now going almost 80 MPH down the road. Autumn leaves uplifted, shooting high above to drift along the gusts of late summer.

Not a single molecule in his body wished to keep driving down the road. He wanted to turn around. He wanted out.

Sure, he'd been through basic training up North and participated a bit regarding Military functions - but never was he in the loop about being deployed. Especially in somewhat of a leader position. He wasn't prepared.

With the landscape flying by and his foot pressing the pedal, tears developed in his eyes and goosepimples patterned his skin. Every flashing memory and distant joy was now so far away that he couldn't feel anything, but the ineffable feeling of anxiety.

He had no clue of what was yet to come.

Driving that distance to the armory engraved the feeling of fear into the folds of his brain. Driving all that way just to be flown out to a city he's never been, to fight people he's never met, and deal with things he's never seen.

One fist gripped the wheel so hard that the veins looked like burst pipes, the other fist had the index and middle finger extended and pressed against his forehead. It felt like blood was about to start pouring from his nose, like his head was going to explode.

Kate was going to be okay, so was Jade. But the thought of being gone disturbed Evan beyond recovery. He couldn't stop cycling through thought after thought, thinking of this and that. Making up scenarios that would never come true, and simply worrying about things that weren't going to happen. His eyebrows settled against his eyes, fiery glow from the pupils as he stared at the rising sun. It wasn't blinding, it was infuriating.

How was time allowed to go on without him at home? It wasn't right.

He wasn't angry at anyone, just angry at the situation. The only person he felt any sort of distain for was the man who called him up to go out West. A high-ranking officer who ripped Evan from his home and planned to use him as a pawn in this civil war. Even then it wasn't anger that Evan felt.

It was resentment.

The men at the top always got to determine how the men near the bottom were allowed to live. The word resentment started to feel too tame for the way Evan was beginning to feel.

He would manage.

Chapter 1

Introduction

Evan had never been this cold in his life.

The frozen and bitter air scraped against his cheeks, leaving them a permanent red as the blood inside tried to stay liquid rather than solid. Not an atom of his being wanted to move from his spot. He was cold, but he was comfy.

First, he heard the howling of the wind, the only thing that he could hear in fact. Second, he felt snowflakes descending upon his face, like tiny needles penetrating their target. Third, he regained his sense of smell; fresh Winter air filled his nostrils and froze the tiny hair within.

He was too exhausted to open his eyes. He sat there for an amount of time that was unable to be measured. It could've been 2 minutes or 2 hours. His eyes darted around in the darkness that his lids created. Suddenly, they shot wide open.

Analyzing his surroundings, seeing only the inside of the helicopter. His weight was shifted to the right and when he looked to see why, he observed a steep incline that led to a twenty-foot drop onto a tiled floor.

His eyes widened and his heart dropped.

The seatbelt that strapped him to the seat was tight and when he tried to loosen it, he was met with resistance. He moved his right foot to hold himself steady enough as to not slide out of the helicopter. Now giving the seatbelt some slack, he wiggled out.

His boot slipped while attempting to free himself, sliding onto the floor towards imminent doom, exclaiming a groan like whimper. He outstretched his left hand to catch himself, successfully gripping a handlebar. As he looked down, his feet just barely dangled outside. Along with all this movement, the helicopter responded accordingly.

Creaking and croaking violent metallic shudders as it began to rock back and forth.

Evan now lifted his legs into the small compartment, pulling himself further out of the steep slope. Using whatever strength he could muster to get himself out of there. His dirtied hands grasped for handlebars and loose straps, he felt screwed. He now managed to see perfectly into the cockpit.

Two men lay dead, both sunk deep into their seats. Frozen blood caked their pale skin. One pilot was pimpled and had probably been out of college for just a couple years. The other one was obviously a senior officer; the gray goatee was shaded a dim scarlet from the blood that had flowed from a forehead laceration.

Evan's eyes blurred and focused, thinking to himself thoughts of terror. He couldn't open his mouth due to how absolutely dehydrated he was. He simply shook his head, closing his eyes and choosing to press on.

He had been in a terrible accident.

Evan's hands were pricked up and riddled with scabs. His fingers were sore and stung at each seam. He avidly chewed his nails, so that didn't help much. The pain in his fingers made it harder to keep moving up, he wanted to give up.

He couldn't.

Evan could now see where the helicopter had landed. He recognized it as the second-floor overhang of…something? He was too zapped of energy to continue assuming where he might be. All he knew was where he needed to be, and that was out of the helicopter and on that overhang.

Just feet away now, Evan reached for the edge of the chopper door, grabbing ahold, and using his feet to bring himself upward.

Suddenly there was a sickening, loud thrash along with instant bending of the chopper. It sounded as if someone had chopped down a tree, a huge one at that. Evan frantically swung his boots under the seats and flung himself further ahead.

He was preparing to jump.

When he heard the overhang concrete floor begin to crack, he gripped the outside door of the helicopter. Using all the strength he had left to leap out of the chopper. Everything slowed to a stutter, the world rotated below him; he could feel every bone in his body being labored with Earth's gravity.

Evan landed about five feet away from the edge, just as the chopper let loose and shot away from him.

Now on the ravaged concrete overhang, the once stable surface cracked and shuddered with Evan on it. He sprawled away, and scrambled to his feet while wiping his nose of snot.

The helicopter made a truly horrifying noise as it plummeted, destroying the tiled flooring; flattening all that was below. Evan rolled onto his back, accidentally slamming his head onto the frigid tile. His chest rose and fell with each and every labored breath. Laying there and staring at the ceiling, he managed to turn his head despite how tight his muscles were, trying to recognize his surroundings.

It had to be a mall, there's no way that it wasn't.

Countless shops and kiosks consumed the walls and corridors. Goofily chosen names for the stores and obviously pointless cosmetic products. The helicopter had crashed through the sunroof, smashing it to pieces and letting all the snow into the small corner of the mall. Evan scrambled to his feet and felt his brain sink like a deflated dodgeball.

While standing on the ravaged corner of the overhang, he gripped his side and then his arm. He took his hand away and saw it wet with fresh, red blood. It was at this point he noticed a horrific gash on his forearm. He held his arm tight now, constricting the blood flow. His teeth grinded, finally noticing the extreme wound. It didn't hurt until he knew it was there.

To his left there was a long winding corridor, and in front of him was yet another corridor that led out of view. Every other direction was what he could assume to be a dead end.

Shops were all around.

Behind him was a small staircase that led to the ground floor, he put his hand to his forehead and rubbed his tired eyes. It was only now he recognized his clothing.

A large military vest with patted sleeves and pants, no helmet, however. There was a small pouch that was slung over his back, heavy in weight but small in size. His vest weighed down his limp body, ensuring that his movements were limited. His cheekbones tightened the skin around his mouth, almost as if his lips were stitched together. His almost clean-shaven face was disrupted by uneven patches of scruff, sandpaper like stubble.

Evan moved his dry hand down from his forehead to his mouth, feeling the rough hair scrape against his hand. His eyelids lifted and before he could limp to the staircase, an unnerving and disturbing noise made his body pimple up.

Words couldn't begin to explain the ferocity and animalistic shudders behind the noise. He flinched, beginning to back away almost as if he'd heard the scream of a banshee. The tattered railing stopped him from backing up, making him slip onto his butt.

He coughed briefly, looking in the direction of where the noise came from. Evan winced his eyes, as if he were trying to see something in greater detail.

Despite his observations, there was nothing to see.

The perpetrator who had made that noise was nonexistent. He looked around, horrified at what he had heard, anticipating another holler. The sheer moments afterword filled him with dread, as if he knew a bullet was headed his way.

After a couple seconds of the wind competing with the peaceful silence of the abandoned mall, the silence won.

The shroud of terror wasn't heard again. For a moment, he thought he might've been going crazy.

His skin was pimpled with fear and his teeth scraped with anticipation. He didn't have the slightest clue as to what had made such a noise, this 'unknowingness' was the scariest part. He used the railing to help himself up, raising above and getting to his feet.

Evan looked around feeling as though someone was watching him; however, he found no watchful eyes. Not a single bone in his body conjured a single identifiable emotion. It was all a blend. Fear, fright, madness, fear again, cluelessness, dismay.

His pupils dilated while staring through the sunroof.

Now slipping his phone out of his pocket, he started to dial the numbers 9-1-1. No ring or even a caller I.D, nobody picked up and the only sound that could be heard was that of a beeping call error. Confused and dazed by the situation, Evan started off toward the stairs. Thoughts still fluttered around in his head, thinking about what had happened and why it happened. He didn't even know what day it was.

He now walked down the steps; his spine would make him want to shout in pain every step he went down. He again looked at the gash, it looked as though someone had taken a katana to it. It left splotches of blood every step of the way, painting the misplaced and powdered snow a dark and dim red.

"How did I not realize that my forearm had literally been gashed open? Maybe I just didn't notice it? Or maybe it was the adrenaline?" Evan thought to himself. He wanted to started chewing his fingernails, but they had already been gnawed to the stub.

Now finding himself at the bottom of the stairs, he approached the chopper wreck. Crushed bodies of the pilots flamed apart in Evan's mind. Their torsos were pinned beneath the heavy mass and their heads were ready to pop like a festering zit. The chopper had slammed down so hard that it had displaced tile and thrown debris all around. He tried to steady himself, leaning against the chopper. His eyes did the tango back and forth looking for the massive red cross.

No first aid kit could be spotted, just an open wound with infection soon to come he thought. He fell to his knees.

Wondering *how on earth* he was where he was.

Evan thought to himself for a quick second, figuring he could find a craft store, one that moms would frequent quite often. Thread and needles were bound to be abundant.

Evan looked down corridor one and corridor two, shops and kiosks galore. Tons of bizarre names and odd designs crowded signs and logos, along with a small fountain in the center of this specific intersection. One thing that disturbed the environment was propaganda banners with big military outfitted soldiers and words hinting to a draft, Evan had seen thousands of these already. He eventually chose to go down the second corridor.

He would struggle walking, the blood loss was beginning to disorient him, light headedness made it difficult to drag each foot forward. He hadn't felt like this before, it was a new sensation. He couldn't focus on more than one thing at a time.

He walked down the winding hallways, the ceiling seemed to be getting higher, and the walls blended with the floor.

He tumbled to his knees while trying to steady himself, gripping his arm. Looking to his right and then to his left. Conveniently discovering a craft store, "*Miranda's Scrapbooking*." Evan tried getting up only to stumble and shake his head.

Despite the cold air, sweat dripped from his hair and curled the longer strands. The dark coils swung in front of his eyes with each step.

Evan crawled over to the store and when he got to the doorway, he used it to his advantage, grappling to the door handles and lifting himself up. His forearm now throbbed and pulsated with an explosive rage.

He scanned the store through the window, everything was mostly intact, which was different from most of the other stores he managed to peer inside off. The cash register had been thrown across the room and picked clean, but everything on the shelves was still present. The last thing people should be worrying about in a civil war is how they're going to scrapbook their memories.

Evan struggled through the door and dodged storage cabinets and shelves. Limited capability and unforeseen weakness made him unbalanced and fumble to his knees. His usually tan face was stained pale.

He managed to find the thread section, figuring that if nothing else, he would use a pin as his suture.

Evan looked back at his gashed arm. His eyes danced around finding and searching for thread. He stood up and held his arm, the pain shot through his nerves like a freight train. Evan reached to his left and grabbed a roll of navy-blue thread, lowering it to where he was sitting. He attached the end of the pin to the end of the thread while whispering to himself.

"Jesus… Christ." He shut his eyes tight and opened them. "What the—" he paused again, "Heck."

His arm shook, holding the makeshift suture. Steady adrenaline pumped through his veins, fearing for his next action. He glanced at the blood gushing out of his forearm and then his eyes rose into his head.

He was terrified.

His eyes dropped down out of his skull and centered on his shaking hand, flexing the muscles and resting them. He lowered his hand down to the gash. Unable to use both of his hands for the procedure proved to be difficult. The needle entered one side of the open wound and then looped through the other side.

Evan was doing something that was unbelievably crazy. Never once in his life did he think he'd be giving himself stitches and following through with every individual suture.

He groaned with each deep threading. The pain was something he'd never felt before. He bit his teeth down, each tooth scraping against another one.

After briefly setting the needle and thread down on his camouflage trousers, he pulled out his wallet and set in in his mouth. Tears wouldn't leave his eyes despite how desperately they needed to leave.

Evan then picked the suture up once more and continued. Loop after loop, steady as can be. Struggling to be exact with the incisions of the needle, his head throbbing ever so hard. Evan bit down on the wallet with such force it felt as though the leather was tearing.

He kept suturing the gash, praying for the pain to end. When he was about halfway done, Evan set the bloody needle and thread onto his pants. He looked at the messy job he'd done.

It was the best he could do with only one hand.

A thought then occurred to him, thinking about the resulting infection. There was no way anything he was using happened to be sterile.

Relentlessly, he picked up the needle and started once again, groaning, and shouting with pain. His eyelids shut closed like a vault door to the most secure facility in the world. His eyebrows lowered to a slant as he pierced his skin again, accidentally touching the open wound. His lips were dry with pain and his heartbeat was becoming faint and weak from the blood loss.

As he neared the end of the procedure, he pulled the string taut and semi-sealed the wound. With his left hand, he searched the infinite pockets of the military vest. His broad and skinny shoulders just barely held the vest up. To his disbelief he found gauze wrap and hydrogen peroxide, this was an absolute miracle. He poured the hydrogen peroxide along his arm and waited for the bubbling to stop. It stung like hell, but he managed to only let a few groans of pain escape his frail body. The peroxide bubbled and fizzed dramatically, oozing out of the slits the stiches left. It fizzed for about a minute or two, then Evan poured more peroxide, making sure that the wound was no longer at risk of infection.

After the second round of the peroxide stopped fizzing, Evan put the now empty bottle back in the pocket that he had found it in. He picked up the roll of gauze and carefully wrapped it around his forearm.

After wrapping several layers of gauze around his arm, he pulled it tight. So tight that it felt like a permanent cast.

His fingers felt like they had fallen asleep, as if every inch of his hand was being punctured with tiny, microscopic needles.

He laid there, his back up against a supply shelf. He couldn't believe what he had just done. He exhaled shallow breaths, sucking air slowly. He could feel the cold air creep down is throat and touch the membrane inside his lungs. His ears were red from the cold Winter fog and each tiny noise was comparable to headphones at full blast.

His self-conscious thoughts were his only friend now.

He tried getting up and slipped, falling onto his knees hard. His empty stomach growled, trying to speak to him. Evan tried getting up once more, feeling defeated. He limped to the doorway, holding his bonded and bandaged arm, and looking back at the tremendous blood splotch where he once sat.

The voice inside his head shouted for *warmth and shelter*.

Evan wandered back to the chopper crash site, thinking of his next meal. His stomach was vacant and in dire need of sustenance.

As Evan turned the corner and saw the ravaged chopper, atop the wreckage were the massive piercing eyes of an owl. Yellow and burning, the owl wouldn't turn its gaze away from Evan, as if it was God looking upon a sinner.

Evan stood there, staring back at the bird. Both of their eyes locked in a strange silent war. The owl somehow had made Evan lose the staring contest, whether by shear spite or the fact that Evan's eyes were beginning to sting. When Evan opened his eyes again, the owl had disappeared. He was unsuccessful in trying to relocate the owl.

Shaking off the possible hallucination, he figured he would need a weapon. He had no idea what could be waiting out there wanting to harm him. Now becoming paranoid, every little noise was a sort of trigger or alarm for his brain. He stumbled, holding onto the chopper to steady his fall. Evan searched the wreck as best as he could, finding a few smashed firearms. He found that either the stock was missing, there was no ammunition, the barrel was bent, or the guarding was shattered.

His hands were perfectly sculpted to fit his face, sinking down into the palms out of disappointment. He looked up at the second level overhang and identified a possible candidate.

A hardware store, he hoped that supplies would still be somewhat copious. "*Hardware Hanks*" was the name.

He struggled to ascend the stairway, walking past the tattered railing and desolate overhand.

The image of his arm slit wide open, the massive gash spewing blood. It was an unexplainable PTSD that burned like an unresolvable forest fire, one that would burn for years.

After reaching the hardware store, he tried to open the door. He gripped the handles and pulled at the glass threshold.

He shook the doors, letting them rattle with each movement. Now with all the strength he had, he shook them as hard as he possibly could. He managed to shatter one door and leave the other slightly damaged. The salt like shards landed on Evan, requiring him to shake off like a wet dog.

He walked around the small hardware store, observing that everything that had any sort of purpose had been taken.

It was a disturbing sight, a store with no products.

Suddenly, this overwhelming stench that burned the hair in his nose surrounded him. He turned his head in disgust, gagging at this odor and now trying to locate where it was coming from.

Alas, behind the service counter lay a pair of boots, limp and lifeless. Stepping closer and having the stench get stronger, Evan closed his eyes and plugged his nose. Now he saw it; the corpse's head was hacked open, right down the middle, with a hatchet imbedded in its head. Evan stood, appalled, frozen in place. Realizing the only weapon in the whole store was imbedded in a dead man's forehead.

Evan took hold of the hatchet and unlatched it out of the cranium. Evan's eyes centered on the hatchet and then the gaping valley in the corpse's skull.

Disgust.

He shook his head and chose not to think about it. As he walked back to the staircase, he attempted to identify a good place to build a fire. He figured he could use the snow that had entered through the sunroof as drinking water.

He thought he could also use the snow has a bed of sorts, using it as a blanket and packing it around himself to conserve heat. He started scanning the environment for something to use as a firestarter. He identified a Zen themed banzai tree kiosk and instantly knew how he was going to build a fire.

He reached the small fountain in the middle of that intersection and set up his camp opposite to the chopper, against the polished stone fountain. He took the pouch off his back and leaned it against the polished bricks. Assembling a small circular indent into snow below the sunroof. He picked apart the numerous banzai trees he'd taken, preparing them. He set them in the middle and set the smaller branches within to be used as kindling.

He sat down for the first time since sewing his arm back together and slipped his huge overweight vest off.

Evan started going through every pocket on that vest. There had to be something that would help him start a fire, right? After five minutes of searching, all that he found was a small coil of rope, some crumbs, and a spare ammo clip for a pistol that was no longer holstered at his hip. He sighed.

"That's it?"

An idea struck him.

Now taking the hatchet, swiftly scraping the polished stone next to him, creating a wave of sparks. He did this repeatedly until the small little trees began to burn. The tiny foreign leaves would slowly ignite with each shower of sparks.

The fire started with a small flame that slowly tiptoed over to the twigs. The fire expanded up one of the sticks and started enlarging. Evan waved his frail hands at the fire, feeding it oxygen. Now the fire had engulfed the entire teepee, despite the cold air that surrounded each flame.

The sun was beginning to set, Evan could tell even through the thick blizzard clouds. Things were always quiet during the Winter. The suffocating landscape dampened all sounds. As the small fire began to illuminate his face, he would cup snow in his hands and put little bite-sized pieces into his mouth, melting them to water.

The fire provided a very minuscule amount of warmth, but Evan tried his best to bask in every bit that he could.

After having his serving of snow pellets, he sat down in a small snow drift close to the fire, establishing this as his bed. Shoveling out a little indent in the snow, then laying within.

A strange thought entered his head as he began situating himself, like he was forgetting something. As if he left the oven on. It was on the tip of his tongue; he just couldn't pinpoint it. Laying there and staring at the wide-open smashed sunroof, he tried to figure it out desperately.

The woman he married, and the daughter they shared.

He figured it out, his wife and his daughter. *How had I forgotten?* It had to have been the shock from the crash, he thought. In that same thought, he felt his eyes start to decay, as if he were looking at the sun.

Evan slipped a small and wrinkled photograph out of his left pocket, almost forgetting it was even there. He set it on the snow next to him.

The faces of the two most valuable people were printed on the photo. Evan had brought it out West when he was deployed so he'd always have the two of them by his side.

"How had I forgotten?"

He wanted to get up and start searching for his family, but his body simply wouldn't allow him. He slipped into a rough slumber.

Chapter 2

Deranged Humanity

Desperate glimmers of light shone through the damaged clouds.

Evan stood up in a desolate field with knee high brush. He looked around into seemingly endless landscape, nothing was in the distance, nothing was nearby.

His hunger was satisfied, his thirst was quenched. He was comfortable.

He was wearing a gray flannel shirt with his sleeves rolled up, and felt almost lightheaded when he came upon a set of ruins. Evan winced to see it clearer, finally recognizing it as his home.

The same place he raised his daughter.

A nice stone foundation complimented the white chipping paint that surrounded the outside.

Except that this wasn't his house, or at least how he remembered it; all the windows had wooden boards nailed over them. No lights were turned on, no life was within.

He walked around to the front of the house and tried knocking on the door. A long silence ensued before someone knocked back.

Evan spoke desperately, "Hello? Is anyone there?"

A body was then thrown through the window next him. Evan had known the body and the face; it was that of his wife. It was indistinguishable from any other person on the planet.

Glass had shattered onto the floor, crashing everywhere. Her pretty and pale face complimented by her noticeably dark and curly hair.

He felt his stomach flip upside down before feeling the urge to vomit.

Suddenly, everything went dark. Everything was silent. Through the winding hallways and corridors of the mall, glass was shattered. Sure, it was far away, but the sound of glass being shattered would wake anyone up.

Evan's eyes shot open in suspense, he glanced around frantically; still being in the exact same position he had fallen asleep in. He cleared off the compacted snow and attempted to stand up. When I (the author) say he *attempted to stand up,* I mean he completely faceplanted into the tile.

More windows shattered.

After his humiliating tumble, Evan got to one knee and used it to stand up. His legs were sore and felt strained as if he had run a marathon the day before. His injured arm felt absolutely stiff. Nothing could get it to move.

He recalled his dream but could barely remember it. He scratched his head while noticing that the wrinkled family photograph had drifted a few feet from where he had set it the night prior.

The first thing he did that day was reclaim that picture.

As Evan awoke and regained all of his senses, he heard another window frame shatter along with a bunch of quiet and distant shooshing. He stumbled to his feet and slung the pouch around to his back. He figured it was just best to get up and get a move on, but every little movement drained more and more energy.

He now followed the previously mentioned noises, creeping through the long halls until he felt like he was getting lost. Out of his peripheral vision he thought he had spotted a tiny wildlife store. It was smooshed between two equally sized clothing stores and blocked off from the outside world by a gated shutter door. The name of the store was "*10,001 Lakes.*"

Evan pressed his face against the glass and used his hands to cover the reflections. He saw a rack of bows near the back of the store, he figured this would be the best option. Before resuming his hunt to discover the origin of smashed windows, he better show up with a way to defend himself. Now walking over to the shutter door and with an idea in his head.

With his fingertips, he began to lift the heavy gated door. He was only able to lift it about a foot off the ground before the gash on his arm started to pulsate with unbearable pain.

Still keeping the shutter door from the ground, he got to his knees and began sliding underneath like a snake between limestones. Now letting go of the heavy gate, he got to his feet and massaged his beat-up arm.

His eyes glanced around and located the bows toward the back. Different colors and different models to pick from. From modern bows to crossbows to simply traditional old-fashioned bows. Trying to pick from all of these narrowed down how much he knew about them—which of course was nothing. He figured he should just go with the traditional bow, knowing that if he chose one of the modern ones, he would easily get confused and probably end up shooting an arrow into his own foot.

Evan was still extremely underdressed, but this was helped by periodically wiggling his toes up and down inside of his boots like a second grader does at recess in February.

The beautiful wood finish was smooth to the touch and the string was tightly taut to the top and bottom. Evan now picked out the appropriate arrow to go along with his bow. He slipped the spare arrows in between the slots in his belt, keeping them perpendicular with his torso.

He used the same technique to exit the store, sliding his bow out first and them himself.

He got back to his feet and groaned with pain. Down the hall was a sign hanging from the ceiling that indicated a food court was ahead. While he came upon the massive plaza, he became increasingly paranoid.

He glanced around, trying to get the upper hand on whoever had entered the mall.

Evan loaded an arrow and had his other hand resting on the string, ready to fire at any given moment. He searched around looking for who had entered the mall, only seeing a couple shattered frames near the front entrance.

Suddenly from behind him, a plate or something fell onto the ground and crashed, making a ton of noise. Evan flung around and pointed his bow at the two fast food shops where the noise emanated from, he couldn't identify which shop it came from.

He thought about talking, about shouting; but that thought was short lived and quickly suppressed.

The food court was quiet; no one spoke at all. Evan wasn't sure what to expect. His eyes watered; he wished his eyes had a windshield wiper to clear away the developing condensation.

It was so quiet that Evan swore he could hear his own thoughts as if they were playing on the intercom.

Finally, the thought was reincarnated and overcame the suppression. Evan spoke, "Hello? Anyone? Is anyone there?"

He was interrupted when a man rolled out from behind a counter in the store to Evan's left. Slow enough to notice, quick enough to be caught off-guard.

The man had a pistol pointed directly at Evan; he could almost see right down the barrel.

The man instantly started shouting, "Put that fucking bow down! Or I'll shoot!" The pistol being wielded by Evan's opponent was quite bland, almost entirely carbon colored.

Evan didn't lower his bow. He at first was shocked at the unveiling of the gun but quickly grew defensive. His training had prepared him for moments like this.

Evan quickly observed this man's appearance, he had a long lengthy black beard, and his hair was buzzed on the sides with a bit longer hair on the top. Evan couldn't analyze every distinguishing feature in such a short amount of time.

Without notice, the man flicked off the safety and gave Evan one last warning.

"Please put the gun down man, come on."

Evan stood there, like a wild West showdown; tumbleweeds and everything. The whistling wind from the broken windows shifted and blew snow around.

Evan wanted to deescalate the situation at any cost as the man readied to fire. After a couple moments of silence and tension, the man and Evan's eyes zeroed in and glared at one another.

Without any sort of way to predict such a move, the man shot at Evan. Missing the first shot, and barely missing the second shot.

Evan of course knew that bullets would be flung his way, he had already analyzed nearest cover and possible flanks. He fled to cover in a hurry, which was only a couple of upturned tables and chairs. He heard a deranged cry of some sort. A womanly cry. "Stop!" she shouted.

Evan had thought the man most likely had his wife or girlfriend traveling with him.

He slowly exited cover, shouting to the man. "Don't shoot!"

The man still held the gun, pointing it firmly at Evan. He stood up but acted injured. Acting as though a bullet had hit him.

The man had fallen for Evan's ploy and started walking toward him. Still waving the gun, telling Evan to throw his hands in the air, "Now jackass! Don't make me put the finishing shot in!"

Evan prepared his attack, readying his trembling hands.

He stopped dead in his tracks the same time the man did. Both stuttered for a moment when the atmosphere fell silent.

All of a sudden, Evan reached back to his pouch and flipped it over his shoulder, striking his opponent and knocking the gun from his hand. Evan then proceeded to tackle the man onto the tile.

All of this quick movement would usually make a man with a gash in his arm yelp like a puppy, but when you've got adrenaline flowing through your veins, you aren't exactly able to recognize what's painful and what isn't.

The womanly voice screamed out in defiance.

Evan hit the man, once, twice, three times! The woman came over with a tray from the store and whopped Evan right in the face.

The man recovered from his embarrassment and scrambled to his feet. "Holy shit," he exclaimed.

He retrieved his gun and instantly directed it at Evan, the wife stepped in front of Evan as she had a natural dislike for violence. Keep in mind, Jackson didn't much like violence either but when faced with a threat, he would do anything to keep it far away from the ones he loved.

Evan could hardly think, his eyelids refused to open and all he could hear was loud inaudible shouting. He blacked out.

He couldn't hear or remember anything. The darkness consumed him as his brain coughed out a few more thoughts. He wondered if he was dead; wondering if this was it. The void in his lids sucked his consciousness downward. Within seconds, he was out.

~ . ~

Saturday date nights in Rochester, making faces at his wife from across the table and playing tag with their feet beneath. Movies after dinner and laughter all throughout. They'd bring home pizza for Jade, and all fall asleep on the couch together.

When Kate would tell stories at dinner, Evan would listen. Chirping in with inciteful quick-witted statements that made her giggle. Never once did a story of hers fail to entertain Evan. Never did a quick-witted quip ever disappoint Kate. They were made to frolic in the comfort they each provided.

If only he could relive just one of those nights.

The void that he had fallen within suddenly puked him out, throwing him onto another cold floor.

His eyes twinkled awake; the great brightness above blinded him. When he heard a voice, he lifted his head and muttered a few inaudible words.

The first person he saw was a new one, it was a kid.

The walls and furniture in the building looked like an ice cream parlor. Pink and blue shades on the walls along with swivel chairs around the front counter.

The boy stood up quickly and spoke to someone whom Evan could not see yet. The kid had dark brown silky hair, tan skin and by looking into his eyes you could tell that he hadn't had a good rest in what could've been days. His hair bounced every time he shifted his head.

"The man—he's awake!"

A women walked over and squatted next to Evan, her golden fluffy hair and pale skin matched perfectly with her baggy sweatshirt, dirty jeans and mismatched socks. Evan couldn't believe that someone like her had knocked him out with a lunch tray.

She spoke, "My name is Ana, this is Matt, my son." She gestured, "I think you can help us."

She had a dimple on her left cheek that would appear and disappear just as fast, never being able to look at it long enough to remember that it was there in the first place.

Evan remembered what had happened. "What- no, what the heck, you guys tried to kill me?! No! I need to find my family, I need to get away, where are the police?"

Ana tried to calm him, "Matt, go get your dad."

Matt got up and followed his mother's direction while Evan babbled on. "Do you know what is going on? Do you guys have fresh water? Any food around here? I'm starving!"

Evan bombarded Ana with questions desperately, as if she knew how to answer anything that was being asked.

"Slow your roll."

The man came stomping in, greeting his wife, and keeping Matt behind him. Evan tried getting up and into a more defensive position before realizing that he was tied down and restrained.

Both the man and the woman's ring finger was protected by a gleaming band, Evan was able to infer that the two were married.

The man glanced down at Evan, "The fucker hits hard."

Evan scoffed back.

"What do you guys want with me anyway?"

"We think that you could help us," Ana was interrupted by her husband.

"More like we think you could get us out of here." Said the man aggressively.

Ana glanced at her husband and then back at Evan, "Jackson, we need him to trust us as much as we need to trust him." This further confused Evan.

The husband whose name was revealed to Evan now being Jackson spoke again, "Mhm, continue," he grumbled.

Evan looked puzzled.

"The military uniform; are you a solider? An officer?" Ana asked.

He spoke, "Why should I tell you guys anything?"

Ana then showed off a peanut butter jar and some crackers. "You tell us what we need, and we'll give you some food, kapeesh?"

Evan's eyes widened at the unveiling of food and instantly spoke. "I was a sergeant major; I was called back from out West because things back here were getting worse, they *were* right."

Ana interrupted Evan saying, "Sergeant Major? You must've been important." Jackson scoffed at that.

"Main thing we wanted to figure out was if you knew about any last resort bunkers or some shit. There's gotta be something out there." Jackson spoke, recovering from the aforementioned scoff. He seemed as if the last thing he wanted to do was speak to Evan.

Evan looked at Jackson, then chuckled, "Emergency hideouts? No of course not, that's what armories are for, or fallout shelters. Listen, what's happening?"

Jackson opened his busted mouth, "Everyone went crazy, I don't know. Shit. Beats me."

"Went crazy?" Evan inquired.

"Some virus; I remember hearing whispers about it on the news, but I just think they tried to cover it up."

Evan looked around at everyone in the room, "…And they went… crazy? What does that mean? You're telling me all of those stories in California were real? I thought they were just propaganda or something, I thought it was made up."

Jackson nodded, "So you know then."

Evan looked back up at him, "I don't… but I've heard about it."

Jackson snarled at Evan, "Probably the Chinese or Russians, fucking propaganda, my guess would be as good as yours."

"What about the armory?" Evan asked, trying to ignore Jackson's meaningless assumptions.

Ana spoke, "That was the first place we went. They started up a quarantine in the city, but the limit had been reached; and by the time we got there… they… they—" she started choking on her own isolated guilt.

Jackson stepped forward, "The government started throwing lead at us, so we ran."

"We just need somewhere to sleep," the boy spoke.

Evan sat there in shock. "What do you mean? '*Throwing lead at you.*' You're telling me they shot at you?"

Jackson murmured a low toned "*yes.*"

"The goddamned *government*," He specified with annoyance in his voice. "Probably them who plotted this whole thing. Listen, do you know anywhere or not?" Jackson spoke in a way that made Evan feel insulted.

Evan nodded, "I might know of a place." Jackson naturally doubted him, nodding off and gesturing Evan to speak more. He had no respect for the military, especially after recent events.

Evan and Matt's eyes met awkwardly but both moved away quickly. "Where is the place you speak of?" Ana asked. Evan turned his attention to her.

"Deep in the woods, near the Cylon wildlife area East of St. Paul. The army made it sound like some sort of secret, so if anything crazy happened, maybe something like a *civil war*," he stopped to briefly emphasize how outrageous the state of their country was. "We would have a place to take our families," Evan revealed. "Are you going to give me the peanut butter or what, I'm starving!"

Ana tossed down the jar of peanut butter and a dozen saltine crackers. Jackson pulled his wife to the side and whispered, "Do you think we can trust him?"

She paused, "Well, I'd like to think we can." They spoke shallow enough for Evan (who was now scarfing down peanut butter and saltines) to not hear them.

"But seriously, what if he's leading us into a trap or something?" He tried to reason pessimistically.

"Look at him," they both turned. "He doesn't have a clue. Nobody's spoken to him."

"Hm…" Jackson growled.

Jackson turned to Evan and left Ana, he changed his tone and spoke. "How'd you get here?"

Evan again looked up, cracker crumbs trickling down from his almost clean-shaven face and peanut butter staining his uniform.

"Uh… um, hold on," he choked up his food. "I woke up yesterday and… hm. Well, I was in this helicopter—"

He had no need to withhold information now that his stomach had something to look forward to.

"Helicopter?" They all asked.

"Oh my god, you guys haven't seen it. The *helicopter*!" He had completely forgotten to tell them. "It'd have a map too!" He started to remember what had happened before the crash. The map was his focal point while being jolted amongst the turbulence.

"Are you serious?" Jackson totally thought that Evan was bullshitting.

"Yes. I can show you."

Jackson felt as though he was being lured, so he of course consulted the best rationalist he knew.

"Babe, should I go with him?"

"You can keep him in the ropes, right? Besides, you're like twice his size."

"Hm." He was reluctant.

"Just keep the ropes tight."

"Yeah…" he was slightly nervous.

Ana told Jackson to stay safe and be cautious, the father then walked over to his son and patted his shoulder.

"I'll see you guys soon." Jackson said as he helped Evan up and loosened the ropes around his ankles. Jackson wished that he wouldn't have to leave the parlor for a second, leaving his family alone was tough.

When they exited, Evan realized he was in a completely different part of the mall. "If you bring me to the food court, I can find my way from there."

Jackson agreed.

While on the way there, Evan tried to start small talk, all exuberant saying, "Your wife, she seems awfully optimistic."

Jackson mumbled, "Mhm, yup." Evan attempted to befriend Jackson despite how irritable it was to have a one-sided conversation.

"Where did you work?"

Jackson replied, "Construction near Lanesboro."

Evan followed up with, "It's beautiful down there." Jackson nodded, not engaged in the conversation at all.

They had finally reached the food court and Evan instantly pointed down the corridor to their right.

Evan trotted back down the hallway, trying to keep pace with Jackson. When the two reached the entrance to the corridor, Evan could see the fire that he had built nearing its final puff of smoke. The little hot embers exited with stuttering frequency. The sky above the sunroof was pale white, maybe a shade of gray, it was hard to tell. It was also quite dim because of the raging blizzard.

Jackson and Evan walked past the chopper, both staring at it as if it were an outstanding painting at an art show.

"How did you make it out of there?" Jackson had finally asked after his vague responses.

Evan thought about it for a second and realized, "I don't know, man, pure luck, I shouldn't have survived that."

Jackson kicked at the fire, releasing hot ash into the air, "The map, where is it?"

After Jackson removed the ropes, Evan tried searching through more of the ruble, lifting metal sheets and now climbing within. He remembered seeing the map before the crash, seeing it as a vivid and random memory.

He knew it had to be somewhere.

Finally, he found it crumpled and smooshed between some baggage. "Ah-ha! I found it, here it is," he praised, lifting it into the air for Jackson to see.

Evan climbed out and offered the map, Jackson spoke "Thanks…" Then questioned Evan about the blood on his sleeve.

"What is that… what the hell is that man?" Suddenly changing subjects.

Jackson seemed to be getting increasingly defensive. Evan responded quickly, "Big cut, why do you ask?"

"Just a cut then?" Jackson was obviously skeptical, Evan had analyzed. And for some reason, Jackson was like an open book, a clear window. Evan could see right through him. Noticing all the little lines and tiny developing wrinkles in Jackson's face with each different emotion.

Jackson scrunched his nose, "I'm not going to ask to see it, I just want to know if it's a bite or not."

Evan was quick to ask why, and Jackson was quick to clarify. "I don't know how it's spread; a lot of the posters just warn that it spreads like Rabies."

"The virus?" Evan questioned while handing Jackson the tattered map.

"Yeah," Jackson said, now sounding somewhat engaged in the conversation for once.

"Is that what I heard yesterday?"

Jackson raised his bushy brow, "What?"

Evan started to explain, "It was this noise, I don't know."

Jackson silently pondered, "Must've been. I've only seen a couple sick people."

Evan raised his eyebrow while inferring what Jackson was saying. He wanted to know more but was interrupted.

An unpleasant screech was heard from a second level shoe store. The same noise that Evan had heard the day before.

Jackson untucked the pistol from between his hip and belt, situating it in his hands. They both stared up from where the screech came from. Evan looked down at his constrained feet.

"Jackson…?"

Jackson stood there, almost frozen. Evan examined that Jackson was in a state of shock. Evan signaled more, "Jackson! Hey?"

An unidentifiable creature ran out of the store on the second level and flipped over the railing, slamming down on the tile. The insanity was immeasurable. Despite its current injured state, the crippled hands were reaching out at Evan. The horrified expression on his face reflected in the glazed eyes.

The hair on both men's necks stood on end, pricking their skin, and taking the breath from their lungs.

Luckily, Jackson snapped out of it, finally responding to Evan.

"Yeah, hold on!" You could tell he was scared.

More horrid shrieks echoed on the second level and within seconds, more of them flung off the balcony. More dead ones clumped up and softened the fall for the rest, allowing them to reach Evan and Jackson. They would break their arms or legs but would still try to get up. This was unlike anything they'd seen before.

Jackson tossed Evan a blade to free himself from the ropes. Evan cut fast, he cut for his life.

"I'll hold them off, keep cutting!" Until now, Evan didn't think that Jackson could even attempt to be somewhat altruistic.

Jackson wanted to run, he wanted to leave Evan, but some deep instinct inside of him prevented him from doing any of that. He wished he was more selfish, but only serial killers are that selfish and Jackson of course, was no serial killer.

Evan flopped like a fish onto his back. His injured arm wasn't helping the situation whatsoever. Jackson aimed his pistol, preparing to use it. While the looming threat grew, Jackson helped Evan back to his feet, making things easier.

Evan saw one of the creatures readying to attack but was put down after a bullet entered its chest. Jackson was quick to defend and even quicker to run. Before the two ran out of there, Evan glanced back at the growing danger. Over half a dozen of those creatures had stumbled to their feet and began to jog after them.

They both scrambled to get out of there; Evan finally cut off both the ropes and could now run at full capacity.

The two of them ran through the corridor and back into the food court while being chased by the growing horde.

Evan shouted, "Where's my bow? My axe?"

Jackson mumbled, "It's back at the ice cream shop, but you can keep the knife if you'd like." Evan smirked at this obvious attempt at humor. That crappy blade could barely slice through rope.

They both sprinted down the hallways, heaving. Evan was a bit jet legged. Jackson was bigger in size compared to Evan, yet he ran faster and more efficiently. Of course, Evan could run, but the helicopter crash surely didn't help things; nor did the pulsating gash on his arm.

He simply couldn't relent, for if he did, he would surely die.

The mutant like beasts would lunge and thrust toward Evan and his newfound 'friend'. Meanwhile on the other spectrum, Jackson was thinking to himself, "I just have to outrun Evan." Surely that wouldn't be his fault if Evan was slain by the crowd.

Despite the air being dry and terribly cold, both men were sweating bullets. One worse than the other. Jackson then reached into his bag, grabbing hold of a walkie talkie. Radioing to his wife, "Come in, come in! pack our shit up and get ready to leave!"

The radio connection was poor, and she was left completely oblivious. The wife and son could still hear the endless ruckus from down the corridor. Ana opened the door and asked for Matt hide away in the back of the parlor.

Ana turned, "Get inside Mathew!" She ran out to the railing and could see Jackson and Evan running helplessly, trying to get away. They were both on the first floor and needed to reach the second. Jackson noticed a torn railing that hung low from the overhang, figuring he could use it as a ladder to reach his wife and son. He leapt onto it and ignored Evan.

"Hey man! What? Help me up!"

Evan shouted; the impending hoard of beasts wasn't far behind. He desperately cried for help, like a helpless dog trapped in a growing pit of cement.

Jackson continued to climb the broken railing and reached the top, meeting his wife who was less than pleased with his most recent decision. She pleaded to her husband, "We can't just leave him."

Jackson didn't want to leave him like that, but it was far more justifiable than any other option he had thought about.

Evan started shouting, "Come on man!"

Ana had pulled her husband into the store, "Why would you do that? He's a human just like us!" She obviously didn't want anyone to be hurt.

Jackson responded, "We have the goddamned map, we can finally get out of this mess and get help!"

Matt tried intervening with his parents, "Dad, you're right but we didn't have to abandon him, he doesn't stand a chance! Did you see him?"

Jackson mumbled, "We have the map, isn't that enough?" he tried again to justify his rationale. He knew what he did wrong but chose to try and avoid the conversation all together.

Meanwhile, Evan sprinted away from the mob of feral monsters. He came to a similar intersection and noticed a flight of stairs to his left, he spun in that direction and headed up straightaway. He hopped up the stairs ever so fast, he could feel his legs and arms begin to shake. He was far too exhausted for this kind of frantic running.

He sprinted down the overhang; looking for the store that Jackson and his family were in. Evan wished to know what had caused all the chaos.

What made things go so wrong?

Running from unidentifiable beasts that incited unmeasurable terror.

The family kept arguing even though Jackson had made up his mind. Slowly they felt the floor begin to rumble. Cabinets shuddered and shook, Jackson turned to the doorway.

"Shit."

Evan had led the mob to the family.

Jackson whipped the door open quickly, pulling Evan in before the hoard got ahold of him. Then shoving him to the floor, all in one swift motion.

"Get away from the windows Matt!" Ana screamed.

Jackson threw cabinets in front of the door, blocking it. He flipped the lock and spun to sink his fist into Evan's cheekbone. Evan was quick to try countering the attack but was simply overpowered by the vastly superior man. When the knuckles contacted his face, he felt every atom in his cheekbone melt.

"How the fuck are we supposed to get out of here now?"

Ana told Jackson to cool down, "There's got to be a way out of here, right?"

Her husband stomped around angerly, a cloud disrupted his critical thinking. Matt struggled, "There's got to be some roof hatch or something right?" He questioned.

"Knock knock, Evan!"

Evan answered while rubbing his face, "Who's there?" rotating his jaw round and round.

Jackson retorted, "A goddamned idiot who got all of us a one-way ticket to our own funerals!"

Evan frowned, "You're the one that left me out there to die! How can you be mad that I saved my own skin?"

Ana nodded and so did Matt, "He's got a point," they both said at the same time.

Jackson stormed off, "There's gotta be away out of here, right?" He reassured himself.

Matt dug back into his pre-quarantine memories. One of his friends who had worked at the same mall had taken pictures of blueprints in the store he worked in. The thought of mall blueprints was hilarious to the boys for some reason. Simply the concept of having the blueprints to a shopping center. Only god knows why mindless middle schoolers would find such joy from such a mundane thing.

"Blueprints!" He exclaimed.

"Blueprints?" His Dad questioned, trying to make sense. "You… you're right!" Jackson spun and scurried into the back of the ice cream parlor.

His wife and Evan looked 100% confused at this.

They were clueless.

Jackson started explaining as if he'd done so thousands of times. "Every room is fitted to have blueprints or at least a fire exit page printed in the back, It's protocol for buildings like this."

Ana nodded, "I see what your stepping in."

Matt subconsciously snapped his fingers while his Dad walked out of the backroom. He held two sheets: one for fire exits and one for ventilation. He set them both on the floor, "See ventilation?" he pointed before finishing what he had to say, "There's a duct that leads out this way—" he swiped his fingers along the paper. "And comes out on the roof, I'm sure we could find our way out from there, right?"

Evan nodded, "Yeah even if that's not possible, we could squeeze that way." He redirected everyone's attention to a slightly larger vent that only led across the mall rather than leading to the roof.

Jackson spoke, "You might be right," he growled. "Vents to the roof seem a bit tight, 2 by 1 feet across, it'd be a tight squeeze."

Ana made a face, "The utility room would be a better place for us to go, the vents are 3 by 2 feet, you think?" She added.

Jackson nodded, "You're right, we'd be better off there."

Evan felt like he should be involved in the conversation, "Where is the utility room?"

Jackson then joked, "We're leaving you for them," joking that he'd leave Evan for the crowd of bloodthirsty sickos outside. Evan suddenly looked worried.

"I'm fucking with you; the room is behind the food court near that weird antique store." They all knew what he was referring to.

Matt pulled the multitool from his parent's bag to unscrew the vented grate.

Evan got to his feet and rubbed his cheek. They heard a metal sheet crash to the floor in the back room and Matt walks out stating, "Those vents should be harder to take off." Evan realized that Matt had the same dimple that Ana had.

She smiled at her son. Jackson headed to the back room and smirked at his son, Evan followed and greeted them with an awkward smile. "My stuff?"

Jackson pointed to the bag, "You can get them when we're all out of the vents."

Evan tried to steer clear of Jackson. To stay somewhat afloat on common ground.

Impending doom arose as the mumbles and groans of the lost souls got louder and louder. They started to bang on the doors while the windows started to crack.

First Jackson tried sliding his bulky self into the vent, it was decently tight but not tight enough to stop him. In line to enter was first Matt and then Ana. Both parents wanted to act as a shield for their son. The boy seemed kind of... well, if Evan could describe it, "*So terrified, he was too embarrassed to admit it.*"

Ana reassured Matt, "The vent isn't as small as we thought, it won't be long before we get out, I promise." Evan raised an eyebrow, Ana started getting ready to enter the vent.

"He's claustrophobic?" Evan asked.

"Yeah," she replied, "I know he'll get over it someday."

She helped Matt crawl into the vent, while up ahead Jackson was cursing his way ahead. "The hell did I just hit my head on?" he grumbled.

With everything that's happened, a kid like Matt shouldn't have to deal with it. Evan figured the kid had enough going on.

Echoes and creaks of the old vents haunted the group's soul. While back in the ice cream parlor, they heard the monsters break through the glass and enter. Evan was glad that Jackson had joked about leaving him in the room rather than following through.

Matt started to heave.

"Son, It's going to be alright," Jackson mumbled from the front, trying to scoot himself through the vent.

Honey" Honey, take deep breaths, don't overthink it."

Evan agreed with Ana, "It's going to be okay, we're safe in here."

After Jackson turned the corner, he could see the duct to the utility room. He pulled the floor plan from his back pocket and made sure he was on the right path. "After this turn, it's easy going, don't worry son."

Dust and cobwebs crowded the large ducts. Just after a few days, the vents had already dirtied up. Each crawl forward froze their arms and provided an unshakable chilling sensation.

Jackson made it to the utility room and started kicking out the vent cover. It scathed the floor as it shot from the wall. Jackson hopped out and made sure the area was clear before helping his son down, eventually helping Ana out. Evan grabbed both edges of the vent and worked his way out. Jackson glanced, seeing the malnourished man struggle to exit the vent. A swift urge to assist washed over him but he ultimately figured that he owed nothing in regard to Evan.

"We're out," Evan exclaimed. "I'll admit I got a bit uneasy."

Matt nodded, "The whole damn thing was uneasy."

Ana scolded her son, "Language, Matt," her son then apologized melancholy and such.

Jackson turned to his left only to see a frozen corpse laying with a wrench stabbed into its eye. Blood pooling in its mouth and the other eye still open, staring at him. Jackson hurried his family away from the horror, allowing them only to catch a glimpse.

When they exited the room, they found themselves in the back of some internet provider store. They all hurried through the joint, not caring for what it contained. When they got out, Evan instantly knew where he was, the view of the shattered sunroof and fragmented overhang told him his exact position. Ruble and carnage stained the once shining and glimmering tile.

Like a once great canvas of modern architecture now splashed with the gore of a slaughterhouse and the destruction of a terrorist attack.

The wind continued to howl like the loneliest wolf in a friendless forest.

Ana was shocked and Matt looked horrified. The pilot's body was mangled from the windshield and the severed metal sheeting hung by just a bolt.

Evan mentioned, "An exit can't be too hard to find." He didn't pay much attention to the carnage as it wasn't anything new to him.

The family nodded while still looking at the disgusting sight.

"Stop looking at that," Jackson sternly said to his family.

They all glanced and analyzed their surroundings, attempting to find an exit sign. "There's one!" Matt exclaimed.

"Yeah, good job but that also leads back to the food court… and back to the hoard," Jackson spoke with a shallow tone.

"Over there," Evan yelped and pointed.

It was situated next to the previously visited hardware store a level below and squeezed between a childcare center. Evan and the group scuttled down the stairs past the fountain that Evan had slept next to the night prior.

The sun was high in the sky at this point but still blinded by the nonstop flurries of snow and the impervious gusts of wind. Ana examined the camp, "You made that fire?"

"Yeah," he started to itch his wounded arm, "All I really did was create sparks off the fountain." Sometimes, Evan wished he was able to come up with quick witted responses but often failed, especially around new people.

"Me and the boys tried starting a fire last night, it was ridiculous. Hardest thing we've ever done." She joked.

Evan chuckled, "Yep, it's hard work, they taught me a couple things in the military, luckily one of them was how to start a fire."

"They may have taught you a few things in the force, but they sure didn't teach you how to be quiet, any of those things could hear you, just so you know, Evan." Jackson walked with his arms, like a lowland gorilla walking to the nearest stream. His arms were like wrecking balls while his body was the thick frame.

Ana frowned, "Let's get a move on."

Evan pondered after replying with a melancholy, "Yeah." Figuring he should keep his questions and thoughts to himself. He silently kept trying to figure out what those creatures were, wondering of their true origin and their true behavior. It was a person on the outside, *sure*, but there was nothing behind the eyes. Not a soul, not a single emotion. Evan didn't realize that he was subconsciously picking at the bonded wrap around his arm while questioning himself.

It came loose and started to unravel. As soon as he would tighten up one part another would come loose. Matt noticed, "What's uh, what's going on there?"

Evan tried covering it up when he realized they had noticed.

Jackson felt the need to tease the possibility of infection. "I know that's not a bite, but please tell me it's not infected."

Evan moped, "I don't know, I poured some disinfectant on it yesterday so it should be fine." He pulled the bottle of hydrogen peroxide from a pocket on his vest, presenting it.

"That's the word that's going around, it's all about infection. My neighbor was bit by a dog and got it, some of my friends in the city were telling me about how they heard people biting other people and just—" Jackson shook his head while sliding his tongue across the roof of his mouth. "Just gross to think about. That's how it spreads though, that's what I've been told. We should still keep an eye on it just in case it is infected. The last thing we need is some infected military prick biting us."

Still unassured about Evan's allegiance, Jackson seemed to function like a teeter totter, swapping between trust and being a hard ass. Evan asked if any of them had some wrapping or bandage to cover up his wound. Jackson offered an old rock band shirt and almost forked it over to Evan before his wife stopped him.

"No, not that shirt, use something else," she said. Jackson rolled his eyes and folded the shirt back, and pulled out a different plain brown shirt to wrap around the injury.   Jackson turned to Evan.

"The first shirt; I bought it for her like seven years ago at some concert. When shit hit the fan, I was packing cans of food and survival shit, she was packing that kind of shit." He remarked, thinking that it was quite funny for someone to pack that sort of stuff in a situation like that.

Evan chuckled, "I'm sure that's what my wife did," pulling out his small family portrait and showing it to Jackson. Nearing their way to the exit doors, Jackson examined the photo. "You guys seem pretty happy, where are they?" He spoke, realizing that Evan was a person just like him.

"Hopefully back home."

Evan spoke again, "A couple months ago before my deployment, I got to spend one last day with them, it was awesome…" It felt like he was leaving a lot of important details out, probably to not bore Jackson. "Then I was out West for a while. Ended up being called back here, god." Evan said in an annoyed tone.

"You got that right, the goddamned government kept trying to cover everything up about that new virus; *bunch of idiots*. Keeping that from us ultimately hurt us all in the long run."

Evan frowned, "Yeah, I don't remember much about the chopper going down, but I remember everything beforehand. I hope they're alright," Evan didn't want to get too deep into his feelings. The trust between the two wasn't there yet.

It was nice talking to him without being cussed at.

"Yeah, it was nothing but chaos for a few days, whatever that virus was wiped out most of Rochester in a day or two. Whatever is left, we'll find out soon enough," Jackson concluded. Evan nodded, putting the photo away in a safe pocket. The big bold letters of the exit sign signaled for an upcoming doorway leading outside. The weather was violent and unforgiving. The wind blew snow around, constructing drifts and walls of powder. With no plows to clear the roads, mostly everything was covered in a foot or two of carpeted snow.

They opened the doors and snow rushed in like waves of ocean water. They all started stomping through the thick and treacherous frosting, almost swimming through it. The powder was up to their knees, reaching their hips in some places. Jackson spotted a grey jeep that was parked across the parking lot, clearly abandoned.

The group started heading for the jeep. Jackson was the first to reach it, swooshing the snow away from the doors and realizing the car was locked. He flipped Matt around and pulled a thin plastic ruler out of his backpack, proceeding to maneuver it down past the window and into the door. A few moments passed while Evan and the members of the family all had their eyes glued to Jackson. Suddenly there was a click and when he tried the handle, it was open.

Evan stood there a little confused but ultimately accepted it. "How'd you learn to do that?" he questioned.

Jackson spoke with snow gathering in his beard. "What are you gonna do? Arrest me?"

Evan stuttered, "Uh…"

Jackson reassured Evan. "I had some sketchy friends growing up."

Evan smirked, "I assume you know how to start the thing then too?"

Jackson chuckled, "Easy." He pulled the plastic covering off from under the wheel and started connecting wires. A small spark occurred as he hopped in the driver's seat. He connected one last wire and the car miraculously started up to his surprise, although with a stutteringly loud mechanical noise. "All this snow, I'm surprised it started." His family and Evan hopped in the car, ready for takeoff.

The jeep slowly drove and pushed snow out of its way as Jackson lowered his foot down on the pedal.

The car compacted snow beneath the tires and made that annoying crunching noise. The car would get stuck and spin in the snow.

Evan sat in the passenger seat while the mother and son sat in the back. He held onto the safety handle that hung from the ceiling as if it would actually save his life or something. Jackson gripped the wheel tightly, pulling it one side to the other.

The car wouldn't follow his command though.

"Damned thing!"

The screeching and noise made such a clatter that the group could now observe several of the creatures clawing their way out of the mall entrance, breaking the glass, and stumbling into the frigid cold outside. Matt looked and glanced around, "Dad, over there, the snowplow!"

Jackson spoke exuberantly, "Shit, you're right!"

The group quickly exited the vehicle and ran through the thick snow. Trudging along. Evan saw several of the beasts now just a dozen paces away. "Jackson, focus on getting that snowplow open, I'll take care of those things."

Jackson inquired, "Are you a good shot?"

Evan reassured him, "Yes," he sternly answered. He didn't exactly know what he was getting into, but he was sure that any kind of bullet would do what needed to be done.

Jackson handed Evan the pistol but before he gave full control, he had one last thing to say, "Don't screw this up, Private, *now get to it*."

Evan accepted the pistol and took aim.

The nearest beast would be his first target, firing his first shot and ignoring the kick of the weapon. Shooting twice and finally three times.

He noticed that he was obscenely cold despite multiple layers of clothing he wore, so cold. Meanwhile, these creatures seemed to have unlimited stamina despite wearing T-shirts. Evan shot again, hitting the creature's neck, and once more finally landing the bullet in its skull. The creature was incapacitated.

Evan noticed more creatures clawing their way out of the doorway, shouting and gargling horrifically. "How's the truck going, Jackson? You gotta hurry it won't be long before—"

Evan was interrupted by the roar of an engine and Jackson yelling, "Ah ha!"

Evan spun around and handed Jackson the pistol as he entered the snowplow. Matt hid in the back with his mother like before. Jackson pleaded with the vehicle, "Come on you bitch!"

Evan thought that Jackson's almost impulsive habit of cussing was often over the top and far too vulgar, but then again that was an opinion coming from a man who had barely sworn in his life.

He put his foot to the floor and as the truck drove off, it cleared the snow out of their way. "This was a good idea!"

Matt smiled.

As the plow sped out of the parking lot and away from the incoming hoard, everyone in the vehicle tried to simmer their adrenaline that was brought on from the near-death experience.

Evan gathered his wits. His injured arm would itch as it scabbed up and tried to heal itself. All he wanted to do was give in and itch, but he simply could not. His back felt stiff, and his muscles were sore. He still held onto the safety handle on the ceiling to stabilize himself. Evan wanted to peel back the fabric on his arm and pick at the scabs, but he knew that would cause more harm than anything else.

The dunes of snow and drifts as tall as street signs made roads difficult to navigate. Evan felt his eyes roll back into his head; he was tired from the long day. Only a few hours had passed since he woke up, but it felt like it had been an entire week since meeting the family.

He was unsure of Jackson, but he thought the other two were okay. He could barely remember their names. He wanted to trust them, but he was unwilling at the moment.

Chapter 3

A Place to Take Shelter

Dust settles in a condemned motel room.

Most of the furniture was wrapped in plastic and the floor had this gross crusty film over the top of it. The Tv had old fingerprints and visible hand marks on the screen. The drapes blinded the window and prevented even the dimmest of light from entering.

Suddenly, the door was bust open like canned corn. The door swung open and slammed the wall behind it. Jackson burst in holding his pistol in one hand and gripping a flashlight in the other. He scanned the room and made sure the coast was clear. Opening the blinds, he allowed the crisp Winter sun to scorch the crusted carpet.

Dust lofted down from every surface as Jackson disturbed the still environment. Like constant rainfall in a jungle of cobwebs and dust.

"This place looks alright, come in," Jackson announced to his family and Evan.

Ana and Matt hopped out of the snowplow; Evan lowered his bow downward while helping them grab their backpacks. His arm was still itchy with the scabs, and he felt pain just to the touch. He soon followed the family's footsteps and kept to himself. No matter how hard he tried to focus on anything else, the same thought always came full circle. He couldn't stop thinking about his wife and daughter, praying that they were still alive somewhere.

Jackson laid the plastic sheets down on the floor so his wife wouldn't have to deal with the disgusting carpet. The second she walked in however, she started cleaning. Evan observed this, glancing but not staring.

"Clean freak! That's what we'd call her at our house. All nice and tidy everything had to be, but if I were honest, we would've been swimming in trash if it wasn't for her."

Matt settled and situated supplies while Jackson kept the coast clear.

Ana cleaned so hard it looked religious.

Evan tended to his wound; you could tell it was trying to heal but was simply unable to. Despite how handsomely Evan had dressed the wound, it refused to act handsome.

The sun began to set. Most sunsets glazed the sky with orange, but the blizzard had other ideas. It blocked out our glorious sun and its wonderful rays with the thick snow-cover, the sky got significantly dimmer by the minute.

The air was frigid, and the snow traveled sideways. Things were soon situated, and Evan cranked the small space heater to the max. Ana tucked herself in the old dusty sheets of the bed which Matt was already dead asleep within, snoring and drooling like a dog. Evan had taken his vest off and was down to tan pants and a stained white T-shirt, standing close to the space heater.

Jackson flung the door open, disturbing the heat that Evan felt. His silhouette was contrasted by the darkness outside and the dim light within. Large flurries of snow were visible as the wind howled. He stepped inside and stomped his boots, closing the door as he did so.

Ana peaked out from under the sheets, sleepy as ever.

Evan pointed at Ana so Jackson would notice. "Oh… didn't mean to disturb you, I'll be there in a sec, sorry dear," Jackson said as he draped his coat over a hook. His red flannel provided enough warmth at the moment.

Ana vanished beneath the sheets once again and moments afterword she was snoring.

Jackson noticed this and chose to go stand by Evan. The space heater was the only thing keeping the room at a comfortable temperature.

When the two met by the space heater, Jackson actually struck up a conversation rather than ignoring Evan's presence. "So, you were deployed out West then huh?"

Evan looked up from his focal point (which was a glowing red button atop the space heater). He briefly recalled his experience there. " Yeah, just North of Denver," he was quite surprised that Jackson had said anything aside from a slur.

"Hm…" Jackson blew warm air into his cupped hands. "What happened in Denver?"

Evan stood quiet for a moment, realizing that Jackson had actually been the first person to ask him about it. "A hostage situation."

"Shit," Jackson was mid chuckle before he realized that it wasn't something he should be chuckling about. "Was anyone hurt?"

"No," Evan said, knowing that he had fabricated a lie. He simply didn't want to think about it. It was somewhat of an uncomfortable question, so Jackson chose to redirect things. "Where'd you live then?"

"Oh, I live down in Elba," Evan spoke of it as if he hadn't visited his house at all in the past six months. "It's down in the Whitewater valley, it's real nice down there."

"I'm sure," Jackson would spin frequently as to evenly heat his body.

Evan inquired, "How about you?"

"Our house was out past Fleet-Farm, but when word got out that Rochester had been placed under martial law, I don't think I'd ever driven that fast," Jackson announced, then stopping to let out a cough. "I was down in Lanesboro helping a friend finish up his deck before the weather came. Then of course news hit, and my phone went off. I ripped out of his driveway so fast I'm pretty sure I got whiplash," he chuckled.

"Yeah, I've been told things were getting a little out of control," Evan related, pausing briefly. "This whole civil war," he scoffed, "I'm glad that you guys in the North are shielded from most of it.

"Tell me about it," Jackson rolled his eyes. "Everyone out West is probably dead by now. Anyways, about the time I rolled up to our house, I didn't even give my truck enough time to stop before I ran out and into the house… and I don't really run… like at all… for anything," Jackson joked, trying to make a dark situation lighthearted.

Evan smirked while glancing at Jackson, "Yeah me either, except when I'm running from an angry mob in the middle of a mall, then I'll jog."

Jackson smirked; he was beginning to actually like Evan.

"Do you know how to use the pistol? Well, I mean obviously you know how to shoot, but do you know how to *use* it?"

Jackson stood dumbfounded for a moment, pretending that he actually knew the ins and outs of his pistol. However, he did not. "Yeah?" He answered as if he had forgotten how to speak.

"You totally don't do you?" Evan teased.

"…No."

Evan motioned his right hand, hoping that Jackson would let him demonstrate how to pull the clip and clear the chamber. His friend was hesitant at first, but soon handed his pistol to Evan.

The shiny inlay of silver complimented the carbon black frame and trigger. It was so smooth and heavy. Evan tossed it up and down in his hand while demonstrating how to pull the clip out, cocking the chamber and releasing the bullet within. He handed both items to Jackson and reset the pistol to its prior state. He set it back in Jackson's hand.

"Now do what I did."

Jackson looked at Evan and then back at the firearm in his hand. After a moment of comprehension, Jackson clicked a switch and the clip fell out onto the floor. Evan was quick to catch it midair, while Jackson tried tucking at the chamber.

"No, you have to—." Evan signaled with his right hand, acting as if he were flicking another lever on the pistol. Jackson caught wind of what Evan was doing and soon cocked back the chamber, sliding it back and presenting his perfect repetition of what Evan had done.

"Good, man."

Jackson reloaded his pistol, "I literally had no clue how to do that, shit, thanks Private."

The two glanced at one another, both flashed a half smile and quietly shuffled away from the space heater as to not wake up the mother and son. Evan gulped down his final cup of melted snow for the night.

"I'd say we stay here for a bit until the storm dies down, then we leave and hit your place, then the military compound," Jackson said; adding Evan's house along the way was comforting. Evan relinquished a smile, relaying it to the bearded man across the room. Jackson then motioned "You can sleep in the tub in the bathroom, it'll be more comfortable that way."

Evan agreed. The real reason Jackson wanted Evan in the bathroom had to do with trust.

Before Evan closed the bathroom door, he stopped to speak to Jackson, "Goodnight, thank you man."

Jackson nodded, "You can thank me by keeping my family safe, goodnight." He shut the door.

Evan sat down in the tub and set his vest on top of him acting as a blanket. Before he was able to close his eyes, his brain forced him to think. Jackson had totally left him to die in that mall, but he redeemed himself somewhat. Jackson was a good guy who made a questionably bad choice, but surely Evan had made questionably bad choices in the past, right?

Forgiveness was appropriate.

The moon made its run across the night sky, blinded by storm clouds and thus another day began with the rising sun. Small fluttery clouds passed by the sun and brutal light reflected off the tall drifts of powder.

Evan laid in the tub, tossing, and turning. Overnight he had developed a sinking feeling in his chest, worrying for his family. Rapid growth of dismay for his family seemed to be chipping away at his soul. He slept just fine but waking up felt like hell. When he heard loud knocking at the bathroom door, his eyes flew open.

"Wake up Private," Jackson's voice bellowed from one side of the door to the other.

Evan spoke up, "One second," he sat up and rubbed his eyes. His injured arm ached with problematic pain and his back felt like a wooden board had been nailed to it. He lifted himself out of the cold tub and realized an aching pain in his neck. This was one of the few times in his adult life that he felt truly old.

He stepped out of the bathroom and tried to straighten his back. "Good morning," he greeted. Noticing some canned stuff and various bags strewn across the TV stand, Evan pondered. "Is this what you guys have left?"

"Yup, this is about it, I'm sure we'll be able to find something out on the road. I never learned how to hunt but we could do that if we get desperate, I guess."

Evan spoke like a politician speaks about problems they don't experience, "I sort of know how to hunt, It's been a few years but if things get bad, I'm sure I could."

Jackson nodded, "I couldn't care less for food, I just need a smoke man," he let out an annoyed laugh. He *really* wanted a cigarette.

Jackson put on his coat and exited the motel room. Ana was already up, organizing stuff in their luggage. She greeted Evan with a friendly smile.

"Good morning."

"How'd you sleep?" She asked.

"Good enough you could say, and you?" Evan replied while scratching his sandpaper like cheek.

"I slept pretty good for what it's worth," Ana said with a smile, the same dimple on her cheek flashed Evan a grateful wink.

Meanwhile outside, Jackson attempted to start the truck. The engine rattled and coughed. It was then that he noticed the flashing *low fuel* sign on the dashboard. "Shit, hey Private?" He inquired.

Evan turned his attention to Jackson, or rather the threshold. He opened the door to check on Jackson, "What's the problem?" He walked over to the truck.

He noticed that the storm had finally passed, the sun reflected blindingly off the snow and the sky was a bright blue without a single cloud passing overhead.

"Goddamn gas tank, is there a siphon in the back?" Evan went to check the bed of the truck

"That's lucky, right here, five-gallon tank and a siphon. We got lucky."

Jackson recruited Evan to go around and collect gasoline out of vehicles.

As he slogged through the thick snow and hooked up the siphon, he sucked in and out came gasoline. After seconds of silence, all he could think of was his family. Whether or not they were alive or not, all he wanted to do was get on the road and begin searching but he kept calm and collected. He didn't want the others to notice how uneasy he felt. He wasn't the kind of person to ask for help anyways. His distant memories and delusions were interrupted by the gas can overflowing and getting all over his hands. He quickly took the siphon out and looked around to make sure nobody had seen him make a fool of himself. He tightened the cap and walked it over to the snowplow. Jackson was still dinking with it as if anything he could do would help.

Evan began fueling the vehicle and still continued to drift off in his own thoughts. Jackson signaled that the can was empty before Evan had even realized, "Go try and squeeze as much gas out of those other cars, we're going to need it."

Evan walked to the next car and began siphoning the gas out. Jackson's wife and son had helped load their stuff into the back seat of the truck.

Evan came back and finished filling the truck with his freshly stolen gasoline. Ana and Matt entered the back seats while Evan occupied shotgun. As they pulled away out of the small motel lot, Evan gave the place one last look.

Chapter 4

The Road

Ice and snow suffocated the landscape

As the truck slid and spun around the vacant roads, Jackson hit the steering wheel while cursing and swearing.

Evan sat in the passenger seat awkwardly, wanting to suggest better ideas or wanting to take the wheel entirely. Spinning and screeching wasn't doing the group any good. Evan started to suggest ideas.

"We could go on foot, maybe get some snowshoes? It wouldn't be that bad right?"

"Listen to me Private, I'm not giving up on this truck, it's going to make it... and where the hell would we find *snowshoes*." Jackson scoffed. Evan turned his attention elsewhere. In the back, Ana and Matt were bracing for every single shift that occurred in the chaos.

It was now that Evan thought he could hear something over the roar of the engine. "Jackson, *stop*."

"Why the hell would I stop?" He said while twisting and turning the wheel from side to side. Evan thought he could hear a faint motor, "Jackson, stop."

Jackson let his foot off the pedal and slammed his hands on the wheel, now looking at Evan with his eyebrows being more expressive than his eyes.

"Does that work for you? Dick," Evan sat there for a moment.

"Do you hear that?"

The truck grew silent. Just as Evan heard the sound of a motor again, Jackson started talking. "I don't hear a damn thing."

"Shut up Jackson." Evan said, more serious than he was last time, "There it is again."

Jackson didn't hear it at all, "What the fuck are you talking about?"

Matt wished he could swear like his Dad. He thought it was so hypocritical when his parents would scold him about swearing. As these thoughts crossed his mind, he also heard the roaring of a motor.

"I hear it," Matt exclaimed.

Ana tried a little harder to listen in.

Suddenly she could hear the shallow rumbling of a motor, and she was sure it wasn't the truck's engine. The noise was far too faint for that to be a possibility.

Jackson's eyes were looking around, getting increasingly paranoid. His eyebrows fluctuated up and down coordinating with which direction he was looking. Now he heard the motor.

"I hear it."

Evan theorized, "I think it's getting closer."

It totally was. The shallow motor now turned into an apparent and overwhelming noise. It sounded as if a squadron of snowmobiles were surrounding the truck. Evan danced his head around the truck, looking through every window, trying to identify where the noise was coming from.

In the distance and just over the hill, two figures appeared, Evan now knew where the noise was coming from.

"There, two guys maybe? I think they're on snowmobiles." Evan spoke to the family.

Jackson sat there for a second, spotting them in the mirrors. Two large snowmobiles, blue trim, and black body paint. A sled was tied to the back of the closest one.

"Shit. Evan, what do we do?"

Evan looked back at Jackson, "Me? I don't have a clue, they obviously heard us. Unless you get this thing moving, we won't really have a choice."

Jackson sighed and switched the truck back into gear. The sound of motors got closer and closer with each passing second. The noise had become so loud they could've sworn they were right next to the live motor. Matt then alerted his parents.

"Three men! Over there!"

Evan peeked over Jackson's seat and identified one man stepping off the first snowmobile and two men stepping off the second, They were all too heavily dressed to truly identify them.

The men cut the motors, letting the atmosphere fall silent. Jackson had stopped the truck. All was quiet for just a moment until a raspy and muffled voice could be heard. The words weren't clear but regardless, it made the hair on everyone's neck stand on end.

Evan whispered to Jackson, "Do you have your pistol?"

Jackson was visibly concerned, "Yes." His voice was dim and low compared to its usual loud and overwhelming tone. It felt as though every organ in his torso was being filled with a reactant ready to explode. He *did not* know what to do.

The raspy and demanding voice outside began to be louder, enabling words to be recognized.

"Get out... we... armed... now!"

Ana and Matt turned their heads, "Dad? What do we do?"

The stress was building for Jackson when suddenly a singular word was audible.

"Military."

Evan observed the look on everyone's face, a sickeningly distressed and hopeless look. The voice had sounded a lot closer than before, and when Matt went to check, a man dressed all in snow equipment went for the back-passenger door.

The door was pried open by the man and Matt was grabbed, being thrown from the car. Jackson leapt out of the driver side door with velocity that shouldn't have been achievable. The pistol had fallen from its hold and onto the driver seat, Evan glared at it and quickly made up his mind. He snatched the pistol and opened his door.

The man who had grabbed Matt was met with a violent right hook from Jackson before being tackled to the ground. Jackson had ripped off the snow goggles and tore the hat off of the man, exposing his eyes and parts of his face.

The two men who were still next to the snowmobiles had raised their firearms, pointed directly at Jackson.

"Get the hell off of him!" The men shouted.

Ana fumbled to the floor of the truck amidst the chaos. She started searching through the duffel bag, knowing that Evan's hatchet was somewhere in it. She scrambled to find it, knowing that it was only a matter of time before doom befell the family.

Evan observed these men. They obviously were not soldiers, there was no way. He looped around the front of the truck and took a tactical position. He peeked out and saw Jackson struggling on the ground with one man and two more demanding for him to stop. Matt had now been freed and had scrambled a couple feet away.

Jackson noticed his attacker reaching for a holstered pistol, he then set his foot against the man's wrist and took the firearm for himself.

"You son of a bitch," Jackson spoke.

Evan noticed the two men getting increasingly unnerved just by the sounds of their voices. Evan stood up and announced his presence, pointing the pistol at the two men.

"You aren't military!" Evan exclaimed.

The men were silent.

Jackson now held the gun, pointing it at the men and holding down his attacker. Matt had now stood up and ran around to the opposite side of the truck. Ana was already armed to slash the hatchet and the impending footsteps only made her get ready to swing. Within a split second, Ana had to recognize the footsteps as that of her son and hold back from swinging the hatchet. Matt spun into his mother's hold, feeling protected once again.

Jackson's attacker was held down, gasping for air.

"What was your plan?" Evan asked dominantly.

"We were just going to take your shit."

Evan's eyelids narrowed as he focused on his target. He analyzed the situation. The two men held their pistols poorly, shaky hands and bad aim was bound to land Evan as the victor if there were to be a shootout.

Jackson glanced over at Evan to see the expression on his face. A grim and grizzled face of serious defense. Proper firearm posture and accurate aim ensured a quick end to a dangerous threat. The two of them made eye contact; Evan nodded as if Jackson were asking a question. The scene was like a standoff, the cityscape in the background and snow blowing across the dunes. It was truly something out of a movie.

Jackson looked back at the two men; long silence followed the tense standoff. Gunfire erupted and before Evan could even identify who had shot first, he had flicked off the safety and dropped one of the men. Bullets hit the truck and made a destructive sound of clamor. Gunsmoke made it unclear whether or not Jackson had been shot, but someone was screaming their head off.

Horrific and distressed screaming echoed around, making Evan's ears jolt from the unsettling discomfort. When the gunfire had ceased, Evan ran to Jackson's position. Upon realizing that Jackson was unscathed, Evan glanced at the duo of armed men. They both were down but only one was still moving.

"Holy shit, holy shit, holy shit." Jackson whispered to himself.

The still moving and obviously injured man was screaming relentlessly, it sounded as if he was tearing his vocal cords.

Jackson seemed bewildered, shellshocked even. Evan stopped before pursuing the last man, checking on Jackson.

"Jackson? Jackson?" Evan demanded.

His eyes were staring at where the two men had previously stood. After Evan had called his name several more times, Jackson finally snapped out of it.

"Yeah... yeah?"

"Keep it together, I'll go deal with him." Evan gestured toward the screaming man, "You go deal with your family."

Jackson nodded quickly with fear in his eyes. Evan of course recognized the emotions being portrayed.

Evan got up and walked over to the pair of snowmobiles, walking past the first body and glaring at it. Blood had been sprayed all across the snow, one snowmobile had been noticeably riddled with bullets and blood while the other was untouched.

The screaming man was crawling away, each staggered motion was met with a blood curdling yelp. Evan simply told him to stop.

When the man stopped and spun to his back, they made eye contact. Evan could see the pain in the man's eyes, even through his dense snow goggles. Still gripping the pistol, Evan glanced at it and glanced back at the poor man.

"Don't—" his bloody mouth sputtered.

Evan stepped closer; the snow was beneath his feet. He stood high above his attacker.

On the ground and in a puddle of his own blood, the man pleaded with Evan hopelessly. "Let me go, I won't—"

Evan cut him off after seeing the bloodied and shot up leg, "You won't be going anywhere bleeding the way you are." Evan frowned.

The man looked down at his own leg. He hadn't realized where he'd been hit, all he knew was that he was hit somewhere. Evan spoke again regrettably. "You won't make it twenty minutes."

It was a mercy killing right? Evan certainly didn't know this man, but he knew that nobody deserved to freeze to death or bleed out slowly. Before shooting the man, Evan looked away. He *hated* this.

He *hated* doing that.

Chapter 5

Bad Things.

Evan went back and forth in his head.

Was it just or unjust to kill that man? There wasn't really a just reason to murder anyone, but Evan thought that the circumstances around it allowed for him to do what he had done. The fear in the eyes of the man he had shot were the only thing he could see; the eyes of a man who was in over his head. When faced with the bewildered eyes that clearly didn't want to die, Evan didn't want to grant that kind of punishment. The only calming thought that Evan could find, was the thought of finding his family. Otherwise, his mind was clouded with thoughts regarding those eyes. Death was a cruel punishment, but it could also be a mercy.

After *killing* those men, he thought back on the West, and the people he had put down over there. Rather the people he helped put down.

That hostage situation.

Denver airport had been taken by some extremists, protesting for their freedom in exchange for a difference to be made. No difference would be made that day however, because when rich politicians are *rich enough,* they don't bother to pay an ounce of attention to anyone beneath them. The group had taken innocent passerby's hostage and were threatening their lives. It was up to Evan and his team to save all the hostages and take the perpetrators in alive.

That job was too big, and far too important for someone like Evan.

So, he continued to think. Not just about the men he killed in Denver but the men who he recently shot. Both acts of murder happened to ensure the safety of others, but that didn't mean they *had to die.*

He looked up from his hands, suddenly distracted by a bump in the road.

Rolling and empty farm fields were disrupted by the sound of a motor. The peaceful grain silos and lonely farmsteads reminded them all of a painted masterpiece. The view reflected off Evan's glossy eyes. Every single structure looked old, as if it was there before the dinosaurs.

Evan lay upon luggage and supplies in a sled that was tied firmly to the back handle of the snowmobile. Jackson drove while his wife and son held tight. It was a smooth, slow and calming ride through the country, driving North to Evan's home.

Evan had informed the family of the town he lived in, telling them that it was on the way. Evan felt purpose being the family's protector but wouldn't be satisfied until he found his wife and daughter.

He didn't want to be the protector of someone else's family, he owed that to his own.

The introspective and internal thoughts that clouded his mind were now beginning to subside. He didn't enjoy thinking *that deeply* about things but would find himself doing so more than he wished. So instead of reflecting, he would keep his eyes on the road.

The handcrafted sign was up on the road ahead, burnt by the cold. The words read:

"Welcome to White Water Valley!"

He recognized it instantly, home was close. Elba was a small town with an even smaller population. As they drove down into the valley, they could all observe a clearing to their left. A large open field cut in half by a tiny creek. A rusted bridge connected both halves and located right next to the bridge was a poor little maple tree. Most of the orange and yellow leaves still clung to the dying branches. The poor thing was underprepared for Winter.

Over the frantic snowmobile chatter, Evan could hear the family gaze in awe at the view. For a split second his mind was clear, not a single thought flashed in his brain.

He didn't know what would be waiting for him at his home, but he was optimistic that he would see his lover and his daughter. He felt both anxious and happy to be in his current position. To think there was a possibility to see his family once more made his heart flutter with joy. But what if they'd been slaughtered or torn apart by those beasts?

Evan wasn't sure, but he tried to stay positive.

They passed a small campground with a lodge and a small summer house. Now, the group sped across a poorly constructed bridge and kept going along the outline of what used to be a road. The two feet of snow made it nearly impossible to tell. The road followed the base of a hill until they would see a gas station up ahead and several small buildings. The Winter-blasted sign read:

"*Now Entering: Elba, MN pop: 154.*"

Evan was met with memories. The first thing they all saw, was a bar, two actually. Then a small gas station and an empty church at the end of the main street.

Jackson was rather amused at the ratio of churches to bars.

Evan recognized the town as his home, He felt extremely anxious. He now directed Jackson to his house. "Take a left and continue to the white house, the one with the painted garage door, you can't miss it."

Jackson pulled up to the home and the first thing that Evan noticed was the lack of light in the house. Not a single light was left on nor was there a clear view into the house through any of the windows. His eyes scanned his home, trying to identify any sign of life. As soon as the snowmobile had rumbled to a stop, Evan leapt off the sled and ran to the house.

He began shouting the names of his two favorite people.

First his lover, "*Kate*"*!*

Then his little girl, "*Jade!*"

Jackson wanted to shoosh him, figuring that they didn't know what kind of people were left in the small town. He ultimately decided not to.

It wouldn't have mattered; Evan still would've shouted for his family.

The garage had a painting or mural, whichever word you prefer. It was two hands almost touching, in the background there were rolling hills and distant pastures.

He knew that the garage would be the best way to get in, a security system was something the family would always talk about but never get around to.

Evan began attempting to lift the garage door when Jackson stepped in and started helping. They lifted it successfully and walked to the door that led into the home.

Eggshell white wallpaper and an overall lived-in atmosphere. Ahead of him was an entrance way under the stairs into the kitchen that wrapped around the backside of the staircase. The staircase made this L shape. The living room was connected to the kitchen and was at the front of the house.

Evan called their names out franticly. He ran to the front door, spun around the staircase, and headed right up. It was split between two rooms and a small intersection between. On the right was the shared room between husband and wife while the room to the left belonged to his daughter.

He first checked his daughter's room, posters and picture frames on the walls, stinky socks, and an old beanbag. "Jade! Hello? Are you in here? I'm home!"

No response. Not even a whisper. No one was there.

Next, he ran to his room, half drawn drafts of beautiful works of art covered the walls. The bed was centered with a nightstand on each side.

"Kate, Jade? Are you guys in here, I'm home, it's Evan! Please, are you guys there?"

He would look through every nook and cranny. He then thought about something, thinking that they've got to be in the basement.

He had never ran so fast down the stairs, spinning around the passage into the kitchen. After passing through the kitchen, he had finally arrived at the basement door.

He flung the door open and saw a figure standing at the threshold near the bottom of the stairs. Every instinct in his body told him to close the door. When her twitching body started to turn around, Evan already knew what had happened.

Long dark, slightly curly hair and layers of cloths. Slow twitching and sudden jolts. Evan feared for the worst.

He said her name.

"Kate."

The figure turned around. *It was her.*

Time stood still for a moment.

Evan met eyes with his wife. She had turned into one of those things. The floating orbits laid still in the socket, glazed over and traumatized. It seemed to reject the urge to move.

Evan stood there, mouth open. His eyes being flooded with emotion. Frozen and unable to move.

It shook him to his very core.

Then, reluctantly looking so, his dead wife began walking up the stairs, one step at a time. Shaking with the urge to stop. As if his wife was still there, but she couldn't control her own body.

Evan didn't know what to do.

He could only assume his daughter was down there too. His heart sunk like a rock in the ocean. As if someone had tied cinderblocks to his ankles and dropped him in the deep end of a swimming pool. His soul hardened like cooling magma. His mind was in constant motion with thought. Like a factory manufacturing doubt.

He felt his world crumble, everything he had been hoping for. All that time and then this. What he could've done and how he could've handled things. Maybe if he were faster or did things differently, maybe his family would still be alive.

The body that once belonged to his wife had now made it halfway up the passage, nearing the top.

Ana had just entered the house when all she could hear was a distant gargle. She knew exactly what had happened. She rushed through the passage and turned the corner. Now just feet away, Evan stood still watching his wife's body approach his. Ana shoved him out of the way and shoved Kate down the stairs to further prevent another tragedy.

"She... how? My daughter, I don't know if she's down there or not... I pray she isn't." This was the first time anyone had heard his voice tremble the way it did.

Evan was in disbelief, complete pain and discomfort. He just wanted to shrivel up like a raisin and crawl away deep in a cave, never to be seen again. He fell to the ground, not crying yet but just frozen in place. His heart and soul had both been chopped away at by a vengeful lumberjack with a grudge.

After shutting the door, she signaled Jackson to come and get Evan. The last thing he needed was to see his wife die a second time.

Jackson hurryingly dragged Evan off, he was yelling and franticly trying to get loose. Jackson held him tight, "This whole situation is fucked right now…" he mumbled while trying to keep Evan in place.

Once Evan was out of sight, Ana led Kate up the stairs, shallow gargles, and weak movements. For some reason, Ana had never seen one of these creatures be as skittish as Kate was.

Now out the back door and into the snowy backyard, Ana kept her distance and made sure there was no possibility of being injured. Kate must've been the first creature to not really fight back, all the others seemed to have an unlimited hatred for the innocent whereas Kate seemed to just accept the circumstances. With a slight pause, Ana flipped Kate around and sunk a blade into the base of her skull.

Ending things.

Small gargles and tragic coughing exited the corpse's mouth as she lowered it to the ground. Ana reluctantly began moving the body. Dragging it from where it previously stood and over to the side of the house. Ana sat it up against the stone foundation and faced Kate to the North, out of sight for the most part. She made sure it had a good view, which was weird considering that she was dealing with a corpse. That didn't stop Ana, she propped Kate's arms up on old building equipment and laid the head upon compacted snow. She thought about taking the ring off of Kate's finger but ultimately decided that the ring's final resting place should lie with the person Evan loved the most.

It was difficult for Ana to kill the wife, but she didn't want to consider it a wife, it was a creature, one of the flesh-eating beasts. She did what was right, or at least she thought she did. Maybe she didn't? She did what was appropriate in the heat of the moment? She didn't know. Ana contemplated.

If only there was a guide on how to handle things like that.

Ana sat in silence, frozen, not from the cold, but from her actions and how this world was affecting people. So deep in thought she didn't notice her son standing by at the backdoor looking outside at her.

"Is that… his wife?"

Ana's lip quivered. Ready to cry but she wanted to show strength in front of her son. "Yeah… I had to do it. it was what was best for Evan, she wasn't coming back."

Matt nodded, "I'm sorry Mom…" Ana could tell that her son was holding something back. He knew that things weren't going to get any better.

She knew that things were only going to get worse. She just hated to see her son that gloomy, it broke her heart. Matt hadn't come outright and said what he thought but his mother already knew what he was thinking. She tried to comfort him.

Meanwhile in the living room, Jackson attempted calming Evan down, but he wouldn't stop sobbing and crying.

He was a crab in a broken shell.

Shriveling up as his body drained of tears. Shouting an inaudible mess.

Jackson tried. "Evan, it's okay, it's alright, it's just that, everything is fucked. And I know you're in pain Evan—"

Evan wasn't listening, "Is… is my daughter down there. Please go check."

Jackson nodded with every vein in his neck constricting, "Okay."

Fearing for what he might see, he walked to the kitchen and began heading down the stairs to the basement. Each step creaked. Uneasy air filled his lungs and was exhaled with a shaking fear. It felt like the whole decade was flashing by while going down those steps.

He made it to the bottom, Evan's daughter wasn't there. He found nothing, except for one note, hanging by a nail on a wooden shelf. He removed the nail and began reading the note.

"Evan, my dear."

Me, and Jade miss you dearly, you were always the best part of both of our lives, I hope you find this—

Jackson couldn't continue reading. He felt his chest sink. He took the note and stood there for a moment, glancing at the note in his hand and then back at the door near the top of the steps. He gulped and headed up. Instead of a decade, it felt like a century passed while going up.

"Is she there?! Is she?" Evan demanded with his shaky voice.

Jackson said, "No, but I found this."

He handed Evan the note, postponing the sobbing for a moment. When he began reading it, the sobbing was resumed.

Evan couldn't handle this kind of pain. He was desperately searching for answers. A tremendous gash in the arm was a big deal but as soon as it came to the loss of his wife, the gash felt insignificant.

Why, how, when, what, but one that stood out of all those, was *why*.

Why did this have to happen? He couldn't find an answer. His mind spun and his heart sunk. He was stunned where he sat, writhing in the floor. The old rug soaked up his tears.

He missed her, even before he knew about her death. He attempted to stand up and his head was so unclear. First it was a murder plaguing his mind and now his wife was dead. How could it happen? Once again, *why* did it happen?

"Why Kate? Why not me?"

He'd switch places with his wife with the snap of a finger. He didn't want to deal with it at all. He just wanted to keep going as if nothing happened. But here was the dilemma… everywhere he looked, he would see his family and past memoires. Anyone could sympathize with this. It seems all his brain can think of is of all the times he had spent with his wife and daughter.

Why did *this* have to happen?

Ana walked back inside, along with Matt following her like a lost dog, tail in between its legs. Jackson stood close to Evan, figuring the least he could do is be there for him. "Evan, do you want to stay here for a bit?"

Evan didn't even hear Jackson; he was so lost in thought. His mind was deep below the surface.

Missing her; missing his daughter.

Jackson noticed this. "Ana go bring the snowmobile in the garage and unpack some of our stuff, we'll stay the night."

Ana stopped for a second, she looked at Evan and saw the pain he was in. She could partly understand his pain, but not of that magnitude.

Matt felt so sorry for Evan, he couldn't correctly empathize with him, he was too young.

Evan just sat there in the fetal position. His arms wrapped around his legs as he pouted. He couldn't register reality; he was blinded by his own misfortune.

Jackson couldn't help but feel sorry for Evan. He wanted to help, or do something, he just wasn't good at expressing himself or helping others in that sense.

Evan's ill heart melted into this gross, caramelized paste. Sheer pain and anger with hints of loss and desperation slugged throughout.

He couldn't move.

He crawled out of the fetal position and began walking slowly to the stairs. His daughter wasn't dead, not for sure at least. She could be anywhere though, and that didn't make him feel any better. He ascended the creaky steps, croaking like a frog in the summer dusk. Ana's eyes darted to him.

Jackson caught this and knew what she was thinking. She wanted to help him of course. He stepped forward, "I'll deal with him."

Ana nodded, "Be careful, he's not in a good place right now." Jackson reassured her and headed up the stairs after Evan.

Matt spoke, asking his mother, "What do you think happens next, mom?"

Ana didn't know if she were honest. "We go to that military base and find help."

Matt of course knew what the next move was, so he tried to clarify, "I mean about Evan," Ana was shocked he was asking about him, "You have a tender heart, Matt. I just think he'll have to figure out how to handle it."

Matt agreed. On the flip side, Jackson tried not to provoke Evan. He figured he could snap at any second. He didn't know. Evan had turned to his right and entered his and Kate's shared room. Jackson followed but kept distance.

He peeked around the corner. Evan lay there, sobbing enough to raise sea levels. Jackson didn't think he was seen, but yet, Evan never failed to surprise him.

"I see you, either stay or leave."

Evan pouted and his chest would do this weird spasm thing, you the reader of course know what I, the author am talking about, because you've probably been there yourself.

Jackson stepped into the room. He felt awkward, like he overstayed his welcome already. He didn't know what to say to Evan. "Hey; I'm so sorry, for this, man."

"Saying sorry doesn't really do anything, maybe if I had done things differently, or if I were faster. Maybe things would've had a different outcome, just… why? Why like this? I hate all of this."

Jackson could do nothing but agree with him. What Evan really wanted to do was go batshit crazy and break something, he knew that wasn't the right way to do things.

"I had to kill my neighbors," Jackson muttered, knowing that he hadn't killed anyone. The only reason he made up this strange lie was to try and relate, to try and provide Evan with the feeling that he wasn't alone.

All Evan did was leave Jackson in the silence of his own words.

"It was a nasty thing, they had turned into those monsters, you know. Even though I'm bad at well, explaining the way I feel, or getting into emotions like this, I want you to know, through all this bullshittery that I'm trying to be here for you, man. You didn't deserve this, I'm sorry, Evan."

Evan still remained silent but realized that was one of the few times that Jackson called him by his actual name. Jackson had meant what he said.

Jackson stood there for a minute, he wanted to make sure Evan was halfway decent before he left the room. There's a big difference between decent and halfway decent, and it was difficult for Jackson to distinguish one from the other. So, he left.

Trembling hands and sore eyes. Evan was weak.

As soon as he felt like he was recovering, the tears would start back up again. Chopping away at his sanity. Sitting at the foot of his bed, noticing a million little things.

Basic things suddenly sparkled with emotion and meaning. A dusty jewelry box, an old painting hung on the wall, remembering his wife straightening the painting and setting jewelry in the box.

Each corner of the room had its own significance and each object within held a memory.

He hadn't realized how much time had passed since they had arrived at the house, the sun had finally ducked below the horizon and the moon had risen above said horizon.

With the windows hiding behind useless drapes, moonlight shone through in thin stripes on the floor. Painting the room in this grotesque atmosphere.

The darkness complimented the moonlit floorboards coated by a fluffy rug stained with remnants of an old Kool-Aid spill.

He didn't know what to think about the situation.

With his wife dead and his daughter nowhere to be seen, it shook him to his core. From the second he arrived at his old home; his heart was pounding on end. Like it wanted to leave his body, this caused a shortness of breath. He couldn't handle it, he began bawling. In a fit of loneliness, he lay motionless in his bed with his eyes streaming tears and his nose leaking snot. It wouldn't be long before the sheer amount of mental exhaustion would send him into a pity sleep.

Brief intervals of sleep and crying began, where he'd wake up in a cold sweat and fall endlessly until his eyes clasped shut. After sorrowful moments of tearful terror, he would end up falling back asleep.

Evan would repeat this pattern all night.

Downstairs, Matt had helped his mother set up a makeshift bed on the floor and made the living room into a makeshift cabin bunk. Sleeping was hard now that they had found a safe place to lay their heads, which was extremely weird. Despite being concealed from the outside chaos, they all struggled falling asleep.

Jackson awoke in the middle of the night.

The hardwood floor hurt to sleep on, but at least his wife and son were comfortable. Most of the electrical appliances still worked despite the apocalyptic background. Jackson figured that most electrical sources were either damaged or failed quickly in wake of the outbreak in the bigger cities. A small valley town like Elba could last longer without existing damage.

Light from a lamp illuminated the room, leaving shadows and dark spots gleaming into the kitchen and pantry. It was quite comfy; however Jackson couldn't sleep. He gave it his hardest try but he knew that regardless, he wouldn't be able to sleep, not anytime soon at least.

Jackson stood up from the couch and rubbed his eyes. Adjusting to the vibrant light.

He stretched and his back imitated cracking ice. He peaked through the drapes blocking the window, still howling winds. Harsh conditions mixed with fowl temperatures made the inside seem like a sanctuary. Being coddled up in a small house protected from the elements made him appreciate all that he had taken for granted before the fall. Jackson yawned as he began digging in Matt's backpack for the bag of chips they had brought from home.

Sour cream and onion: his favorite.

He quietly munched, trying not to wake his family. He tiptoed to the stairs and started walking up, he was on his way to check on Evan. The light from the lamp below creeped up the stairway in segments restricted by the steps.

The light provided dim guidelines of where to step. Jackson tried to stick to these guidelines while being covert, not knowing whether or not Evan was awake.

Small sounds exited the bedroom, delicate snores, and minor mumbles. The snot that plugged Evan's nose limited his breathing. Jackson creaked open the threshold, peaking in, making sure everything was okay. He quietly closed the door.

He remembered that his wife liked to jot down in a journal she kept in her purse. She had lost it when fleeing from their home, so he figured a replacement wouldn't be too hard to find. He simply wanted his wife to be comfortable during the end of the world.

He figured there's got to be some sort of journal or notebook somewhere in the house. So he first searched the upstairs, looking in the small bookshelf at the peak of the stairway in between the two rooms; peering into Evan's daughter's room, deciding he shouldn't enter. Then steadily tiptoeing back down the stairs to the main level. Still holding the bag of chips, he tried to be as quiet as he could with the loud bag.

He wandered into the kitchen, assuming there wouldn't be any form of notebook or paper material just lying around in a room such as the kitchen.

After every other choice was no longer viable, he opened the door to the basement. Figuring there has to be something down there, right? It looked used for storage more than anything else.

As he made his way down the steps, he flicked on an old switch and illuminated the small cobble room.

Small dried/frozen droplets of Kate's blood stained the floor. Jackson looked away, noticing a piece of paper that was tacked to a small wooden shelf, sitting on top of a small cardboard box that housed Christmas decorations. The note read:

"Dad."

He set the bag of chips on the shelf, standing like a photographed sasquatch.

His natural instinct was to begin reading it, despite that, he resisted, not wanting to intrude on something that was clearly meant for Evan. His curiosity was starting to overtake his morality and without delay he glanced down at the paper, reading just the first few sentences.

He looked at the page, eyes watering. Not knowing what to say or do, reading the first couple of sentences and stopped. He couldn't handle it. The guilt he had was too much, he folded the note in half and prepared to bring it upstairs.

Evan's daughter was alive.

Traversing back up the stairs into the daughter's room, he set the note on the foot of her bed. Figuring that Evan should be the one to uncover it. Jackson made one final glance out of the poorly covered windows. The moonlit sky trying to peak through the dense blizzard storm. Being stuck inside the house invoked a cozy feeling.

Jackson steadily slipped back into his sleeping bag and let out a long sigh. Stress was already building and seemed to be adding up with every passing day. His eyes scanned the same school picture of Evan's daughter up and down for about an hour until he finally fell back asleep. For some reason, she was the focal point.

He didn't know what he had gotten himself into.

~ . ~

The sun rose over the tall trees that stood at the top of the hills surrounding Elba. All the winds had left the area and the calmness of morning Winter had set in. Despite all the death the group had encountered over the past week, the sun still rose and set. To them it was the end of the world, to the universe it was a minor inconvenience for a planet nobody cared about.

When the snowstorm had hit the region, every critter scurried into the closest natural fallout shelter. Ana was the first one to wake up, rubbing her tired eyes and finding the encouragement to stand up. The storm had finally passed, knowing this made her feel at ease, like things weren't so tense.

She remained quiet while she dotted her eyes around in the kitchen and inferring that a coffee maker had to be somewhere. "Yes!" she celebrated silently while tossing her arms up in the air. Almost completely forgetting about the day before.

Scuttling the pantry for coffee grains and finding a small, red container, she put the correct amount in the machine and filled the pot with water. She was surprised that the water still worked when she flicked the knob. Actually astonished, figuring the house must operate off a well system.

The smell of coffee soon drifted into the living room; the sound of the dripping water filled the house. Ana stood there, leaning on the counter, and soon spacing off into oblivion. Staring out off into the forest that was at the foot of a hill a few paces from the house. All the trees were coated in snow and all the were branches smothered in icy crystals. There was something so artistic and calming about literally nothing. Sure, there are trees and snow but other than that, there was nothing.

Something was so beautiful about something so simple and plain.

Jackson soon arose from the hardwood floor and wandered into the kitchen, lured by the scent of coffee. He greeted his wife normally, which was odd considering the past few days had been rocky. It felt comforting.

She opened her arms hoping to receive a hug. Jackson walked toward her, wrapping his huge arms around his wife, and setting his head on top of hers. While she embraced the hug, all he could think about was Evan. He couldn't imagine what he must be going through. The hug was brief.

Jackson spoke to her, "I need to check on the Private."

Ana nodded, wishing the hug was more genuine and a bit longer, but understood the situation.

As Jackson stepped out of the kitchen, he stopped and turned his head halfway around and spoke, "You know I love you."

"I love you too, bimbo," Ana responded with a smile and her cheeks grew rosy. Jackson did a little half smile, letting his soft side shine through.

The stairway that led upstairs felt as if it led to the sky.

Finally, after the tough walk, he stopped himself before opening the door, he couldn't do it. This deep gut feeling struck remembering what was in the daughter's note; he began to overthink.

He conjured up the bravery to attempt opening the door and of course, the door made the creakiest croak ever.

Evan lifted his head from the sheets, a total mess. Jackson tried his quickest to shut the door and avoid being spotted.

Evan knew better, "Come in."

Jackson took a big stressful gulp. "Shit," he whispered under his breath. He propped the door open with his foot. Naturally terrible at empathizing or conversing in general.

Even though he sucked at those things, he wanted to try and help Evan.

"How'd you sleep?"

Evan knew Jackson didn't care about how he slept. "Be real Jackson, ask me what you want to ask me."

"What?"

With a straight face he confessed, "I was many things out West… things I was good at and things I wasn't so good at. One thing I was incredible at was interrogating. You're easy to read, ask what you were going to ask." Evan's face remained neutrally hopeless.

Jackson looked as if he had no clue what to say next. "I wasn't going to ask anything."

"You were. I know you were." Evan stopped to look out the window, then back at the burly and bearded man in the doorway, the eyes of a man who wanted to know how the man in the bed felt. "I know what you were going to ask."

Before Jackson could intervene, Evan had answered the question he proposed to himself.

"My wife, she's… gone. My daughter, well I don't have a clue where she is and I'm just trying to figure out what I should do next."

With Evan's face looking tired, Jackson offered coffee… But Evan seemed to ignore the offer and went straight into something else. "I wonder if anyone else is here, in this town I mean." Jackson thought it over.

"There probably is," Jackson agreed.

"Small town like this, I doubt it was evacuated." Evan nodded with what little energy he was currently in possession of. "Do that today while I stay here."

Jackson accepted the terms.

He got up to leave the room, but a stroke of empathy blew over Jackson, he turned to Evan.

"I'm here for you man," and just like that he left and was down the stairs. Evan let out a sigh, barely changing his facial expression.

Jackson called his wife's name, she jolted her head to him and asked, "Yeah? What's up?"

"I'm taking Matt out; we're going to see what we can find out there." Ana began thinking up ideas about how she could help. "Should I start making some breakfast?"

Jackson nodded, "Good idea." He walked over to Matt who still was fast asleep and got a devilish idea. He firmly gripped the couch from the armrest to the back and shook it violently. Matt's eyes opened wide, and Jackson chuckled, "Earthquake!" He exclaimed while being awoken at such a wild shake.

For mere seconds, Jackson didn't have a worry in the world. Matt tumbled onto the floor; now being shell shocked, his father   lent   a   hand, "We're going out."

"Isn't it still snowing?" he was interrupted by his own observation. Clear sight from the living room and out the kitchen window indicated the storm had finally passed. "Shit," Matt said, thinking he'd get out of having to go leave the warm house.

Jackson chuckled, "Watch your language and go get your snow gear on." Matt rubbed his eyes and stumbled up. He had the impulse to check his phone only to take it out of his pocket and realize it had low battery combined with no signal.

"Matt, try 9-1-1 again," Ana spoke.

"No" No signal here," he began dressing himself in snow pants, boots, gloves, and an oversized blue patterned coat with streaks of gray. Jackson wore similar items of attire and figured they should exit through the garage to avoid passing Kate's corpse out back.

Within ten minutes, Matt had nearly woken up completely, he was ready to start the day. Him/He and his father exited through the garage but before leaving, Ana made sure to kiss them both on the cheek.

The wind had finally stopped, the worst storm that had hit the area in years just happened to fall on the very week that things took a turn for the worse.

Now the aftermath; intense snow drifts combined with that dense and dry snow that covered the ground and suffocated the landscape. The unforgiving snow lay vertically suspended on trees while the branches were struggling to keep up their integrity. Sheer weight and intense winds left most small trees in shambles and took some telephone poles down.

The storm left the small valley town shaken up and in shambles, Jackson analyzed the town from his first couple steps out of the property. Matt asked his father, "You think those things will be here?"

"It's a small town, I doubt many people have left or entered, especially with the storm fucking things up like this." Matt nodded and agreed with his father.

The road they took into town led to a small gas station and two buildings that resemble/d that of a bar. Almost three feet of snow, Jackson and Matt trudged through it. They hoped to find some folk to speak with or perhaps some food.

Jackson could remember hearing things on the news about mass cover ups but chose to ignore it. Overall, it cost him his home, his city and if he didn't keep his act up, it could cost him his family.

The coverups should've mattered more to him but at the time he figured it was government bullshit, you know? The usual shady government stuff that often goes unreported. His ignorance costed him so much. Small thoughts entered his head while he walked through the annoying powder.

He would often suppress those thoughts, "*Now is not the fucking time, gotta stay focused on finding supplies. Can't deal with this shit right now.*" He thought to himself.

Back at the house, Evan lay there, he couldn't get back to sleep after Jackson had walked in. The gravity of the situation weighed down his chest as if he were on Jupiter. He tried to find the courage to fumble out of bed and yet, was too sore and too tired to do anything at all. His chest felt like an elephant had decided to sit on it, compressing his organs and making it difficult to breathe.

He had heard all the footsteps out of the door and at first, he thought the family had abandoned him. Small clanking and muffled clatter would find its way into Evan's ears from the floor below, leading him to believe someone had stayed behind.

Suddenly the creaky old steps began creaking in the way they always have. It was weird, Evan wanted someone to talk to, but he didn't at the same time.

He heard the steps reach the bedroom door. There was a small part of Evan that wanted to tell whoever it might be to come in and a bigger part that wanted to shout for them to go away.

As he waited for her to enter, the time seemed to stop. She stood on the opposite side of the door debating if she should enter, not knowing he'd already noticed her presence. After thinking she had gathered the confidence to open the door and she soon realized that the same confidence had disappeared.

Ana walked back down the stairs and decided to stay away. Even though he thought he wanted her gone, he wanted her there and talking to him, distracting from the grim reality.

Chapter 6

Weather Wasted Town

Elba was desolate.

The small local bar across the 'T' shaped intersection still had its lights on. Jackson saw this and felt sick, he instantly made Matt stand behind him. Trudging through the snow together they made it to the entrance. Jackson noticed the configuration of this establishment was very strange. Figured it was one of those double story high ceiling bars.

"Lights?" Matt asked.

"Yeah," Jackson sighed.

They looped around the back of the building and found the kitchen entrance. Jackson untucked the pistol from his belt and prepared to open the door. The crammed alleyway had enough room for them both to stand on opposite sides of the door as a precaution.

He banged on the door with the butt of the gun to attract any possible beings inside. Before anything serious happened, Jackson directed his son to hide behind the dumpster off to their left.

Suddenly, a figure appeared at the door, an older man peered through the small glass pane. From what Jackson could observe, he had all those manly wrinkles, you know. The forehead and cheek wrinkles of an elderly gentleman.

He called out, "Hello? Is anybody there? I thought everybody left for the city."

Jackson quickly and carefully debated his next course of action, not knowing what to say as a response, "We've actually come from the city."

"Are you an officer?" Jackson was confused, he wondered why the man would ask that, "No, we aren't, I am not an officer."

"Then why should I trust you? You're only here to rob us," Jackson backed up, confused and baffled, "What have they been broadcasting on the radio?" He demanded.

"Not to trust men like you, to not open the door for anybody and to stay inside, and that's exactly what I'm going to do," assertively the man said.

"You don't know the half of it, they shot at me and my family—" He signaled Matt to come out from behind the dumpster.

Confused and on edge, Matt exited the dumpster and presented himself to the old man. His expression changed to dismay, now asking, "Is this true kid?"

"Yeah, why would we lie to you about something like this?" Jackson backed away to let his son talk. Not fearing much of the old man anymore, the conversation continued without a hitch.

The old man was beginning to show signs of trust; nodding and losing the somewhat disgruntle expression. Jackson took this how he would, with a grain of salt but with hope this time. As Matt continued to speak, Jackson was analyzing the situation, hoping betrayal or theft would be out of the question.

As the man started to crack open the door to provide entry, he stopped to speak, "Just you guys then?"

Jackson hadn't thought this part through and scrambled to come up with something to say, "Two more at the house," Matt said before his Dad could get the words out. Fearing that Evan and his wife could now be in danger. He then realized he would need to conceal Evan's military background as the man would no longer trust a military official.

The man was preoccupied with jolting the door open. The amount of snow was staggering, they had to clear the way just so the door could open.

Matt continued about the military and how evil they seemed to become considering recent events and Jackson pulled him aside and out of audible distance from the man, "Don't talk about Evan."

He nodded, agreeing with his father, and realizing everything would fall apart if they knew of Evan's prior military involvement.

The man hadn't heard a word because of his ongoing struggle with the door.

Jackson slid in and held the door for Matt. The kitchen they stomped into was obviously not up to code, but you could tell that some kickass burgers were once cooked on the stovetop. The man led Jackson and Matt further through the kitchen, looping back and around into the main bar. Jackson's eyes widened when he identified two different men taking refuge.

The unveiling of two additional men pushed Jackson even further to the edge. The room was two stories high and had a large round bar table with many side booths. Tv's filled the corners of the wall and animal mounts crowded the upper walls.

"Hey Johnny! This the guy who was knocking at the back door?" His name being revealed as Johnny spoke up.

"Yeah, he says he's got two other people back where he's staying."

Jackson wanted to speak up and tell everybody to slow down but he was nervous. Based on his last encounter with people, he didn't exactly jump to trust all that fast anymore.

"So, these are my two best employees, we got caught in this damn blizzard while all the TV's and radios were telling us to evacuate, and ever since we've been stuck here." Johnny pointed to a short, probably 5'5 man with a stocking cap on his greasy head.

"This is Ethan," The most distinguishable feature about him was the drink in his hand and cigarette in the other.

"And this here is George," The man who was pointed out and identified had a blonde beard shorter than Jackson's and a crew cut. He greeted Jackson opposed to Ethan who just briefly glanced at him. Jackson instantly didn't like Ethan and thought of him as a no-good drunk who didn't have much regard for anyone around him.

"Ethan doesn't talk much but my oh my can he serve drinks!"

Jackson knew what kind of man Ethan was and put himself in front of Matt.

"So, what's your name big guy?"

Growing more and more timid, Jackson acted as a wall between the men and his son. He stood stiff as a wall and tall as a tower. "Oh, I almost forgot, my name is Jim, and this is Hayden," Jackson said, not budging to show the men who his son was. Matt thought it was stupid for his Dad to miscommunicate their names, but he understood what his father was trying to do.

Everything was fine but this weird overarching fear for him, his son and the people back home was eating away at him. Itching to leave, Jackson's eyes darted around, trying to identify as many exits as possible, growing restless as he did so. Matt noticed his distressed father. Now this made him uncomfortable, based on the last couple days things were about to take a turn for the worse.

"Can we set you up with anything?" Johnny asked, "We've got enough stuff in the back to cook a couple more meals for you and your kid there."

They were relieved to hear this; Matt was surprised to hear that someone had offered him a meal. "Yes!"

"What'll you have?". In shock, Matt shouted, "A burger!" Jackson didn't quite trust it yet and decided to speak up, "Hey son, maybe we should quick go check on the others."

His stomach twisted and turned with fear and doubt, preventing him from being hungry in the slightest.

Matt wanted that burger the man spoke of, but he understood what his Dad was doing. Figuring it might be better to go along with it. They felt lured and actively persuaded to stay.

The one man was practically drunk and the other could possibly overpower Jackson, his eyes darted around the room. Figuring he could take the old man and make a break for it, putting his son in front of him on the way back to the house. The mountain of tension and distrust built and built. Jackson stood there like the floor beneath him was turning into lava and his only escape was a risky path.

Trust is a tough one. Trusting strangers was one thing but trusting strangers amidst a global epidemic after the end of the world was another.

As the world spun around him, Jackson stepped back and located a saltshaker on the table behind him and gripped it covertly, he prepared to make his move.

He threw the saltshaker at... hm... Jackson had totally forgot his name, either way he threw it at the sober blonde guy and tossed a tablecloth on top of the drunk.

The old man seemed confused, "The hell?" Jackson darted around bringing his son with him. "Hey, what are you doing?" Johnny shouted.

They darted back through the kitchen and out back into the alleyway to safety.

The drunk threw himself upward to chase after Jackson and Matt while the blonde, George, sat there dumbfounded, "Did the guy really just throw a saltshaker at me, what the hell."

"I'm gonna get that son of a bitch!" Ethan exclaimed. Johnny spoke up, "I don't know what's going on, but it isn't good."

Ethan went up to go chase after them, but was nearly stopped by Johnny, only to be shoved out of the way. "Stay out of it Johnny!"

When Ethan drunkenly jogged around and into the kitchen, Johnny ordered for George to make sure Ethan didn't get into too much trouble.

"Those folk seemed on edge from the get-go—I don't even want to know what's going on the city."

George sighed and went to follow, figuring his 'friend' was going to get himself into a fight, Déjà vu form every night at the bar. Jackson and Matt stormed off through the snow trying to get back to the house as fast as possible when shouting came from behind them

"Come back here and fucking fight me!"

Jackson quickly turned around, looking at the drunken fool chasing him and his son. His first instinct was to turn back around and get his son to the house as fast as possible. He briefly thought about unholstering his pistol and *using it*.

Instead of *using* the pistol for its intended purpose, he chose to rather fire a round into the air to scare his attacker. This however did not inflict its hoped-for effect.

Evan's eyes blew open after hearing the gunshot while Ana whipped out of the living room to peer out of the window. The sight was something out of a nightmare.

A man stumbled after her husband and son. Now, Jackson and Matt banged on the door, begging to be let in. She rushed over to begin unlocking the door.

Evan came rushing down the stairs completely leaving his sorrow in the room. He quick unlocked the door with one swift motion and flung the door open. At this point Ethan was out in front of the house babbling curse words. Jackson was turned to him looking down with Matt behind him, safe from harm. Jackson told Ethan to back off and when he started walking up the steps, Jackson aimed his pistol.

He wasn't going to shoot until Ethan darted toward him. Evan threw Jackson out of the way and swung his foot toward Ethan, instantly recognizing him as the town drunk, he'd had to hold his tongue for countless times. Oh, how Evan had distain for a man like Ethan, knocking him down the steps and into the snow. The pistol still fired a stray bullet as it all happened so fast. Both Evan and the attacker were underdressed and unprepared for the weather.

Evan focused all his anger on this poor individual. Outsourcing his pain in this horrible way felt good but he knew it was wrong. The drunkard tried fighting back but was met with brutality. Ethan tried pulling a switchblade to slash Evan, only to be disarmed and get his forearm snapped like a twig. The constant cracking and snapping of the bones horrified George who was just a couple paces behind Ethan when this happened. Jackson focused his aim on George who was now frozen in his tracks.

Ethan sputtered a drunken slur while Evan backhanded him. The meaty punches had been accompanied with a downpour of red upon the white.

Jackson felt vulnerable during this encounter. Evan had somewhat proven himself but as a result, Jackson began to question his own skill regarding his ability to keep his family safe. When Evan's target was rendered, "Immobile," he turned to George with fire in his eyes.

George pleaded with his hands up, blinking a few times to recognize Evan. It was the same man he'd seen around town; how on earth did things get to this extent? "I was coming to stop that fool! I had nothing to do with this!"

Jackson stood there without knowing what to do next. His son stepped out from behind him and stared at Ethan on the ground.

"Drag him back and don't set foot near this house… or I'll kill him next time." George complied, scared out of his mind he began dragging Ethan back toward the bar. Evan grinded his teeth while stepping away from the man he had just beaten to a pulp.

He hadn't even thought about his image and how badly it had been tattered by this act of violence. The few people left in Elba who knew him were now *scared* of him.

Ana stood on the porch now with her family. They all stood there fearfully.

Heaving with lust knee deep in the snow and trace amounts of blood on his knuckles; each breath made his head throb. Every limb ached with pain and the blood that flowed through his veins carried adrenaline throughout.

Ana rushed Matt inside to clean him up as a motherly instinct. Jackson was frozen, for the first time during this crisis he stood there like a tree. He had nearly failed to protect his family and was saved by some guy they'd only known for a couple days. He tucked his pistol away and couldn't stop looking at Evan. Things had escalated so quickly that it left him no time to comprehend. On edge and feeling sick to his stomach, he turned around into the house and went straight to the bathroom.

He shut the door and began undressing the layers he had put on prior. He set the gun on the shelf and ripped off his shirt. He did all this without even taking a breath. After a couple seconds of standing there, he looked up at his reflection and finally took a couple of deep breaths. Disappointed in how he handled that situation, he just stood there, holding the sink for stability.

Out in the cold, the wind whistled, and Evan watched George drag the limp and bloodied body down the vague street outlined by the displacement of snow. The young afternoon was so quiet. So very quiet. Dropping to his knees and realizing this was the wrong way to outsource his pain, he began to think to himself. After the hopeless night in that bed, he flung out of it so fast he'd forgotten to put shoes on. He stood there looking at his feet covered in snow. Strangely focusing on this as a focal point. Nearly in the middle of the street with blood-stained snow all around him, he stopped breathing.

The cold was almost unnoticeable for him. Standing there like a statue. His lungs started breathing again after the blood vessels in his head began to throb.

Ana was inside questioning Matt, "What happened? Why were they chasing you guys?"

Matt told her to slow down, and he believed it was just a misunderstanding. Ana was so confused by this, everything seemed so simple and easy going before this incident. The morning was delightful before Jackson and Matt went out. She hadn't even realized she burnt breakfast either, so now the house smelt of charred toast and disintegrated eggs.

While Ana finished tending to her son, Evan stepped through the threshold of the front door. Shellshocked and unwilling to speak.

Matt and his mother both stood there wanting to ask the same thing, to ask if he was okay or not, they already knew the response would be a silent one.

He shook his clothes off, leaving snow chunks all over the hardwood floor. One of his knuckles split and the gash in his arm seemed as though it had opened again. Blood dripped from the breaks in his skin. He went to use the bathroom only to be greeted by Jackson exiting. They both made brief awkward eye contact as they passed by one another.

Jackson could feel the heat in Evan's eyes while looking into them.

Once Evan entered, he shut the door fast and did all of this without a thought. Not a word at all was spoken from anyone.

He did the same thing that Jackson did, holding the sides of the sink to stabilize himself. He gazed into his reflection deeply. Small mumbles and grumbles from outside the bathroom door let Evan know that they were talking about him in secret, all he could do was assume.

He assumed correctly. The others spoke of the incident behind his back believing he wasn't eavesdropping beyond the bathroom door.

"I didn't know he was capable of much more than what he'd already shown us," Ana spoke.

"That was…" Matt tried to search for the right word to describe what just happened, but nothing quite fit.

Jackson didn't wish to relinquish his thoughts regarding it, he was ashamed of what he did, rather what he didn't do to prevent the situation from unfolding the way it did. He was completely and utterly silent.

Ana tried asking him questions about it, but Jackson mostly blocked it out. He had a habit of rejecting contact when something was bothering him. Ana had mostly figured out how to handle this side of him but by no means was she good at it.

Jackson sat down on the couch and remained there. Letting out deep breaths and sighs occasionally. Ana tried sitting down next to him to comfort him but ended up fighting briefly with him instead.

"What happened?" She softly asked.

He was quiet. She tried poking again.

"Hey," she wished he wasn't so despondent.

He glanced at her without turning his head, mumbling a sound without opening his mouth.

"What happened?" She knew he didn't want to talk about it, but she needed to know what happened.

"We came here, Ana." She didn't like it when he used her name. "And I think we need to get back on the road." He folded his arms.

Most of the time when faced with internal issues, instead of dealing with them, he'd find something to distract himself from it. That's why he liked traveling/driving/working. It helped him from dealing with things.

"I also need a fucking smoke," he said with a sigh. Ana sat there next to her husband, not really knowing what to do next.

Evan sat on the side of bathtub shirtless and licking his wounds. He had patched up his knuckle and was currently working on his forearm gash. Hearing Jackson outside saying they should keep moving, he stopped binding the cloth for a second. Looking at the door as if he were looking at Jackson.

Maybe he was right. Maybe moving forward would be the best course of action.

Evan contemplated. Now hearing Ana reason, "I don't think it would be healthy for him." Evan clearly knew who she was talking about.

He wrapped the cloth around once more, unraveling the thoughts that plagued his mind. Maybe getting on the road would take his mind off his wife, maybe it would cure him. The tranquil release of travel often distracted him, but the thought of leaving his house was what really held him back. He didn't want to leave his town and her, certainly didn't want to leave home.

With the bathroom light illuminating him poorly, he went back and forth in his head. Now thinking of his self-interest rather than his wife. What would be best for him? A nice vacation would be nice but as of now, that seemed to be something that he wouldn't experience ever again; so that was off the table. He knew moving forward to the military base would be in the family's best interest. But leaving his home behind would be difficult.

It was his only safe space in a world full of harm, but sometimes you need to step out of the box to see the scope of things.

His brutality was now just a distant thought that he figured wasn't worth thinking about. He was far more concerned with moving forward, like beating that man had made him realize that if he stayed there any longer it wouldn't get better. Not by a long shot.

Evan finished bandaging up his arm and put his shirt back on. He splashed his face with water and again looked at his reflection, now seeing his wife with him, a part of him. Knowing that Kate would want him to do what's best for Jackson's family.

Slowly, he opened the bathroom door and presented himself to the family, Ana and Jackson sat on the couch and Matt sat on the floor going through his bag. Evan noticed the snow he shook off was now fully melted into the hardwood floor. He stood there looking at them, while they sat there looking at him as if a confession was in store. Evan spoke not a word about what he did to Ethan but rather demanded them to do as he said.

"Be ready before sunrise tomorrow, we're leaving," he turned and went up the stairs. He left the family without a response or ability to question him.

Jackson didn't even change his expression. Matt spoke, "Tomorrow before sunrise?"

"Should we talk to him?" Ana questioned.

"I think his mind is made up, besides I'm ready to leave." Jackson murmured.

"Is this what's best for Evan?"

"Who gives a damn, you heard him, Ana."

The decision was made. By sunrise tomorrow the group was to leave, and this decision was mostly favored by Jackson. Matt and his mom on the other hand weren't too fond of it, they were just getting comfy at the house.

Up in his room, Evan rustled through his dresser hoping to pack some clothes for the trip. He figured that leaving his military uniform behind would be a wise choice considering how the government had made themselves look recently. He tore his rank patch off and set it on his night table. He hung up his uniform and began going through the closet now looking for Winter clothing.

A nice, big gray jacket with the inner lining being a blue flannel pattern revealed itself to Evan, completely forgotten by him, "No way... I forgot she bought this for me."

He put it on and noticed it fit astonishingly well. Perfectly cuffed sleeves and collar. Brass buttons and beautifully placed pockets informed Evan that this was indeed the jacket that would get him through the Winter.

He took the coat off and draped it over a hook in the closet. He grabbed a few earthy colored t-shirts and tossed them in the duffel bag. This duffel bag he planned to take with was a dark green with leather stitches, complimented with its overall quality. It used to be his Dad's duffel bag that had become his over time.

He packed a pair of boots and in a small, secluded side pocket, he packed a picture of his family, still in the frame. He set the trapper hat he planned to bring on the same hook the jacket was draped over. A small hand sized military radio was set in comfortable side pocket.

Evan loaded a spare belt and an old holster of his that lay hidden under many boxes. He packed an old dark green hoodie along with this small snub nose revolver he had. Silver tint around the chamber, disrupted by common scratches from repeated rotation. The frame was equally silver but had less wear and tear. The wooden handle was a dark whiskey oak color. He had three boxes of ammunition for it, those of which he packed in the bag and loaded 6 into the chamber. It was properly sighted in and ready to use at a moment's notice. All Evan wanted was to be prepared for what they would come to face in the open world now ravaged by chaos.

Evan set the revolver on his night table and packed a couple more articles of clothing. Doing all this like an automated machine programmed to accomplish a task.

He stood up and took the rank patch off the night table, then slipping it into his wallet. Evan still carried his wallet with him despite recent circumstances.

It appeared as though only seconds had passed since beating that man to the brink of death, but Evan was caught off guard by the passage of time. The Winter evening had set in fast, dimming the landscape with its blue gleam.

Now figuring he should check out his daughter's room, he walked in between the threshold. The family downstairs heard him cross from one room into the other, wondering what he was doing, Ana theorized.

They all sat down there; quiet and cautious, afraid of Evan. Jackson most of all, believing himself to be the most powerful one in the group now renouncing his title. Seeing the now afternoon sun slowly sneak behind the trees, Jackson realized he should find something to eat.

He beckoned Ana to help him find something to make. They found a box of mac and cheese within the pantry. It wasn't apocalypse food, but it would totally hit the spot otherwise. They asked Matt if mac and cheese would do it for him and he replied a solid, "Definitely."

Sitting at the foot of his daughter's bed lay a note attached to a journal labeled '*Dad*,' tattered and tiny dots of blood around the top right edge, his eyes quickly rendered the handwriting as Jade's. He removed the note from her bed and hesitated to bring it closer to his face, now having tears develop in his eyes. Now with blurring vision and increasingly intense emotions, he read the first couple lines of writing, it read:

"Dad,

The odds of you finding this are next to none."

"Mom didn't make it and told me to get out of here before the storm arrives. This past month has been the quickest and yet, the slowest of my life. Mom got bit. She's screwed and so am I if I don't get out of here. I pray you find this."

"The news guy will not shut up about Minneapolis and how safe it is. I guess we'll find out. And apparently there's this big quarantine zone there. Who fucking knows? I'll either make it, or I'll die just like Mom."

"I'm trying to remain optimistic how you taught me to be. I don't know what I'm meant to do dad. I miss you. I wish that nasty fucking military guy hadn't taken you from us. Maybe we'd have more of a fucking chance if you were still here."

"I want some gummy bears."

"With hope,

Jade."

"P.S: Sorry for all the swearing, super fed up at the time of writing this"

Every word seemed to impact Evan one way or another. Each second spent reading that page imbedded knives into his back that cut deeper than should've been possible. Jade didn't seem hopeful, this was terrible news to Evan, usually she was optimistic about things. Overly optimistic if he was being completely honest.

"Minneapolis?" he questioned himself. Thinking it over and over in his head. *"If the military there is like the military here, she'd have been shot by the time she arrived."* This made the situation less hopeful for his daughter. He was on his knees at the foot of the bed, pouting like a sick dog who'd been scolded for puking.

He wished he knew what to do.

The worst thing ever is knowing *which paths you can take*, but not knowing *where they will lead.*

Small mumbles from downstairs made their way into the room, Evan glanced over at the light shining through the doorway, gleaming onto his face as he stood up.

Holding the note, he wandered his way down the stairs to speak to the others.

Tears streaming down his face, now knowing where his daughter went off to, each step down felt like he was sinking deeper into a pit with no bottom to it. Now reaching the bottom of the staircase, he turned to face the family.

In the midst of cooking Ana walked out from the kitchen to see what Jackson and Matt were staring at. Evan, now a shell of who he once was stood there holding his daughters note.

"Minneapolis," his lips quivered, and his hands shook. If only it were easier to be that direct.

Jackson of course knew what this meant, but it left his family puzzled wondering what Evan meant by, "Minneapolis."

The first words muttered from anyone was, "What?" From Matt.

They all stood there in the living room, darting eyes at one another hoping to make sense of it, all besides Evan. His eyes were focused on a focal point which was unknown to everyone in the room.

"That's where she is."

They all figured the same thing, that he was speaking about his daughter. Jackson and Ana made eye contact reading each other's minds in the process. He knew she wanted to ask and speak to Evan, he tried urging her not to with just his eyes and small head movements.

She of course did it anyways. "Your daughter?"

"Yeah."

"Well, if you'd like, we could accompany you there if you'd like."

This was exactly what Jackson was worried about, he didn't want his wife signing up his family for something that (in his eyes) wasn't worth it.

Jackson visibly rolled his eyes at his wife. He cared about Evan but not enough to go and try to rescue someone who he believed was probably dead.

Matt was in between all of this. Not knowing what to do or say. When his Mom made this offer, he whipped his head to look at her, thinking to himself, "*No way.*"

Evan spoke up now that everything was tense.

"If you feel that you want to, you can."

Jackson wanted to speak to his wife about it but was unable to currently due to Evan being present.

Matt danced his eyes around at his parents and at Evan, he wanted to speak up but figured it would be better if he didn't.

Evan seemed disillusioned with himself, he turned around and walked back up the stairs without a word to anyone else in the room.

They were all frozen. Suddenly the timer Ana had set up for the macaroni began blaring and ringing. She jumped and ran to strain the noodles. Jackson cleared his throat loudly trying to get his partner's attention. She pretended not to notice while straining the macaroni and preparing the pot with the cheese powder. Setting 1/8 a stick of butter and a fourth cup of milk into the pot, Jackson cleared his throat again.

"Ahem."

"Jackson," she said while mixing all the ingredients together, "I know he wouldn't make it alone."

"The fuck makes you think we'll make it surviving out there? We've barely made it here!"

"I just thought... I don't know. I thought maybe we could help him..."

"And put us in danger? Are you serious?" Jackson moved his right hand to press it against his forehead, slightly annoyed. Often when he was upset, he handled it by arguing.

Ana now separated the mac and cheese into four bowls and set spoons in them.

"Here guys," she said as she gave her son and husband each a bowl of mac and cheese. Jackson knew she didn't want to talk about it.

"If that safe compound even exists, shouldn't we see it through before we chase a rumor."

Ana was now conflicted, "I guess I didn't mean anything by it, I just knew he needed comfort."

Jackson now knew why she said what she did. "I'll speak to him in the morning."

Ana told her husband to bring Evan his serving of food, "Maybe you could bring it up to him now, sorry for saying what I did."

Jackson was comforted by her apology, thinking to himself, "Maybe I can talk us out of this, or at least convince him to wait."

He got up from the couch and headed for the stairs, stopping just as he was about to walk up, apologizing to his wife.

"Sorry Ana, you just have to remember it's him or us, and I figure I'd rather have us survive than him." He spoke in a tone that ensured Evan wouldn't hear him.

Each time that Jackson had to walk up those damn stairs, it felt as though they had been elongated further. It got harder and harder to walk up those steps every time.

He twisted the handle and entered. Evan sat with his legs crossed, reading through the same note addressed to him over and over. Jackson set the bowl of macaroni on the dresser and tried speaking to him.

"You know I value the safety of my family over your safety right, and you also know that if Rochester turned out the way it did, Minneapolis is likely much worse. You understand that I can't let my family follow you into a death trap, right?"

Evan nodded, "I figured you'd have something to say. I need to see it through Jackson."

"I understand Private, but I won't let my family be put in harm's way for you to follow a lead. Besides man, a city of that size would be impossible to navigate just for one person."

"She's in there, or somewhere in between."

Moments of silence concluded the conversation. Both now being divided on what to do about things, Jackson left Evan and continued down the stairs leaving the conversation open ended and unfinished.

When Jackson reached the bottom of the stairs, both Ana and Matt looked up from their bowls of macaroni. His sunken eyebrows and ill faded facial features had let them know that the conversation between him and Evan wasn't exactly what he had been hoping for.

He spoke to his family, "It's best that we rest up, we're leaving in the morning."

Before everyone had fallen asleep, Ana tried poking at Jackson to talk to him. She figured she could maybe change his mind; she knew he was upset with her.

They didn't touch each other all night.

Chapter 7

The Road to Minneapolis

At least there wouldn't be traffic.

The sun hadn't yet begun to peer over the blanketed hills, yet Evan was wide awake. Making sure his bag was packed with everything he wished to bring along. The holster lay hidden beneath his thick gray coat.

He trudged down the steps carrying everything. Jackson was also awake at this hour, though his family remained asleep. He was preparing coffee for everyone and quietly washing their mac and cheese-stained bowls.

Jackson stopped Evan just as he was about to drop his stuff at the door asking him, "Hey, is there a spare unused notebook anywhere? My wife would love to keep writing."

Evan scratched the stubble on his face, "If there was, I'd bet it would be somewhere in Jade's school stuff upstairs. I'll get one for you." While saying this, Evan examined that Jackson had been doing the dishes. He let a smile shine through but didn't let it shine for long.

Jackson thanked him and tried to keep common ground with Evan, especially after seeing his violent side the day prior.

The duffel bag was dropped off by the door and Evan trotted up the stairs, eager to get on the road. He swiped an unused notebook from Jade's school backpack but before going back downstairs he noticed something on her bed. Her favorite stuffed animal from her childhood sat on her windowsill, staring back at him. This small bunny rabbit stuffed animal that Jade had grown up with; his daughter had somehow left it behind during her departure.

He knew she would never leave something so important like that, figuring she must've forgotten it, he picked it up and planned to put it in the duffel bag.

He walked back across the 2nd floor intersection and snatched his dirty bowl. Coming down the stairs significantly slower than he had gone up them, he handed Jackson a red spiral notebook and his dirty bowl; He knelt to the duffel bag.

He set the stuffed animal in a small side pocket that felt as though it was designed to perfectly fit it.

Jackson took the notebook and bowl, now thanking Evan and questioning him at the same time, "What's that?"

"Jade's stuffed animal, she must've left it behind."

"Yeah," Jackson spoke, "For what it's worth, Private, I hope you find her, I just want to be able to save my family before we chase after yours."

The two remained quiet now. With the room growing more and more silent by the minute, Jackson figured it would be best to wake his family up for the day. He brought the dish to the kitchen and resumed his current task.

Matt of course fought waking up and all it took for Ana to wake up was the realization that coffee was brewing.

She sat up and rubbed her eyes, looking around the room and letting the pleasurable scent of brewing coffee fill her nose.

Jackson spoke while combing his gruff beard through his fingers, "Good morning babe, I got coffee on the cooker already."

Ana smiled and her dimple winked. "You're too sweet you big ole' hunk."

Her husband smiled at what she said. Smile might not have been the right word; it was more of a shallow fluctuation of gratitude, but smiles like that were the norm, so Ana knew it still made him fuzzy inside.

Matt groaned, "Ugh." Ana turned to him, naturally being better at waking him up as it was her daily duty back at home. "I promise we'll find somewhere to stop and get some chips or something…" She spoke in a persuasive tone.

Evan was silent, usually he'd be talking to everyone a heavy bunch but as of now, all he could muster was a quiet, "Good morning," to the family.

Her husband already had a full mug, so she got up to get herself one, searching through numerous cupboards until Evan corrected her.

"Top left, Ana." He sounded like he had been smoking for years, but in reality, he'd never smoked a cigarette in his life. He was just tired.

"Thanks, found it."

It was all so quiet and awkward. Ana didn't like the atmosphere in the room, Matt didn't care much because he figured he could catch up on sleep while everyone was concerned about Evan. The light coming from the lamp illuminated the room with yellow light, while the threshold into the kitchen was blinding compared to the living room. Ana began filling a mug with coffee, then scrounging to find creamer.

She hated the natural taste of coffee and would almost fill half the cup with creamer. The ratio of coffee to creamer was that of ocean to land.

Evan opened the front door, as soon as he did this, a rush of cold air entered the home. He stepped outside and stomped down the front steps, heading to start up the snowmobile.

He dropped the duffel bag on the sled and revved the engine, putting it into proper gear as he awaited the family's arrival. Light winds traversed the hillside and swept dry snow along the landscape. Eager to leave and being dressed in layers, he stood there leaning against the snowmobile.

Sweatpants, jeans, double socks, t shirt, sweatshirt, coat and gloves, the holster being concealed beneath all this and out of sight. He was prepared for whatever they would face. Minneapolis was roughly a day's trip away, maybe two if they chose to stop somewhere. The dark sky was now beginning to be illuminated by the flourishment of daylight. Coloring the sky dim dark blue with vibrant and shaded lines of pink dancing off the low hanging clouds.

Evan was just ready to leave. His eyes glanced around the property; images of distant family memories flashed to him in quick succession.

An old swing set peeking out from the backyard and the painted mural on the garage. The front steps that led to the small porch and each second-floor window. Nostalgia had a strange way of making mundane things glimmer with that of extraordinary proportion.

The family now stepped out of the front door, interrupting Evan's reflection. They hadn't realized how much time had passed.

"So, do you have a specific path in mind Private?" Jackson said while stepping over the bloodied snow from the day before.

"We hit uh... I'm trying to think of what it's called... I-35 I believe, that's where I'm shooting for." Thoughts in his mind threw his train of thought off the rails, almost forgetting what highway he was planning on traveling to.

"Will that get us near the compound?"

Evan lied despite the trust that the family had in him, "Yeah that'll get us close."

Jackson sat behind Evan on the snowmobile, realizing that he was unable to prove or disprove Evan, but he knew something was off

He chose to trust what Evan said.

Ana and Matt recognized there was no room for either of them, so they got comfortable on the sled along with all the luggage. Evan asked if they were all ready, and of course they knew he was eager to get out of there, so they replied with a simple, "Yep."

The motor let out a powerful shout as they ripped out of the small loop at the end of that street.

Passing the small bar on their way out, Jackson and Matt glared at it, knowing the significance of it. They sped down the country road passing a small gas station and an increasingly more beautiful view as they made it up and over each hill. A small campground with a creek splitting it was too scenic to avoid eye contact with. The decreasingly dim environment still allowed for things to be seen.

Rising over the hill and now being greeted with the elegantly rising sun over the powdery plowed fields, they were in awe. The horrors of their journey thus far were now being contrasted with never-before-seen beauty that provided enough dopamine for them to keep pushing. Seeing the whole countryside, small family farms and grain silos blocking light with their shadows. The landmarks remained so still as they gazed upon all of it, like a portrait.

The windmills rotated still, ever so gently and without a noise. Matt couldn't take his eyes off the splendor. Almost tuning out the roar of the snowmobile as his eyes tried to look at everything all at once, taking it all in.

His wonder and love of a good view was truly pleasured during this moment. Ana noticed her son with a partial smile, being one of the only times during this mess that he was enjoying it. She smirked a warm expression, Experiencing complete and utter kalopsia.

Passing the sign that read: "*Leaving White Water Valley,*" Signified the beginning of their journey.

Jackson also attempted to enjoy the view but was sidetracked on the past day. So much had happened, yet so little was discussed. He felt like he got no closure for what happened and knew that bringing it up would make him sound weak, he chose to suppress the emotions.

Evan just kept his eyes on the road, the same way he had the day of his deployment. Except this time, he was headed toward his family instead of leaving them. He wanted to get to Minneapolis as fast as he possibly could. Though he took a little bit of the scenery in, he mostly had his hand on the throttle and his eyes on the road. The beauty didn't distract him how he wished it had.

They sped all down the road swiftly and without delay, traversing the roads that led to Minneapolis.

~ . ~

They didn't encounter a problem until they reached the township of Castle Rock. Taking side roads and gravel pathways in and around every town that was in their way. Finally, after smart time management and clever path taking, the fuel meter had sunk to the big red E.

The small flutters of the engine's last breath were audible enough to be heard by the group. Matt had fallen asleep during the trip and Ana simply took in the view along with every new town. Jackson hopped off the snowmobile and darted his eyes looking around for a price tower that is often associated with a nearby gas station. Just barely a half-mile outside of Castle Rock, he saw a distant gas station, situated within the town.

"Over there," Jackson remarked.

"In the town? Are you sure that's a good idea?" Evan replied.

"What other choice do we have?"

Evan agreed, "I'll go get some, give me twenty minutes tops, doesn't look too far from here." He was a little annoyed about the time that they were wasting.

Jackson agreed, "So just... uh? Are me and my family meant to stay here while you do that?"

Evan grabbed the gas canister and nodded, "Bonding time perhaps?" He said while walking off into the snow flooded road that led to the town.

Jackson figured it might be nice for his family to talk about things, so he of course tried starting a conversation with his wife.

Evan was now a couple dozen paces down the road; Ana started up a conversation regarding Matt.

"He hasn't slept this good in days, not even at the house."

"I know, I hope this all comes to an end soon, maybe this is just a *right now* thing, you know?"

Optimistically, his wife replied, "Yeah, who knows, maybe by this time next week we'll be sitting around a fire drinking hot cocoa."

"Yeah, I hope that's how things *turn out*," Jackson replied, knowing her foresight into the future most likely won't *turn out*.

Their son was all snuggled up amongst backpacks and duffel bags, snot being frozen down his to his chin and snoring as if he were a diesel motor.

Ana and Jackson embraced one another as they thought similar thoughts, caring for Matt. She knew her husband wasn't exactly one for affection, but when he let his soft side shine through, it made it all the more worth it.

Based off his watch, Jackson knew it was noon, the sun was high in the sky and the wind had mostly calmed for now. They observed Evan, now near the gas station, gasoline jug in hand and making quick time.

Big pine trees provided shade for the family, hiding them from the bright Winter sun.

Matt awoke, quickly shooting up wondering where they were.

"D-d-dad?" he asked frantically.

"I'm here son, no need to shit your pants. We're just outside of Castle Rock, we just ran out of gas, that's all."

Matt took a sigh of relief while getting himself into a comfier position, stretching his arms and mid-yawn he asked, "What time is it?"

"Quarter past noon, we're on track. If we're lucky we'll make it to the compound by sundown."

Matt nodded, "That's good I guess." Now fully awake, he got up from his makeshift bed and announced he was going to find somewhere to take a leak. Jackson pointed by a distant tree.

"Might as well mark our spot huh?" Jackson proclaimed.

Matt wandered off into the brush to find a tree where he would soon *mark his spot*. Ana walked out into the road and began shuffling her feet along in a pattern. Jackson picked up on this and asked her, "Stick person huh?"

"Yes! Now get out here and help me draw a little hat on the stick guy's head."

Jackson rolled his eyes playfully and started shuffling out to where his wife was. He tiptoed carefully across the established carvings in the dusty snow, now in the stick man's torso, his wife invited him to progress further to meet her by the head.

Together now, they shuffled separately to both do at least half of the hat. Ana giggled her shy and soft chuckle while thinking about the absurdity of what they were doing. Jackson smiled softly, cherishing the moment.

Matt got back from taking a leak and noticed his parents shuffling around in specific patterns.

"What... are you guys doing?" He said with a grin.

"Get over here and help up draw this stick guy!" Ana shouted.

"Give it fingers or something!" Jackson played along.

From down the road, Evan could hear them laughing amongst each other. He turned his head and ignored it. This permanent feeling within him made the fun times in the distance seem annoying.

He analyzed the small town, seeing evacuation notices and several posters indicating many places offering quarantine zones.

Among these posters and various signs, Minneapolis was strongly indicated as a place to go. Silent as he did so, filling up the gas canister after manipulating the *pay inside* option.

Glaring at the family as the gasoline splattered within the can, he hoped they would get on the road as quick as possible. Selfishly rushing things, he let gasoline spew out of the can as it filled up, shutting off the valve and now standing up to continue back to the family.

He pulled out the folded map that lay inside of his coat pocket. Trying to decide the most fuel-efficient route to reach Minneapolis as soon as possible. He also knew the family was under the impression that they were headed toward the military hideout, he knew this was a selfish action but all he wanted was to find his daughter.

Being selfish wasn't who Evan was, but the need to find his daughter overpowered that of what was best for everyone else.

Our protagonist began walking back to the group. A heavier jug this time made things a tad bit more difficult, but he continued.

After completing the stick man, the family had launched a snowball fight at this point, balls of snow flying through the air like tank shells in a world war.

Almost back now, Evan saw this, the choice to join and the choice to keep driving to Minneapolis weighed on his shoulders.

He knew that joining the snowball fight would be the best option, maybe it would help ease him; but even if he did, he got the feeling that he wouldn't be able to get his daughter off his mind for even 5 minutes. The constant flashing image in his head blinded his eyes and deafened his ears.

"Let's get a move on," Evan said with an orderly tone.

Everyone stopped what they were doing.

"The hell'd you say Private?"

"I said we should get a move on. We'll be lucky to make it there by tonight."

Matt and Ana stood there, shockingly Matt spoke up.

"Buzzkill man," tossing a snowball Evan's way.

Pelting his jacket and looking at the chucks float down, Evan relayed a sigh, "You can keep playing, I'm just eager to get going."

Matt smiled a devious smirk as he formed another snowball with his hands, whipping it at his Dad, then ducking for cover behind a snow drift.

Evan walked over and started filling up the snowmobile. Jackson noticed his miserable tone and attempted to preoccupy his family with the snow war.

"Hey Matt! I heard Mom plans on destroying your snow drift, you better get her before she gets you!"

Knowing that he wasn't currently needed in the war, Jackson walked over to Evan. Hoping to strike up a worthy conversation.

Ana knew what her husband was doing, so she decided to distract Matt. She never thought she'd be so thoroughly engaged in a snowball fight and yet, there she was.

"You know we're just trying to make things easier for him, right?"

"I know, I know."

"If he's having a good time during a time as terrible as this," Jackson motioned at Matt, "That's a good thing and that's something I want to maintain. You gotta understand that man."

Evan nodded.

"It might do you some good to join us."

Jackson jogged back into the warzone, inciting many snowballs to be thrown.

After Evan finished filling up the snowmobile, he leaned against it, waiting for time to pass. He took his gloves off and twiddled his thumbs anxiously. Watching the snowball fight rage on, he began to envision his family in place of the current one. Seeing Kate throw snowballs at Jade and having himself take the bullet for her instead in a dramatic showdown that will never be. Creating an illusion based on what he currently saw, he blinked many times to clear it out.

He tried to focus on something different, now staring at a telephone wire, noticing three tiny birds using it as a place so sit. Of course, he thought, now watching one of the three birds fly off, never to be seen by Evan again. The two birds played back and forth almost human like, as if they were teasing one another about something.

Small innocent chirps bellowed from the birds, relaxing up on that wire without a care in the world, almost like they had no knowledge of the imminent doom that faced humanity. Maybe they were happy about humans suddenly leaving. Evan could admit that it was more peaceful with streets being as barren as they are now.

His focal point of that telephone wire was interrupted by the impact of a snowball. Now zeroing in on Matt, his grumpy face turned to that of confusion, then looking down at his coat and the fragments of snow tumbling down, confusion turned to his sorrowful attempt at a *game on face*.

Evan figured he should try to play along and maybe push his negative emotions aside. He pushed himself up and bent down to form a snowball in his hand, then launched it toward Matt.

Inserting himself into the fight, he fought hard, trying to hit anyone and everyone with huge snowballs. Evan actually found himself laughing during this. He was surprised.

Evan rolled behind a snow drift and took cover from impending snow strikes. Waiting for his moment to strike, he molded many snowballs with his hands, collecting them in mass for his attack. He jolted up from the drift and began whipping them every which way. Hitting everyone but Matt, who was hiding behind a monstrous snow drift. Evan began to plan his attack, looping behind the tree line to get the flank on him, he executed his strategy.

Unknowing of his imminent doom, Matt stayed on the lookout for his opponents. Without delay, Evan struck Matt several times with many snowballs. Both giggled with joy and carefree attitude.

About half an hour of this whimsical mayhem passed when everyone started to calm down.

Evan had actually enjoyed himself. He was surprised. He didn't think that he'd be able to laugh the way he did ever again. A small part deep inside of him wished that the fun didn't end, because it kept him distracted from his grim thoughts. If only the snowball war lasted longer, but all good things come to an end, and all wars stop being fought at some point.

They all began heading back to the snowmobile and sled.

Matt and Ana both assumed their previous positions on the sled, snuggled up with the baggage. Jackson and Evan both went for the driver's seat, now bumping into each other, dialogue began.

"Oh, I figured I'd drive there, considering that you drove here the whole way."

"No, don't worry." Evan said, he selfishly just wanted to make it to Minneapolis without the others knowing.

"You sure?"

Evan nodded while situating himself on the snowmobile and putting his trapper hat back on his head. Jackson followed suit.

The engine started up with a sputter. Evan flexed the throttle and forced it into gear. The group ripped and raced down the snow flooded midwestern road. The sun was high in the sky and all the clouds were hiding, allowing the reflection off the snow to be blindingly bright. They all accounted for this by squinting their eyes or shutting them completely.

The atmosphere was so arid, so incredibly dry despite the immeasurable amount of snow that flooded the landscape.

~ . ~

Jackson looked at his watch, seeing the time, 3:53 PM. He yelled ahead to Evan an inquiry. "How close do you think?"

Evan didn't respond, Jackson figured maybe that he didn't hear him, or maybe he was too focused on the road.

All Evan was focused on was the thought of reuniting with his daughter, hoping that Minneapolis was somewhat intact by the time that they'd arrive.

"Hey! How close are we?" Jackson said for a second time.

Evan snapped out of his deep thoughts, blinking three times, and shaking his head. "I'd say roughly a couple more hours!"

Jackson sighed, he figured they'd all be a lot closer than they really were. He knew something was off.

At about 6:00 O'clock, they made it to I-35, just as Evan had so expertly planned.

The sun had begun to set by now, leaving what little number of clouds there were in the sky painted an easter pink. The distant trees and structures were becoming ever so dim with the clouded dusk.

They had all noticed that the further they headed from Southern Minnesota, the better the weather had gotten. Matt felt as though he would be perfectly fine without his snow pants and gloves.

Now driving on I-35 and coming up on the crest of the hill, knowing he would be able to see the entirety of the city, Evan was excited, yet nervous for what he would see.

Dim clouds had slowly rolled in and overcast the sunset, making everything gray. The further North that you would look, the darker it would be.

The road leading into the city was crowded with many vehicles, big and large. All were vacant and abandoned of course.

They rolled over the crest on the hill and what they saw was earth shatteringly disgusting to look at.

The whole city was a shell of what it once was.

Taller buildings were noticeably damaged, whether it be glass panes shattered, or a fire raging. The flames grappled to many of the buildings, blowing and whipping in the wind. Skinny and fat plumes of smoke all came from separate fires.

The distant bellows of nonstop and erratic gunfire was audible from the crest of I-35. Evan stepped off the snowmobile, trying to analyze the situation more.

Fire and smoke were the only lighting, aside from the numerous flood lights and buildings still left with electricity. In the outskirts of the madness, he could observe military like vehicles entering the city. Several explosions totaled buildings and structures in the distance, only to be followed by the delayed *boom*.

Evan dropped to his knees without expelling a word nor a sound. His hands shook as he dropped to his knees.

The sight was disturbing. All they could do is estimate the death count based off their observations of the ravaged city.

The road ahead seemed even worse, cars blocking every path along with what they could only assume to be those creatures, waddling in between cars and barricades. Shadowed figures limping through the damaged environment.

A large sign was suspended above traffic down the road. Alerting them to a supposed mandatory infection check ahead, though by the looks of the highway, it hadn't been used in weeks.

He couldn't believe his eyes. Terror and doubt befell his mind, he spiraled out of control. Jackson noticed this and hopped off the snowmobile, gesturing to Evan.

"I tried to tell you, if Rochester was that bad, the cities had to have been far worse."

All Jackson got in return was stuttering silence.

Matt and Ana got up from their little seats on the sled, only to be greeted with the city on fire.

Ana was the first to gasp.

"Oh my god…"

Matt followed in line with an even louder, "Oh my god!"

"What happened here"

Evan was silent, not thinking about what to say next or even registering that anyone had spoken.

He scrambled to the duffle bag and pulled out a pair of binoculars and proceeded to put them up to his eyes. Scanning the city, looking at every tall building, seeing if he could find out what had happened, in all reality he was looking for Jade. Maybe seeing her by complete random chance would be a possibility.

Praying and hoping to see her, alas she was nowhere to be seen. The few civilians he saw were far away and blurry, but he could tell they were distressed.

Shooting firearms or running from something, every single person that Evan observed was doing one or the other. The sight shellshocked him. Distant screams were heard, indicating that the area was not safe under any circumstance. The screams could only be described as cries of murder.

Jackson spoke softly but firmly.

"*We should leave.*"

Evan wasn't going to leave after finally arriving at his destination, not unless he were to see it through.

He was *not* going to turn around.

Silence followed Jackson's statement.

"I said *we should leave.*"

Louder this time, Matt and Ana stuck close to each other slowly making their way behind Jackson. No way they were going to follow Evan into the city.

Standing still and staring at the city, Evan didn't respond. Jackson felt pressured, backing away, and getting near the snowmobile.

"Evan," Jackson asserted.

Distant clammors and booms were all that could be heard atop the crest. "We need to get out of here."

Jackson didn't care that Evan had flat out lied to him and his family, he understood why Evan would do that. All he knew was that the entering the city should be the last thing they do.

Evan started walking toward the snowmobile without a word, planning to take it and get a head start into the city. Jackson told Ana to get out of the way as he now approached Evan.

"Fuck do you think you're doing?"

Evan shoved Jackson out of the way.

"I gotta go in there."

Jackson bounced back and grabbed Evan by his arm, redirecting him away from the snowmobile. Evan spun and struck Jackson hard.

He was staggered and honestly surprised at what had just happened. His friend had just hit him, it wasn't a held punch either.

Jackson lunged at Evan, grappling him and they both struggled to overpower the other. Ana gasped and started to yell at them both to stop.

"You're fucking crazy!"

Evan got a hit in, Jackson got a hit in. Both struggled and whipped one another back and forth. Evan swung his right leg behind Jackson and brought him to the ground. Evan quickly ripped his jacket open and unholstered his revolver, standing over Jackson now.

Swiftly, he aimed it toward his target on the ground. Jackson had done the same, untucking his pistol out of his jeans and aiming it at Evan from the wet ground. Pulling and aiming at each other simultaneously.

Ana shouted for them to stop, tears forming in her eyes begun dripping out.

"You put that fucking gun down asshole!"

Evan gripped the pistol, fire in his eyes. Still not a word coming from him at all.

Matt wanted to speak up or do something about the situation, anything at all to deescalate it. He jolted from his mother's hold and went to get the better of Evan amongst his rage.

He grappled Evan's arm that held the revolver, taking the aim away from his Dad. Jackson stumbled to his feet fast and shoved Matt out of harm's way.

Evan tried aiming the revolver back at his friend, but before he could, Jackson had gotten the advantage. Running at Evan, the burley-built man easily tackled the malnourished and weak one.

Getting him to the ground now, Jackson disarmed Evan and tossed the revolver a couple meters away just out of reach. One hit, two hits! Multiple strikes to Evan's skull.

"God... damn it!"

Evan preformed a kick maneuver into Jackson's ribcage, knocking the wind out of him. He scrambled out and over to his revolver, picking it up and aiming it at Jackson once again.

Jackson had already bolted to his feet and already had his gun trained on Evan. Adrenaline rushed through them both.

Evan was cornered between parked and vacant cars; Jackson had the advantage.

"I'm taking my family and I'm leaving... you wanna get in the way of that? You'll die here."

Evan stood there, heaving like a wounded bear. Jackson backed his family toward the snowmobile, he kept his aim targeted at Evan. He stumbled back, took the duffel bag off the sled, and tossed it several meters, as far as he could.

The family boarded the snowmobile and pulled it into gear, revving the motor while still pointing his pistol at Evan. It was tense, like a wild West standoff. They locked eye contact, angry and reserved looks from both men.

Without a word back to each other, Jackson ripped out of the highway and dodged cars all the way up the on ramp. Matt eyeballed Evan as they pulled away.

Both men were hurt, not only because of the wounds that had been inflicted, but because of the severe harm done to their relationship. They had become friends in a world devoid of such, now separated because of one selfish choice.

Chapter 8

Heads

Shaking in the cold, grinding his teeth.

Evan stood there, pointing his gun at the spot where Jackson used to be, he lowered it and glared at the displaced snow on the ground. Despite the conflict that had just occurred, the bigger and more important one raged on in the city.

His body was sore, so sore. Aching to let him know that something was horribly wrong. The gash on his arm was pulsing with pain, knowing that every time it got close to healing, he would do something to mess up the whole process.

Silence followed the fight.

The slow realization hit Evan slow but very hard. His friends had left him due to his own actions. Knowing he shouldn't have started the fight and screwed everything up, he kicked at the ground in anger. He holstered his firearm and struggled to hold back tears from how hurt he was inside.

His sadness turned to misunderstood anger and determination. Afterall, he only knew them for a relatively small amount of time, right? Why should he care? He's certainly forgotten people more important than the family before.

It doesn't matter, right? He attempted to convince himself that Jackson and his family were significantly less important than they really were, and somehow by trying to justify his actions, it made him feel a little less guilty for inciting the fight and causing them to leave.

Isn't this what he wanted? To be in Minneapolis? Well yes, it was what he wanted, but was it really worth it? He could possibly find his daughter, but he selfishly severed the relationship he built with the people that saved his life.

Evan reflected on it heavily, now sitting down at the spot he once stood, trying to make sense of how he was acting. It wasn't like him to act this way, he then stood up and figured he might as well prove Jackson wrong by finding his daughter.

He staggered over to the duffel bag. As he scrambled through it, an idea struck him. While doing this, he chose to push his negative thoughts out of the way, he figured he'd have plenty of time to dwell on things in the future. He knew that it was the wrong choice, but also figured he shouldn't sit there and boil about it.

Out he pulled his military radio and began tuning it to commonly used channels to see if he could tune into anything.

After tuning through roughly a dozen frequencies, a voice blared out of the radio.

"—Can anyone spare some numbers for Lindin Hills? They just keep coming! I don't know how much longer we can keep things in order here—"

There was an abrupt cutoff followed by a bright and vibrant explosion where what Evan could only assume Lindon Hills was located.

Not a word from Evan, only his eyes being widened beyond regular proportion.

Another voice blared directly after this event.

"Linden Hills outpost come in! Come in! Is anyone there! God damn it! Them too? Fucking hell."

Raising his eyebrow and staring at the radio device in the palm of his hand, he began to think to himself.

"What exactly is going on in the city?"

Tuning his radio to more frequencies to see if he could get any more glimpses into the seemingly hopeless situation. Twisting the side knob on the radio, hearing only static as he swapped through the countless frequencies.

Suddenly as he tuned in to 184.6 VHF, a deep bellowing voice was speaking with a sorrowful and depressive undertone.

The constant noise began attracting the creatures, unknown to Evan of course and without delay, one of the creatures had squeezed through a gap in the parked cars.

It slid out and fell onto his face, raising its gaze at Evan who was still distracted by the radio.

The voice bellowed several phrases along the lines of:

"Numbers are down, on both sides."

"I don't know how much longer we can keep this up."

While listening, Evan finally realized that Jackson had sped off with his bow still in the sled. He briefly frowned and shook his head, shutting his eyes and sighing.

"Lieutenant general Johansson just tells us to keep fighting, and I can confidently say that this is a fight we will not win."

Before Evan could learn anything more about the situation, the creature had announced its presence by a gravely gargle, as if it had eaten nothing but shards of glass for the past week. Its limbs and extremities clearly had frostbite, the nose had been ripped or rotted off. The skin was blackened with the frozen contents within. A t-shirt and jeans were the only thing separating its body from the outside cold. Chapped and bloodied lips, blood crusted eyes with this indescribably disgusting color, zeroed in on its target.

Evan jolted up and left the radio on the ground, the monster seemed to switch its focal point from the blaring radio to Evan back and forth, like it couldn't decide which it hated more.

Stepping back steadily, one foot behind the other, Evan figured he would have to find a way to take it down. Struggling to walk forward and twitching relentlessly, the creature stared Evan down. It began to jog at him, now swinging its frozen arms. Ultimately, it decided that Evan was the one it hated more.

Evan dodged its first attack and tripped it, bringing it to the snow below, its facial wounds and scratches that had been frozen shut by the cold had now opened, staining the snow a dark red.

It spun around on its back and Evan put his boot to its neck, keeping it nailed to the ground. He undid the belt strap that kept his blade safe, raising it high in the air and staring down at the monster. The axe gleamed orange, reflecting the distant fires.

The person inside this beast was still there, it had to still be there, *right?* Evan thought.

On the ground, the creatures twitching, and bloodied face resembled a sad and scared one in certain aspects. Like it was afraid. As it struggled and convulsed on the ground, a red and white colored foam began to spew out of its mouth.

Evan tried to figure it out before he got the chance though, he could hear several more of the creatures scuttling to his position. He sunk the hatchet into the monster's head regrettably. As he pulled the hatchet out of that bloodied stump of a skull, built up liquids and chunks flung out into the air. Evan coughed at this disgusting sight.

He quickly moved into a tactical fight position, ready to land the first shot to whatever may be coming his way. His right side was protected by a large SUV. He hadn't realized the tiny chunks of flesh that had landed on his jacket.

Before he could think his next thought, three humanoid monsters had hopped and climbed over cars, hollering with their shredded vocal cords. They hopped down and descended upon the blaring radio.

Not even noticing Evan who stood about 15 feet away, they shook their bloody fists in the air and shouted.

Evan backed away and behind the SUV, now in a prone position, looking at the creatures from beneath the vehicle. For what felt like an eternity, he laid there, hoping they would leave. After a couple minutes of silent observation, Evan heard a new set of footsteps.

Like a set of twigs tapping the ground with each swift stride, he heard it ascend upon the hood of a car. Now, its feet tapped and rattled on the metallic car surface, scraping against the paint. It hopped down and Evan saw what it was. Fear overcame him, it made the peach fuzz on the back of his neck stand on end.

Four jutted legs with infected claws protruding from each toe; it moved without delay. Finally, it made a noise, this sickeningly spiteful bark that echoed through the crowded highway lanes, Evan could only see from its legs down, but he could tell its fur was greased up and bloodied. Ravaged and fluffed out randomly.

It poked its nose at the radio and flipped it over onto its side. Now that its head was visible to Evan, he made several more observations. This filthy and deranged K-9 police dog still had its collar and tiny vest on from what he could tell. Its teeth bared as it began to growl a sick, deafening, and damaged snarl.

Suddenly, its head pointed in the air, Evan stopped all his motion, trying to make zero noise, he held his breath.

Through the startling and twitching of the creature's altered voices, Evan heard the deranged mutt sniffing the air.

His eyes widened, shock and fear clouded his mind. He tried to quietly scoot out and away from the SUV. Now crouching

6

and leaning beside the car; he tried to peak around the corner, seeing the K-9's nose high in the air.

The radio still blared the low-pitched voice, when suddenly it stopped, along with the signature, *"over and out,"* from the unnamed speaker. The creatures did this weird action that could only be described as an insane sneeze as the noise ended.

Evan unholstered his snub nose revolver and held it by his side. He glanced at it and began to cock the hammer.

Click

The hammer cocking back had made a small but audible noise; from this Evan heard the dog turn its head swiftly, facing the SUV.

Turning their heads, the creatures now focused on the car. Just as Evan turned the corner to shoot his targets, the infected K-9 had started running at him, seeming to already know he was there. Before Evan got the chance to aim, the dog had leapt off the ground and trampled him, pinning him to the ground. He held back the dog's chomping teeth by its collar when he noticed the handle of a blade sticking out of its side.

Noises of struggle came from Evan's mouth; he carefully held the dog back with one arm and snatched the blade that was buried deep in the dog's ribcage. Struggling to hold back the chomping jaws, he managed to rip the blade out.

Blood showered from the wound.

He slashed its leg and tried to knee the mutt off of him. Several of the dog's ribs cracked after multiple knee attacks, now kicking it off, he flew up and dodged several of the creatures just in the nick of time.

The pistol had been knocked from his hand during the chaos. He tripped the first monster and whipped around to roundhouse kick the other in its torso; it tumbled backwards and fell on its side.

He then used the blade to fend the dog off, playing tag almost. As soon as the dog would lunge and try to bite Evan, he would slash another cut into it. They played this back-and-forth game until Evan mustered the confidence to swing his boot at the dog's face, knocking it a couple meters away now.

He fled to his pistol and without a second thought, he shot a bullet directly into the skull of the poor infected animal. The final noise that left the dog's mouth was that of a sour whimper.

The monsters that followed swung their arms clumsily at Evan, he still noted that for some unknown reason, they seemed to hold back. Unlike the dog, they seemed like they didn't want to behave the way they did. Killing them was something he didn't really want to do. He knew he was wasting time by even contemplating.

He shot the first creature in the neck; it fell to the ground with a gaping hole from the wound. The second however, he landed a perfect shot right between the eyes.

The third was a teenager he assumed, baggy clothes and a goofy attempt at facial hair. He could just tell that it was a teenager.

For this one, he felt this guilt for even pointing the revolver at it. Chomping and slashing its arms back and forth while it stumbled toward Evan, it tripped onto its knees and he put the nose of the gun to its head, pulling the trigger.

This gunshot finalized the encounter. Evan figured there would be more within minutes. He grabbed the duffel bag, then slung it around his back and tightened the strap. Slipping the military radio onto the same strap.

As the cold air of the Winter night floated into the city, Evan braced for it, using an old plain black colored bandana as a windbreaker for his face.

The lights that were meant to keep the highway lit were sporadically brightened. Every other one was providing light, very few provided less than adequate light. The lights from the city still shown through the cold fog of the evening dusk. The twinkling of distant gleams was bright enough to puncture the fog and shine on through.

It was like that the whole way leading into Minneapolis. He crouched in between cars and hid from the oblivious and countless creatures that roamed the desolate road. Up ahead, what he could gage as roughly a mile, he could observe a makeshift military setup gate.

The floodlights blinded him, even from a distance. He had not a clue whether the gate was manned or not. Large mandatory infection check signs were all over the place.

He unlatched the radio and spun through various frequencies, saying things like:

"Come in I-35 Gate."

"Come in highway outpost."

"Come in."

Evan did this for five minutes or so minutes while progressing toward the possibly guarded gate. He was relatively close now, just outside the floodlights gleaming barrier.

Suddenly there was a figure walking amongst the flood light, stuttering and staggering, clearly it was one of those things. His question was answered by the bright flash of a firearm.

First the flash and then the gunshot. Evan quick ducked down behind cover, barely seeing where the shot came from. Along with the shot, several humanoid shouts came with it.

The opposing monsters were shot down swiftly by an automatic rifle. The stakes were raised by this. Hyperventilating now, Evan crouched behind a car, had to decide what to do.

As the gunfire continued, taking down more and more of those creatures, Evan sat there trying to decide what to do. There was no way of telling how many soldiers were at the gated outpost. What could he do?

He peaked over the trunk of the car, seeing several creatures approaching the gate, all being mowed down by what he could see as two streams of gunfire.

Scared out of his mind, he tried to figure out what to do. The gunfire softened and became increasingly irregular.

A lightbulb appeared over his head. He quickly pulled his wallet out and slid the military patch into his hand.

When the gunfire ceased completely, he carefully stood up with the patch held high. His fear had subsided into confidence. As he entered the floodlights barrier, he heard one of the soldiers tell the other not to shoot.

"The fuck?"

Evan kept walking before one of the voices demanded him to stop and to stay frozen where he stood

"Stay there or we'll fucking shoot you."

Evan listened closely, hearing them whisper back and forth to each other covertly. "Is he holding a badge?"

"Yeah, I think so… ask him—" the last part wasn't audible.

From what he saw, there were only two soldiers. His odds had increased.

"State your name and rank! Followed by your DOD card and member Id number! Also remove that fucking bandana!"

Evan pulled the bandana down, being met with the brutally frosted air. He raised his patch high, "Evan James Smith is my name! My rank is a sergeant major! I am now going to reach into my back pocket to get my DOD card! Is that okay?"

The tension was immense, before he knew it, the soldiers had given him a response.

"Yes! Turn around as you do that! We can't take any chances."

Evan did as they said, turning around and reaching into his back pocket, while he did all this, he tried to keep his pistol hidden. He figured unless they searched him, he'd be fine. He gulped to release stress.

He pulled out his wallet and slipped the DOD card out, announcing that he was going to turn back around.

"Before you do that, tell us what's in the bag!"

Evan was facing opposite the gate, scared out of his mind.

"Fella's gotta stay dressed right? Just some clothes and stuff."

The soldiers started to grow somewhat suspicious, Evan could read this just from their tone of voice.

Silence followed, figuring it was most likely his turn to speak, he began reading his member ID.

"8-7-5-8-3-4-0-1-8-4-4!"

The soldiers then asked, "Are you armed?"

A second or two passed and Evan answered, "No!"

"What about them shots bout a half hour ago? They came from back that way. It wasn't you? Huh?"

Evan's brain kicked into high response mode, "Wasn't me, though I recall hearing the same shots."

The soldiers looked at each other and he could briefly hear them exchange inaudible dialogue. Fearing for what they may decide, he knew he was going to get through this gate, and if they wanted to die trying to stop him, so be it.

"It wasn't you then? What was it?"

"Your guess is as good as mine, man."

Evan tried to play cool even though the situation was red hot, he stood still holding his IDs in the air. The gleaming golden star along with the lines reflected the flood light's blinding rays.

"One of us will come down and search you, stay put!"

"One of us" Evan thought. That must mean it's just them, right?

As one of the soldiers descended a makeshift steel grated stairway, he removed the duffel bag from his shoulder and set it on the hood of a car close by.

A scrawny kid that was far too tall for his uniform began walking toward Evan; his hair was short and fluffy, and from the reflection off his hair, appeared to be blonde. He couldn't make out the face due to the extreme lighting contrast.

The soldier approached Evan with a rifle slung over his shoulder, at a moment's notice, he could pull and shoot. The rifle was carbon black and seemed state of the art, iron sights with a metal stock cage around the barrel along with the long straight clip protruding from the bottom.

"Sorry about this, we just can't take chances these days."

The other solider on the catwalk kept his rifle trained on Evan during this process. The soldier patted him down from top to bottom, finding the hatchet and taking it, he set it on the same hood where the duffel bag was located. As the solider poked and prodded every inch of Evan's body, Evan kept his eyes staring up at the solider on the catwalk, looking to see if the other soldier would let his guard down.

"What's going on in the cities?" Evan asked.

"Beats me man. Fucking people… I just do what I'm told."

Evan quickly responded, "And what was it you were told to do?"

"I shouldn't even be talking to you right now."

As this ill hearted conversation took place, Evan witnessed the soldier on the catwalk walk off and enter a small compartment located right of the catwalk. Muffled words could be heard. Meanwhile, the conversation concluded.

"What do you mean?"

"You shouldn't have come here."

Just as the soldier spoke, his hand ended up patting the revolver, still concealed by the jacket at this point.

"What's that?"

Evan thought fast, debating his options. He could either escalate or deescalate the situation. Analyzing every angle as fast as he could.

Before anything else could be said, Evan spun and ripped the rifle from the man's shoulder, dropping the DOD card and military patch. He whipped behind the soldier to use him as a human shield. With one hand on the rifle and using the soldier's body as stability, Evan prepared to make his move.

The second solider heard the ruckus and ran out of the small compartment, sliding into a defensive position and using the catwalk railing as a stable surface for his rifle.

Evan aimed the automatic rifle toward every floodlight he could find, shooting a barrage of bullets and destroying every single source of light. Riddling every light heavily, the noise was extremely loud. After the rifle ran out of bullets, there was all but two floodlights destroyed.

"The fuck is wrong with you!"

Located far from him, one light shallowly illuminated everything to Evan's left. The other was illuminated above the soldier on the catwalk.

"What the fuck! Hey! Show your hands!"

Evan hid behind the soldier, now begging for his life. "I don't want to die please!"

"Don't worry, so long as your friend up there keeps his cool, I'll keep mine," Evan reassured. He didn't want to hurt anyone if he didn't have to.

The soldier on the catwalk began speaking to his radio, requesting backup of course.

"I-35 gate requesting backup! Dangerous and armed tourist!"

He was interrupted by Evan unholstering his pistol and dropping the automatic rifle, shouting demands at him.

"Put your rifle down!"

"You're fucking crazy man!"

Evan got a bright idea. Aiming his pistol at the overhanging light above the catwalk, he took a shot.

The light shattered, huge shards of glass and sparks rained down upon the soldier.

He shouted in pain as the glass slammed onto his head and cut his skin, Evan then swapped his aim to the soldier, shooting him once in the shoulder. A red mist shot out from the wound as the bullet tore through his skin and flesh.

Evan let the Private go, shoving him away and disassembling the rifle he previously used. He tossed the parts sporadically around, making it impossible to reassemble.

"This is your shot, get out of here."

The 20 something year old kid pleaded, scrambling away like a wounded animal.

Evan reassured him. "Stay in the shadows and stay quiet," he tossed the hatchet a couple feet in front of him toward the kid.

"Go!"

The kid stood up, took the hatchet carefully, and ran out of view. Evan got down to business now, he picked up the ID's and stuffed them in his back pocket. Slinging the duffel bag around his back, he walked toward the gate, staying out of view and flank.

Through the darkness, a voice was heard.

"Requesting backup!"

A voice bellowed back to him all static-y, "We simply cannot spare anyone right now."

Stepping under the grated stairway, Evan spotted the soldier… or rather his shadow from beneath. Now using the grated stairway to ascend, Evan came around the bend with his pistol drawn. Now seeing the soldier, he observed his appearance. Black matted hair and a deranged look on his face, as if he bit into a lemon and squeezed the rest of the juice into his eyes.

"I'm not going to kill you," Evan clarified.

Now reaching the top of the stairs, he grabbed the rifle from the ground and away from the soldier. Slinging it around his shoulder, the soldier didn't even try to fight back.

Observing this, Evan asked, "Why didn't you even try to shoot me?"

Holding his shoulder with blood gushing from it, the soldier spoke with a hurting tone.

"Us soldiers, especially us Privates are as good as dead, we're basically just fucking bait. I figured it was my time. I'd rather die than continue to live this way, they haven't fed us in two days."

Now shocked by this and thinking to himself that he should've aimed for the head.

"They?" Evan questioned.

"The higher ups."

Astonished and quite frankly shocked by this, Evan told the kid to run as far away as he could, "There's got to be a first aid kit somewhere here, take it and get out of here."

Without another word to each other, the kid stood up and ran into a side compartment, sliding right out with said first aid kit. Before the kid ran down the stairs, Evan stopped him.

"Radio frequencies, which ones do you use?"

The kid stuttered before speaking, "In there," he pointed at the compartment he had run out of prior. Evan now turned away without a second thought, he walked into the cramped room and observed his surroundings. Now hearing the kid continue down the stairs, he dedicated all his attention to the room.

In one corner, two unkempt sleeping bags on the cold floor. In the other corner, adjacent to this one, lay a desk with unorganized papers on it, a large box radio with several sectioned off switches and microphones.

There was a an old and torn up piece of paper tacked to a tack board; on it were radio frequencies along with the locations they coordinated to, all in uneven and shaky handwriting. Around twenty different locations were written down.

Evan took the paper and set in on the desk, now leaning over the radio and picking up the microphone. Twisting the knob to the frequencies written on the paper, he was quiet as he did so.

Sheridan was labeled as 'main base.' He figured it would be a good place to start.

Simply listening in to begin with, he didn't want to alert anyone to his presence. After a couple moments of radio static, a voice began giving orders to an unnamed recipient.

"This is lieutenant general Johannsson, can anyone spare numbers? The University is struggling to keep the fight going, the civilians are overwhelming their barricades. They need help."

Evan instantly looked over to the paper on the desk, searching for a radio frequency related to the University. He knew that he'd heard that name before, recalling to when he initially used the radio.

'Lieutenant General Johannsson.'

Twisting the knob to the University's radio frequency labeled as 'medical center,' he wondered why the hospital wasn't labeled as such, now scanning the paper briefly. The hospital frequency was scribbled out, Evan began to wonder why. Before he had time to think about it, he had to begin listening.

"Ay—come in! anyone? This is the college territory! There is a considerable amount of people outside our walls! We need some fucking help here!"

Another voice piped in angerly.

"God damnit Johannsson! Send some goddamned fucking men here now!" In the background of all the yelling, Evan distinctively heard someone shout, *"Is that a fucking tank?"*

Now somewhat familiar with Johannsson's voice, Evan recognized it right away.

"You morons are seriously impatient. Nobody has responded to my call for backup, and by the looks of it, nobody will. I've received a call for backup at 4 different districts right now, If I were you, I wouldn't expect backup anytime soon."

Evan sat there, experiencing all this from such a far distance. Observing how dysfunctional the remaining military was, he knew that if they kept this up, it wouldn't last long.

"You son of a bitch Johannsson! I hope you feel all comfy and content with yourself sitting up there in that goddamned hotel!"

The soldier on the University side of things switched his tone from angry and aggressive to this sarcastic, hateful tone.

"Whatever, you're not worth the fucking trouble, we're all dead here anyways, so why don't I start drinking huh? Wouldn't want to waste this here bottle. Fuck you Johannsson, fuck you and your ego."

In the middle of that, Evan faintly heard the speaker unscrew and pop off the cap to what he could only assume to be a bottle of alcohol. He could hear the cap drop to the floor and clank around.

"Yeah, that's a great idea. Drink yourself to death before you get yourself and those around you killed. Fool."

Johannsson's response was so cold and heartless, Evan couldn't believe it was even said.

A separate section on the box radio began blinking, a voice spoke after several quiet and spaced beeping noises. Evan's ears flopped outward as the new noise filled the cramped room.

"Come in gate I-35! Come in now! Tell me the state of the tourist situation. This is King field outpost, pick up!"

Evan stood there, dumbfounded.

"We heard gunshots."

Picking up the radio now, he took a breath. Closing his eyes and thinking of what to say. Even though it was barely 10 degrees outside, sweat had built up on his forehead.

"We handled it."

"Handled it? What do you mean?"

"We killed him, the intruder," Evan stuttered.

"Oh… the situation is fine?"

"Yeah, I-35 signing off."

Evan took a sigh of relief, rubbing his eyes. Taking the radio frequency sheet and folding it into a rectangle, he put it into his pocket. He glanced over at the sleeping bags on the floor, tired now after his crazy day. His eyes felt like they'd roll back into his head if he closed his lids.

Figuring that at first light he'd wake up and get into the city. He ripped the closest sleeping bag into two equally sized slices. Like little square cut pizza.

He folded them into squares and though he wanted to keep listening to the radio, he could barely keep his eyes open. He limped out onto the catwalk, trying to identify somewhere to sleep, if he chose to sleep at the outpost, it would clearly be too risky. Instead of that, he figured a car would service his needs better.

Seeing a nice sized dark blue Tahoe, he descended from the catwalk and headed for it.

He hoped it would be unlocked. Now reaching the Tahoe, he tried the handle. Of course, it was locked, the door wouldn't budge. Looking around like what he was doing was illegal, he used the butt of his pistol to shatter the driver door window. The already trashed car had trace amounts of rust building up around the usual spots and dirt splatters all across each side of it. The dirty windows indicated a once clean and prestigious vehicle that has now fallen into the realm of obsolescence.

Climbing in and throwing the harvested sleeping bag slices into the back seat, he closed the door, he used the window switches on the driver door to slightly lower each window. He didn't want to suffocate on his own breath as he slept, now putting the duffel bag in the passenger seat, he pulled out a t-shirt and began tying it to the top handle on the driver side door.

He couldn't leave the window just wide open. Evan strategically tied the shirt to different corners of the car window, now blocking the entirety of it. He knew he could sleep sound now.

He crawled goofily from the driver's seat to the set of three seats in the back. One half of the sleeping bag went to the creation of a makeshift pillow. The other half was used simply as a blanket. Laying his head down and propping his foot up on the door, all relaxed and comfortable, he started to reflect.

"Jackson and his family... I wonder if they're thinking about me. Probably, I'd bet they are." He hoped they had made it to the safe house. He set the assault rifle on the floor, leaning against the seat while thinking.

"They deserve to rest; I shouldn't have gone and ruined things." Deep down inside, Evan knew that his daughter was probably dead. All he wanted was to believe she was alive, so that's what he chose to believe. Deciding to shut his eyes and staying low, away from the windows; he felt himself drifting to sleep.

Now opening his eyes once more, he blankly stared at the ceiling of the Tahoe. He took his trapper hat off and tossed it to the front of the car, now closing his lids, the darkness consumed his vision and provided him with what little peace he was allowed to feel.

Hatred wasn't the right word to describe how Evan felt about Jackson, it was more or less distain and even that was too hateful of a word to describe how he felt. If anything, Evan just wanted to reverse things, to go back and choose a different route to go down.

He wished maybe he had stayed another night outside of Minneapolis, because after all, Evan kind of liked Jackson.

Evan wished that things had happened differently, again.

Chapter 9

Tails

He kept his eyes on the trail.

Jackson sped down the desert like snow tundra with drifts as tall as him while he tried his hardest to keep to the route on the map.

The sunlight was sinking beneath the horizon, trying his hardest and pushing down on the throttle as he drove up a hill. Reaching atop this distant crest, he turned back to look at where he had come from. The silhouette of Minneapolis in the distance was still in flames, extremely faint gunshots were still audible, even over the roaring motor.

As he came to a stop, he wondered what Evan was currently doing; wondering if he was already dead or not. The family hadn't spoken a word to each other since the fight. The sky had fallen mostly dark with black streaks painting over the dim gray clouds.

"Jackson honey, shut it off."

Jackson turned to look at his wife who sat behind him.

"Okay."

With the motor falling silent, the bombing and consistent barrage of bullets grew louder. Ana tried speaking to her husband.

"Should we at least talk about it."

Matt remained silent as his parents spoke, meanwhile on the inside he was still overcome with insane adrenaline. Putting his life on the line had spiked an emotion had hadn't really felt before.

"I guess," he said, not exactly wanting to converse at all about it, turning his head away from his wife.

"Okay," Ana said softly.

Jackson didn't speak, he simply kept his lips shut. Ana widened her eyes and squinted at Jackson, "I just can't sit here and keep all these thoughts to myself, it's sickening."

"Then tell me," angered by the fight, Jackson didn't much want to speak on it.

"He's going to die in there Jackson, and you know it."

"Good, fuck if I care. That son of a bitch Evan."

Ana knew that Jackson was better than that, "I know that you care more than that, be human at least."

Jackson knew that he cared more than that. He knew that Evan mattered to him more than he was honest about. Though Jackson wasn't the most agreeable person to be around, Evan saw past it and was able to agree with him on multiple occasions. Through all the purely dangerous things the group had encountered, Evan was there and able to make sure that Jackson's family made it through whatever roadblock they encountered.

Jackson of course knew this. "Yeah? So what? If he wanted to sign up to die in that *fucking city*, he can be buried there for all I care!"

Matt didn't want to get involved; he didn't like it when his Dad raised his voice.

Jackson never really let go of his true thoughts, truly what he wanted was to tell his wife how he really felt.

He tried to keep hope alive for everyone but himself. This task he chose to fulfil benefitted those around him, but when his mentality surrounding things is brought into question, he doesn't even want to try to resolve his problems.

"Not now, Ana."

"When Jackson? Then seriously tell me, when?"

Jackson displayed distancing behavior, not keeping eye contact, and generally keeping away from his wife.

He felt weak when discussing his issues; like the whole world was caving in on him. As if he was wedged between two walls and they kept closing around him no matter what he did to stop it.

"Ana, what's done is done. It's not like I'm about to turn back to go save his dumbass again," Jackson said, being quite profane.

Speaking up with a louder tone, "I'm not asking you to go back for him, I'm asking you what he meant to you!"

His eyes widened with the new question, "Obviously… fuck. Ana are you really going to make me say it?"

Ana nodded, "Yes."

Jackson closed his eyes and sighed. "He was a friend..." you could tell that he was holding back how he truly felt. "He got us out of shit that I wouldn't have been able to, he was good."

He was stuttering and choking up just trying to get the words out of his mouth.

His lip quivered and the bottom half of his eyes began to build up tears that so desperately needed to leave.

"Worst part is, I doubt that military base would even let us in without him, I doubt the place is even still standing." He turned, now facing opposite Matt, whispering to his wife, "I'm honestly surprised that I've kept you guy alive this long."

Matt however heard it, figuring his Dad just didn't want to diminish whatever hope was left in his son.

Stuttering and muttering dialect of words that Ana could barely make out anymore, she embraced her husband with a tight meaningful hug. He pouted and cried into her shoulder as if his mother was holding him.

"I don't know how much longer we'll all make it."

Ana just closed her eyes and tried to soothe her husband with a quiet and shallow, "Shhhh shhhh."

This however made Jackson cry harder, despite the fact that she was comforting him, he simply needed to cry.

Standing there and holding each other, their heartbeats synchronized perfectly beating in rhythm. Matt lifted himself from the sled he sat in, now trudging through the snow over to his Mom and Dad.

He wrapped his arms around the both of them, he knew It was an extremely rare occasion for his father to be crying, he chose to try and comfort his hurting Dad.

Feeling the warmth of his family, Jackson closed his eyes and finally started to let it all out.

The darkness of night began dimming the region. The family separated after an appropriate amount of time, Jackson had now been relieved about things, crying really helped his mental state.

"I knew you needed to let it out," Ana said.

"Yeah… I knew you were right," he chuckled and cleared his throat.

The distant fires and light from the militarized and ravaged city were still bright. Smoke bellowed and rose from many sources. Jackson observed this, trying to make sense of it all as he walked back to the snowmobile.

While Ana and Matt spoke quietly back to each other, their dialogue was interrupted. Big and loud scrapes of metallic sounding motorized machinery pierced their ears. They could hear it getting closer,

Jackson ran over to his wife and son, getting them down and close to the ground, he swiftly unholstered his pistol and prepared to fight for his family. He was ready to fend off anything that set foot close to his loved ones.

Atop the hill they were all on, Jackson had a view onto this small double lane wide street about thirty meters away. As the noise grew louder, he located the source.

Large treads shielded by a sheet of steel rolled along the double lane street. Tan colored with slight discolorations all around. The large, oversized barrel swung with each jerk of the frighteningly large vehicle.

Located next to the barrel was this side compartment with a mounted machine gun, Jackson identified the first person he'd seen since Evan departed. Clearly, he wasn't a soldier, the man had a dark brown coat on with a branded hat on backwards.

Jackson squinted to make sure he wasn't hallucinating.

Following the tank, were three jeeps. Obviously, all normal people, not a single person Jackson saw was wearing a military uniform, they were all dressed casually. The jeeps only went as fast as the tank in front of them. As the convoy took the curve on the street, Jackson realized they were headed for the city.

The convoy rolled to stop very slowly, a latch atop the tank flew open and a lanky malnourished looking woman stepped out. She was dressed in a maroon sweatshirt with blue jeans, concealed by a large, oversized, and unbuttoned coat that flashed the University of MN logo. She hopped down and off the tank.

Ana and Matt peered their heads up to Jackson, "Why'd they stop?"

"I don't quite know babe, all I know is, we have to stay still."

The woman who previously exited the tank appeared to be speaking to the men in the jeeps.

Jackson tried to eavesdrop. On the back of the closest jeep, there was a kid, his eyes scanned the tree line that sat on the hill, Jackson began sweating bullets, nearly connecting eye contact with the kid.

The kid had a 'Twins' baseball cap on and an oversized vest that was hung over his baggy sweatshirt.

Suddenly, their eyes connected. Jackson's eyes widened and so did the kid's. He seemed frozen. Before hopping off the back of the jeep, the kid tried shooting his eyes elsewhere, pretending as if he hadn't seen Jackson. He walked up to the woman who had previously left the tank; Jackson stood up and began rushing his family to the snowmobile, he had to get them out of there. He knew that the kid was going to rat them out.

Within seconds, Jackson heard the footsteps of nearly a dozen men running up the hill, most likely armed.

Jackson pulled his pistol and told his family to get behind the snowmobile. Ana and Matt both ran and dove behind the snowmobile, Ana whispered firmly to Jackson.

"What about you?"

Jackson murmured back, "I guess I was right babe."

When the first people reached the top of the hill, they pointed their rifles at Jackson while realizing he had a gun.

"Shit! Gun!"

Nobody had fired yet, though Jackson was ready to shoot at a moment's notice, he couldn't push himself to fire the first shot. One of the men in the crowd of a dozen spoke something like, "The fuck? He doesn't look military."

Silence filled the air, the flashlight attachments from the rifles illuminated every aspect of Jackson's appearance.

His teeth grinded against each other as he kept his aim straight at the crowd. Everyone remained silent and at bay, lasting for what felt like an eternity.

In the distance, gunshots and explosions could be heard, faint screams of distress and horrible cries of agony. It pushed everyone to a tense edge. The aforementioned woman made her way through the dozen or so men by clearing a path. Stepping forward and out of the crowd, she took a pistol that was probably twice the size of her hand out of her belt strap and pointed it at Jackson.

"Military?"

Jackson's fearful and angered face turned to confusion.

"Did you ask if I was military?"

"Yes." she sternly replied to him, "Answer."

Jackson analyzed her appearance in between each following reply, seeing that she was on the older side of things, black hair with random strands of gray. Facial wrinkles and chapped lips, she wore thick rimmed glasses that made her look like an owl.

"No. I'm not military." He said, mildly annoyed now.

While he said that, he glared at the kid that had spotted him just moments earlier.

"I figured you wouldn't be," the woman spoke, "Before anything else happens, you need to lower your piece there."

Jackson glanced at his gun, still out in front of him. "And... give it to you?"

The woman shook her head, "If you think it's better for me to take it, I will... and so help me God, if you don't know how to use it, please let me know."

Jackson stood there in shock, not registering that anything had happened. The woman lifted her head to peak behind the snowmobile. Seeing Ana holding Matt, she spoke, "You, ma'am, come out slowly with the kid, we aren't going to hurt you."

Jackson stood there still, frozen as if every atom in his body had ceased motion.

"Sir, put it away."

Jackson snapped out of it and tucked the pistol back into his belt. The woman told the crowd behind her to lower their guns, gesturing them to do as she says.

"Your name sir."

"Jackson," he stuttered.

"Is that your wife? Your son?"

Jackson nodded.

"What're their names?"

Ana spoke up, "I'm Ana and this here is Matthew," she said while looking at her son.

"…and you are?" Jackson asked.

The woman straightened her glasses while clearing her throat, "My name is Liv, I was a professor at the University, of course that doesn't matter anymore but hey, maybe after tonight it will."

Ana raised her eyebrow, "What happens tonight?"

Liv informed them, "Well… me and this fine group behind me are headed for the University. Others are heading there as we speak. The plan is to take it back from those who took it from us. Before things got bad, the university was being used as a triage of sorts, there are surely enough medical supplies there for me to help the fine people still breathing."

Matt stayed quiet and simply listened, he had questions of his own but couldn't muster the confidence to ask them.

"You're a doctor?" Jackson inquired.

"Not a doctor, but I taught basic anatomical knowledge there, if you ask me, I should've been working at the hospital but I'm glad I wasn't. The hospital was ground zero for everything."

Before the family got a chance to ask even more questions, Liv abruptly ended the conversation.

"I'm sure we'll all have enough time for questions later, but our little encounter pushed us behind schedule. You're all set to come with us—"

She was interrupted by Jackson, "How do we know if we want to come with you or not, the city looks like hell."

"I was just getting to that, you may not want to come with us, as the city is a warzone, but do keep in mind that the whole place isn't like that."

"What do you mean?" Ana wanted to know.

"What I mean is: we have a safe place where the weak can go, a place for them to rest. Just South of Longfellow, a district called Howe, there are families similar to yours, it's up to you."

Jackson turned away from the woman, he brought his family close and huddled them, "What do you guys think?"

Ana didn't really know what to think, Jackson was pretty skeptical, and Matt held back his thoughts.

"Come on guys, I need your input."

Before the family could decide, Liv had turned around and said, "Decide fast because we have to get going here pretty quick."

"It's worth a shot," Ana reasoned. Liv turned and walked away; the armed men followed her down the hill.

"What if it's a trap just like everything else?" Matt piped in.

Jackson agreed with his son, well… he partially agreed. He had this weird gut feeling like it was a trap but that quickly subsided and he felt hope that it might be what Liv said it was.

Ana remained optimistic regarding it, "I think it's legitimate, I think we should go for it."

Matt spoke up, "How do we know for sure?"

Jackson knew they were running out of time, he figured that the compound they were originally headed for would be comparable to buying a lottery ticket, but the place that Liv spoke of was more of a coin flip.

The odds were better if they were to go with the convoy rather than to go off on their own. Jackson had decided.

"We're going with them," he announced. Matt stood there disappointed and felt like he was doomed.

Matt followed his Dad to the sled, trying to reason, "What if they just choose to kill us or something?"

Jackson spoke down to his son, "Who knows if that compound out East is real? We have a real chance with what that woman was talking about."

Matt frowned, not knowing what to think. He sighed and picked up his little backpack, he proceeded to follow Jackson and the others to the convoy. They completely left the snowmobile behind while they jogged down the hill with their belongings.

The convoy group were all getting situated in their jeeps and just as Liv was about to close the latch to the tank, she noticed the family coming down from the hill.

She shouted, "Head to the last jeep!"

Jackson briefly stopped and turned his attention to the jeep furthest to the back.

He climbed over the roadblock and frantically announced his presence to the driver, "Where do we get on?"

The driver, who had a Kevlar vest and aviator glasses then pointed to the back, "Around the ass end."

Jackson nodded quickly; he didn't want the entire convoy to be held up on him. He walked around back swiftly with his family following him closely and clumsily.

The kid who had previously spotted him lent a hand, Jackson looked up at him, a brief wave of anger overcame him, but the emotion was quick and short lived.

"My name is Randall, get up here." The kid's voice flamboyant and light.

Jackson took his hand and helped the rest of his family into the bed of the military jeep. They sat in the open part; the sky was painted dim blue and black above them.

The now faint visible stars twinkled above oh so elegantly. Clouds drifted across the dark sky, revealing the moon from time to time, Ana kept the sky as her focal point.

Randall set his rifle against his seat, now straightening his baseball cap while he tried speaking to Jackson as the jeep started up. The most prominent feature on the kid was his huge nose, almost like an elongated shark fin. A long skinny face with brown pupiled orbits. His hair was short and black, the acne on his face crowded his cheeks and his mouth was smaller than it should've been for someone who talked as much as he did. It made his face resemble that of a mouse.

The convoy remained uniform while they dodged vacant cars and slowly entered the city.

"Hey sir, I'm er- sorry for telling them about you."

Jackson looked at him, then back at his hands, "There's no problem, if what Liv was talking about is true, I should be thanking you."

"Er… well how'd you guys get here?"

Jackson pondered for a second, "If I were to be honest, I'm not quite sure, we were aiming for somewhere completely different."

His wife and son glanced at him; they knew the story was far too complicated to explain.

The city grew closer and closer with each passing minute. Jackson noticed Randall twiddling his thumbs, his hands looked so young, so unscathed.

"How old are you kid?"

Randall answered with a stutter, "Nineteen sir, why?"

Jackson looked at him for a second, "Nineteen?... and they've got you in the line of fire?"

Randall corrected Jackson, "Well er—it was my choice, I guess. I sort of volunteered for this."

The driver up front could hear the conversation through the shattered back window, "Yeah, kid's good like that."

Jackson now thought a little higher of Randall for this. Relevant questions now came to mind.

"Why'd Liv ask if I was military or not?"

Randall chirped back with his high-pitched melancholy voice, "You don't know what's going on in the city do you sir."

"No."

"Long story short, after things got bad, they set up a bunch of quarantine zones in pretty much every district… then things got worse when rations started to become scarce." While speaking, Randall waved his hands around sporadically. "The same military that was supposed to save us were slowly killing us, so we fought back."

Jackson looked at his family and then back at Randall, "We've experienced something like that as well. We were in

Rochester when things went downhill, the military shot at us, told us that they'd reached their fuckin limit."

"Yeah... seems that a lot of people aren't that fond of the government these days, damn."

Jackson just shook his head, disappointed he said, "Probably them that caused this whole damn thing."

Randall agreed, "I just wished I would've had more of a heads up, you know?"

Jackson nodded, "I just wish that I'd paid more attention to the news, I had stopped watching because of all the fuckin political drama."

Randall spoke, "Just a couple of eyebrow-raising news stories was all it was at first..." Jackson noticed a small scar on Randall's nose while he spoke. "Then I started hearing rumors, then the city was put under martial law as neighbors on the same floor as me were being ripped out of their homes and I don't remember ever seeing them again."

"Well, why were you in the city?"

Randall started popping his finger joints, "Well originally I'm from Grand Rapids, but I was here for the College."

Imitating a half smile, Jackson inquired.

"What did you major?"

After cracking all his fingers thoroughly, Randall took his baseball cap off and started dinking around with his hair.

"Oh—er I was trying to get just a bachelor's degree at first but found myself attending veterinary classes. Talked to my Mom and Dad about it and they pushed me to start pursuing that."

Jackson's opinion regarding the kid started to change, "Veterinary school huh?"

Randall nodded and before he could talk anymore, the convoy came to an abrupt stop.

They were all now placed in between a ravaged intersection. Cars flipped and charred. Traffic lights bashed and stores looked as though there had been a tornado that swept through. Most light posts didn't shine as they should, but some still gleamed.

Suddenly, Liv's voice began blaring over the jeep radio. "Tell Randall to get on a different jeep, we need him. After we roll out, take Jackson and his family to Longfellow," Liv ordered.

Randall's expression turned to that of dread and worry, he put his baseball cap back on and straightened it. He picked his rifle up and slung it over his shoulder, he now hopped out of the back of the jeep.

"Good talk, Jackson I think your name was. Hopefully we run into each other back in Longfellow," Randall said optimistically.

Jackson leaned over and shook his hand, "For sure, kid."

Randall jogged to the jeep ahead, positioning himself in the back, he sat down and set his rifle to the floor He sat in between two significantly larger men, Jackson watched as the convoy continued without him.

Jackson knew that Randall was worried, he knew that this was the last place that a kid like him should be.

Randall stared back into Jackson's eyes as the convoy took a left turn out of sight.

Ana gazed at her husband; she spoke up, "Good kid?"

"Good kid," Jackson said, still looking at the corner that the convoy had turned down.

Matt sat there, now beginning to calm down from the adrenaline that had coursed through his veins.

"Dad?"

Jackson turned his head, "Yeah son?"

"What happens when we get there? I mean what do we do?"

The driver switched the jeep into gear, they turned right and down an extremely dark street.

"I guess we just try our best to make good impressions."

The headlights on the jeep were the only thing illuminating the dark road ahead, with buildings on each side of them, they made observations.

Many of the apartment buildings had bodies out front, laying there dead. They were all uniform with one another, as if someone had lined them up and put them down like a sick herd of livestock. Countless bodies lined the streets.

"Holy fucking shit," Jackson gasped.

"Come on you shouldn't be looking at that," Ana said while covering Matt's eyes.

The dried blood had all stained the snow and drained onto the curb. Jackson demanded the driver to tell them what had happened.

"The fuck happened here?"

Responding with a reluctant tone, the driver spoke. "Cases of the disease or virus or whatever the hell you wanna call it, broke out in small buildings like this. The military's only solution was to keep it contained for as long as possible... I guess it didn't exactly work the way that they'd planned."

"When your only tool is a hammer, I guess every problem looks like a fuckin nail," Jackson retorted. With each passing street and avenue, more and more bodies could be seen, observing this, Jackson knew exactly why the civilians fought back.

Some apartments and tiny shops were obviously burned to the ground, and some were just in shambles. Mandatory evacuation signs hung from street poles and countless propaganda themed flyers were stapled to telephone poles.

Now that they were in the city, the explosions and gunfire felt way more real. With each gunshot and minor noise that they could hear over the engine, they turned their heads.

Ana naturally being the more worrisome of the group, stayed on high alert. Jackson simply scanned the environment, up and down, side to side. Ten minutes passed of these horrible sights. Most people wouldn't be able to believe that the military had done such horrible things.

Up ahead, they all could now see light. Slight illumination on their faces signaled that they were close to their destination. As the jeep made the left turn onto a side street, Jackson observed their new home.

Big floodlights illuminated the surrounding streets, large walls constructed of sheet metal and various furniture protected the community.

The driver flashed his headlights at the guard post three times before the massive gates slowly began opening. Tall buildings with men walking along the rooftops surrounded the perimeter. The words, "North Longfellow" were spray painted on the gated threshold.

Within the buildings, Jackson could see lights on and people living their lives. The place was huge from what they observed. The jeep slowly traversed into the makeshift but sturdy gates. One of the heavier built guards shouted, "New people!"

Now inside the encampment, they saw at least a couple city blocks being used as housing and whatever else they needed it to be used for. The central park was being used to station military vehicles that had most likely been stolen. Multiple tarps set up along with massive supply crates.

Four more tanks could be seen, shocked and stunned by this, Jackson didn't speak a word.

The jeep stopped inside the walls, the gate closed behind them, and heavily dressed men and women descended from the guard post.

They instantly ordered, "Newcomers, get off the jeep with your hands in the air."

Jackson was confused at first but quickly understood the instructions. He told his family to do as they said.

Jackson grabbed his family's luggage and tossed it in front of the guards, "This is all we're worth right now."

"Derrick!" One of the guards spoke to the driver of the jeep, "Who are these people"

"Liv told me to send them here," one of the three guards started going through the family's luggage. Ana of course told them, "Quit going through our stuff!"

The guard, who was dressed in a university sweatshirt and cargo pants, told her, "Chill out, it's just a precaution."

Another guard began patting Jackson down from head to toe, discovering his pistol. He gripped it and pulled it from Jackson.

Jackson went to stop him.

"The fuck-," before Jackson could finish his sentence, the guard reassured him that he'd get it back.

"You'll get it back at some point."

Jackson snarled. Matt was the next to be patted down. The guard discovered a set of house keys and a phone.

"You can have these back, kid."

Matt accepted it back without a word. His mother was now the next person to be patted down. All they found on her was a pen, pocketknife, and a rather small flask of water.

"You two can keep all your stuff."

Jackson tapped the guard on the shoulder, "When do I get my gun back man?"

"Really depends on how fast you settle in."

Jackson stood there dumbfounded, "I feel a little weird without it, so if you could give it back, that'd be fuckin great."

"Can't do that," the guard said while handing Ana back her possessions.

Another guard stepped in, "There was nothing I didn't expect to find in your bags, housing is over there," he pointed toward the townhouse looking apartment buildings. All made from brick and masonry.

"Down 2nd Street, someone will show you to your room, have a good night sir, you and your family."

Jackson stopped for a second, thinking to himself, "It was that easy? What the hell?"

Ana and Matt thought the same thing. They all grabbed their bags and began walking toward 2nd Street. Their surroundings were unfamiliar.

Jackson observed that this settlement was doing way better than pretty much the entire outside world. People were outside, shoveling the sidewalk and there were plows going up and down the streets, clearing it of snow. The family now stepped onto the sidewalk of 2nd Street. At the end of this particular street there was a blockade with a similar guard situation.

As they all walked down the street, a shoveler greeted them, "New here?"

Dressed in a scarf and poufy hat, she had glasses and an oversized trench coat on.

"Yeah… just got here actually," Ana said.

"Oh great, head right over there and Nicole will show you where you can hang your hats."

"Thanks ma'am," Matt said.

"No problem, honey," the woman responded.

The building she spoke of was across the street and illuminated by some cleverly positioned Christmas lights. They trailed up and down the fencing and up over the doorway. Yellow jolly light.

Jackson steadied his wife as she was almost taken out by a patch of slippery ice. They made it across the street and stepped up onto the curb. Ana spoke to them, "Everyone here seems nice."

Jackson nodded and Matt agreed, "Yeah they are."

They made their way up the stairs and Jackson held the door open for his family. Upon entry, they realized the building had heat. They scurried in fast and stomped their boots on the carpeted mat, leaving all the snow at the door.

A bigger woman greeted them, "New here?"

"What gives it away?" Jackson said with a chuckle.

"Well, I wish I had some quick-witted response, but the truth is: I haven't seen you guys in here before."

Ana smiled and shook the woman's hand, introducing her husband and son.

"And my name is Nicole, you guys seem sweet; I'll show you to your room."

Jackson, Matt, and Ana all smiled at each other, they followed her up a flight of stairs and while they were walking, the woman struck up a conversation.

"Where're you from?"

Jackson answered, "Rochester, place went to hell so we get out while we still could."

"Hm, seems like every newcomer has a similar story."

"What do you mean?" Ana asked.

"Every person who ends up here tells me about how they had to flee home, or they would've died."

Jackson nodded, "I just wish it wasn't that way."

Nicole agreed.

By now, Ana had noticed the way that Nicole looked at Jackson. She didn't like it. Jackson of course knew that this was happening but simply chose to ignore his admirer.

They arrived at their room, Nicole opened it with a master key and handed Jackson the actual key to the room, "Everything mostly works except the tv and phone. We ration our food every morning at 8 by the library building, first come, first serve."

Jackson and Ana gazed into each other's eyes, realizing they'd be able to get the first good night's sleep they'd had in days. Matt rushed in to check out the bed situation.

One queen sized bed and a long couch that was up against the wall, the window as open and facing the street outside. The room was compact but suitable.

Ana would've instantly started tidying the place up and making sure everything was in tip top shape if the place wasn't already spotless.

The window provided a perfect view to the city, many big buildings were visible, the mayhem within the city continued. The gunfire and constant chatter of everything was like white noise to them now.

Jackson and Ana entered the room after thanking Nicole.

"We call the bed," referring to him and Ana.

Matt offered to win it over a game of rock paper scissors, Jackson rejected it, telling him, "You and Mom can have the bed, I'll take the couch, it doesn't look too bad."

Matt cheered on with his victory, "Yes!"

Ana firstly checked out the bathroom, "Looks nice in here."

Jackson didn't much care about the bathroom situation, he was simple like that.

The walls were eggshell white and there were various paintings hung on the walls. Matt undressed down to just a t-shirt and underwear telling his parents, "You know, this place seems alright to me."

Jackson was still somewhat suspicious of their newfound home. He picked up the ironing table from the closet and stuffed it against the door, making sure if the door was being forced open, it wouldn't budge.

Ana took her coat off and hung it in the closet, now undressing the rest of her body, she slipped under the sheets.

Jackson observed his family, taking his jacket off and making himself somewhat comfortable.

He sat down on the sofa and Ana started talking to him from across the room, "Come over here baby."

Jackson got up while scratching his head. She told him to reassure her, "I just need a voice to tell me it's all going to be alright."

Jackson spoke, "Yeah babe, I think we'll do alright here." She turned to him, he kneeled and leaned over her face while she lay in the bed.

"I mean really tell me that things are going to be okay."

"They are," he said, trying to sound convincing.

"I know you don't believe that." She put her hands on his face as she flipped reassurance onto him.

"We *will* be okay babe, we *will* make it," she said confidently.

Jackson smiled and put his hand on her face as well, they came closer to kiss one another. A long meaningful kiss ensued.

Pulling away only when they both felt content, Jackson stood up and kissed her forehead.

"Hey, I've got something for you." Jackson began walking over to his bag that had been left by the couch. Swiping it up and removing a red notebook and a pen. Until that point, he had almost forgotten that it even existed.

Her tired eyes widened with glee, "A notebook?"

"A notebook," he confirmed.

He waltzed back, like a waddling statue. When he handed her the notebook with the pen tucked in the spiral, she told him that she loved him.

"I love you babe," she said, whole heartedly.

"I love you too," he retorted.

She set the notebook on the nightstand,

Jackson laid down on the couch and plopped his legs on the arm of the sofa, relaxing finally and positioning his head, he started to feel himself drift off into a low slumber.

A pleasant night of sleep befell the family.

Chapter 10

J-35 Sunrise

The sky was considerably dim for a city that was on fire.

The eastern horizon started to gleam, painting all the clouds a dim red. The atmosphere was still dark, but you could tell it was getting brighter by the minute.

Staring through the sunroof at the heavens above, Evan rubbed his eyes. Yesterday had seemed like a blip, as if it didn't happen at all. The cold air that filled the vehicle overnight hung low and made his fingers feel like they were going to fall off.

Before Evan could fully wake up, gunshots pounded nearby. His head spun up and he was now wide awake. He quickly grabbed his pistol and darted his eyes around, looking through every single window in the car. It sounded super close, as if it was right next to him.

He held the snub nose revolver firmly, staying low and away from the windows, yet making sure he could see all his peripherals.

One floodlight remained functional; it illuminated the I-35 gate poorly. He kept his eyes trained on the dark spots. All of a sudden, a barrage of several more shots bellowed throughout the region, followed by some flamboyant laughter.

Now hearing the human laughter, his ears twitched, analyzing where it came from.

Now seeing three men followed by two women appear from out of the darkness, Evan hid behind the driver's seat. They had come out from under the I-35 gate catwalk.

Military caps on with heavy clothing to protect them from the cold. The group chattered back and forth; Evan picked up on some of their muffled dialogue.

"Why the fuck are all the lights turned off?"

One of the woman soldiers shrugged.

Evan's head pounded with a headache. Now put into another tactical situation, he figured he might just have to wait it out.

One of the men ascended the grated stairway, shining a flashlight. He called out to his friends, "There's blood up here! Stay on high alert!"

The blood from the previous night's events had hardened on the catwalk. The solider then called out a pair of names, whom Evan could only assume to be the two men that he'd encountered the night before.

"Jake? Daniel? Hello? Are you guys there?"

The soldiers drew their rifles and were prepared to shoot anything that moved. "They were fine last night what the hell? They said they had the situation under control."

When Evan saw that the other soldiers were shining their flashlights into cars, he instantly started looking for ways to exit the Tahoe safely. He got ahold of his duffel bag and clicked open the back door facing away from the military group.

Grabbing the rifle that was still on the car floor, Evan slung it over his shoulder along with the duffel bag around his back. He retrieved the trapper hat while stepping out of the car, not bothering to shut the door.

Pistol in hand, he crouched behind the Tahoe. He positioned the trapper hat on his head and stuffed his cowlicks and fluffed morning hair back into the hat. It was still dark enough for a shadow to not appear. Evan could not see an opponent if they were twenty feet away. Suddenly a pair of footsteps began approaching the car, Evan quickly aimed his revolver toward the hood of the vehicle, preparing for what was to come.

He observed light coming into the car, shining from every angle. Tense as can be, Evan gripped the pistol.

Just as the footsteps directed away from the car, they came to a stop. Evan sighed to himself. He was just beginning feel relief when the set of footsteps had turned around. He thought quick.

He started picking a large scab on his hand until it bled, then scraping at it with his nails, it started producing a steady amount of blood.

He wiped it all over his neck and face, trying to make it look like he had been dead for days. He then laid himself against the cement barrier, leaving one hand hidden holding the pistol.

The flashlight now approached from the backside of the vehicle, getting closer and closer as the radius of the beam increased. Evan closed his eyes and steadied his breathing enough so that his torso barely fluctuated. He hung his mouth slightly open and stayed as still has he possibly could.

He heard the solider give out a "Hm." Now approaching Evan with the light shining on his face. His closed eyelid's interior that was usually black was now a bright red with the light shining upon it.

"Score," exclaimed the soldier when seeing Evan's stolen rifle. When Evan felt that the time was right, he shot his eyes open and quickly pulled the rifle from the soldier, ripping it from his arms and tossing it away. Uncomfortably, with his left hand holding the pistol, he pointed it at the solider, pulling him closer with his right hand.

Evan grabbed him by the collar, his expression was that of a snarled angry old man.

"Stay quiet and you'll stay alive, Understand?"

The soldier nodded his head, he was absolutely terrified. Evan narrowed his eyes and pushed the soldier against the Tahoe, keeping the gun to his neck.

A voice bellowed in their direction, "Hey Henry? Did you find anything man?"

Evan instructed the soldier to respond back, "Tell them... tell them that you're taking a leak, now."

The soldiers whose name now being revealed as Henry looked at Evan and then back to the ground, "Okay okay." He whispered.

"Nah I didn't find anything; I'm just taking a leak."

The other unnamed soldier simply responded, "Don't wander too far kid, don't expect me to save your ass again."

The kid, Henry, had gingerly bright orange hair with a pathetic attempt at a mustache. Evan wondered why all these soldiers were just kids.

"How many kids are a part of this?" Evan demanded to know.

Henry whispered back, "Y-you want me to talk?"

"Yes."

"I don't know...? A lot? Me and a bunch of other kids, I'm not even supposed to be telling you this."

Evan pondered for a minute before being interrupted.

"Are you a part of the Revolutionists?"

Evan turned his head, "What?"

"The Revolutionists."

Evan was confused, he tightened his grip on the kid's collar. "What are you talking about?"

"You don't know?"

Evan pressed the kid against the car, "No, I don't know."

The kid stuttered before Evan told him to shut up. "Listen, you're going to stay here, count to 100 and pretend like you never saw me? Do you understand?"

The kid instantly chipped in, "Where are you going?"

"What does it matter?"

Henry grabbed Evan's arm that held his collar, "Because I don't think I want to be like this anymore."

Evan whispered aggressively, "What?"

Henry nodded, "Yeah."

After a couple of seconds considering what the kid said, Evan spoke, "Why would you want to come with me?"

"Because man," The kid whispered, "I just can't fight for this cause anymore."

Evan fought with his inner turmoil, understanding the kid's situation. Wanting to take Henry with him, he went back and forth in his head between pros and cons.

"Alright kid, I'm going to throw you a one-time deal. We'll run, and when I say run, I mean run like you're running from a tiger."

The kid sat there and nodded, "Okay... Also, I didn't catch your name man?"

Evan simply replied with his name, "Evan."

"Get ready to run like you've never ran before," Evan retorted.

Before standing and taking his gun away from Henry's throat, he made sure the coast was clear.

"If I hand you your rifle back, can I trust that you won't shoot me?"

Henry answered quick and stern, "Yes."

"Trust me kid, if you change your mind about that, I won't hesitate to return the favor."

Henry nodded. Evan reluctantly handed the rifle to him, making sure the safety was on.

Evan prepared to hop over the cement highway barrier and make a break for it. The temples of his head pounded. He secured his duffel bag and holstered his pistol before buttoning his coat. Grabbing hold of his rifle, he crawled over the barrier and Henry followed suit.

Now in the opposite lane of traffic, Evan was sure the other soldiers hadn't noticed until someone called out for Henry to respond.

"Henry?" A woman shouted, "Are you done over there?"

Evan ducked and dove behind a truck, Henry stood there like a deer in the headlights.

"Get down!" Evan whispered aggressively.

Henry glanced at Evan, the flashlight settled on Henry's face, a voice requested that he return to the group.

"C'mon Henry? What are you doing over there?"

Henry glanced at the bright light aimed at him, now speaking out to his group, "I'm sorry."

Evan stared at the kid, when all of a sudden, Henry shouted.

"Run!"

With such short notice, Evan got up and ran as fast as his malnourished self could. Henry bolted quicker than Evan, now ahead of him. The military group was confused at first but quickly noticed that Henry wasn't the only one running from them. They all swiftly moved up to the catwalk preparing to start unloading rounds.

With the sun now barely peaking over the horizon, it unevenly illuminated the highway. Some of the path could be seen easily while other parts were as dark as they were at midnight. The soldiers ordered Henry and Evan to stop and surrender.

"Stop now!"

The kid ran ahead of Evan, dodging cars and sliding over barricades. Evan upped his game and increased his pace.

Twenty feet ahead, Henry spotted a creature. This one was drenched in blood and was severely underdressed. The dark toned skin made the scratches and cuts seem significantly more red.

It shouted and growled a sickening snarl. Henry tried his best alerting Evan.

"There's a dead one!"

Evan did not know what he was talking about at first. Henry leapt ahead and quickly pulled the rifle up to his shoulder, shooting the monster twice in the head. Its face turned into a smashed potpie mess.

"Keep running!" Henry shouted.

Evan kept pace now, squeezing in between cars, and sliding across the hoods of sideways vehicles.

The soldiers on the catwalk began to open fire, shooting a barrage of bullets toward Evan and the kid. Striking the cars next to them and shattering car windows. All that the bullets were, was encouragement to run faster.

They stopped briefly to look at the catwalk, the shooting had stopped. Suddenly they observed a bright flash. Before Evan could react and realize what the flash was, Henry dove and tackled him to the ground. The bright flash was that of a scope to a sniper rifle, which then shot a high-powered round just inches above them.

"Sniper?" Evan shouted.

"Yeah, I sort of forgot to mention that."

The duo now hid behind a misplaced vacant car. Evan picked up a piece of fabric that lay strung across the ground, he folded it into a square and prepared to toss it in the air.

Evan tossed the fabric in the air and within a split second, they heard the powerful bang of the rifle. The fabric was struck, and the bullet went clean through, leaving the fabric destroyed.

Henry put his palm to his forehead, "Sheeeit."

Evan sighed, trying to think of ways he could get out of their current predicament. Another bullet struck clean through the driver side window and shattered the passenger side window, throwing shards of glass upon Henry and Evan.

Henry's radio started going crazy.

"Kid, what the fuck are you doing?"

"Henry? Get back here! Who is that?"

Henry remained silent, looking over at Evan.

A voice shouted from the catwalk, presumably the sniper. "Get them! I think they're armed!"

"Get them?" Evan thought. Henry tried peaking over the hood of the car, seeing several beams of light quickly approaching.

Before Henry was able to lower his head back to safety, a bullet skidded off the hood and ricocheted into the windshield, shattering it. Henry ducked his head below, announcing to Evan his discovery.

"We need to get out of here, Evan."

Henry spoke worryingly, scared of what was to come. His adrenaline kicked in, ushering Evan to get up and run.

The soldiers that were now on foot could clearly see the duo. The rising sun now provided enough luminosity to see most of Minneapolis and the surrounding area.

Now on their feet, Evan and Henry sprinted from walls made out of bullets. Turning his head to look at what was behind him, Evan saw the sniper scope flare.

A bullet ripped through the car next to him. The soldiers now hot on their trail yelled after the two.

"Hands in the fucking air!"

Evan and Henry had nothing to say to the soldiers, just focusing on their escape. They were looking for viable routes to evade their pursuers.

Despite all the bullets that were being flung their way, not one hit. The route they had taken led to two choices: Continue the road or head up the on ramp.

All the gunfire started to attract the monsters, hearing their nasty growls and sickening shouts of anger made the chase that much more intense.

Evan spun around and shouldered his rifle, popping shots off just above the soldier's heads. Not trying to kill them, he just wanted to scare them off. He noticed this made some of them duck behind cover, giving him and Henry a chance to bolt up the on ramp.

"Get going Henry!"

The soldiers exited cover quickly and fired several more shots, striking the pavement in front of them. Uplifting the concrete and shooting the dust in the air.

Running through the dust clouds, they ducked their heads as they ran up the incline.

Henry exclaimed, "Keep going! I'll cover you!"

Evan nodded, "Okay!"

Henry took to his knee, clipping one of the soldiers in their leg and forcing another to duck under a car. The sniper flare zeroed in on Henry, as quickly as he could, he aimed at the catwalk, shooting five or six times before the sniper's gunshot erupted a bullet from its barrel. The stray bullet struck the taillight of a car next to him and the scope flare disappeared.

He didn't know if he injured or killed the sniper, but he figured it was better if he didn't know.

Evan yelled out to him from the top of the on ramp, "Get up here now man!"

With what ammo was left in the rifle, Evan shot beyond Henry at the other soldiers, again only shooting above their heads to freak them out. After making it atop the on ramp, Henry took a breath of relief and spoke to Evan, "If we keep running like this, it won't be long before they catch up to us."

Evan agreed, "Let's just find somewhere to chill out for a minute, you and your friends woke me up a little earlier than I wanted."

Henry nodded. The road ahead looked just as you could imagine, evacuation signs and propaganda posters. A large city block with buildings packed next to each other on either side. Up ahead and to the right, there was a pizza parlor.

"That could work. Maybe there's food in there too," Henry pointed out optimistically,

"Let's just get out of here first," Evan said while beginning to jog down the street. He unloaded the empty clip from the rifle and slipped it into a side pocket on the duffel bag.

"Do you have any more rounds for this gun?"

Henry now recognized Evan's stolen rifle, seeing that it has the same make and model as the one he held. He tossed Evan one of the two spare clips he had.

"Make it count, it's all I have left."

The duffel bag and rifle slung over Evan's shoulder bounced up and down with each stride. The soldiers had stopped pursuit finally.

"Good aim back there, kid."

Henry grinned a shallow expression of pride, "Thanks."

"Where'd you learn to shoot like that," Evan asked while taking the trapper hat from his head and snuggling it deep into the duffel bag.

Henry answered confidently, "My Dad used to take me duck hunting, I don't know if you've ever done that but you've gotta be fast and accurate."

Evan nodded, "I've been a couple times. I prefer deer hunting though, it's a little more peaceful."

Henry agreed.

Now within walking distance to the pizza parlor, a pair of headlights could be seen at the end of this lengthy road. From down the road, the vehicle looked like a military grade Humvee. Henry's radio started going crazy again.

"Humvee inbound to I-35 gate outpost, over and out."

"We need to get off the streets, now." Evan announced.

Evan analyzed the situation same as Henry, now bolting to the inside of the pizza parlor. When the door didn't open, Evan used the butt of his rifle to shatter the glass pane.

Henry entered first, closely followed by Evan. They took both sides of the doorway and stayed away from the front wall, which was almost entirely made of shiny glass windows.

They held their rifles, ready to fight if the Humvee stopped. As they heard the massive wheels press against the pavement outside, they tightened their grip.

For what felt like an eon worth of time, the Humvee approached the store. Evan ground his teeth and readied himself for more combat.

Soon the Humvee simply rolled past and turned down the ramp that the duo had previously ran up. Both men were quiet for some time, making sure that the coast was completely clear before even thinking about what to say next. Henry tried to speak but Evan quickly shooshed him, it was nothing personal, it simply was to protect both of them.

When the atmosphere finally became less tense, Evan was the first to speak. "Those fucking things can hold almost 5 guys."

Evan snarled, "You don't have to tell me."

"What's that supposed to mean?" Henry asked while wiping his forehead, cleaning the built-up sweat droplets from his forehead.

"I was in the military." He slung the rifle over his shoulder once more and pulled his patch out, tossing it to Henry who caught it perfectly. Spinning it in his hand like a Pokémon card, he handed it back to Evan. The atmosphere had started to become less tense. The rumbling of the Humvee had passed, and the kid's radio fell silent.

Henry took a breath and shook his head back and forth while Evan dropped his duffel bag and reloaded a full clip into his rifle. The strange Italian paintings on the wall and stained-glass lamps were off-putting. Henry began walking around in the darkness, looking for a light switch. While Evan slipped the patch back into his back pocket, he questioned Henry.

"Why'd you want to come with?"

Henry turned to Evan from across the room. "I'm hungry. I mean just look at me, I'm a couple more days without food from going crazy." Henry displayed his abnormally thin torso.

"About a month or two ago, I had some meat on these bones," he spread his arms. "Then grocery stores couldn't get shit in, and when I mean shit, I mean they couldn't get *anything* in. I'm fucking hungry man."

Henry took his padded vest off and stretched his bony back, his voice fluctuated with each crack. "They hadn't fed us in almost two days—"

Evan interrupted Henry, "I've heard it's pretty bad." Recalling to the brief conversation with the soldier on the catwalk the night prior. Henry spoke while flipping a switch, lighting up the small parlor and having the stained glass illuminate his fluffed, short ginger hair.

"You don't know the half of it, and if you did—you wouldn't be trying so damn hard to get into the city. We hadn't dealt with a douchebag trying to get into the city in probably two weeks, what are you doing here man?"

Evan remained close to the front of the store, while Henry hung around the back.

"I'm *looking* for someone."

"Oh, well—" Henry paused while making his way into the kitchen. His echoey voice followed up, "Whoever it is, they're probably dead."

Evan nodded, "I know," he said while looking out the huge main window, strangely fixating on a propaganda poster. It had a Devil themed soldier who held a poor helpless child from a noose, Evan thought that propaganda like this only widened the divide.

Now opening the slitted kitchen door, Henry asked, "So? Does that do it for you *Evan*?"

Silence filled the restaurant, Henry hated silence. He chose to maybe turn around the conversation. "There's some pizza crusts back here, some stuff to make sauce and some cheese in the fridge, we could probably—" Henry was interrupted.

"I don't know or trust you, *Henry*." Evan said his name in a different tone, just as Henry had done. "Talk to me."

Evan didn't exactly know where to take the situation. His brain had already analyzed Henry's voice. Evan would be able to tell if something was off. Awkwardly standing at the opposite end of the shop, Henry asked again, "Pizza?"

Moments earlier they had been running from certain doom, and now the kid was asking if Evan wanted to make pizza. Oddly enough, without knowing this kid at all and being stuck in the middle of a war-torn city, Evan felt that eating pizza was the right next move. He was hungry after all.

Evan had started to slowly tiptoe his way to the back of the restaurant, striking conversation with the kid.

"So, you're in high school then?"

Evan felt weird striking conversation, but what else could he do?

"Yeah, I had only just started my senior year. I'm sorta pissed that I don't get to see what life is like without school, I guess this is it."

Evan smirked while changing his fixation from the poster to the patterned wallpaper, "Straight A's or no?"

"Fuck no, of course not." Henry said.

"I never really had good grades, but I guess I never really put in the time either, I always had something else going on." He continued.

Henry's slim physique was amplified by his pencil thin shadow. Evan's shadow crossed Henry's as he walked over toward the back of the parlor. "I never had the best grades either."

When Henry sat down at a table near the kitchen, the hanging lamp had shown Evan more features of Henry's face.

The pointed nose was covered in freckles and the fluffed ginger hair just barely hung in front of his gaze. His extremely white eyes complimented the baby blue pupils in the center and just by looking at the kid, you could tell he played a sport at one time or another.

As Henry walked back into the kitchen to preheat the oven, he analyzed Evan's face from the back.

His salt and pepper stubble pricked his face. His tired eyes had purple bags underneath while the small cuts had scabbed up on his face. Evan took his hand and rubbed his sandpaper like face, closing his eyes and opening them after a couple seconds. His gray jacket made his weak torso seem built while his brown hair had been ruffled out. His blue jeans had some blood stained on the knees and his dark leather boots had been scathed with scratches.

"Military you said?" Henry's voice echoed, eager to make this pizza and finally have some food in his belly.

"Yes," Evan said. Before Henry could make any more conversation, he was interrupted.

"So where were you—"

"Do you have a map?"

Henry looked at Evan through the serving window, finally making eye contact with each other. "Oh—uh—er check my vest pockets."

Evan reached for Henry's Kevlar vest that he had discarded moments earlier, pulling it up and tossing it on the table. Each pocket was empty, he searched through them relentlessly. When a horribly folded piece of paper slid out and onto the table, Evan's eyes widened.

The districts had been conveniently outlined and along with each distinct section, they were labeled. Pink, yellow, orange, and green highlighter had been used for key locations.

"Flip it over for the key," Henry spoke, following it up with, "You care about what toppings I use?"

There was a pause of silence. Once Henry had finished creating the sauce from the ingredients in the kitchen, he lathered it heavily, making sure that every square centimeter of the pizza crust had been covered; it was his favorite part after all. Now he sprinkled the cheese on, bit by bit, licking his lips as he did so.

"Hey, what toppings?"

Evan stopping looking at the folded map for a second, snapping out of his fixation. "Anything works, just no sausage."

Henry now opened the fridge once more, taking pepperoni and tossing the meat circles all across the pizza.

"Hey Henry, where do they keep the civilians?"

Henry snapped back as he put the pizza into the oven. "They don't really keep people around anymore, they either use them as soldiers like me or people run. Most of them end up dying though."

"What do you mean?" Evan said with his left eyebrow slightly inclined.

Henry set the timer on the oven and exited the kitchen, pulling up a chair to the small round table. "What I mean is: everyone who didn't stay already left." He plopped down on the chair like a water balloon hitting the floor, "The closest thing those *goatfuckers* up in Sheridan have to a civilian camp, is where they keep all the wrongdoers. I don't know if this place exists, but there was talk about a prison... sort of. Not really a prison but a lockup of sorts. I don't fucking know man."

"Sheridan?" Evan asked.

He knew he had heard of that before, thinking back on the previous night. Evan pulled the radio frequencies sheet from his pocket, unfolding the poorly treated paper and scanning through the list of named locations. He identified Sheridan, circled as 'Main Base.'

"Lieutenant General Johannsson? Does that name mean anything to you?" Evan asked, now putting the pieces in place.

"Yeah, he's the dick who runs the show."

Evan reflected, "Tell me more, Henry."

"Well, before things got really bad, a different guy was rolling our dice. He died, or was killed, or got sick, I have no clue. Regardless, that prick Johannsson only got to be in charge because he was next in line."

Without warning, the ground began to rumble, as if the entire planet had gotten the shivers. Henry shot up from his chair and without a moment's notice, he flipped the light switch. The entire parlor had fallen dark, and the only available light was from the progressively rising sun. Overcast clouds made the lighting a dim gray that was bright only in the darkness.

The huge main window at the front of the restaurant was bright with the dim sun. Henry urged Evan to duck behind something and before they knew what was coming, it came.

The Humvee that previously passed had come back. Rolling slowly and steadily. The massive tires crushed the snow beneath the treads. Compacting it into ice and continuing on its path. As soon as the Humvee had surpassed the store window, Henry stood up.

His baggy clothes complimented the ugly underneath and the shadows made from the outside light cast his outline on the wall behind him. Evan stood up next, everything looked like a black-and-white movie. When the roaring engine could no longer be heard, Henry flipped the switch, enabling saturation to compliment the Italian setting.

"If I'm being completely honest, I'm surprised that the power here works. Last I heard, Johannsson was trying to get into the Utilities center. So long as this oven makes it to the end of the timer, I don't care."

"The power?"

"Yeah, if Johannsson can control the electricity and shit, he'll have the entire city to its knees; including those who chose to revolt."

"So, it's basically a warzone here?" Evan inquired. Henry noticed that Evan had been absolutely unphased by the death machine that had just rolled by. He expected that Evan's voice would at least be a little shaky.

"A warzone would be a good way to explain it, yes." Evan demanded Henry to explain a bit more.

"Well, I guess things took a turn for the worst one day. Must've been almost a month ago that Johannsson took control and people fought back, I don't know. People just decided that they'd rather die out there than in here, pathetically."

"Why did things get so out of hand? I mean seriously?" Evan itched a scab on his chin.

"Because Johannsson has a big fat fucking ego, I heard he was a complete and total failure when he was deployed out West, that's why he came back here.

It all started making sense to Evan. "Basically... Johannsson is the root of why things got bad here?"

"For sure, that dude is *such* a motherfucker. I mean things were bad here even before he got a say in things, like shit, they separated me from my family when we got here. *What the hell*. You don't do that."

Evan agreed, "Yeah, that's hard kid... why did you and your family come here?"

"Well, the reason you gave for coming here was extremely vague and made almost zero sense, but I'll go along with it." Henry paused to rub his nose. "My parents were divorced, so I don't exactly know where my Dad went, but my Mom took me and my baby sister here. She thought it was a safe zone, or some shit."

He straitened his hair with his left hand and rubbed his nose again with his right hand. "Anyways, turns out she was sick, and my sister had barely just turned 2, so they took both of them and sent me in a different direction. They said they needed those who were fit enough to help the situation. At the time I had enough meat on my bones, but the last good meal I had was..." Henry paused to think.

"I actually can't remember the last good meal I had." Evan nodded, letting Henry know he was listening.

"So, you want to get out? Like out of here?" Evan asked.

Henry nodded, "Yeah, maybe my Dad is still rocking it in Rochester."

Evan knew that the likelihood of Henry's Dad still being alive was basically zero to none. "Rochester didn't fare too good, kid."

"Oh, well shit. I heard that too, but who knows."

Despite this kid losing his Mom and sister, and most likely his father too, he seemed as if he didn't care. Evan sat there at the round table, "You seem like you couldn't care less."

"Well of course I care, of course I fucking miss them. I just don't think I should dump it all on some random dude like you. I'm sure you've got your hands full with shit anyways."

Evan saw this distinct twinkle in Henry's eye when he spoke about missing his family.

"Yeah."

The timer that Henry had set up for the pizza began to ring, unsettling both of them at the table. Henry got up and spoke again.

"Who are you looking for anyways?" He entered the kitchen and unwound the timer.

Evan hesitated. He figured that the kid hadn't shared too much of his sob story, so neither should he. Patiently, Evan awaited the pizza. Henry must've been waiting for a response, because after a couple seconds he asked, "Touchy subject or…?"

"Get the pizza out here and I'll tell you."

As Henry walked out of the kitchen with the pizza on a circular dish, he also brought a tiny basket with parmesan and pepper flakes. He set the dish down on the table, along with the basket. Upon realizing that the pizza had already been cut into slices, Evan snatched the biggest slice he could and instantly started stuffing it into his face.

Henry did the same but powdered his with the parmesan that melted into the cheese, taking the color of the pepperoni grease. The sauce blended beautifully with the perfectly melted cheese.

The slices of pepperoni were crisp and crunchy with each bite, driving poor nutrition but delightful flavor into both bellies. Evan was the first to move onto slice 2, while Henry followed close behind.

Minutes later… they had both devoured the entire pizza, both bellies full and entirely stuffed. Henry let out a greasy belch while Evan put his rough hands on his belly, slouching back in his chair.

"Who er—are you looking for?"

Evan looked up from the grease-stained circular dish only having crumbs left.

"My daughter."

"Shit," Henry responded.

The two sat at the round table, glancing out the window and across the street. "Why'd she come here?"

Henry instantly saw Evan's tone change, "She came here for the same reason you did. She thought it was safe."

Evan wanted to rise from the chair he sat in, but he was glued to it. It was as if his full stomach was an anchor, and he were a ship at sea. Evan tilted his head back and let the stained-glass lighting bask his face. Henry wanted to lighten the mood, he felt like his last question left things off on the wrong note.

"I make some kick ass pizza, don't I?"

Evan opened his eyelids and resumed from his momentary rest; he tilted his head back toward Henry.

"No joke, you really do…" after a long pause, Evan continued. "You taught yourself to cook it?" He didn't really know where else to take the conversation.

"My grandpa actually, he was the most stereotypical Italian dude ever."

"We're talking about like, he would attend operas and shit. Plays and all. He would make his own pasta and create his own sauce, all kinds of shit. It was incredible to watch. He had a big curly mustache too."

Evan chuckled at how outstandingly stereotypical Henry's grandpa was, he thought it was even funnier how Henry chose to describe it.

"He was a sucker for pizza, he thought American joints like this," he said motioning the parlor they currently sat in. "He thought they were *Mucchi Di Merda*." He did his best to imitate an Italian accent.

Henry nor Evan knew what it meant, yet it still made them chuckle. When silence befell the room, Evan spoke about his grandpa.

"My grandpa never spoke much. He didn't have much to spend either. He did have a dog though. A beagle named Bob; he loved that dog. Did you have a dog, Henry?"

Henry spoke, "No, my mother was allergic. We had some fish though. Which of course were a headache to take care of. I feel like the fish know that they're a headache too."

"Yeah no, fish are ridiculous. My daughter, Jade, went through a fish phase. We got one from the fair in Rochester when she was about… hm. She must've been 6 years old or so. Anyways, she won a goldfish off of some stupid ring toss game and we kept it for a while." Henry nodded to let Evan know he was listening.

"She was too small to take care of the tank and stuff, so I became the fella for the job. She named the fish Fiona, and well…

the goldfish lasted way longer than I thought. The fish got so old that it turned silver by the time I was deployed out West." Evan paused, realizing that the goldfish tank was no longer in the spot that it had been, thinking back on his house. The tank was gone. He didn't remember seeing it.

"Wow, it was just a goldfish too. That's pretty cool."

Evan snapped out of it, figuring that it shouldn't disrupt the conversation he was having now. He figured that maybe Jade had just forgotten to take care of the fish or something.

"Yeah, it was pretty cool," Evan spoke.

His belly had begun to digest all the pizza he had consumed. Reaching over and snatching papers to lay them flat.

Henry looked at the papers he had laid down, then glancing back up at Evan. The mood had shifted from fish to something entirely unrelated. Henry wanted to talk more about fish, but Evan wanted to find his daughter.

He started tuning his radio to different frequencies, tuning back to Sheridan, and hearing only silence. He asked Henry what had happened at the University the night prior.

"Some battle or something, the rebels wanted it back because of all the shit we had stored there. It was basically a hospital."

"We'll start there."

Evan then tuned to the University frequency and waited.

Chapter 11

The Line.

On the other side of the city, the sun had no clouds to hide behind.

The rays had shot through the poorly made drapes and illuminated all of Jackson's face. Outlining every tiny developing wrinkle and presenting his chapped lips. His bushy eyebrows moved around as he began to wake up. Side to side and finally his lids opened.

His pupils dilated to the bright sun, glancing around at the room he slept in and the couch he rests upon. The soft snoring voice indicated that Matt was still asleep and the little almost chipmunk whimpers told him that Ana was also still asleep. He groaned while stretching his arms.

His shoulders were sore, and his face had been bruised from Evan's punches. He rubbed the bruises, it felt almost good to massage despite the equivocal pain. The more he rubbed the discolored skin, the better it felt. Jackson glanced at his wristwatch to look at the time, it was 8:13 AM.

He forced himself up from the couch and flopped his legs off to the floor. Before getting up fully, he flung his arms out and cracked his back. Popping as if he had added milk to a bowl of rice krispies.

Rations were distributed at 8 AM, he remembered. Then standing up and stabilizing himself. Now walking over to the door, he slipped on his boots and thick dark blue coat. He tried to remember what the woman had said about rations, or rather where to go. It was on the tip of his tongue, recalling the short conversation the night before. Jackson grabbed hold of the doorknob and twisted it slowly, trying to not wake his family.

He still was flabbergasted by what had happened; they had been saved by a group of altruistic civilians. He got lucky.

The carpeted floor had been stained with dirty boot marks from the night before. He found the stairwell and descended to the ground floor, crossing the reception desk that Nicole was no longer standing at. Jackson had finally recalled where the rations were being handed out.

The library had to be it; he couldn't think of where else it could possibly be. When he opened the front door to the apartment complex, he noticed there was no wind, or almost none at least.

His short hair remained stationary as he walked against the almost unnoticeable gusts. His beard on the other hand waved around with each progressive gust. To his left was a long city block that led to a gated wall that seemed impenetrable. To his right was the rest of Longfellow.

It led to a long street with the main entrance and adjacent to the small park where the stolen military equipment was stored was a long line that expanded all the way through the sidewalk. Jackson figured that it had to be where the rations were distributed. He jogged up to the end of the line and secured his spot in the growing string of people.

Everyone who stood in line came in all different shapes and sizes. Some were tall and bald; others were short with incredibly long hair. Some had coats and others didn't. Some were men and some were women, some were built so similarly that Jackson could've swore they were twins. Some had guns and others had knives; some had beards like his and some had no facial hair at all. One thing that everyone had in common was that they all looked hungry.

Whispers and distinct names were being thrown out in the jumble of quiet conversations. Jackson tried his best to eavesdrop but could barely manage to pick apart a handful of things.

He knew that they were talking about the University, it seemed like a common word that was being thrown out of everyone's mouth. He recalled that Liv had been planning her attack on the University, but he was curious of whether or not the attack was successful.

The trio in front of him consisted of an elderly looking man with muttonchop maintained facial hair, a younger looking man with an oversized stocking cap, and another young man who couldn't be a day over 25. Jackson had overheard them talking about the University and wanted to know more.

"Hey fellas."

The elderly looking man spun around first, looking Jackson up and down as he did so.

"Hey big guy." The two younger men didn't bother to turn around or even say hi.

Jackson's mouth hung open with a friendly and awkward smile, hoping to figure out what happened at the university. "So, you guys know how the University turned out?"

The old man turned his gaze back to Jackson again, his old, wrinkled mouth spoke. "I think our guys came out on top, which would be my best bet." The old man's turkey gizzard like throat wagged back and forth with each movement. "Can't tell for sure unless someone returns with news of any kind. I'm a no news is good news kind of guy."

Jackson nodded, "I'm Jackson by the way," the old man outstretched his right hand.

"Nice to meet you," they shook hands.

The older man turned back to the two younger men, Jackson minded his own business now, looking around and seeing everything in the morning sun. He noticed the several guard towers at the entrance with heavily armed guards. They all looked like extremely normal people.

The silent mumbles in the line continued as Jackson waddled in place to keep warm, seeing the vapor float from his mouth in the cold. From his eavesdropping ears, he could distinguish the word, "Utilities." He was unsure of what this meant. Distant shouts from the towers distracted Jackson from the pattern he was making in the snow.

Suddenly, the massive sheet metal doors were opening, and he could now hear the sound of many engines. Hijacked and manned Humvees drove in, one after the other. All who exited the vehicles were dressed in casual Winter clothing; they were not soldiers, they were civilians. The massive doors closed without delay.

Everyone standing in the ration line glanced and peered above one another, not bothering to move from their spot in line. Jackson had completely spun around to look at what was happening. Seeing all of the heavily built men exit the vehicles; one stood out.

His weak and lanky frame hopped off the Humvee and nearly slipped on a patch of ice while doing so. The sun bounced off one side of his nose and shadowed the other. The little acne craters on his face were all complimented with their own tiny shadows.

Everyone in line reached out for the arriving soldiers, demanding to know how the battle had gone. The soldiers rejoiced.

All cutting in front of Jackson of course, he eyeballed the individuals that cut. Suddenly he heard his name.

"Jackson? Er-- I think your name was."

The kid was standing there, Jackson turned to him, "Randall? Right? I think."

"Yep, hello again sir," his tiny mouth fluctuated.

"Why do they all get to cut in line? What the fuck." Jackson whispered to the kid.

"Because people want to talk to them."

Jackson raised his bushy eyebrows. "Why didn't you cut?"

"Because nobody wants to talk to me, I don't think any of them really know me at all… I guess I haven't taken the time to know them either." The kid was an outcast despite his upbeat nature.

There was a moment of silence between the two while the entire line was talking and discussing the events of the prior night.

"So, you guys won right?" Jackson inferred.

"Yeah, it got a little sketchy at some points but overall, we came out on top. I think Liv is happy about having the University back."

Jackson rolled his eyes, figuring it might be entertaining to talk to someone new. Regardless, he knew Randall would've chewed his ear off anyway.

"Well kid, if you want to talk about it, I'll listen."

Randall was excited to talk to someone about it, he didn't much get to express his view on things, nobody was willing to listen. "Well sir, we got there right, and I think all the little greenies got pretty fuckin' scared by the massive tank we brought, they surrendered pretty quickly, it was the assholes that decided they wanted to go down in a blaze of glory that made the fight long." Randall stopped to adjust his hat. "Whole thing should've been done and over with in ten minutes, but of course a couple asshole green-caps decided to make it more difficult than needed."

Jackson figured that the phrase 'green-cap' must mean soldier, or a slur used for them. "Did anyone on your side get hurt?"

"Well, I heard one of the dudes going in through the North wing was injured in an ambush, but other than that, the University was taken by us pretty easily. Liv wanted to take the University because of all the medical supplies there."

The line shuffled forward, and Jackson followed close behind. Then questioning, "Is Liv the leader? Or what's the deal with her?"

"She's not necessarily the leader... I guess she's one of the few people here that we look to for direction. She's got a smart head on her shoulders, that's for sure." He plucked an eyelash and toyed with a pimple on his cheek.

As the line moved along, Jackson processed the information slowly. As he made sense of things, he was trying to remember what Randall had told him the night before on the jeep.

"You guys are fighting against the military, right?"

"Pretty much, sir."

"Hm."

Randall scratched his ear like a dog and then put the hat back on his head, "I was here from the beginning. Up here for college, I'm pretty sure I told you this last night, er whatever. Anyways, things were alright for a while, they just told us to stay in our dorms and to not really leave, the infection rate was too high er something like that. Couldn't tell you, I was too busy studying for this huge mid quarter exam I had scheduled, I thought everything was going to blow over in no time."

The line shuffled forward while everyone rambled on about their specific timeline regarding the battle. "Anyways..."

Jackson knew he was in for a story.

"Some of my neighbors in the dorm I was staying in got sick, like really sick. I tried talking to them, but it seemed like they weren't themselves anymore. By some miracle, I survived. That's not the point, I always get off track, shit. Anyways—"

Jackson chuckled, "Yes, yes you do."

"Well, anyways—er. All those dirt faced greenies were taking the sick people and just shooting them, like they were sick cattle or some shit. They'd take the bodies and throw them in these massive burn piles, it was sick."

"You're getting sidetracked again aren't you kid?" Jackson pointed out. The line shuffled forward and the two bumped into one another. He wasn't the least bit surprised at the atrocities of the Military.

"Oh, I am. Okay so, let me get down to it. We are fighting the military because they went bananas, that's the simplest way I can put it. They thought they could treat us like sheep, they thought they could be shepherds. There we go, that was my point."

It stooped Jackson, he stood there and tried to process it all. "Hm, I knew it was bad up here, but it was pretty bad down in Rochester too."

"Oh, I heard about that crap. Sorry about that man."

"It's alright, my wife and my kid made it so, that's all that matters. I don't know how the city is doing right now, but either way, I'm here for now."

Randall nodded, "That's right, your wife and son," Randall remembered from the night before. "Make sure to get 2 extra ration bags for them." Jackson nodded, thanking him.

The two didn't speak for a couple minutes while the line moved along steadily. Randall kicked at the hardened snow and fiddled with the straps on his vest.

Jackson stood there, analyzing his surroundings. The nice brick pillars that guarded the park had snow crawling halfway up, the running engines had finally been shut off, the silent street soon was loud again with the reemergence of mumbling voices. Johannsson was a name that was thrown around quite often, Jackson had recognized.

As Jackson and Randall slowly followed the line to the front doors of the library, conversation started up again.

"Don't expect to be thrilled with the rations, it's nothing fancy but it sure gets the bones moving."

This prompted Jackson to look ahead to the table set up at the door, small bags of oatmeal, bottled water, and some other unrecognizable food items.

"Do you have a radio?"

Jackson turned, confused at the question. "No… I don't."

"You can have mine," Randall tossed his tiny radio to Jackson, being caught perfectly. "Tune to the University frequency at... hm... in like... 20 minutes, wait no just tune in at 9 am on the dot."

"Well shit, thanks, also what do you mean University frequency? I don't know how to use this thing." Jackson looked like an old man trying to figure out an iPhone.

Randall demonstrated without a fuss, showing him which knob did what and how to pull the tiny antenna out. "143.8 FM, that's what you gotta put in to reach the University. Liv is going to direct a statement to that Johannsson asshat."

Jackson nodded, "I assume Johannsson is in charge of the military?" Randall nodded.

"You'd be right."

As the two moved closer to the ration distribution table, Jackson thought that Randall might never shut up. Talking to the kid was alright, but it certainly wasn't something Jackson wanted to do that early in the morning.

"What do you think about the West sir?"

"You can knock it off with the 'sir' shit, I'm not even 40 yet."

"Oh, okay sir—er I mean Jackson."

Jackson smirked, "I guess I didn't care before everyone started getting sick, and I care even less now that the tv isn't constantly blaring."

"So... you did care?"

"Well of course I have my opinions, but those pretty much get you killed... or would've gotten you killed. I guess we have bigger things to worry about other than an opinion."

"So, what side did you lean toward?"

"It doesn't matter kid, not anymore. I lean toward whatever side gets me a pack of cigarettes."

For whatever reason, the kid was *persistent* about Jackson's political view. However, Jackson was smart enough to not outright advertise his thoughts about things.

"Well, sir--," Randall stopping himself, "I mean Jackson, I'm just trying to make conversation. Personally, I think that the West were in the right for protesting."

"Me too, but I think the last thing you should be talking about is politics, especially in a line full of people who might think different."

"Yeah, er—you're right. I just hate the silence, it's unnerving to me."

Jackson was on the opposite side of the spectrum; silence was peaceful to him. As they stood there, the remaining line to the ration desk became shorter and shorter.

Soon, the two had reached from the front of the line. The large woman greeted Randall first while Jackson recognized her. It was the woman that had welcomed his family the night before. Small talk ensued while Jackson prepared a greeting.

Randall moved out of the way after he received his rations, Nicole greeted Jackson. "You came in last night, right? Jacob, was it?"

"Jackson actually, it's okay," he chuckled. "Hi, I'm pretty sure your name was Nicole?"

She made a sweet face; her big cheeks squeezed her facial features together. The sun complimented her dark toned skin and shone off the highest point on her cheeks.

"How was your first night?"

Jackson responded, "I slept great, my wife and son slept even better, they probably aren't even up yet."

Nicole giggled as she collected his rations, "3 portions for you and your family? How's that sound?"

"Sounds great, thanks Nicole."

She handed him several Ziplock bags with various oats and other things within along with a bag full of water bottles, 6 count. Nicole spoke to Jackson as he turned away. "Have a great rest of your day, see you later."

"Oh yeah right, you too! Thanks."

Randall had been waiting for Jackson to be done in the ration line. *Of course he had been.*

"Man, you should see the way she looks at you."

Jackson looked up as he started heading home. "Yeah, I saw."

Randall wished that a woman would look at him that way. "I never really was a looker, even before."

"Yeah kid, I see that" Jackson poked fun at the kid. Randall smirked, seeing the obvious sarcasm. They parted ways as they headed home.

"See you later sir!"

The kid clearly had forgotten what Jackson had said about calling him 'sir.' Jackson responded, "Yep."

As he walked back to his momentary room at the apartment building, he got to see his street in the daylight. The nice brick buildings all reflected the sun beautifully. He stepped through the front door and ascended the stairs. After reaching his room, he stuck the key in the door and flung it open, slipping his boots off and setting everything on the foot of the bed.

Ana was nowhere to be seen while Matt was still knocked out cold. Jackson looked around the room for his wife, seeing the bathroom door closed, assuming she was within. He unpacked a bottle of water and chugged it in less than a second.

When Ana exited the bathroom, she snuck up behind Jackson and wrapped her arms around him, squeezing him with her vice grip hug. He exhaled a groan, but it was a lovely groan.

He put his hand on her arm and told her, "I got us some shit to eat, I think this place is alright."

She agreed, "For sure honey."

When the hug ended, Jackson glanced at his watch, seeing the time as 8:57 AM. He retrieved the radio that Randall had gifted to him, tuning it exactly how he had been shown. The radio static was unnerving to say the least.

He stood it atop the TV stand and started munching on some of the oats, filling his stomach with nutrition. Ana sat with him on the bed, she knew Jackson was mildly annoyed, but clearly not enough to outright share.

Ana poked him, "What's up?" Jackson of course knew she'd ask this.

"That Randall kid kept trying to get me to talk politics, I didn't think he'd ever shut up." He surprisingly didn't hide any of his annoyance like usual.

Ana flopped her head on Jackson's beefy shoulder, "So you didn't let him know what you think then?"

"Not really, I'd rather we don't get thrown out of here because of our opinion or some stupid shit like that."

"Yeah… that would be dumb…" Ana stopped to lift her head from his shoulder and eat a handful of oats. "Why do you have the radio on?"

"That kid Randall told me Liv was going to *talk* to everyone at 9, so I guess we have to wait."

"They won last night, right?" Ana questioned.

"Yeah, he said the military fell pretty quick."

In the midst of them speaking, a voice began to speak over the radio. *It was Liv.*

"This message is directed at Lieutenant General Johannsson and all the others who contribute to his reign."

Silence followed the statement. Jackson and Ana glanced at each other, not knowing what to expect.

~ . ~

"This is Liv, or rather Olivia Sullivan. I was a professor at the University, I taught basic anatomical knowledge and medical skills for students who wanted to save lives."

"Things were fine before you became the de facto leader. You have demoralized the people of this city and continue to destroy all that we love, you have failed as a leader, and you have failed as a person. This place is our home, and you are a foreign invader."

"Lieutenant General Johannsson, if you're listening to this broadcast, I can guarantee that you and your city will fall if we keep fighting each other. Give up and let us decide our fate instead of taking that liberty from us."

"If you keep fighting…"

"I can assure you a slow death from the hands of all those you have wronged."

~ . ~

Evan looked up from the radio, meeting eyes with Henry. They both looked shocked, as if they had just listened to a live declaration of war, and that's just what the speech was about. It was about *war*.

After the radio fell silent and the brutal static ensued, Evan started looking around at the other frequencies on the sheet. The map outlined exactly where the sections were located while the other sheet contained the proper frequency information.

"What was the other group in the city? I can't remember what you called them."

"The Revolutionists?" Henry spoke while picking at a zit right under his left cheek.

"Yeah, them. Would they know if my daughter was alive?"

Henry scoffed at Evan, "I wouldn't bet on it, man. What makes you so sure that she even made it here?"

Evan remained silent. Jade had to be in the city... she had to be. Before he spoke again, he put the trapper hat back on his head. The dark green undershirt complimented the blue plaid patterns on the inside of the jacket. The gray outside created vast shadows with all the folds in the fabric.

"The map says that the Utilities are near Northern Calhoun Isles," Henry went to look at the map. His eyes scanned the paper, making sure Evan's theory was right.

A small square box was outlined in green highlighter along with a drawn pointed arrow. *Utilities* was circled right next to it.

"Where are we at right now Henry?"

"Man, I'm not coming with you. I gotta get out of the city; As far as they're concerned, I've gone AWOL, they probably think I ran to join the Revolutionists. I've seen men die for way fucking less."

"I don't expect you to come with me, that's not what I'm asking. I'm asking you to tell me where we are right now."

"We're right here," Henry pointed at the Southwestern side of the metro area." Evan, that's a day's walk at least..."

"Calhoun Isles are closer than Longfellow, right?"

Henry agreed, "You're right, but still man."

Evan had an idea; he knew that walking across the entire city alone would be a poor choice, so he had to find a way to make Henry come with him. At this point, he trusted Henry... kind of. He knew that Henry wouldn't want to be alone either.

"They've got to have trucks there, right? Or cars at least, right?" Evan tried to reason.

"Yeah... probably."

"If you help me get to the Utilities center, I'll help you steal a car to get out of here." Evan proposed a deal.

"So, you are asking me to come with you huh?"

"I guess I am," Evan admitted.

Henry stopped for a second, realizing that he wouldn't exactly want to walk all the way to Rochester. Nor did he think that walking all that distance on foot would be safe. Henry gave it some thought and eventually agreed to go with Evan.

"I'll go," Henry muttered. He didn't necessarily want to put himself at risk but heading out of the city on foot would be just as bad.

"Thank you, Henry."

Evan situated his trapper hat while slinging the duffel bag over his back, grabbing his rifle, and buttoning his coat.

Henry simply slipped his vest back on and unrolled his sweatshirt sleeves, letting them hang. He flung the rifle over his back and followed Evan out the previously shattered door.

Before starting on down the street, they looked both ways as if a car of any kind would be coming their way.

There was nothing to look out for.

Chapter 12

A Professor's Invitation

A single declaration.

Liv's earth-shattering speech left all who had heard it completely shocked. Shortly before starting it, she had called a favor in to Longfellow.

Jackson and Ana sat on the bed, trying to process the words that had come from the radio. "They're serious, aren't they?"

Jackson replied to his wife, "Yeah, Randall was telling me about it in line. They want Johannsson dead."

"I was just about to as who that was, he sounds like he isn't the most popular guy."

"Yeah, they hate his guts."

Knocking fists struck the door and the two of them spun their heads at the same time, like dogs hearing the mailman. Jackson got up first to answer the door. With each stride, he grew strangely nervous.

When Jackson opened the door, a tall man in sweats with a heavy vest draped over his torso greeted him. His voice was way deeper than Jackson's.

"I was told that Jackson + 2 were staying in this room."

Jackson nodded awkwardly.

"Liv radioed in on a separate line before her broadcast, she insists that you and your family visit her at the University."

Jackson stood still, "She wants us to go to the University?"

"That's correct, yes. You would receive a safe escort to and from of course. She also informed me to give you back your pistol, she knew that we would take it." The soldier outstretched his hand, revealing the pistol that had been taken the night prior.

Jackson glanced at the pistol before taking it, "Why does she want to see us?"

"If I'm being honest, I don't know. She might just want to check up on you guys, seeing how you're new and all."

"Fuck, okay, okay. When do we leave?"

"As soon as you can, that would be nice."

"Mhm, we'll be out." Jackson shut the door and before he got the chance to speak to his wife, the soldier knocked at the door again. When Jackson opened the door, he was informed.

"Plug the bathtub and sinks, fill them with water."

"Why would I ?"

"If the Utilities get attacked, our water will be cut off. We have to save as much as we can."

"Okay, I'll be sure to do that."

Jackson shut the door again, ensuring now that he would be able to speak to his wife undisturbed.

"Get Mathew up and we'll head to the University." Ana stopped Jackson, "Do you think this is a good idea?"

"Listen, Liv is asking for us to see her, she runs things, I think… we should go see her."

Ana was a little sketched out by the thought of it. Jackson was nervous as well, though he chose to drown that emotion. It would all be okay.

Ana silently disagreed but reluctantly decided to wake her son up. She put her hand on his forehead slowly to get him awake. His open and drooling mouth muttered some inaudible words.

"m…what…"

"Sweetie, it's time to get up. We have to go to the University. Get some pants on." Matt originally fought getting up but soon after Jackson advertised some oats and raisins, he was up in a second.

Matt picked up the pants he had discarded the night before while ripping a bag of oats from his Dad's grasp. Entering the bathroom with his eyes half closed and drool still dripping from his mouth. After about five minutes in the bathroom, Matt exited with wet hair. He shook off as if he were a dog and proceeded to crunch dry his hair. He grabbed another bag of oats and raisins and scarfed it down.

"I thought that kid only ate chips and pop, what the hell," Jackson exclaimed.

Ana giggled and tossed him a new t-shirt, saying, "Throw your coat on too, you'll need it."

Jackson started filling the bathtub and sink with water, plugging the drains and waiting for them to rise. Once the water had reached an appropriate limit, he turned the faucets off accordingly and exited the bathroom.

Jackson spent the time they had left tucking his pistol in a discreet location in between his belt and his torso. It was invisible to the naked eye, especially under the coat and sweatshirt.

The three got up and took a water battle from the ration stash while leaving their room. As they made their way down the stairs, Jackson noticed that each room they walked past had the sound of running water coming from within.

"The Utilities?" Ana asked.

"Yeah, I'm pretty sure they're expecting an attack, guys in line earlier were talking about it."

Matt announced that he was about to ask the same question, "Is that why you were filling up the bathtub and stuff?"

"Yeah, I don't think it'll be good if other people are in charge of our water."

They all silently agreed. The trio swung the front door open and observed a Humvee out front waiting for them, exhaust vapor flowing from the pipes. The driver waved his arms as he propped open the door, "Get in the back, guys."

Before they all knew it, they sat scrunched together in the back of a Humvee. The engine roared as they peeled out of the dead-end street, now making it through the huge, gated exit from Longfellow.

The man-made gates were large and heavily armored with sheet metal and other tough materials.

As the Humvee rolled out onto the street, it turned right and began speeding down the path to the University. The horrific sights they all had seen the night before were now amplified by the growing sunlight. Illuminating all the gruesome features of every gunned down corpse. The entirety of the blood that had drained from these bodies was frozen in the streets.

"Hello, driver?" Jackson asked.

"Yeah?"

"Do you have any idea why Liv wants to see us?"

"No clue, man."

The cab grew silent

Matt used this to his advantage and tried to catch a couple Z's.

As the driver took a route onto the ramp heading North, taller buildings and the downtown area of Minneapolis was observable. It still looked just as ravaged as it did the day before. The fire was less noticeable while the broken windows were fare more noticeable than before. The city looked *dirty*.

Military barricades that blocked off city streets were now vacant and abandoned Humvees were a regular thing to see. Sandbag walls with large camouflage trucks suffocated sidewalks.

The highway that led to the University became increasingly packed with cars. Paths were tight and by some miracle, they were able to squeeze by.

Matt struggled to sleep because of how tight the back of the Humvee felt, he wanted to explode. His claustrophobia was overpowering.

They drove along the river that split the Eastern side of the city and observed a few dozen unlucky geese who were too late to fly South. It seemed like overnight, the gunfire had become almost non-existent. The tall buildings shadowed all that was West of their stature and blinded the sun's attempt to clear the air.

While Jackson peered out the window at the hopeless surroundings and the now somewhat quiet city, Ana did the same. She saw things differently; she noticed the absence of people. Nobody was walking the streets, as if everyone was hiding. The shadows were exceedingly dark, and the sun illuminated things until they were blinding to look at.

Jackson noticed his wife doing the same thing he was, he nudged her with his elbow. She stopped from her gaze and now looked into Jackson's eyes.

"What?" She said with a twang in her voice.

"Even though you haven't showered in days," he whispered. "I would still kiss every inch of your body."

She smiled, blushing, and getting goosebumps all over her arms and legs. Ana made sure Matt was dead asleep before making a move on her husband.

She leaned over to Jackson, meeting eyes with him in the back of that Humvee. When their eyes connected, they waved and fluttered, as if they couldn't decide which eye to look at, right or left. When she came closer to him, he closed his eyes.

Their lips connected and soon did their tongues. They felt each and every warm release of air on each other's face, hitting their skin and spreading throughout. Within the vacuum their mouths created, their tongues played tag back and forth. Both pairs of eyes were closed and when their hands connected simultaneously, their lips separated to giggle. Ana's pointed nose fought with Jackson's brick wall of a face.

Their lips were sculpted to fit one another.

A bump in the road made their mouths disconnect for a moment, Jackson opened his eyes and Ana did the same. They both smiled and giggled, cheeks red. Their flirty moment was interrupted by the man driving the Humvee.

"We're approaching the University. Come in." The radio static ensued once the words stopped.

Jackson looked down at his hand that was still holding Ana's, "That was good."

She smiled, "Sure was," she nudged him.

The radio blared a low voice, *"Come to the Southern gate, by the main entrance. You brought the family that Liv wanted to see, right?"*

"Yup."

Still smiling at one another and red, they both glanced out the window at the upcoming University. As the Humvee crossed a bridge, more and more of the campus was becoming visible. Almost every building was made of brick and guarded by tall stone pillars. Aside from the architectural beauty, small markings on every building indicated that a fight had went down.

As they approached the massive gate, guards could be seen walking the perimeter, making sure that a looming invasion could not be had.

The Humvee's brakes kept it from rolling any further, the driver announced his presence over the radio and soon the gates folded in, allowing entry. The cab was beginning to get a little too warm for comfort, Matt awoke with sweaty armpits. He shook his head and noticed the surroundings outside the window.

Brick buildings and snow crowding the streets. "Mom? Dad? Are we at the University?"

"Yes, sweetie," Ana said while adjusting her legs into a more comfortable position.

A voice spoke on the radio, telling the driver to unlock the doors.

"Now tell the family to exit."

"Alright, get out. I guess they'll take it from here."

Jackson raised his bushy eyebrow, "Where are we supposed to go? What the hell?"

"I don't know man; they'll probably send someone to come get you."

Jackson was initially confused and rather pissed at the miscommunication, but eventually opened the Humvee door to let him and his family out. They stepped out of the Humvee and felt the snow crush beneath their feet, looking out in all directions, having zero clue about where they were meant to go. Matt rubbed his eyes, groaning about how he should still be in bed.

A guard approached the trio, dressed heavily and with a rather flat voice he spoke. "Head to the science building, it's over there," the guard pointed at a building with many brick pillars separating long windows made from untouched glass panes that reflected the sun perfectly into everyone's eyes.

"Okay, thanks," Jackson said while ushering his family to begin heading that way.

"What do you think she wants to see us for?" Matt questioned.

"Beats me, I just hope we aren't in trouble or some stupid shit."

"I don't really know what we would be in trouble for, I mean think about it, we just got here," Ana added optimistically.

"I guess, I don't know. Maybe she's got some answers for us about all of this shit. She said she was a doctor, or should've been one or something, I can't remember for shit. So, I'd assume she knows a little bit more than us, I guess I'd just like to know what the fuck is going on." They all approached the building, growing closer.

You could tell where the grassed areas were meant to be and where the walkways that once harbored countless students were located just by the displacement of snow. They couldn't tell whether the lights were on or not, all they could notice was the absence of people. Usually, a campus is filled with people, walking about and socializing. Not this one, however.

The atmosphere was silent, as if they were attending a funeral. The trees didn't move and neither did the snow on the ground, everything was still. The only thing moving was the family. It sounded like during the battle overnight, everyone had gotten their tongues cut out as a punishment.

When they finally reached the science building door, they noticed that the threshold had been riddled with bullets and the brick surrounding the door was chipped with punctures. Jackson awkwardly raised his fist to knock at it, but before his hand contacted the door, Ana redirected his attention.

Liv was standing at the other end of the building, facing them. "Jackson? Get over here." She said his name as if she'd forgotten it.

She stood as if she had a wooden pole nailed to her back, profoundly perfect posture. Jackson's eyes widened, "Okay!"

The family waddled to Liv, making sure not to slip and embarrass themselves. The first thing Jackson did was outstretch his hand, hoping to shake hands with Liv. His hand joined hers in a firm hold.

"I heard your broadcast, it was badass."

"Well, I'm glad you think so, that was the intended effect," Liv adjusted her glasses and smiled with only half her face.

Ana shook the scientist's hand after Jackson had his share, reminding Liv of her name.

"Your name is? My apologies."

"Oh, it's fine. My name is Ana," she smiled with hope.

"Ana? Nice to officially meet you all."

"And this is Mathew," Ana presented her son. Matt rubbed his eyes again, asking Liv, "How are you awake at this hour?"

"Well to be fair, I haven't slept since…" Liv paused, "Well, I don't quite remember, I'm just happy there was some leftover coffee from those military jokers." Liv reassured Matt, "Don't worry, I don't think I had the best sleeping schedule when I was your age either."

Matt smiled as a reassuring gesture, he didn't really know this lady, she was a stranger to him. Liv ushered everyone indoors, insisting that it was warmer inside. It certainly didn't feel like it.

Once they all entered the building, they observed more brick themed architecture. The tile floor looked dirty from the snow that had been tracked in and the halls were dark, only having certain lights turned on to conserve energy and to not cause a shortage.

"I'm positive that you guys want to know what's going on here, all new arrivals have the same look on their face."

Jackson walked closest to Liv and kept his family behind him as they followed her down the halls, heading up stairs and turning down different corridors. The artwork on the walls was mostly abstract, which Jackson thought was stupid.

"Originally, it was my students and I who were held out here during the initial call for martial law. After the first week had passed and we were putting a dent in the cafeteria food, the military had come knocking. The weak ran, the strong fought, and the smart hid—"

Ana interrupted Liv, "What did you do?"

"I tried to fight but resorted to hiding and before I knew it, they had found me. Turns out within the first month or two of this outbreak they were trying to cover up; the major hospitals had become ground zero for everything. They figured someone with my skillset could end up being a doctor for their men… and I was. Up until stories got around about how bad things were getting. I couldn't sit here and help those who were hurting the city. Me and a couple other trusted individuals devised a plan and got out. We only killed one man while escaping, that I am proud of."

"You were a part of the military?" Jackson confusingly asked.

"No, not at all. They were forcing me to treat their wounded for a time. Anyhow, I ended up finding the Revolutionists shortly after escaping. Ever since… it's been my goal to recapture the University, I knew about all the supplies that had been stored here and luckily, they hadn't moved since my time here. I've been treating people all morning, there are more injured on the way."

"Why did you want to see us?" Ana asked while popping her joints on her right hand.

"It seems like I'm the only person in this city who knows about what's really going on. I wanted to make sure that you guys had your questions answered, I wanted to make sure that your wounds had been sutured and your bruises had been healed, I hope that was a good enough answer, Ana."

"Yeah, okay, if you know what's going on, please tell us. We've been here almost a full day and I still don't really know what's going on." Ana was stern with her request.

Before Liv could answer Ana's statement with another remark, Jackson interrupted it all.

"The same thing that happened in Rochester, babe. The military became far too incompetent and way too selfish, those bunch of dicks," Jackson whispered the last part under his breath.

"Bingo," Liv added. "He nailed it. Basically, me and hundreds more would rather fight back than be shot in the street like sick cattle."

Liv directed them into a huge open room that must've been the top floor, the ceiling was high and the view outside the window indicated a 40-foot drop. There was a huge sunroof at the top of the room that let only the brightest sunlight through, reflecting off the walls and presenting how dirty they were.

Many cots and coma beds were arranged in a pattern, head to foot with minor space in between the bedside. Many were resting in the beds, all had patches or wraps of some kind around their arms or legs, some unlucky people had wraps around their faces.

Ana spoke with her hands over her mouth, "Jesus Christ."

The sunlight illuminated all the victims from the prior night in horrific, yet delicate lighting.

"Before I start treating any of you, is there any chance that any of you could be infected. If one of you are, then most likely all of you are."

"How do we know? All I was told was to stay away from rabid animals and shit like that," Jackson tried to relate.

"You would know if you were, so I'm guessing you aren't."

"But… how could we tell?" Ana worryingly asked.

Liv adjusted her glasses while brushing her hair with her bony fingers, looping it behind her ears and continuing. "It works a lot like rabies; think of it like rabies on steroids, supped up. You'd notice right away; first the infected person or persons aren't acting like themselves. As if they had been hit on the head with a frying pan and someone had knocked a screw loose."

Jackson and Ana looked like they were taking mental notes, writing it down and memorizing. Matt on the other hand thought back on school before the quarantine was set. Some of his classmates seemed completely different or more aggressive leading up to the day school was cancelled.

He interrupted Liv, "I remember friends of mine coming to school, they seemed like, extra angry. I mean some of my friends were just jerks, but it seemed like in the last week or whatever, they had become worse."

She paused, "Well, yes, the virus effects kids differently from what I've seen. It seems to have more of an incubation period because of how strong a child's immune systems is. On the other side of the coin though, old, or unhealthy people would simply die from the symptoms, or at least I think so…" she paused to slip on a pair of latex gloves. "Rabies turns the brain into a fragile and useless balloon, while this virus turns the brain into an animalistic and primitive dodgeball with spikes on it. Regardless, nobody exactly knows where it came from; personally, I've got a few ideas. Could've been made in a lab or a product of the climate, it doesn't matter now, nor does it make a difference. I'd hope that wherever the virus came from, a day comes that we'll be able to treat it."

"Well, can you treat it? Shit seems grim enough as it is."

"No, well… not exactly. Keeping the infected person healthy prior and after exposure to the virus can extend the incubation period which is anywhere from a couple days to a week, but whether or not you keep the person healthy, their body submits to the virus at one point or another. Right now, a cure is out of the realm of possibility, I simply don't have the skills required to synthesize such a thing, nor do I have the resources or the time. The day will come, but that day is far ahead and will come after Johannsson is gone."

Her voice echoed around the huge room; everyone could hear what she was saying clear as day regardless of where they were in relation to her. Jackson questioned, "What's the deal with this *Johannsson* clown?"

"I couldn't talk enough about how much he has done to deserve the hatred he receives. That jackass," Liv's voice had twang when she used profanity. "He doesn't deserve to be at the top, he didn't earn it. There were stories of him out West, deserting like a coward. None of it was proven of course so he ended up coming here for whatever goddamned reason. He is a spoiled kid with far too much power at his disposal."

"I struck a nerve there, didn't I?" Jackson joked.

"Yeah, a few nerves if I'm being honest."

She started to examine Jackson first, pointing out the noticeable bruises on his face and minor cuts, making sure his nose wasn't broken.

"How'd you get these? Did you get into a bar fight recently?"

"Some asshole jumped me when we got to the city." His family knew who he was talking about.

"Did you kill this *asshole*?"

"What kind of question is that?" Jackson flinched while being repulsed at what Liv had asked. She was prepping to clean his face with a washcloth.

"The kind of questions I ask everyone, I like to know what kind of people I'm talking to. So, did you kill him or anyone else for that matter?"

She took a rag with soap water and cleaned his hands, Jackson made eye contact with his wife, looking to see if he should be honest or not. That was another conflicting factor, he didn't know if he had or not. A few days ago, when they were attacked by those three men on the snowmobiles, he didn't know whether or not he had killed one of them. He simply didn't know.

"I didn't kill the asshole who jumped me, but a couple days ago, I think I killed someone."

"What do you mean you think you killed someone?"

"Yeah, I think I did, I'm not sure."

"Well, did you intend to kill whoever it was."

Jackson paused to think, "Yes."

"That's all I was looking for, Jackson." Liv stopped to fold the washcloth. "It was done to protect them I assume." She gestured to the family.

"Yes."

"Well, I'm glad that my assumptions about you were right. You seem exactly how you are. The beard adds to the way you're built though. You look like you're meant to work as a lumberjack up North, but rather you seem almost opposite."

"What's that supposed to mean?"

"When I first saw you on that hill, looking as if you had just bawled your eyes out, I read you like a book. I've been told I'm almost too good at reading people."

Jackson at first was a little pissed off at Liv for figuring him out but chose to not show it. "Good job I guess," he said while sighing in a ridiculous way.

"Mhm, anyhow, where are you three from?"

Jackson looked at his wife, letting her know that she could talk. "We came from Rochester."

"Southern Minnesota I think, right?"

"Yup, yeah. Well, we didn't leave by choice, we left because it was our only choice."

"Seems like a lot of people ran."

"A lot of people ran?"

"Well, of course. Everyone has a similar story really, some ran, some sprinted and some died. Those who were unlucky ended up here, Minneapolis was hailed as a completely safe quarantine zone before things got bad, and it wasn't long before things got worse."

Liv finished with Jackson and moved on to Ana only for a quick response, "Get Mathew first."

"Oh, alright."

There were a few moments of blank silence, until questions filled the air again.

Ana spoke, "Do they know how this virus or whatever started?" She flopped her hair behind her ear and put both of her hands in her pockets, tiptoeing to Jackson and leaning against him.

"It came from the water is what I heard, which basically confirms my main theory regarding that. First the fish got sick and over time, the same fish were mixed in with the seafood that was eaten at restaurants and the puppy chow of domesticated animals. We made it all too easy for the virus to jump the gap from animals to humans, and we allowed it to be that way."

"Your main theory?"

"I sure hope none of you guys are as simple minded as some of the other morons here, and I certainly hope you believe in climate change."

Even though Jackson thought it was borderline mumbo jumbo, he believed aspects of it. Regardless, he chose to close his mouth. Ana had similar views to her husband while Matt only knew what his teachers told him.

"The ice in the North, the huge glaciers that have been there since mankind started walking on two legs had to have contained viruses and pathogens that we would have no natural immunity to. The same viruses that have been trapped in ice and isolated from all of us, are now the ones destroying our way of life. That's my theory."

"Glacier viruses? Sounds a little far fetched to me, it's gotta be horseshit."

"The evidence shows, colleagues of mine were doing research at the time and discovered that most of the coverups were near the coasts. Places like the Philippines have been doing as bad as we are now for a long time. It isn't horseshit."

Jackson paused, analyzing the evidence that was put before him. Matt started asking questions, "You said something about the hospital here, what happened to it?"

"It was ground zero for the whole city, I have no clue as to how many poor souls are trapped there, sick or not. I was supposed to go there, but that's when the military showed up."

"Are they all dead?"

Liv was quiet, she knew the answer and so did everyone else.

She cleaned Matt's face, his eyes squinted and for the first time in a while, he felt somewhat clean. Jackson picked at his nails while Ana fiddled with her fingers. A question disrupted the silence.

"How do you get sick?" Matt questioned.

Liv moved on to Ana, putting her hair up in a bun and answering the question. "Do you know how rabies works? I mentioned this already, but I'll run back through it. The virus works like crazy rabies, infecting those by transferring DNA. Bites, scratches, spit, blood, and any other bodily fluid transfer. There's something in the basement that I would like you to see, we found it after we cleared the place out. It's shocking to say the least."

Jackson agreed but was confused at the offer. Wondering why Liv had thought of it as 'shocking.' He stood there, leaning against a raised cot, watching Liv clean his son, disinfecting any cuts. He observed more features of Liv's face during the silence.

Her temples were gray and every strand of hair on her head was curled down to where the hair ended. Her glasses were thick and made her eyes seem massive. Her fingers were wrinkled, and her hands were shaky. You could tell she was tired.

"What did they tell you in school, Mathew?"

Matt looked up from his now clean hands, "Some teachers were just crazy it felt like, they would just talk and talk but say nothing. You could tell how some of them felt just by the way they talked. All they told us was that things were getting bad in the big cities, like L.A and Miami. That's all they really told us." Matt played tag with his fingers.

"Sounds about right."

Time was going by fast, way quicker than Jackson had thought. It didn't seem like they had been there for that long of a time but when he looked at his watch, he was blown away. Maybe the Humvee ride was longer than he thought or maybe his watch was fast? When he looked at Liv's watch, he realized that it read the same time as his, he wasn't going crazy not yet at least, he thought.

12:38 PM

When Liv finished cleaning Ana up, she made sure everyone was okay before directing them to the door.

"Do you guys need anything else?"

Matt was about to ask for chips before Jackson nudged him. "We're all set, Liv."

As they all exited the huge room, Ana thanked Liv again and Matt gave a shallow, "Thank you."

The dark hallways were tolerably okay to walk through because every couple other lights barely illuminated the halls just enough to see. Liv told them to go left and head for the stairs. Ana and Jackson were somewhat skeptical of this, Matt was skeptical too, but said nothing.

When they reached the stairwell, Liv simply told them to go down. They did just that and nothing more.

"What's down here, Liv?"

"You'll want to Leave Matt out of what I'm going to show you, it's pretty gruesome."

Repulsed at this, Ana spoke. "I think I'll sit this out, same goes with Mathew. You can go down with Liv, I'll stay outside with Matt, babe."

Jackson agreed, though he didn't want to go alone, it would feel a lot better going with his wife than just going with Liv. He heard his wife and son ascend without him.

As they descended, they could all feel the air getting colder and the stairs looking more and more beat down. Small splotches of blood had stained the concrete and they became more and more frequent.

"What's all that shit about?"

"Hm?" Liv mumbled.

"The blood."

"You'll see."

A fowl and incredibly overwhelming odor lit their nose hair, making their eyes water.

He was repulsed and on the verge of vomiting. The acid in his stomach was boiling like steam in a crockpot.

He questioned where him and Liv were headed. "What's down there?" The steps finally stopped, and in front of them was a huge metal door with blood sprayed all across the entryway.

She pulled a keycard from her pocket and swiped it through the panel attached to the wall. The small red light flashed green, and the door popped, releasing a lock or something. Liv cracked the door open, and all that could be seen beyond the threshold was darkness. She reached in and flipped the light switch. Everything was illuminated instantly. It could all be seen now as Jackson peaked his head in.

Carnage was all over the floor, bodies on stainless steel tables and chained up remains. Cries and shallow moans could be heard from within. The floor was caked dark red, and the smell was repulsive. He thought he was going to pass out when Liv patted his face.

"Walk in here with me, I need a second opinion."

Jackson rolled his eyes back into his skull, gulping and pinching his nose. It was equally repulsive to smell and look at. It made his stomach bounce around like it was trying to escape, it made his lungs choke up with the sick air.

Jackson and Liv stepped into the basement and their shoes stuck to the floor, as if it was coated with caramel. While they tried to pull their shoes off the ground, it felt as though they had entered a human sized mouse trap.

More of the room was visible now; in one corner was a chain-link fence with plywood stacked around it. Within the cage was one of those monsters. Before he could pull his gun, Liv told him it was okay.

"No need, it's trapped in there for good."

"What the fuck, did you do this? What the fuck?"

"I got here last night, and the smell lured me down here, this wasn't my doing. It's my belief that the military got overly curious, same as I." She rubbed her eyes and adjusted her glasses, "I want to understand the virus, Jackson… But not like this."

Jackson took his hand off his nose and swept his beard, combing the hair between his fingers. "Why did you show me?"

"I told you, I need a second opinion."

His eyes couldn't scan the room all at once. It was more carnage than he'd ever seen, more carnage than anyone he knew had ever seen. It was *so* much. All the tables had limbs on it and every single hacked up carcass was caved in, like a collapsed mineshaft.

"You want my second opinion?"

"Mhm, I would."

"This is sick, I get it that people get curious but, but these men must've been mad, or crazy. Sure, I've been curious about things, but I've never ripped apart the neighborhood fucking cat because I was curious."

"I think that things were getting desperate. Some of the samples I found had burn marks on it and were nearly cooked… and I think that poor bastard," she pointed to the confined monster in the cage. "I think he got hungry, I think he ate the meat and I think he got sick. I think they confined him, and I think they were running experiments down here."

Jackson looked at the humanoid monster in the cage. The camo pants and bludgeoned body made Liv's theory make sense.

The presumed soldier had his vest and shirt ripped off, leaning against the wall in the corner. The skin was similar to Swiss cheese, holes, and slices that tattered the skin. The eyes were bloodshot, and each pupil was focused on a different thing. When Liv moved closer to the cage, the monster convulsed and shouted briefly before backing off against the wall. Jackson was used to seeing these creatures charging without a second thought and not relenting. Seeing it back away and give up like that gave him the chills.

"Why'd it do that?"

"Why'd it do what?"

"It fucking backed away; you have to know how these fuckers behave right? They never back away. What the hell."

"I have a theory; even though most of the brain is under the influence of the virus, some parts are still present. It's clear that the soldier was tortured and beaten as some sort of sick way of seeing how much it took to kill one of those things. I think that because of the continued torment and ridicule. I think that it's scared of us."

It made sense to Jackson. It all made sense, and yet he was still confused. "I thought you said the virus is in control of the brain?"

"It is, but that doesn't mean that the brain is destroyed completely."

"What do you mean?" Jackson whispered a cuss word under his breath, insulting the horrid stench.

"I think that these *creatures* feel the pain that people inflict, and they feel the emotions that correspond with the pain. Our brains love patterns, they're constantly searching for patterns, I believe that some small part in that virus ridden brain is still searching for patterns. The pattern in question would be human = pain. That's why he's scared," she gestured to the monster behind the fence. "That means that they can retain memory, or some form of memory. I don't think you understand how big this is."

Jackson didn't exactly know or care about what this meant, he wasn't exactly an expert in what Liv was talking about, yet he chose to listen because it was somewhat interesting. "Get closer to him," she spoke.

Jackson at first redirected her to do it, but after some clever worded persuasion, Liv finally got Jackson to do as she said.

He stepped closer to the fence, the corrupted man at first had no reaction, but when Jackson got within reaching distance to the fence, the man stumbled back and hit the wall. He groaned and choked up bloody remnants of what was inside. Jackson took another step forward, placing his hand on the fence and shaking it. This made the creature go crazy. It started writhing back and forth in the corner, shouting, and scraping at his scalp as if bugs were crawling under the skin.

Jackson shouted a primal grunt to further terrify the creature, he liked feeling in control when face to face with the things that had ripped countless people apart. The creature hid its face in his bloodied hands and placed itself in the fetal position, it sounded as if Jackson had made it cry, and the tears were made of venomous poison. He then stepped away, feeling his shoes stick to the floor and turning to Liv he spoke.

"I think you could be right, but what exactly does that mean? Sure, they can remember shit, but in the long run, everything has a memory, right?"

"It's shown that animals in the wilderness that analyze patterns and can recognize safe and unsafe situations based on those memories are the same ones that have spent the most time evolving their brain. Of course, big cats evolved to be biological killing machines, but animals like octopi have evolved to problem solve."

Jackson nodded to let her know he was listening.

"If that shell of a brain can still analyze patterns, being scared of things that have previously hurt them, that means that they're more intelligent than a mindless zombie. Do you understand?"

Before answering, he scratched his nose and glanced back at the man in the cage, still in the fetal position and crying. "Yeah, sorta."

"Now, what is your second opinion."

"I think you're right, Liv."

Chapter 13

Mongrel Pack

The sun was a bright, vibrant white.

An hour past noon, the two had been walking since the early morning. The sun was high in the sky but provided no warmth. Evan made sure that they wouldn't walk past any military hideouts, using the map to his advantage. The conversations between the two were small, short, and simple. Nothing more and nothing less. They had taken turns starting the conversations, coming up with questions and topics as they walked. They avoided main roads and stuck mostly to buildings and alleys, slithering their way to the Utilities center.

One question stood out: "Where were you deployed?"

Evan was interrupted from his deliberately patterned pace, he decided to reveal where he was deployed. It would be boring if he didn't.

"Denver."

"Oh… well why? What was going on there?"

Evan felt like he could be open with Henry, it was nice confiding in someone. It helped ease his troubles.

"The Westerners had taken the airport, some had taken employees hostage and demanded *true justice*. They called upon our leaders to show up, or let innocents die."

"Shit."

"See, here's where they got it all wrong—" He began talking with his hands, waving them up and down with a repulsed and disgusted look on his face. "You can protest, you can do whatever you please in the name of change… But once you bring unwilling people into your cause and put their lives at risk, that's where you cross the line."

"What did you do there? What happened?"

Evan scoffed; he partly wished that Henry would stop asking those kinds of questions. "I put those men down, me and the other men I fought with. I don't like talking about this stuff, just letting you know."

"Oh, sorry…" Henry felt awkward. "That's where you were when things got bad back here?"

"Yes."

"Damn."

"If I hadn't been deployed, I can confidently say that my family would be alive, my wife at least and my daughter for sure."

Henry silently agreed. The two walked in silence now, continuing North, checking street signs, and checking the map every now and then. They had already passed a few large bodies of water and assumed that they were within a few hours from reaching the Utilities center.

Some buildings looked as though they had been torched, as if someone had soaked every floor with gasoline and tossed a match. Bodies lined some streets while others were untouched.

"I'm surprised we haven't encountered anyone; I know that some people still squat in the ruined houses."

"Yeah? How do you know that?" Evan answered, wanting to recover from how awkward he had made it.

"Me and a couple guys were out one day, about two weeks ago, we had been ordered to raid houses for food and other shit, anything that we could carry. Anyways, some asshole came out of nowhere." Henry started rolling up his sleeve while maintaining the rifle's balance on his shoulder. "The fucker had a knife and almost killed the one guy, then he came at me."

Henry showed off the nasty healing wound on his forearm. "If he got the bottom of my forearm, I'd be dead as shit."

Evan chuckled, "Yeah, you would be."

"Am I right?" Henry joked.

Henry walked along, not knowing where to take the conversation from there, being interrupted mid-thought by a question from Evan.

"If they catch us--the military--I'm talking about—what's the likelihood that they'd kill us?"

"Oh, they would for sure kill us... well," Henry stopped himself to elaborate further. "They'd question us first, then kill us."

"Of course they'd want to question us." He scoffed.

"On the bright side, we won't have any valuable info for them."

"Right," Evan said while trying to get something out of his eye.

Walking along the streets and sticking close to buildings, the two would peak around corners to make sure the coast was clear. Henry was tired and the only energy he had left was from that wonderful pizza the two had scarfed down that morning. Evan was running purely on the thought of reuniting with his daughter.

After hours of walking and hours left of walking, they reached a rundown section of the city. All the buildings were smooshed together with poorly constructed fences in between and overfilling trash bins. You could see the outline of bodies in the street, protruding through the snow that had fallen days earlier. Henry and Evan looked down the street, imagining what had happened to the inhabitants. They were obviously murdered, but the question was how?

The two were about to begin walking again when they were stopped by a revolting and primal bark. It was the same horrifying bark that Evan had heard back on the highway. They were both frozen in place before they ushered away. Ducking behind a group of stacked trash bins directly next to a poorly cared for jeep. They kept their heads below the bins and stayed as still as they possibly could.

The battering of the snow and playful yet terrifying barks made both men get goosebumps on the entirety of their bodies. Again, just like Evan had encountered on the highway, the barks were so similar. The shredded vocal cords pierced his ears, making them ring.

"Shit shit shit shit." Henry whispered, "We need to get out of here."

"Man, what's the deal with these crazy dogs? Are they sick too?" Evan adjusted his crouching stance.

Henry sighed, "Yes, just… fuck man, I'll tell you later. We need to get the fuck out of here."

Evan peaked out from the bin, thinking that there was just one dog like last time, but was surprised to see that there were many. There was an entire *Mongrel Pack*, all walking and trotting around with their horrific appearances.

The first dog that Evan observed was a husky, its massive teeth would bare at the other dogs when they strayed too close. The collar was still wrapped around its neck and the fluffed hair had snow gathering on it.

The second dog that Evan observed was a tiny lap dog, smaller than a dodgeball but still feral. The third dog looked the most deranged. The fur was fluffed beyond combing and the mouth leaked a disgusting blood and puss mixture; its eyes were glazed over. Before Evan could view anymore of this primal dog pack, Henry pulled him back behind the bins.

"You'll get us killed; we need to leave."

Evan nodded, knowing that if they stuck around any longer, they'd be ripped to shreds. There was some curious part inside him that wanted to know more about the dogs, but Henry urged him to simply back out with him and avoid the conflict entirely. The two stayed low and slithered behind the jeep, trying to stay as quiet as possible.

Henry led while Evan followed. His plan was to sneak around the house and through the alley that separated the two townhouses. While leading, Henry slipped on a patch of ice, reaching to stop his fall, and grabbing hold of the jeep door, ripping it open and making an extremely noticeable clamor.

They made eye contact as the dogs barking became a lot more apparent following the ruckus. Henry ushered up and told Evan to head for the alley. Now in between the houses, the only way out of the alley was over the chain link fence that proved to be a worthy obstacle. Evan quickly offered to boost Henry over the vastly taller fence, lacing his fingers and leaning over.

Amidst the silence, Henry placed his foot on Evan's laced fingers, pushing himself up and climbing over the fence no problem. Just as Evan was about to start climbing up, several of the dogs had already leapt the yard and now stood at the end of the alleyway. It's almost like they knew that they had won. The way that they profoundly stood, guarding the only exit, and growling a menacing snarl.

Henry stood on the opposite side of the fence, brainstorming any possible way he could help Evan.

Instead of laying down his will and giving up, Evan unholstered his pistol and prepared to fight. He allowed the duffel back to slip from his shoulder and flung the trapper hat to the ground.

"Evan? Fucking shit!"

Evan's rifle plummeted from his shoulder and plopped onto the duffel bag. He readied to shoot his first target when the dogs started charging him; barking and shouting their hideous coughs. Henry yelled for Evan to duck.

"Evan! Get the fuck down!"

Before Evan could do anything, he heard the safety to Henry's rifle flick off and he knew what was about to happen. He dropped to the ground while Henry unloaded half his clip into the dogs, making them scream and cry. The spiteful cries were somehow louder than the noise of Henry's rifle blaring the fireworks.

When Henry's rifle ran out of bullets, all but three dogs were left at the end of the alleyway. Growling and angered by the murder of their packmates. They started to bark and jump while Evan pointed his pistol at them, shooting the tiny lap dog and putting it down. The second dog to be shot down was one that Evan didn't have the chance to observe before. It was a small golden retriever, must've been no more than a few months old when it got sick. He planted his second bullet into the skull of that miserable puppy.

The final and third dog was the one that Evan had observed previously, the most deranged looking one. The disgusting mouth widened, revealing yellow and red teeth, coated with blood and puss.

Henry struggled to reload his rifle quick enough to save Evan, it was already too late.

They both knew it.

Evan shot not once, but twice into the dog's chest, sputtering the blood all across the snow. For some reason, the sick canine just kept coming. Nothing was going to stop it, not even a wall of bullets. It planted his paws in the snow briefly and then jolted forward, aiming its jaws at Evan's face.

The only thing blocking his face from being shredded was his forearm. It all happened so fast. The teeth pierced the coat's fabric, and he felt a horrible pinching sensation. Without warning, the dog began to tug back and forth, ripping the coat and causing Evan to shout.

Evan cocked the hammer to his pistol and pinned it to the base of the dog's skull. When he pulled the trigger, he felt the jaws release and the responding shock of the bullet send tremors to his arm. When the empty corpse of the canine flopped onto the snow, caking the white with red, Evan kicked it away and stared at it for a few moments.

Henry was on his knees behind the fence, he had finally reloaded another clip into his rifle, but he was too late. After the gunshots and the barking stopped, it was all silent.

Evan stood up as if nothing had happened. He didn't even know that he was injured until his entire arm felt hot, almost like someone had poured lava down his sleeve. He ripped his coat off, only to see the source of the heat.

He was met with a red canvas.

The blood had dripped all the way down, painting his hand and sleeve with the red syrup. The gash right next to it was still patched appropriately, however.

"Evan?"

He couldn't hear Henry, or anything else for that matter. Staring down at his forearm dripping blood onto the white below. He must've forgot to breathe because soon he found himself gasping for air and his eyes watering. His chest fluttered up and down with each labored breath. Finally, his ears heard Henry calling his name.

"Evan?"

"Henry?" Evan said while swiping his hand over the source of the blood, revealing the skin beneath. The tiny teeth intrusions left four slim crevices in his forearm.

"Yes, Evan?"

It hurt like hell.

He steadied himself on the fence, removing his belt and tossing his snub-nosed revolver on the duffel bag. Then wrapping the belt around his biceps to cut off the blood to his forearm, he requested to know if Henry had anything to help.

Evan mumbled one thing or another, "You got anything to wrap this up man?"

Henry just saw a man get bit, he knew that a bite is 100% fatal and that within a few days, Evan wouldn't exist anymore. He thought Evan would react a bit more irrational, but rather, Evan was somewhat calm about all of it.

It was so unsettling.

"No, I mean I have an almost used roll of gauze, but that's about it man."

Evan murmured, "Can I have it?"

"Yeah."

Henry slipped the small roll from his pocket after setting his rifle against the fence. He handed it to Evan through the chain-link barrier, telling him, "Dude, you just got bit, what the fuck."

Evan figured that he should get it patched up quick, not reflecting too much on it.

"Yeah? It's just a dog bite? I should be fine. I mean sure it hurts, but I'm alive so?" He had inferred what Henry was about to say and all he wanted to do was downplay the bite.

"Man."

As Evan went through his duffel bag, searching for some fabric to tie around the wound, Henry tried telling him.

"It's the same as getting bit by one of those things, man. The fucking crazies out there."

Evan looked up from his situation, asking Henry to repeat what he had said. "Repeat that."

"It's the same fucking thing, Evan."

A small wave of distain for Henry flashed over Evan, he shouldn't have boosted him over the fence, but if he let Henry die, he wouldn't be able to live with himself. His hateful side wanted to blame Henry for getting bit, but his rational side wanted to keep his mouth shut and simply move on.

"Oh."

"That's all man? Just a fucking *oh*," Henry mocked Evan.

Evan remained silent. He had no clue how long it took to transform into one of those beasts but either way, his goal was cut short. There was no way that he'd be able to find his daughter, and especially like this.

"There's no way they'd let you into the Utilities center with a fucking bite man, some of us barely know how this thing transmits."

"How long do I have left?"

Henry was interrupted, "Well that depends, man."

"How long do I have left," Evan repeated. This time with some vulnerable twang in his voice.

"I don't fucking know; I'd be the last person to know. Shit. I've seen a bite kill a man in less than a day and another man in about a week. Fuck man, I'm sorry."

"You have nothing to be sorry about," Evan said while wanting to blame Henry. "So basically, you're saying you don't know how long it'll be before I turn into one of those things?"

"I don't know man, it's different for everyone from the shit I've seen. I don't know man."

Evan wrapped what was left of the gauze tightly around his arm, tying it taut with an old t-shirt from his duffel bag. "Listen, why don't you get over this fence and we'll keep walking?"

Henry thought it was so odd that Evan had virtually no reaction, all he could do was agree to keep walking.

"Okay, Evan."

After Henry climbed back over the fence and Evan reclaimed his belongings, they resumed walking to their destination. Evan was silent while he put his coat back on and stuffed the trapper hat into the duffel bag; he was somewhat humiliated at his handling of the situation. Henry didn't know what to say either, he wanted to apologize but he knew it was no use.

They walked out of the rundown street without a word to each other.

His arm felt like it was on fire, he wanted to cuss so badly. Not just at himself, but at Henry and the at the whole world. He wanted to climb to the top of a mountain and yell at God for doing this to him. Though he knew that God ultimately was not to blame, neither was the world or the people in it.

It was his fault.

He wanted to tell the entire world to fuck off. He wanted to see his kid and to hold his wife. He wanted to be done. He wanted to see them again. With this new bite, he knew that he would most likely never see Jade again, but he surely would be reunited with his wife soon enough.

"We won't have to worry about anyone coming after those gunshots you know. The military stopped giving a shit after the war started here."

Henry wanted desperately for Evan to talk, to show any sign of humanity. At this point, Henry was scared. He didn't know if Evan would fly off the handle and kill him or if he would go crazy before then, subsiding to the infection and tearing Henry apart with his bare hands.

"Good."

Evan replied with a gravely choked up voice as he combed his fluffed-out hair between his fingers. He sighed.

"So... a couple days then?" He asked to confirm.

Evan didn't want to deter Henry, though he was angry, he still didn't want to die alone. It didn't matter how he died, but if someone was there with him as he went, he would feel okay about it.

"I guess man," Henry rubbed his nose, somewhat nervous to speak. "You seem like you couldn't give less of a shit."

"I care, I mean of course I do, I just can't let it get in the way. I could still find her before I go."

Henry didn't want to downplay Evan's strange and almost unheard-of optimism. "Yeah man, maybe."

Evan turned to Henry while walking, "Is it noticeable?" He showed off his sleeve, hoping to make the bite close to invisible.

"Not really, I guess I wouldn't take off the coat if I were you."

It felt so awkward between them.

"Okay."

Henry wanted to keep the conversation going, he hated the silence and would much rather talk, even if it was uncomfortable.

"What would you do if you find your daughter?"

Evan looked over at him, having to squint because of the bright sun reflecting off the snow. "Probably uh, I don't know. I'd tell her I love her, and that Mom loved her. It sounds cheesy, I don't know. I'd want her to know that though."

"Yeah, I mean even though it is cheesy, I think it'd be good to hear that coming from you." The conversation felt so weird to Henry, it felt so alien to him, simply listening and responding; Evan was just bit and they're talking about something that probably won't happen.

"What would you want your Mom to say to you if you got to see her again?" Evan asked. It was a risky question, but to be fair, Henry had basically asked the same thing moments earlier.

"Heavy ass question."

"Yeah, I mean what else should I ask? What's your favorite color?" Evan joked, trying to lighten the mood.

Henry chuckled, "Well, if I'm honest..." he hummed while he thought about what to respond with. "I'd just want her to recall all of our best days I guess; hearing all of the good things again would be a good way to say goodbye."

Evan agreed with a "Yep."

"My favorite color is blue by the way," Henry said jokingly.

Evan chucked, "Blue is a good color." After a couple solid moments of silent chuckling, he pulled the map from his pocket and unfolded it in his hands. He used his finger to determine where him and Henry were currently located, they still had roughly a couple miles left until they reached the Utilities building.

Henry noticed Evan pondering at the map, "How much further till we're there?"

"We still have awhile I'd say."

The sun was still high above, but you could tell it was preparing to drop soon. Small clouds would pass over periodically, tiny, and white. The streets were almost devoid of vehicles, no cabs, or trucks, not even police cars.

It felt like a ghost town, even though hundreds of thousands of people had once inhabited the city, it was now baren. Windows were dusted, doors were shut, clouds were heavy, and the air was cold.

It was a cemetery.

The injury had certainly made him weaker. His arm once again throbbed with each heartbeat, and it stung with each movement.

What disturbed Evan was the fact that the bite wasn't all that deep, yet it stung as if someone had poured salt into the wound. His legs also seemed weaker than before, trembling when he mis-stepped.

"What does it feel like dude?"

Evan glanced back at Henry, "I don't know... like a bite?"

Henry sighed obnoxiously; Evan's answer clearly wasn't what Henry was looking for. "I mean, what does it *feel* like?"

Evan didn't precisely know how to describe it, of course he was mildly afraid but for some indescribable reason, he didn't believe that he'd die. He still felt like he was invincible, like nothing could take him down. Despite being infected with the single most deadly virus in the history of humanity, he felt impervious. He will find his daughter; he will get to speak to her, and he will succeed.

That's how he felt, anyways.

"I don't feel any different, actually."

~ - ~

After giving Liv *a second opinion,* they both ascended back up the stairs. "You have to understand that I needed your opinion. I had to know if I was going crazy or not."

"I understand, Liv. Just fucking crazy is all."

Ana and Matt were both standing there, having a very competitive game of rock, paper, scissors. Ana's flustered expression indicated that Matt was winning. When Liv and Jackson exited the stairwell to the ground floor, he greeted his wife and son.

"He's kicking my butt," his thin eyebrows waved at his bushy ones.

"Start cheating," Jackson offered his solution.

"He'd still beat me," she mocked.

Jackson quick offered to play Matt, putting his hand into a first and placing the other below. He spoke the words to initiate the game. When Matt threw down rock, Jackson delayed his attack to ultimately beat Matt, though he cheated, he won.

"Ah what," Matt complained jokingly.

Ana had her mouth wide open, "Cheater," she spoke.

Liv smiled briefly at the family. "You guys could stay here for a bit, or you could go back to Longfellow."

Both the thin and the bushy eyebrows stopped waving.

Ana and Matt both agreed that going home and lying down would be great, they made this connection based purely on eye contact. Jackson preferred to go back to Longfellow rather than stick around.

"I can see that you guys are tired, that's understandable. You've all been through a lot. I'll line up a truck to take you back there."

Ana and Matt thanked Liv as she walked over to them, telling the family to stay put. His wife was curious of the contents within the basement, and when she asked her husband, she got a vague answer.

"Nothing much was down there." She knew he was lying. He didn't know if he should discuss what he saw down there.

Matt was also curious, "What? Was there a dinosaur down there or something? Don't tell me she showed you a ghost or a sea monster or something."

Jackson chuckled at his son's charisma, "None of that; it would've been cool if it was though." He joked.

Ana knew that he saw something shocking down there. She could tell by the way he spoke. He tried to hide his vaguely cautious tone with a voice he used very rarely.

Liv walked back down the stairs after a few minutes of the family going back and forth.

"The truck should be outside those doors any minute, get ready to leave." She paused, "Jackson, can I see you for a moment?"

Jackson nodded and waved his eyebrows back at Ana's, while her and Matt shuffled to the doors down the hall. He then walked over to Liv and asked what she needed. He shrugged and raised his brows.

"Hm?"

"Please tell your wife what you saw, tell others if they ask. If your son is curious, tell him what I said. Thank you for your second opinion." She outstretched her hand for Jackson to shake before relinquishing one final piece of information.

Ana stood at the end of the hallway, watching the interaction between Jackson and Liv. Trying to pick apart the words she was able to eavesdrop.

Liv leaned in and whispered to him, her wrinkled and chapped lips expelled warm breath onto the side of Jackson's face.

"It's very possible that after the military attacks the Utilities, whenever that may be, they will go for Longfellow next. Keep your family close but keep your pistol closer, that gun will become your last line of defense if invaders come to take what we have. Stay safe Jackson, I will do my part to keep everyone at Longfellow safe. You have my word."

Jackson shook her hand and smiled briefly.

"Thank you, Liv."

He turned his back to her and walked back down the hallway toward his wife and son. He thought his chest was going to explode if he took another deep breath. He was basically just told that at one point or another, he'd be forced to protect his family. He was equipped to do so, but in the past when it came to protecting his family, the only thing that kept his family safe was Evan.

He reflected as he walked further from Liv and closer to his family.

The snowmobile men who had come, Evan handled it. The drunkard from the bar in Elba; Jackson ran off and Evan handled it. What did Jackson do in both scenarios? He was a coward. Sure, he was twice the size of any other man he'd seen in Longfellow, but truly, it was all show. He knew that if it came down to it, he would not be able to kill a man.

His appearance was that of a lion, but he was a sheep.

He greeted his family, all melancholy and when they heard the truck pull up, he ushered them out the door. Liv was still standing at the end of the hallway when Jackson turned around to look.

It had gotten significantly windier since they'd last been outside, the sunlight was still present, but it made no difference.

Jackson helped his son in first, then his wife and finally lifted himself in.

The driver up front asked Jackson, "Longfellow right?"

"Yup, thanks."

Ana turned to Jackson when the Humvee switched into gear and slowed to a roll. Matt was preoccupied drawing on the window, fogging it up with his breath each time he wanted to draw something new.

"What did she show you? And please don't beat around the bush. I know whatever it was must've been bad, but just spell it out for me."

"It was bad."

Jackson continued whispering, "Matt should know too, but it was really bad, and I want to talk about it, but it was just horrible."

"We can tell Matt later, he seems busy right now anyways," they both turned to look at their son, drawing on the fog his breath created on the bullet resistant glass. First, he drew Spider-man, next he drew Batman. Ana turned back to her husband, putting her hand on his leg as a comforting gesture.

"One of those fucking—" Ana stopped him, signaling him to lower his speaking voice.

Jackson changed his tone, "Okay so, it was one of those fucking monsters. It was locked up in a cage and it was scared. When I got close, it would back away and fucking... it would cry." He struggled to continue. "The whole room had dead bodies and dried blood. It was fucking crazy. All that shit in there was from the military."

Ana stopped to make him clarify, "The military had caught and trapped one of those things?"

"Yeah, and Liv thought that they were running tests on the poor thing. She thinks that the monsters feel pain and basic human emotion, that's what she said. She compared it to octopuses and said some shit about how animals that recognize patterns have the biggest brains or something like that."

Ana asked him to clarify again, she wanted to make sure what she was hearing was right.

"They're *smart* you mean?"

"They're smart enough to understand patterns. They can see the difference between safe and unsafe I think is what she said."

"Oh my—"

Jackson interrupted her. Briefly he thought about telling her what Liv told him in the hallway, about an attack on Longfellow. He figured he shouldn't alert his family to any danger.

"The monster in the cage, I stared at him—his face I mean. It was so human yet so far gone. You could still see the fear in the eyes."

"Jeez… Well now I know why you were so friggen quiet."

Jackson raised his bushy eyebrows sarcastically, indicating that his wife had guessed correctly.

The torn apart city looked different on the drive back, having the shadows shift from where they were hours previously. The sun was preparing to set while the air became dimmer in the afternoon atmosphere. As if the city was torn apart enough, it seemed as though the concrete beneath them would start ripping away to leave ravines deep enough to swallow the city whole.

Snow engulfed and suffocated trees and foliage. Tall buildings were now targets of ongoing wars to secure territory. Anarchists ran loose and basked in the newfound freedom that the new world provided.

They all made it back to Longfellow safely.

Chapter 14

Hotel Minneapolis

Not a bone in their bodies wanted to keep walking.

Henry and Evan were both tired, the Utilities were still a rough distance away and they were making bad use of their time.

Evan was stern against Henry's request to find somewhere to rest but soon found himself struggling to keep his eyes open. So, the two embarked on a journey in the middle of their already ongoing one to find a place to stay the night. It was getting dim out and the Winter sunset was blotted out by distant nimbus.

"You've been on a plane right?" Henry said while identifying a shaken down hotel on the block to their left, proposing it with his hands as a possible candidate.

"A plane? Yeah, why?"

"I just wonder what the city looks like from above." Henry said while staring at a distant fire that was grappling to the Capella Tower.

The two arrived at the rundown hotel that Henry had pointed out. Evan tried the door while responding to his friend, "I'm sure it'd look crazy."

The door flung open on his first try.

Henry was the first to enter, utilizing the flashlight that was attached to his rifle to search the darkness for any possible threats. The clamor of the door flying open would've been enough for anyone living there to be alerted to both intruders.

"Where've you been..." he paused to rephrase, "I mean traveled to, for like a vacation." The dark entrance to the hotel made his ginger hair a lame darker orange.

"Hm... Let me think," Evan said, beginning to walk up the stairs carefully, only having Henry illuminate what was to come and the dim light coming from the minimal windows placed throughout. "Florida, hm... Las Vegas, also Montana about a couple years ago. Not much compared to some other guys I know, but eh, I enjoyed my time in all those places... How about you kid?"

"If I'm honest, I've only ever left Minnesota once, and that was with my Dad to this smoke shop down in Lyle. Otherwise, I've never left the state."

"Yeah?" Evan said while multitasking. He walked throughout the second-floor hallways and tried to be as quiet as he could with each progressive step. Evan assumed: "Parents couldn't take time off work or what?"

"Oh, they had time, my Mom at least. But we were always doing stuff for my sports. It was a different town every week, I don't think we would've ever had the chance to go on a vacation. Before the big ass quarantine, we were actually planning on going over to Michigan before Autumn. But shit happens I guess."

Evan frowned at this, thinking about the possible fun Henry had missed out on. "Well, Henry," the ginger faced kid looked at Evan. "I wish you could've gone on that trip."

He cracked open the door at the end of the hall and attempted to keep the conversation going despite his constant distractions. "What sports did you play?"

Henry looked up from his rifle while entering the room and shutting the door, "I played a little bit of everything if I'm honest, but I was really good at Lacrosse."

Evan interrupted the kid while firmly closing the door and further blocking it with a chair, "Isn't that where you use those weird-looking net staffs or whatever they're called."

"Yeah yeah, it seems weird, and it honestly is, but man I had a shit ton of fun playing Lacrosse."

"Sounds like it," Evan took his duffel bag off, setting it near the bed closest to the window, then sitting on the bed.

"What about you?"

"Sports I played?"

"Yeah."

Evan readjusted his trapper hat a then set it on the nightstand. "I played a little bit of football in high school, but sports weren't ever my thing. I was good at pool though."

"Pool?"

"Yeah, I was pretty good at it. I never went competitive or anything, but I knew how to jab my friends out of a couple dollars."

Henry plopped his rifle against the bed closest to the door, turning off the flashlight and then laying down. The bed that relaxed his body turned his voice down a few notches and the pillow folded in half under his head was enough to knock him out.

"My Dad was good at pool; he had a special stick and everything." He specified.

"Man, what I'd give to play a game of pool right now," Evan groaned while stretching his back and letting it crack.

Evan was eager to keep pushing, but even ambitious men need to sleep sometimes. Though, it would be a bumpy night to come, the two soon fell asleep and traded a simple, "Goodnight," to each other.

~ . ~

Jackson used his key on the door to his family's temporary home, twisting the knob and propping the door open for his wife and son. He flicked the light switch, illuminating the small apartment room. Ana and Matt waltzed in, followed by Jackson. He pulled the pistol from its tucked place and set it on the TV stand, removing the clip and chambered bullet, setting those right next to the pistol itself just how Evan had shown him.

The first thing Matt did was dive into the bed, ready to sleep or chow down on rations; he of course ended up doing both. Jackson tiptoed to the bathroom, wanting to rinse his face off only to be met with the full sink of standing water. He totally forgot about having to fill the bathtub and sink. This reminded him of the looming threat.

Both Ana and Jackson had discussed the basement during the whole ride back to Longfellow. Matt had nearly fallen asleep just before they arrived.

Jackson went to slump himself over the couch, Ana took his hand before getting too far and reminded him. "I know we've all been going through a ton lately, just let me know if there's anything I can do."

If Jackson were honest, a back massage would be first followed by an elegantly prepared meal. However, he knew that was out of the realm of possibility. He also didn't want to ask for anything. He figured it'd be better if he just handled it on his own.

Though the sight in the basement was traumatizing, he knew that so long as he wasn't reminded of it, he wouldn't think about it.

"Just tell me about your dog you had as a kid, babe."

Ana was confused but understood. She followed him to the couch to sit with him. The two plopped down and Jackson flopped his head onto the back cushion, relaxing his tense neck. Ana laid her legs on Jackson's lap with her back against the armrest and began telling a story that had been retold countless times before.

"Her name was Collie, and Collie loved apples. Cut, uncut, apple sauce, apple pie, anything apple," she rested her hand on Jackson's shoulder, rubbing her thumb against his tight muscles.

"Collie was always a good dog, she never went potty inside or tracked in mud, but every chance she got, she would try to smuggle an apple without us seeing." She stopped to make sure Jackson was listening. His eyes were closed, he knew why she paused of course.

"Keep going, I'm still listening," his low tone expelled.

She smiled, "We never caught her either, I think that was the best part. Her apple heists were always top secret, we wouldn't know one was taken until we did a head count. Indiana Jones type stuff, replacing a relic with an equally weighted stone to not trigger a booby trap."

Jackson chuckled, "Ah, that's great." He *loved* this story.

"One time, we found Collie under the couch with a dozen apples, all from the fruit dish that was on the counter. Collie was small too, not much bigger than a shoe box. The counter was tall, and we had no clue how she got up there. That's why we kept the apple dish up there too, was to keep her away from the apples," she giggled. She knew the story was absurd and she wouldn't believe it herself if she hadn't experienced it firsthand as a child.

"Collie would always find a way to get those apples, no matter where we put them or how we hid them. Collie would stop at nothing. She was mischievous, but she was a good dog." Ana kept her gaze focused on Jackson despite his eyes being closed. He knew she was looking at him purely based off of the way she spoke.

His bearded face produced a shallow smile, forcing his upper face to scrunch and his developing eye wrinkles to squint. She knew her story had done its job.

"When she got older, we let her have as many apples as she wanted; apple pie, apple juice, all kinds of apples—except granny smith apples, she hated those… I loved Collie, she was a goofy dog," Ana giggled.

"Collie and the great apple heist," Jackson joked, "Would've made a great movie."

His wife agreed with a smile. "We'd be the only two to buy tickets for that movie," she giggled.

"Nah, the whole town would've packed the theater babe."

Matt piped in from beneath the bed covers, "I wish we got to meet Collie."

Jackson agreed, "Would've been awesome."

The three chuckled in unison, admiring the story that had just been told. Jackson rested his eyes, finally getting to relax. Ana combed his rough beard with her long fingers, brushing every stand to relax him. He kicked off his shoes and kept his eyes closed.

It is a good story.

Jackson and Ana soon fell asleep on one another, and Matt got the entire bed to himself.

~ . ~

Gunshots were still loud, but they were almost white noise to the two of them while they slept. They didn't lift their heads for anything, but Evan's eyes were shot awake randomly. He had a feeling as if someone was watching him. His eyes danced around in their orbits, but he didn't move, he remained still and tried to whisper Henry's name.

"Henry… Henry…"

Silence followed. The kid was dead asleep. It would've been fine, and Evan would've gone back to bed if it weren't for the following noises that emanated from outside the same building they slept within. Shallow knocking and the destruction of furniture alerted Evan further, making him shoot out of bed. Not wanting anyone know that two dudes were asleep on the second floor. It sounded like people were just destroying things, throwing them about and smashing whatever you can imagine.

Evan tiptoed over to his rifle that had been set up against the window and slung it over his shoulder, unholstering his pistol and moving to the door. He removed the chair slowly and set it off to the side. He slithered out cautiously and closed the door as slow as he could, perusing this ruckus.

When he reached the stairs, the destruction was amplified by the sound of voices. Small bellows coming from radios made Evan believe that the Military was tossing the hotel in search of supplies.

Then, terror filled his veins.

Flashlights pointed up the stairwell and Evan was forced to scurry back down the hall as fast as he could, creating a small but noticeable ruckus of his own. He shut the hotel door fast and thrashed Henry awake. He didn't know how many men or what kind of men he'd be dealing with. Henry barely even awoke at Evan's desperation.

"Henry, get up, we need to get up." He begged.

"Huh," he rolled over.

What Evan didn't know was that the military had been alerted to his presence by how clumsily he had run down the hallway. The only thing that Evan noticed was the numerous footsteps coming down the hall, like a menacing parade of death-givers.

Evan flew up and snatched the chair, firmly placing it back where it had been. The door was stopped right as it jolted open. The oak door thrashed as whoever was trying to open it struggled with its sturdy hold.

Henry had tried to open his eyes, seeing Evan pressed against the door and holding the chair in place, preventing certain doom from entering. He rubbed his eyes to make sure he wasn't dreaming and realized that Evan was indeed holding back certain doom.

An enate fear overtook Henry and he flung out of bed. Tossing the rifle into his hands, and assisting Evan hold the door shut.

Meanwhile, on the other side of the door, a tall man in a heavy vest was bashing the door, getting closer and closer to entering each time. Speaking a low, "What the fuck, who's in there?"

Henry was shocked at what he had just woken up to; trying to hold the door closed and prevent the both of them from doom.

"Should I shoot the door?" Henry whispered to Evan, loud enough for him to hear but quiet enough for the men on the other side of the door to remain oblivious.

This gave Evan an idea. He took his pistol and made sure every slot in the revolving chamber had a bullet within. He told Henry to, "Keep it shut."

He prepared to sink rounds into the door.

Before any gunshots fired, a voice from the other side of the door sounded, saying, "What if it's just locked?"

Evan paused for a moment. He didn't shoot, he didn't point his gun, he simply listened. The bashing stopped for a moment, but Henry interrupted the short-lived silence.

"Fuck you! And fuck Johannsson!"

The bashing started right up, far more aggressive than before, nearly shoving Henry onto his back and allowing the intruders to enter.

Evan reluctantly pointed his pistol at the door, just inches above Henry's head. Pulling the trigger, he fired all 6 of his bullets into the door.

The view on the other side of the door was gruesome. The door basher was first pummeled with 3 bullets to the torso, two of them were stopped by the Kevlar vest while the third punctured and went through his body, chopping his spine in two like a crop being harvested by a combine.

The other three bullets however had struck above the vest's protective cover. One shot through his collarbone, another blew a gaping hole in his neck while the final shot blasted through his forehead. Skull fragments and brain fabric painted the wall and the closest men with a red and white mess that resulted from Evan's cowardice.

It wasn't like Evan had the choice to be brave, he and Henry didn't stand a chance against all the soldiers in that hallway. Their cowardice was understandable.

The bashing was silenced and when Evan's pistol had discharged for the last time, the whole building had fallen silent. The soldiers in the hallway were mortified at what had just happened, all but one cocky kid, one who barely knew how to use the rifle he held.

He charged forward, looking for trouble and looking to avenge the door basher.

He cocked his riffle back and prepared to fire a barrage through the door. Evan and Henry both heard this, scuttling away from the threshold, and taking cover on the opposite side of the room. Evan had to actually pull Henry backward in order to avoid the wall of bullets about to be fired.

The loud soldier stood over the dead and deflated door basher, holding the rifle near his hip Rambo-style, and preparing to riddle the room with a spray of bullets.

Evan flopped quickly to the floor that Henry was already level with.

It was quiet, but just for a moment. Before anyone had a chance to inhale again, the air was stripped from their lungs.

Bullets sprayed feathers from the old beds and shattered one of the two windows within the room. Shrapnel and glass rained upon the two of them, they covered their faces with their cold hands and remained still.

When the stream of bullets was finally cutoff, a voice bellowed loudly, "Did I fucking kill you or what?"

Evan motioned for Henry to be quiet, to not start another conflict. The two of them had barely heard what the soldier had said anyways. Both men's ears were ringing. On the other side of the room, a noise emanated, filling their deafened ears with fear.

The soldier was trying to pry the door open to assure himself that the threat had been taken care of.

He had made the wrong move, same as the door basher.

Evan was the first to get to his feet, he didn't have time to help Henry up because before he knew it, the soldier had managed to smash the door open.

He ran in while trying to reload his rifle, intending to sink a final bullet into whatever would come his way. Evan took cover behind the perpendicular wall opposite to the door, so when the soldier had waltzed right into his trap, he had the upper hand. Evan was a wolf spider; the soldier was an oblivious insect.

Evan grappled with the soldier by choking him with one hand and stabilizing the rifle with the other. The soldier tried squeezing the trigger but only managed to riddle the ceiling with a spray of armor piercing rounds. Not a single soldier attempted to enter after hearing a spray of bullets and the sound of struggle.

Evan's only option was to choke his attacker to death, or to snap his neck; both of which were undignified.

"Henry!" Evan yelped.

Henry stumbled to his feet, first pointing his rifle but ultimately deciding to use the stock to rather injure his opponent instead of blowing his face off. He slammed the stock against the temple of his opponent, knocking him out cold and forcing him to the ground.

Evan retrieved the rifle that was slung over his back and swiftly aimed it toward the door, shooting twice through the smashed threshold. Telling any and every soldier to not enter,

Not if they wanted to keep their lives.

Henry did the same, mimicking Evan's actions. "Get out! Leave! Get the fuck out!" He shouted.

Evan stood there, letting the unconscious body of the cocky kid fall to the floor. He glanced out slightly, staying close to available cover and peaking. The door basher's tattered corpse was motionless while blood spewed from the bullet wounds.

Evan had murdered a man, again. He knew that he *hated* doing this, but it kept happening.

These uncontrollable circumstances forced Evan into these difficult situations that often forced him to kill. Trauma from these incidents was one thing, but what ultimately stood out to him was the noises.

The *blood*, the *gunshots*, the *yelps of pain* and the *cries of murder*.

He stepped over the shattered door frame and mangled threshold, pointing his rifle out into the hall, and soon stood over the man he shot to death. He held the rifle close to his face, aiming it at the scared crowd of nameless soldiers. The only thing illuminating that hallway was the shallow Winter moonlight. Each wrinkle in the making was defined on his face, showing his stubble that was nearing beard status. They looked like they had all just witnessed a spine chilling and disturbing top secret bomb test. They were frozen.

"Get... out," his grim voice mumbled.

All dozen or so of them scurried out in a swift motion, leaving a trail of dust in their wake. Evan heard a trio of vehicles sound their engines and roll out just as fast. He stumbled back into the room and glanced at Henry, who was still standing over the soldier he had knocked out.

"We're leaving."

Henry accepted the terms without a word, picking up his rifle and moving to the door, passing the desecrated remains of a man. Evan slung the duffel bag over his shoulder while taking a spare box of ammo from within. After reloading his snub nose, he slipped the rest of the ammo into the pocket of his coat.

The two exited the hotel through the back entrance and tried to walk uniform enough to stay awake, but this proved too difficult to manage. The air was thick with the cold and the snow on the ground made their shoes damp. The city was still alive with gunshots and the noise of erratic mayhem.

It didn't bother either of them anymore.

Henry knew that Evan was silent because of what he had to do, so he figured it would be best to match that same silence.

But he simply couldn't let Evan suffer, not like that, not without trying to combat his suffering.

"You okay?"

The question had caught Evan off guard. He wasn't prepared to speak or answer such a simple but heavy question. Was he okay? Obviously, he wasn't, but did Henry deserve to hear that he wasn't? Was Evan even comfortable with telling Henry he wasn't okay?

"I'm doing alright."

He had been bitten, almost shot, shot at, and shot someone all in one day; Henry knew that he wasn't doing *alright*. "Are you?"

The two stomped around in clumsy lines through the dirty alleyway between buildings, looking for a new place to sleep. "Henry?"

"Yeah Evan?" His previous question was about to be repeated.

"Are you okay?"

There was a long pause between the following words. Henry wasn't exactly expecting to be asked that. He found his nose soon burning and his eyes beginning to water. He wasn't doing okay, but he didn't want Evan to see that.

"Oh yeah, I'm okay," his voice broke. "I'm good."

Evan knew that Henry wasn't okay either, both of them were different sides of the same coin. A man striving to find his daughter, a boy missing his family.

Walking among the broken city during the midnight gleam was a thought-provoking path that ensured them both a hard time. Each tall building to their right was a tower that shielded the moonlight and left huge shadows in their wake.

"You're alright."

Henry looked over at Evan, whose head remained forward, focused on the path they were currently on. No expression could've made Evan know how much that statement impacted Henry. He was alright, of course he was. He didn't want to cry, or crawl away into a hole, he just wanted some food and maybe a bed.

His eyes glanced back over from Evan, dancing in front of him and making various focal points.

However, Evan had shot his eyes over to Henry, whom he could now see the face of a boy who clearly shouldn't be in such a situation in a place like that. A burning city with few good people left to inhabit it.

Evan thought highly of this kid he managed to bump in to.

~ . ~

Jackson had a dream; it was a weird one. He had found himself driving an uncontrolled vehicle, wobbling back and forth down the interstate. He shook with each tremor. It felt like at any minute he could crash. He felt breathless in the dream, a weak man who could do nothing to save himself.

He woke up and never got to know how his dream ended, but in the process of waking up, his body tugged as if he was actually in the car he dreamt about. His wife was still fast asleep with her legs draped over his. Jackson thought he had woken his wife up, but he got lucky and as it turns out, he didn't. Ana was having a dream of her own, it wasn't a bad one, nor a good one. The dream was simply an escape from the room she slept in and the city that was torn amongst itself.

He wanted to get up, to maybe go get the rations or simply stretch his legs, but he also wanted Ana to sleep sound. She deserved it. So he didn't move, he stayed put for her. He tried to close his eyes but couldn't fall back asleep. It got boring, so he attempted to pass the time by trying to remember his favorite movie scenes. There was this movie he saw before the world fell apart; it was about a time traveling mafia.

He thought about zombie movies, and how damn goofy they seemed now that it had become a reality. Then he thought about whether or not the humanoid monsters they encountered would want to eat his brains, if so, he got a kick out of it.

If they ate his brain, he thought, they'd have to first chew through his thick skull to get to it. Too much work for a brain not all that big, he thought.

He glanced at his watch and saw that it was 9:15 AM, he was far behind getting rations. It didn't matter. He sat for a while, waiting for his wife to wake up.

He was comfy.

~ . ~

Pressed against a brick wall and sandwiched between dumpsters, Evan awoke to dogs barking. They were far, but loud. It didn't sound like any regular barking dog, it sounded like the one he came across on the highway and the one that had bit him. His eyes fluttered open and across the alley was Henry, sitting in a similar position.

The kid was obviously dead asleep, so Evan chose to get up and quick try to find something to eat. His leg muscles stretched as he straightened his back, then flopping his arms out to stretch

Three people had died because of him; he couldn't get it off his mind. Though he tried to occupy his brain with the search for food, he simply couldn't get the image of that mangled door basher out of his head.

He tried a couple doors in that alley, all were locked, and all were loud when he shook them. He must've walked up and down that alley three times before giving up. When he walked back to grab his duffel bag, he noticed that Henry was gone.

The place where the kid had slept was now vacant.

Evan first looked around, trying to spot Henry with his eyes, but he was unsuccessful. Panic started to build in his chest, making it feel full and quite heavy. He spun around, looking for the ginger haze that was Henry's hair. The sudden fear that he was alone made him believe that he would die alone.

Finally, Evan couldn't take it, he shouted Henry's name as loud as he could several times.

"Henry! … Henry! … *Henry!"*

The ginger haired kid spoke up from Evan's left, "Over here man!"

Henry heard the upcoming footsteps and warned Evan to steer clear, "I'm taking a piss, don't come over here." Now upright behind the pile of milk crates.

Evan stepped back, relieved to see that he hadn't been abandoned in the wake of a new day. "Oh, okay."

"You sounded worried man."

"Oh, uh, I just didn't know where you went." Evan didn't want Henry to know truly how worried he was.

"Okay."

"Let's get going here pretty soon; do you know what time it is?"

While Henry squeezed the rest of his piss out, he checked the military radio he'd been issued and recited the time. "Almost 10 AM."

"Okay."

Chapter 15

The Battle for Calhoun Isles

They had been walking all day.

Nothing too eventful happened other than an explosion that swept through the top floor of the bank building and the firefight that erupted as a result. Evan and Henry had made bets to see if anyone would fall from the tower. Nobody fell, so the bet was called off.

Evan had slipped his trapper hat back on with the increase in wind chill and the slowly setting sun offering less heat. Earlier in the day they had been basking in the light, but now they had been walking in the shadows of each building they passed. The pain from the bite had almost completely stopped and the two were mostly quiet. They weren't quiet because it was awkward or because they didn't want to talk to each other, they were quiet because of how exhausted they were. They were both hungry for another pizza.

Evan balanced the rifle strap on his shoulder while he adjusted the tattered sleeve, Henry watched as he did so, then asking a question that Evan's daughter would ask on long car trips.

"How much longer until we're there man, my legs are killing me."

This interrupted Evan, who was currently thinking about mentioning his wife to Henry.

"Should be any minute now, I think it's around the block up a few. Let me check," Evan pulled the map from his pocket. He unfolded it once more to verify his statement. "Yup, up here we take a right and we should be able to see the joint."

He still wanted to talk about his wife but figured that he should keep it to himself. Henry didn't need to bare that trauma as well.

"Good. Fuck, I need a nap and a sandwich. I'm surprised I haven't had to shit after that pizza."

Evan looked over at him, seeing his serious face about *'not needing to* shit' Evan chuckled. "Me too, man."

"There was a friend of mine back at the camp in Sheridan who hadn't shit in…" Henry had to stop and think, "6 days I think he said, or 8 I can't remember. He gloated about trying to set a record."

"Some of my buddies back in high-school would try to see how long they could go without taking a dump." Evan smirked.

"How long did they go?"

"My one friend went… hm, I think he went 4 days I want to say. Yeah 4 days It had to have been."

"Jesus, impressive"

"Not as impressive as 8 days."

After the two turned the corner, they saw the Utilities center. A firm gated in warehouse looking factory with floodlights illuminating the entire perimeter. The cement used to make the building looked as old as the sky itself and it was so bright in the increasingly dim city that they both had to squint and shield their eyes.

They could see men up on the catwalks and the cement spires, all armed with rifles. They stood still as a tree, observing from a distance before walking any closer. The stolen Humvees that were parked out front looked as if they could become mobile at a moment's notice. There were two tanks out front as well, armed, and ready to defend if a threat were to arise.

The enormous building had been constructed over a section of the river, using its flow as hydroelectricity. It had a back entrance that was connected to the other side of the river and the front entrance was facing the city. Behind this facility was many neighborhoods crowded with residential housing. The place was big enough to store a few hundred men for sure, but there clearly wasn't enough food to go around, certainly not enough to support a few hundred men.

It was a beacon in the middle of the growing darkness. Its bright perimeter contrasted that of the dark surroundings, the floodlights cascaded the towering walls and the outside fencing had barbed wire at the top, ensuring no men on foot would get in without slicing their hands to shreds.

Evan nudged Henry, "Let's get going."

Henry stuttered for a moment, worried that his previous occupation as a solider would surely get him killed when going behind Revolutionist lines. Evan reassured the scared boy, "I'm sure they'd understand. We could lie too, I'm sure it won't be a big deal. I think we should just start walking over there though," Evan gestured to the compound, "We'll put our hands up to let them know we mean no harm, okay?"

Henry reluctantly agreed, "You better steal me a sick ass ride for all the trouble we've been through today."

"Don't worry, kid. I'll get you a blue hot rod. Black racing stripes and all."

"That's what I like to hear," Henry smirked. The two started walking toward the compound, hands in the air with no bad intention.

The final jaunt to the compound was for some reason more difficult than the entire walk there. It's almost like the last hundred yards were the hardest, even though salvation was surely beyond the fence. Both were anxious and didn't know what to expect. Evan worried that his military background would get him killed while Henry worried the same thing. Each step, right foot over left, was more difficult than the last. Just as they felt their journey was about to end, a shockwave rocked both of them to their backs, slamming onto the concrete behind them.

A deafening and explosive strike had hit the Utilities center. Before Evan and Henry had realized what had just happened, they felt heat. Intense heat that singed their small eyelashes and blew their hair back. Then within seconds, the heat was gone, it ceased. Evan and Henry laid there, staring at the compound now in flames. Their pupils reflected the fire identically.

Henry could only observe so much before Evan was pulling him back around the corner they had come from previously. Henry saw every window shattered and observed bullets whizzing back and forth between unknown marksmen. When they both were back behind the corner, Evan peeked out to see the destruction. Yelling and screaming of unseen injured men and women were all that they could hear.

"What the fuck happened?" Henry shouted, trying to overpower the sound of gunfire.

Evan was unresponsive, all he could do was look at the bullets being exchanged. While trying to think of a clever way out, he spun away from the corner, ultimately determining that him and Henry needed go back the way they came.

Two blinding headlights were approaching from down the street, then four and finally six. This added up fast, telling Evan that there were 3 manned Humvees heading their way. Evan tugged the duffel bag further up on his shoulder while swapping the rifle into his hands, helping Henry up and telling him to move fast.

"Shit man," Henry exclaimed.

They scurred back around the corner to avoid the military convoy. When they turned the corner, the heat of the raging fire was enough to shield them from the cold, despite being over 100 meters away. They hid next to the building, gluing themselves to the wall. The Humvees flew around the corner, zooming up and parking just outside the fence, unloading the men within and leaving only the driver and the gunner in all three Humvees. Evan leaned against the wall while Henry looked to him for direction.

"Okay man, how do we get out of here?" Henry asked with worry in his voice.

Evan glanced around, slowly losing focus and trying to zero in on a way out. As he analyzed every path, his eyes landed on one of the Humvees, Henry saw this.

"No way man, there's no chance."

"Have you ever shot a man? Have you ever killed a man Henry?" Evan asked, indicating that he was about to make a risky move.

"No, I haven't killed anyone…" Henry tried to clarify, "I haven't I've shot anyone before either." His voice broke.

"Okay well," Evan removed the clip from his rifle, making sure it was full before continuing. "Don't overthink it, don't kill them unless you have to and make sure to always shoot them in the leg if you can. *We* are going to take one of those Humvees and *we* are going to get out of here Henry."

Before mustering the courage to actually act on his idea, Evan had to pause and breathe. He closed his eyes and saw his daughter. He *saw* her in the front yard, playing in the dirt. He *saw* her in the living room watching SpongeBob in the early morning. He *saw* Jade.

He opened his eyes and resumed to action, looking down at Henry and telling him to get his rifle ready. Henry didn't exactly know what Evan had in mind, but he had a good idea. He was nervous, same as Evan. When Henry tried to grasp at his safe space, just like Evan had; he saw his Mom, his sister, and his Dad. He was going to get out of there, he had to.

Evan nodded, asking if he was ready, Henry gave a thumbs up. The gunfire and clamor of lost lives were far too loud for either of them to communicate their thoughts verbally. They both charged to the nearest Humvee, rifles in hand.

The heat was far stronger than it was before, moving closer enhanced things. Destruction was all around.

Each bullet that hit the compound deflected dust and concrete chips into the air. Each bullet that struck the ground lifted a cloud of soot into the air and threw gravel around. Each step closer spiked both men's adrenaline to its limit. The Humvee that sat furthest from the compound was their target. As they both approached the Humvee, Evan slowed down, gesturing for Henry to do the same.

They snuck up to the back of the Humvee, before Evan could direct Henry, the machine gun mounted on top began firing. The loud clamor rocked both men in their chests. As if a firework was set off within arm's length away, except the fireworks wouldn't stop going off. Each abhorrently loud gunshot made their ears ring and only when the gunfire stopped was it that the two could finally resume their mission. Looping around to the driver-side door and ducking beneath the small bulletproof windows.

Before acting, Evan tried to shout instructions to Henry. "When I open the driver's door, you open the back door. I'll take care of the driver while you take care of the gunner, pull him down from his perch and disarm him. Shoot him if necessary but only kill if you have to!"

Henry nodded, he had only gotten about half of what Evan had said, but he knew what to do.

In sequence, Evan ripped open the driver's door and the expression on the soldier's face was that of surprise. Evan slammed the driver's face onto the steering wheel before ripping him out of the seat and tossing him to the ground. Henry had whipped the back door open, reaching for the gunner's dangling legs and pulling until he gave way.

All the gunfire and commotion enabled them to pull this off without any trouble. Henry had tumbled back when the soldier fell from the gunner's perch, he scrambled to his feet and drug the soldier from the back seat of the Humvee. Evan kept one eye on Henry and another on the soldier in the dirt. When the soldier's hand went for his holstered Glock, Evan kicked the pistol away, knocking it out of reach and putting a bullet into the leg of his victim. Henry was now on top of the soldier, driving his fist into the jaw of his opponent. Evan went to remove Henry and almost received a haymaker himself.

He disarmed the soldier and plunged a bullet deep into his calf, rendering both soldiers immobile and no longer a threat. Evan shouted to Henry, "I'll drive, get in!"

"Okay!"

Henry scurried around the Humvee to the passenger's seat, while Evan leapt into the driver's seat. He plopped his duffel bag onto the gunner's platform in the back and leaned his rifle next to his leg, pinning it against the center counsel. Henry bounced into the seat and shut the door, setting his rifle against the door, barrel facing up. Evan grasped the gear shifter and put the Humvee into drive.

He peeled out of there, throwing gravel up from the rapidly rotating wheels. The Humvee squealed and bounced around as Evan pinned the pedal to the floor. Henry flopped around with each vicious turn of the vehicle, using the hand supports to stabilize himself.

The sudden realization that one of their Humvee's had been hijacked caused the military to pound Evan and Henry's getaway vehicle with bullets, making their ears ring with each powerful strike. The bulletproof glass stood strong despite the bullet casings spent attempting to ensure a single crack.

A split second passed where Evan and Henry had glanced at one another, they exchanged a soft, mutual smile. What they were doing was crazy, but in some sick profound way, they were having fun.

The Humvee hit every single pothole in the road while Evan looked at the speedometer, he was passing almost 60 miles an hour. He could see the Utilities building in flames out of the driver-side mirror. Their escape was within reach.

"Holy shit Evan!" Henry exclaimed.

Evan smirked cockily, strangely he was enjoying this adventure.

Through all the gunfire and commotion, one indistinguishable noise could be heard. An overwhelmingly loud whistle after the dynamic boom. Evan knew what was coming. There was no escape now. As the whistle became more and more deafening, Evan prepared for impact.

The tank shell struck the front passenger-side wheel, throwing the Humvee 20 feet into the air and causing the vehicle to roll over itself when it struck the ground.

For what felt like just seconds, Evan and Henry were suspended mid-air, trapped within a flying bulletproof capsule. During that brief time, the two of them truly felt weightless and for just a moment, they were floating.

When they struck the pavement, the rattling of steel and tearing of metal was enough to make their ears bleed. Henry tried to hold himself steady as the vehicle tumbled over itself, thrashing him all around. Evan did the same, trying to prevent himself from further injury. It felt like they rolled for 10 minutes. Evan kept his eyes shut.

When the rolling finally stopped and they came to a halt, the two couldn't believe what had just happened. Their hair hung in front of their faces; the Humvee had come to rest upside down and tilted forward. Evan unbuckled his seatbelt and flopped onto his back, the first thing he went to grab was his rifle, but soon he realized it had been smashed to pieces during the crash. Bullets laid on the roof as Evan got to his knees, Henry mimicked Evan's movements. Unbuckling his seatbelt and rolling into a more defensive position.

"We need to get the fuck out of here Evan!"

"I know."

They scrambled to decide what their next course of action would be. Evan unbuttoned his coat and unholstered his pistol. "I think we have to run!"

Evan knew that within moments, the crashed vehicle they sat in would be swarmed with soldiers, ready to kill or take hostage. "Is your rifle intact?"

"Yeah!"

"Okay, we might need to shoot. Be ready Henry!"

Evan kicked his tattered door open and waited for his friend to do the same, the two exited at the same time only to be met with almost half a dozen soldiers pointing their rifles back at them. The odds stood against the two of them. Despite shooting them on the spot, the soldiers demanded that Evan and Henry put their guns down.

"Put that shit down or we'll spray your brains all over the street!"

"...Now!"

It took a moment or two for those words to sink in. Evan had a brief thought, imagining himself taking all the guards down in tremendous fashion, he knew that it was all a false reality created by his imaginative side, however. Before he even had a chance to draw and aim, he had already been defeated. Henry stood on the opposite side of the downed Humvee, rifle in hand and teeth grinding against one another.

Evan closed his eyes, seeing his defeat in masterful detail as he was now forced to lay down his weapon, forced to lay down his life and forced to lay down his will. It was over.

Henry turned to looked at Evan, who was standing perfectly still. Another solider demanded for them to disarm themselves.

"Do not make us kill you! Don't do anything stupid. Lay your guns down and show us your hands!"

"Do as they say, Henry," Evan muttered from across the toppled Humvee. He tossed his pistol to the ground, progressing his hands upward into the air before finally showing the soldiers his face. Henry let go of the rifle with his left palm, presenting it high in the air, while setting the rifle against the damaged Humvee door. Now presenting his right palm to the armed men.

They hadn't even gotten a chance to prove themselves, to defend themselves. Their escape was foiled and their time on this planet had been cut short. Both men were sure that they were going to be executed.

"Walk toward us now!"

Evan's trembling legs dragged forward, slowly. He was disappointed in his defeat. He wanted to cry. Henry kicked a rock forward, pissed off at his defenseless position.

"Now both of you get on your fucking knees!"

Evan and Henry stopped dead in their tracks, they did not want to get on their knees, they did not want to surrender. Every bone in their weak bodies told them to not follow the soldier's instruction. They wanted to disobey what they'd been directed to do. They knew it would surely kill them whether or not they got on their knees. They were sure that this was it. Reluctantly so, the two of them dropped to their knees with their hands still above their heads. When they had finally dropped to their knees, the two glanced at each other while a duo of soldiers approached them from behind.

Their eyes connected in a way that they could read one another in perfect detail. Evan relayed his apology, Henry relayed back to Evan, letting him know it was okay. The two prepared to be wiped off the face of the planet together.

Being completely disconnected from one another before the outbreak and now being connected almost like family. Evan had only ever felt this with his close friends, including Jackson. In his final moments, he hoped that Jackson and his family had made it somewhere safe, he was glad that he pushed them away; if he hadn't, they might be there alongside him, on the brink of total annihilation.

Henry wished for Evan to know that he was an alright guy, he wished for his family to know he missed them, and he wished for his little sister to know how much he loved her, even though he knew they were dead.

The two prepared for the orgasm of death, kneeling side by side they closed their eyes. Before experiencing what they thought was the end, the two were struck in the back of the head; being knocked to the ground and seeing only black as their minds drifted into unconsciousness.

Chapter 16

The Slaughter at Longfellow

They didn't know what was coming.

After Ana had finally awoken, Jackson pretended that he'd just woken up as well. The two of them ate some oats and Jackson announced that he was going to find something to do. He ended up helping Randall barricade a weak part on the rinky-dink fortifications.

Randall of course spouted and spewed about this and that and his views about things while Jackson kept quiet most of the time. Only piping in when he felt it was appropriate. Most of the work involved him stacking wooden pallets against the walls and tying them with rope. Using street signs as support and parking cars against the wall, then stacking stuff on top of the cars.

The two of them had also seen an explosion rock the top floor of a distant building. Randall didn't pay much attention to it, but Jackson however was fixated on it. A question distracted him.

"What do you want to talk about?"

Jackson was caught extremely off guard by this offer, the kid had just spent nothing short of a few hours talking about things that only he found interesting, and all Jackson did was listen. Jackson gave it a hard thought, actually thinking about something to talk about.

"Music?"

"Oh music, I love music sir. I used to listen to mostly punk rock, I love that stuff. Have you ever heard of the band uh... er... what was it? I can't remember. Damnit."

Jackson tied a pallet to the already established wall, "I liked 80's rock."

"My Dad you know, he was into that psychedelic shit, some more obscure stuff. He had a bunch of vinyl stuff back home." The kid talked more than he worked.

Randall obviously didn't get Jackson's firm hint that he wasn't interested in the slightest. He liked talking to people, but he didn't like when people took it upon themselves to talk to him more than he spoke to them, and especially as much as Randall chose to speak.

Jackson wasn't going to be rude and tell Randall to shut up, despite how badly he wanted to. He simply kept the conversation going. "Where'd you say you lived again?"

"Grand Rapids."

"I've been there once or twice."

"Once or twice?"

"Yeah."

"Hm, and you said you lived over by Rochester?"

"Yeah."

Randall still wouldn't take the hint. "Have you lived there your whole life sir?" Jackson had almost forgotten to respond, "No."

"Well, where'd you live before?"

"Iowa."

"Hm." Randall suddenly seemed stumped, as if he'd ran out of things to ask or to talk about. Jackson simply kept stacking things and making sure they were sturdy. The silence went on for a bit, but eventually Randall found something new to talk about. "Have you ever been to the zoo here?"

Jackson subtly rolled his eyes, "Yup, I've been there." His words were closely chased by a sigh.

"What's your favorite part?"

The kind of questions that Randall asked were the ones you couldn't brush off without an answer, so Jackson was forced to say something. "The Aquarium."

"Oh, sir, I love the aquarium. I always liked the tropical exhibit though."

The relentless questions plagued their afternoon and when the sun became dim as it sunk below the horizon, the wind had picked up. Flags blew about and snow drifts were being blown away, flooding the shoveled streets with more snow. The sky was dark a dark pink with rivers of deep blue throughout.

Jackson had completely forgot about Liv's warning until he saw the streetlights flicker, not once, but twice and then three times. He turned to Randall as they were just finishing up their day's work.

He was talking on and on about something that Jackson didn't quite care for when he decided to disrupt the constant babbling.

"Well then, my dog started spinning--."

"Did you see that?"

"See what?" Randall was oblivious until the whole street flickered once more. The lamps inside the buildings flickered too, all the electronics were slowly losing their luminosity.

"Oh... oh shit."

Jackson was silent on that ladder, still as a melting glacier. The wind drifted his beard along and suddenly they all flickered in unison, briefly drenching the street in darkness.

"Randall?"

Now Randall was frozen, not speaking a word and barely even registering that Jackson had spoken to him. He knew what was happening. He glanced across the city only to see a yellow beam, dim in luminosity but bright when compared to the deep and dark background.

"Jackson, get in your room, lock the doors, don't open them for anyone. *I mean it.*"

"What?"

Randall hopped off the ladder, "Get in your apartment, stay the fuck in there, and keep the door shut." He rushed down the street as every single light in Longfellow ceased function. It was almost as if someone had flipped a breaker to the entire suburb. The once bright sanctuary was now cloaked in darkness.

"Okay! Okay!" He didn't bother to ask why because he already knew. Jackson turned and ran down the street to the apartment building, hearing the mayhem ensue as every man who could shoot prepared to defend their home. He bolted up the stairs and down the hall, entering the room. He shut the door and locked it, walking over to the closet, then ripping out an ironing table from its home.

He shoved the table against the door, ensuring it to be locked in place. Ana got up from her spot on the floor, "Jackson, what're you doing? What happened to the lights?"

Before Jackson had even got the chance to respond, he tripped over a board game that Matt and Ana were playing and accidentally stepping on the notebook he gifted to his wife. She would scribble and doodle on it whenever it was Matt's turn to roll the dice. "I need you and Matt to get in the bathroom, I need you guys to lock the door and I need you guys to stay quiet."

The darkness that suffocated the room made the outside moonlight a gift for their eyes.

Ana was confused, Matt was ready to take a nap. "Why...?"

"Because I said so, because you need to. Just get in there," Jackson opened the bathroom door for them to enter. Ana got up, looking at Jackson out of the corner of her eye. She could only assume why. "Are they coming?"

Jackson was silent but Ana had already gotten her answer. "Just get in," he said while helping his son out of bed. Matt looked up at his Dad, What's going on?"

"People are coming, and you need to get in the bathroom with your Mom." He grabbed hold of Matt's arm, pulling him into the bathroom while Ana followed, begging for an answer.

Jackson initially hesitated but gave in and told his son, "The military is coming, you guys are going to hide in there while I sit on the couch, if anything happens, you need to promise me that you'll stay quiet, promise me Ana."

Matt overheard, "They're coming?" he asked. The teenager's voice was shallow enough to sense the fear within each word. Ana looked at him, his glossy brown eyes were now gray with an ever-growing sense of fear and danger. Jackson nodded to them, "Get in there and lock the door." Ana now understood why Jackson was doing what he was doing.

"Okay," she said, leading Matt to the bathroom while she held Jackson's hand. She knew that protecting Matt was all that mattered. Her husband would rather get himself killed than let any harm befall her or their son.

Marrying him was a good choice.

She made Jackson and Matt hug, she didn't know if it would be the last time or not. Then she wrapped her hands around her husband, nearly squeezing the life out of him.

"When the night is over, promise me you'll make me breakfast in bed," she whispered to him.

He chuckled at first, finding it quite silly to promise such a thing, "Breakfast in bed?"

"Yep mhm, breakfast in bed. Promise me."

"I promise—" Ana stopped him, telling him, "Take it serious."

Jackson rolled his eyes while smiling, he loved her. "I promise… that tomorrow I'll wake you up with bacon, eggs, and toast. A glass of orange juice too!"

"Over easy eggs, okay?" She made him do this to provide a sense of hope for the two of them. She wanted to create a false sense of tomorrow, because she wasn't sure if tomorrow would happen.

"Okay babe," Jackson smirked, "I promise."

Ana unlatched her arms from Jackson, almost like a bear trap being released. Jackson went to tell Ana that he loved her but was stopped, "Save it for when you serve me breakfast tomorrow," she pressed her lips against his. Their souls were warmed by this kiss. A final embrace before being engulfed by the frightening unknown.

The door closed, and Jackson stood there for a moment, staring and the nice oak patterned bathroom door, before turning around and heading for the TV stand.

He grasped the pistol, loading the clip through the bottom and heading for the couch. He was going to sit there and stand guard until the tectonic plates pulled so far apart that he'd fall into a ravine full of lava. He wasn't going to leave his post.

It was quiet, for a long time actually. He found himself playing thumb wars with his right and left thumb, trying to cure his boredom. Checking out the window to make sure sure he wasn't missing anything.

He was genuinely bored.

For what felt like hours he sat there, waiting for an attack to come. Ana and Matt sat in the bathroom wondering the same thing Jackson was. Wondering where the gunshots were, why wasn't anybody shooting. The silence was *unnerving*, almost annoying. Jackson liked silence, so it felt so damn weird to all of a sudden hate it.

Jackson sat in the painful silence when it was interrupted by a powerful and indistinguishable bang.

One gunshot started it all.

First it was one, then it was two and finally a barrage. After the barrage, the gunfire didn't stop. The slaughter at Longfellow had begun.

The breaks in gunfire were far more disturbing than the gunfire itself. It was almost comfortable at times because it allowed for the silence to not be so unnerving. In the silence, Jackson noticed every single creak and every single tiny noise, but when the gunfire was present, it distracted his ears from the fear that lurked in the unknown.

Louder explosions let everyone know that tanks had officially entered the fight. In between the explosions, Jackson could hear grown men screaming for their mothers. The pain and suffering were too great to be measured. Jackson wished he had a window to observe everything, he wanted to see what was happening. The only window he had however was one that was looking away from the action.

Truly what he wanted to do was to take his wife and son and get out of there. He wanted to flee. He wanted to run. He wanted to escape certain death, but he knew that sitting still right where he was would ensure a shield between him and the military's violent reign.

Every second that passed was a long one. Every minute that passed was even longer. Measuring time felt like measuring distance between star systems, there was no telling how much time had passed since the first shot was fired. Jackson couldn't remember when, but at some point, the air had started to smell like smoke. As if someone had lit a barbeque in the apartment hallway.

Every bone in his body wanted to get up and check, wanting to put the fire out. But the thought of opening the door was too terrifying, he had no clue what was out there. The thought was manageable enough until extremely loud gunshots were heard, they had to have been fired within the apartment complex itself. It was too loud not to. First it sounded below, and after a few minutes it moved to the same floor. Several gunshots sporadically discharged.

It felt like God was playing with Jackson, as to make him even more paranoid by the following gunshots. The shots wouldn't be nearly as horrifying if it weren't for the screams that followed, it wasn't like people were being mowed down, it was almost like whoever was invading was placing warning shots. Nobody was being killed, otherwise the screaming would've stopped long ago. This was weird. Why weren't people being killed? Isn't that what happens in a war?

Jackson readied to protect his family and to *die* for them.

The door was locked and barricaded, if someone wanted to enter, they'd be met with resistance and a few gunshots through the door. Jackson thought he had the upper hand. He had no clue what he was doing.

He liked to think that he had grown up on the streets and was forced to fight kids twice his size, but in truth, he had never been in a true fight. The only fight he could think of was the one he had with Evan. He was a big man, but he was a gentle one.

The room was beginning to feel like an oven, starting to cook Jackson alive. The screaming was now distant and faint, Jackson figured maybe his family was in the clear, but before he had the chance to get up, sets of footsteps had reached the apartment door. Heavy footsteps that were audible despite the gunfire outside.

Jackson aimed his pistol at the door and prepared to shoot at anyone attempted to break in. His teeth were clenched, and his muscles were tense.

The door croaked open while the ironing table stopped it halfway, Jackson fired a barrage of bullets all striking different parts of the door and shooting chunks of wood from the responding bullet holes. When he stopped shooting, a canister was thrown inside the room, it was dispensing a white gas that made his eyes water and sting. His nose started dripping snot and he couldn't open his eyes, no matter how hard he tried.. He heard shouting from where the apartment door was and every time his eyes peaked from his swollen eyelids, he saw the fire beyond the door and dark silhouettes moving into the room. All of his senses were gone, aside from his hearing.

He tried firing his gun, but someone had disarmed him, tossing the pistol far away. Shouting words like, "Get on your knees!"

Jackson waved his arms around but was soon restricted and detained. He couldn't see anything; he couldn't open his mouth without tasting the foul fumes from the canister. He couldn't even smell the smoke from the raging fire anymore.

He figured that the soldiers taking him wouldn't dare check the bathroom, he thought his family was safe.

They were not.

After the ruckus, Ana had screamed out for them to stop, followed by her opening the door and trying to rescue her husband. She was met with brutality. Jackson couldn't see what was going on, all he could do was listen. This was the part that was killing him inside. Maybe it was better for him to not see what was happening, but the noise of his wife and son being detained destroyed him. He shouted for them to stop, his drunken slurred and senseless mouth tainted by the tear gas made his words unintelligible. He tried to save his family despite being as weak as he was.

Jackson had been defeated. Not because of how he lost, but what he lost. His family would surely be killed, and it was his fault. He would cry if his eyes would let him. The snot from his nose and spit from his mouth had started to coat his beard. He thrashed back and forth as the soldiers dragged him out of the room and down the stairs, hearing his wife and son screaming out in pain manically following him out to the street.

Once they had taken him and his family outside, the gunfire had become much louder, sounding as if his ears were right next to the barrel of every gun being discharged.

He didn't know where he was, he didn't know what was happening and worst of all, he couldn't see his family in what he thought were their final moments alive.

The solider that had dragged him outside had shoved him to the floor, stepping away. Jackson heard close wallows of fear and pain, he realized that he was a part of a crowd now. He tried to listen in to find his wife and son, only to realize they were right next to him. They had called his name, pressing against him in the crowd of men and women in the street.

"Jackson!" Ana had shouted. "Dad!" Matt had shouted. They didn't know where they were headed, but before too long, they were being herded into school busses at gunpoint. Jackson was still weak and defenseless from the tear gas attack, all he had was his wife and son to lead him.

This was not how this was supposed to go at all.

Chapter 17

The Survivor

The ineffable fear he felt was unknown until that point.

He didn't know if he had been banished to hell or not because if he were honest, death would've felt better than what he was going through.

His eyelids didn't want to open, nor could they. His whole face felt like it was about to explode. His head was pounding and every small cut on his body throbbed simultaneously with each heartbeat. When he finally forced his eyes to open, he couldn't see a thing. His head had been encased with a poorly made fabric, so poor in fact that he was able to see through if he squinted hard enough.

The floor was concrete, droplets of blood were visible despite the poor vision through the cloth. When he went to reach and take the cloth off, the rope that restricted him snapped taut and kept his hands from reaching anywhere near his face. He turned his head to analyze the situation. His hands were both tied to adjacent sides of the room on barely visible pipes protruding from the walls.

He groaned, closing his eyes again when his hands clasped shut and made iron fists. He tugged back and forth to try and release himself from his state of capture.

In front of him was a big door, blood covering the knob. He could only imagine what was behind him. He wanted to speak, he wanted to shout, and he wanted to yell. He was afraid of who would respond.

For what felt like days, he was there, strapped to the wall and dangling just barely enough to place his knees to the floor, granting him a minor rest. He closed his eyes again, hoping that he would be able to fall asleep and pass the time. He thought maybe he was being questioned, or interrogated, but the only memory he had was being in that rollover accident and surrendering. This thought then led him to think about Henry, and where he might be. He hoped that Henry was still alive or had escaped at some point. These thoughts occupied his mind enough to subside the jarring pain he felt all around his body.

He shivered as his teeth chattered, cackling loudly within the small concrete box that surrounded him. Not a single breath left his lungs that wasn't visible, the exhaled breath contrasted the cold so intensely, it looked like steam. Evan hadn't been this cold since he woke up in that mall.

While he tried to stay warm, he heard a clamor outside the door in front of him. He stopped everything. He stopped shivering, he stopped his teeth from chattering, and he stopped all motion. He was completely and totally silent. Shallow footsteps could be heard tiptoeing on the other side of the threshold, they stopped when they reached the door. Evan hung his head low, he tried to portray as if he hadn't woken up.

The metal doorknob twisted and screeched as it did so. When the door finally opened, he stayed as still as humanely possible.

"Evan… James… Smith…"

Subconsciously, Evan raised his head, alerted by the man who had just recited his full name. The voice was low, he had heard it before, he just couldn't quite nail where he had heard it from.

"Sargent Major. You know, we could've used someone like you when this all started. Too bad you've been on the wrong side this whole time."'

Evan debated talking, after a long silence followed the man's menacing monologue, he decided to speak. "I'm not on anyone's side, if given the choice, I certainly wouldn't join you." Evan had made the connection; he was speaking to Johannsson.

"So, you know then?"

Evan was silent, talking to this corrupt devil was the last thing he wanted to do.

"You've heard all the nasty things they say about me, all the nasty things they said I've done."

Evan felt weak and powerless in the presence of a man who brought an entire city to its knees. For the first time in his life, he felt fragile. His fate was in the hands of an egotistical maniac who had no regard for human life.

He stayed true to himself in the face of certain destruction. "I don't need to know every evil thing you've done to know what kind of man you are."

"…and what kind of man do you think I am?"

"A weak man. A man who uses others to protect himself."

"Hm... well truly we all use others to protect ourselves. I'm sure that's exactly why you had that kid with you. He helped you steal that Humvee and you nearly had him get into a losing shootout with my men." Evan could tell that Johannsson was using his hands to amplify what he was saying. *"That sounds an awful lot like using others to protect yourself, now doesn't it?"*

"You used the entire city," Evan's mouth tasted of iron as he sputtered those words.

"You used an innocent kid."

Evan clearly lost the dispute, he was in no condition to win, however. He was a fish on a hook.

"You're telling me that I'm evil, you don't even know what I look like."

Evan lifted his head, trying to squint to see through the cloth. All he got was a dim and blurry outline of a tall statured man in a uniform. Wide shoulders and a towering build. Johannsson shadowed his hostage.

"You're telling me that I made the city this way; I'm telling you that the civilians made it this way. I tried to help them, I tried to show them the way and I was met with resistance. They didn't want to be saved." Johannsson had an almost unnoticeable lisp, extremely faint and undisguisable from a minor slip of the tongue.

"They didn't want to die."

Johannsson snarled, almost working up a laugh. *"So that's what they've been telling you?"*

Evan snapped back quick, this deliberate teasing from Johannsson was beginning to annoy him. "What's your story then?"

"My story?" He mocked, *"I did what I did because they forced my hand. I wouldn't have had to kill anyone if they all just complied."*

Before Evan could get a defensive reply out, Johannsson had parried him.

"And don't you dare bring up all the people who were taken from their homes and shot. That wasn't me. It was standard quarantine procedure given from the head of national security himself. If one hog gets sick, then the rest will surely fall ill with the same sickness, that's how it works."

Evan was stunned, still trying to squint hard enough to make out specific features of Johannsson's face. *"So what? Did I finally get through to you? No rebuttal this time?"*

"What do you need from me, Johannsson?"

"I already know who you are, now I need to know why you're here. You already told me you weren't with us, nor those damn Revolutionists." When he mentioned his opposing faction, his voice was filtered with distain and hatred. *"So then answer me this: why are you here."*

Johannsson wasted no time beating around the bush, Evan figured neither should he. "I was only here looking for someone." Johannsson chuckled as if he had heard a joke.

"And for some reason, that caused you to injure two of my men, steal one of our precious Humvees and speed out of there like a bat out of hell." Johannsson moved closer to Evan, soon consuming, and shadowing the cloth bag. Nothing could be seen now, even if Evan squinted as hard as he could.

"So, you tell me that you're looking for someone without telling me who this person is? This isn't a game."

Shirtless Evan felt the pointed edge of a knife drag across his shoulder, now being met with the entire length of the blade, he stayed quiet while being intimidated. *"I came in here for answers, and you scrutinize me based purely off the thing's others have said. You're a bad judge of character, now, before I split open your shoulder and open you up like a pig, tell me why you are here. I don't have any respect for men like you."*

Evan turned his head toward Johannsson's shadow, trying to look as menacing as a half-naked man could with a bag over his head.

"My daughter."

"Oh, fucking joy. Your daughter, really?"

Evan wanted claw his opponent's eyes out. "Yes, my daughter."

Johannsson then moved the serrated blade down Evan's arm, just barely dragging across the gash he earned from the mall and now poking near the bite mark.

"I haven't seen a kid in this city since it went on lockdown, why would your daughter be here? What? Did she run away?" He mocked.

Evan wanted to rip the ropes that constricted his arms and show Johannsson his wrath, he wanted to wrap his hands around the throat of the devil and squeeze the life from his lungs.

"From my understanding, nobody with a bite fights this hard to chase around a little girl inside a city like this. Now the next thing that comes from your mouth better not sound like a lie, or I'll start filleting your arm until every ounce of blood is drained from your body."

Evan was on a leash; he was a shackled dog while Johannsson teased him with bait. "I'm here to find my daughter, *asshole.*"

The vulgar tone that went along with the first cuss word he'd used in a long time was menacing. Something that made a man like Johannsson get goosebumps.

Johannsson didn't even bother to chuckle this time, he just stared down at Evan. As if he felt a surge of power coinciding with the insult he just received.

He wanted to kill Evan now.

First, he thought about stabbing Evan, then he thought about choking him to death. Finally, he settled on a truly harsh punishment.

He lowered himself down to Evan's ears, shouting as loud as he could before slapping the weak man several times only on his left cheek, making it sting. Screaming in both ears and occasionally cupping his hands around the chosen ear to further deafen Evan. In between the shouting, he would strike Evan with his palm, stretching his arm back nearly knocking himself off balance to deliver a blow that nearly made Evan's cheekbone split his skin open.

Evan saw bright lights following each strike to his face, barely being able to hear Johannsson screaming at this point. When the torture finally stopped, Johannsson stepped back. Evan's ears rang and his face stung, he was penalized for telling the truth.

"You done?"

Evan didn't reply, he didn't even know that he was being spoken to. The ropes were the only thing keeping Evan upright now.

Evan went to spit blood from his mouth, but the cloth bag caught it. "I'm looking for my daughter," he sounded like he was choking on all the snot in his sinuses.

Johannsson knew that Evan was telling the truth, he went through all of Evan's stuff in the duffel bag. The children's stuffed animal and family portrait was enough to confirm what Evan was saying, yet Johannsson chose to continue the relentless beating. He knew that Evan was telling the truth, but he felt like he could get a better answer from him. All Johannsson was truly doing, was blowing off steam.

"You better not say another thing about your fucking daughter, I don't care about her. She isn't here and if she was, she's already dead."

Johannsson placed his hand on Evan's face, pulling the two closer than before. *"Tell me why you're here, or else I'm going to—"*

"You aren't going to anything to me," Evan mocked while coughing a red mist into the bag around his head. Johannsson began to unsheathe the blade from his belt. Though his darkened view beyond the cloth was dim, he saw the blade gleam in the light. Just as the blade was brought to Evan's throat, a voice hollered from beyond the door.

Johannsson jolted aback, still pressing the edge of the blade against his prisoner's throat. The door croaked open, and a man demanded that Johannsson come check something out.

"Sir, they're getting rowdy. It looks like a riot is about to break out!"

Johannsson turned back to Evan, flashing a blurry smile through the fabric, and pulling the knife away. If Evan had gotten the chance to be free from those ropes, he would've tackled Johannsson and made him beg for his life. He would have ended the conflict.

Johannsson stood up, "Is *it worth my time?"*

"It's urgent. Follow me sir."

Evan saw his opening; this is how he would manage an escape. Johannsson quickly turned to Evan before leaving the room, hawking the fattest loogy before spitting in onto Evan. The gross blob was the only warmth Evan had felt in a long time. His shirtless skin felt frozen, the loogy was almost warm enough to unthaw him.

Johannsson left the room, slamming the door without a word and winning the encounter. Evan didn't care if he lost, he simply cared about getting out of there. After waiting a few moments and thinking to himself, he started to struggle back and forth, trying to undo the knotted ropes.

The thoughts that crossed his mind consisted of Henry, wondering where he may be. Also wondering what the soldier had meant by, "They're getting rowdy. "Who was the solider referring to? And why were they getting rowdy?

In the midst of his thoughts, the rope that constricted his right arm became relatively limp alongside the clamor of metal and concrete colliding. When Evan turned to look, his neck cracked.

He could barely see what had happened, but it seemed like the pipe that the rope was tied to had begun to give way. When he tugged harder, he noticed the outline of the pipe wiggling around, scraping the concrete stone walls. Then, with all of his strength and pent-up anger, he pulled. It felt as if he pulled any harder, he'd rip his arm out of socket. He tugged and thrashed until the pipe came loose and fell onto the floor, ripping chunks of chiseled stone from the wall. The sound of it all falling to the floor was enough to alert anyone nearby so he quickly snatched the bag off his head.

His eyes fluttered open and shut until his vision became unblurred. He quickly untied the knot tied around his left hand and undid the one around his right. He was free again.

His hair was fluffed and greased. He looked like a mangy dog with his shirt off. Ribcage showing and every single bruise that discolored his skin made him look like an abstract piece of artwork. Every scrape and cut were swollen while he could only imagine what his face looked like.

After a few moments of recuperating his dignity, he figured that nobody was around. The clamor for sure would have lured somebody to his position by now. He shook off his pain and leaned to pick up the pipe that had ripped from the wall. He walked over to the beaten-up door and tried the handle before smashing the locked doorknob. Finally, the door jolted open, revealing a small room beyond the threshold. There was a desk, a small shelf, and all of his stuff. The torn-up duffel bag had all of its contents strewn across the desk.

Jade's childhood stuffed animal, the family portrait, the military radio, and all of his identification cards. He sifted through all of it, finding an almost untouched white T-shirt of his. He draped it over himself, slipping his arms through the holes and finally hiding the ugliness beneath. On the opposing side of the room was another door.

Evan quickly searched the desk for his revolver, checking drawers and peering up onto the shelf. It was nowhere to be found. He turned back around toward the door, facing it, and holding the pipe as a weapon. He switched the lock open, placing his hand on the knob and preparing to open the door.

When Evan had finally opened the door, he peaked in. Henry had been strung up similarly to how Evan had been. Arms tied and rope taut.

His friend was trapped like a bird in a cage, one that desperately needed to be free. Someone as wholehearted as

Henry didn't deserve to be strung up as if his life meant nothing.

He rushed to help the kid, to help his friend. He ripped the bag from Henry's head and started to untie the ropes, saying reassuring things like, "It's going to be okay," and, "You're going to be alright." Evan only said these things to comfort himself, however.

Henry was almost completely unresponsive, his head hung low. The once vibrantly and sort of obnoxious orange hair was now that of autumn leaves. A dead orange.

He rushed to save his friend, finally freeing Henry of the ropes. His limp body flushed to the ground while Evan stabilized his head, making sure the descent was slow and painless. Evan poked around, "Henry? Henry man? Come on."

Silence followed Evan's pleas; it was too quiet for comfort. Evan was used to Henry starting conversation and having a spark but seeing him like this was truly bewildering. Henry was shirtless, just as Evan had been. There were significantly more bruises than Evan had received though, it looked like Henry had received the brunt of Johannsson's fury. Evan sat there, holding his friend.

Henry's left eye twitched, followed by an opening. His eyes opened, revealing one eye being bloodied and the other bruised. Henry motioned with his right hand to Evan, raising it slightly before flopping back down. He now spoke.

"Evan?"

He was quick to respond, "Yeah man?"

"Did you..." Henry coughed. "Did you kill him?"

"Johannsson?" Evan thought about lying. He thought about forging the truth to lift Henry's spirits. For a brief moment, he enjoyed a false reality.

"Yeah, he's dead. He got what he deserved." Evan lied.

Both men knew that Henry wasn't going to make it out of there. For the first time since Elba, Evan wanted to cry. He had only known the kid for a day but that was all it took for Evan to start caring.

"Good, I wished I at least got to bitch slap him or something," Henry tried to chuckle. Despite Evan knowing that the chances of Henry getting out of there were slim, he tried to help him up. Henry coughed as Evan tried to lift him to his feet. It was no use.

"You know, for some guy so dead set on finding his daughter, you sure want me to come with." Henry stopped Evan, "I'm not making it out of here, and you know it. Just stop."

Evan's hands had now been slicked with dark red syrup from trying to lift his friend. He knew that there was no chance of getting Henry out of that room, but relentlessly he tried.

"This is it, Evan." Henry hawked up a blood loogy and spat it on the ground, showering the cold floor with an unsettling red shower. Evan noticed his friend's usually pale face growing blue. Not sky blue or water blue, it was slowly being tinted the dead blue that is associated with corpses. Evan tried and tried but without Henry's willingness to get up, the task was impossible. He knew what was coming, he knew it was inevitable.

Yet he chose to fight it.

Henry would die, just like Evan's wife did. Except the difference was: Henry wouldn't die alone.

Though Evan might be alone when his time comes, he wanted to make absolutely sure that Henry was not alone while he passed on, it was the least he could do.

Henry outstretched his hand, offering something to Evan. "Take it, don't let his recipe die with me."

It was a tattered and folded piece of paper, Evan unfolded it to see the contents within. The instructions on the paper perfectly outlined how to create the perfect pizza sauce. It was Henry's grandfather's original pizza sauce recipe.

Evan wanted to chuckle at this, he wanted to cry too, but both emotions ended up fusing into this ugly combination. He smiled while the salty tears drenched his face.

"It's all about the sauce, Evan. Not the cheese or the crust, it's about the sauce."

Evan knew he was ugly crying, but he didn't care. He just wanted to embrace Henry in his final moments. "You know…" Evan couldn't get more than a few words out without his voice breaking, "You're a good kid, the sort of kid who didn't deserve to…" he had to pause again. "The sort of kid who didn't deserve to be stuck in a place like this." Evan cried.

Henry gave Evan a gingerly smile, but he couldn't hold it for long, he was tired.

He held his friend, both sitting on the dirty concrete floor of the torture room. Evan felt like a mother holding a newborn, Henry felt like his mother was holding him once more before facing oblivion. The two were quiet now, simply enjoying their last moments with one another. Minutes passed with the two still silent.

When Evan went to look down at Henry after this brief moment of silence, the eyes of his friend were locked in place. The eyelids were relaxed and despite the amount of physical damage that had been done, Henry seemed tranquil. Evan called his name.

There was no response.

~ . ~

It smelt so bad.

Everyone was sweating despite the cold; some were bleeding, and some were crying, all were hungry. The crowd was dense, almost like a herd of cows on a ranch. Jackson looked all around.

Overnight, they had been transported to the baseball field in the Target Stadium. When I say they, I mean Jackson and his family, followed by all the innocent men, women, and children who had been living at Longfellow. There were hundreds of people; Jackson was only able to estimate based on how many heads he saw in the crowd.

People stood, people sat, people laid down. Truly all that anyone wanted was to rest one night peacefully.

A thin layer of armed gunman surrounded the perimeter of the field, meanwhile up in the bleachers near the top of the stadium sat several snipers all prepared to shoot the next overly suspicious civilian. Most people were huddled around the center, keeping the children warm and protecting the weak; the courageous and dumb would veer to the edges near the guards, teasing them.

Jackson kept his wife close and the two of them kept their son even closer, acting like a penguin protecting their egg. It was cold, far colder than it had been at Longfellow. The huddling helped though. Jackson's face was cold, despite the huge beard that hung over it. His eyes were sore and every orifice on his face stung from the tear gas that was used against him the night prior.

The sky was weather-less, dim, and white with overcast clouds but no rain or snow, not yet. The air was chill, like the air after you get out of the shower. The family tried desperately to cover every exposed part of their body, trying to hide from the brutal cold.

Jackson was thankful that he was still with his family, and that they were still alive.

He started asking around to the others huddling around him, "Do you know why we're here? What the fuck."

Nobody had a true answer, not a reliable one at least. Not many people even responded, they only shivered in place. Everyone was weak and demoralized. Then suddenly something had caught his attention, a fluttering face. The eyes of a girl he had seen before. The eyes of a lost girl. Her clear skin stood out when put into a batch of pimple faced and grease covered people. Not a single face stood out aside from her.

He had recognized her almost instantly and when they locked eyes, he darted his head away quick. After a moment, he looked back at her, trying to do a double take to make sure it was really her.

The two nights that were spent in Elba had exposed him to enough family portraits to instantaneously recognize this stranger. She didn't know him, but he knew her. Every time he'd stop and turn to look, she'd glance back at him. He knew that he was making her uncomfortable by looking, but he didn't know what else to do. He wanted to walk over and talk to her as if they'd known one another for years but that would simply be too weird.

He was looking at the daughter of his friend.

Jackson tried desperately to work up the courage to walk over to Jade and introduce himself. Ana had noticed Jackson peering away and when she went to see why, she saw what he saw. The eyes of a scared teenage girl, alone in the middle of a captured crowd. For a second, it felt like the whole world revolved around the stadium they were stuck in.

"I should go talk to her."

"I'll do it," Ana rebutted, knowing that some soft blonde would look less threatening than some burly He-man. Jackson looked down at her as if her consideration was idiotic. She looked up at her husband.

"I'll go talk to her honey," she said again, reassuring him.

Ana released from Jackson's stiff arms, telling her son that she'd be right back. When she started walking toward Jade, Matt looked up to his father. Both of them were staring at the exchange about to take place.

"Is that Evan's daughter?"

"It's her," he said, shaky voice and anxious tone.

Ana approached slowly. Jade stood all alone amongst the sea of people. She was an orphan looking for someone to cling to. She was snuggled in a tattered coat with a fur hood. Her olive skin contrasted her emerald eyes ever so dreamily.

"Hey…" Ana greeted, "Your name is Jade and I'm Ana."

Jade looked confused while she raised both her eyebrows, wondering who she was talking to and why she knew her name.

"Who are you?" Jade's response felt defensive.

"Your Dad is Evan."

"Who are you and why are you telling me this? How do you know me?" She was growing weary now.

"He helped me and my family," she spun and gestured to her husband and son, they smiled awkwardly. "He helped us, and…" she paused, "He was looking for you."

There was a long silence while everything processed in Jade's head. Her Dad was alive, and he was looking for her.

Everything that had happened only assured Jade that her Dad had died long ago. That he was stuck far away and out of reach. Now he was alive and looking for her? It didn't make any sense.

"He's here?"

"Sweetie, I don't know where he is, but he's in the city. He came here to look for you."

Her Dad was trying to find her, in a city like this with as many dangers as there were. She was thoroughly aware of how bad the situation was. She knew that all it took was hunger and an overly competent attitude to get you killed in the city. She'd seen it happen countless times since she'd arrived in that *damned* city.

"What do you mean you don't know where he is? You guys were with him," Jade exclaimed, trying to control her shallow anger. Ana spoke, "We got split up."

"Split up? What? You didn't see where he went?"

Ana understood why Jade was getting irritable, she shrugged her arms, letting Jade know that she truly had no clue where Evan could have been. "Sweetie—"

"He isn't alive, I know he isn't." Jade was stubborn like her father, Ana realized.

Jade didn't know whether or not to trust this complete and total stranger, the other part of her didn't know whether or not to believe what Ana was saying about her Dad. She hadn't seen him for months and suddenly by complete coincidence, he made it all the way to Minneapolis to find her. Jade was skeptical.

"He brought us to your home, in Elba I think the town was. That's how we got here." Ana didn't want to mention anything about Jackson and Evan fighting, or any of the drama that had happened.

"He found my note."

"He did."

Jade looked all around with her bright green feline eyes, everywhere besides Ana's eyes. She could tell that the kid was trying to make sense of everything. "Why don't you come with us, this is no place to be alone." Jade looked up, "How can I be sure he's here."

"We could try to find him," Ana reasoned. Truly she knew that the odds of finding Evan were zero to none. She simply didn't want Jade to be alone in a crowd like this. Jade was so young; you could tell just from her skin. It was so undamaged and smooth compared to every other soul on the field. She wasn't a child; she was more of a teen than anything. She certainly had to grow up faster than she'd planned on and all because of the new unforgiving world. Ana outstretched her equally smooth skinned hand, offering it to Jade, convincing her to come with.

Jade looked up, wanting to grab hold of it, a mother's hand. She wanted to, but it was hard. Jade didn't know why, or what made it so difficult to take Ana's hand, but it was just inherently hard to accept this random act of kindness from a stranger after so long of living in a city full of backstabbers.

Jade's hand grasped Ana's after a moment of stubbornness.

Ana took Jade to go meet Jackson and Matt, walking her through the thick crowd.

Jade was nervous and still a little stubborn regarding her Dad but hoped for the best. She tried to be as optimistic as possible, just like her Dad had taught her.

Jackson waved awkwardly, almost like he didn't know if he should embarrass himself first or puke from how equally nervous he felt.

What was he going to say? The girl was made an orphan during the Winter and most likely wouldn't take too kind to strangers telling her that her father was alive months after she thought he was dead. How would he even speak to her?

The lost girl approached Jackson, being followed by his wife. Matt let out an awkward wave, not as awkward as his father's wave, however. Jade waved back, she looked extremely uncomfortable. Ana shot her lover a look, telling him with her eyes that he needs to act normal. An aggressive but controlling look, one that made Jackson snap out of it.

"Your Dad traveled with us."

"My Dad traveled with you; your wife already told me." Jade had already forgotten Ana's name.

"Yeah, he was looking for you," Jackson didn't normally speak this quiet. It felt like he was talking to a friend at a funeral. It was quiet, but then Jade brought up the note meant for her Dad. "You guys came here because of the note?"

"Your Dad would've swam across the ocean if the note said you were headed to England. He would've gone anywhere," Jackson spoke highly of Evan despite their last heated encounter. The fight didn't matter anymore, the bruises had healed. Jackson understood why Evan fought to stay here, especially with Jade now being alive. The fight didn't matter anymore.

Jackson tried to clarify to Jade, "He's probably still out there trying to find you." For a split second, Jackson saw the same twinkle that he'd seen in Matt's eyes thousands of times before in Jade's eyes. The twinkle was gone just as fast as it had arrived. Her eyes now fell back into the dark rich green.

While the two spoke, the crowd in the field sounded like it was beginning to get louder. The usual chatter was beginning to increase.

It sounded like everyone was starting to talk to themselves, it wasn't innocent mumbles or mumbles of conversation. It sounded as if everyone was beginning to plot something.

A plan of escape.

Jackson and Jade started to look all around, trying to analyze what was happening. Ana was focused on a single group, about 30 yards to their left, looking significantly more menacing than the rest. The first man in the group had pulled a 9mm from his boot that the soldiers had missed while patting down. The other men fashioned weapons from their shoes and the laces. Jackson soon noticed the same group his wife was looking at, soon the whole family was fixated on this group.

The chatter was now loud, the hollering and screaming now overpowered the wallowing and cries of the hurt. The Revolutionists were planning their revolution.

Small trios of men had gone around, informing others of the soon to be riot. After some time, one of the trios had reached Jackson and his family, telling them to follow the crowd out of there.

"We're getting out of here, over there," the janky homeless looking man spoke, gesturing to one of the several barricades on the Northern side of the field. *"Keep your kids under your wing and stay near the middle of the group. Be prepared to fight. We're getting out of here!"*

Before Jackson could stop the man and ask him further questions, he had already moved on to inform a different group of people. They were in no condition to take on the armed military, and if they thought so, they were just as delusional as Johannsson.

Maybe that's what it took? To have an estranged delusion of grandeur.

Maybe a delusion is what the people needed to turn the tides and escape. They all figured that the manpower of every soul on the field combined with their pure determination would surely overpower the military's incompetence.

Jade looked to Jackson, as if he had all the answers.

He did not.

~ . ~

Evan folded Henry's sauce recipe paper into a square and situated it into his back pocket. He let go of his friend, gently gliding him down onto the concrete. He stood up with red eyes and a wet face.

A boy had been taken from this world because of something Evan wanted. Henry would've followed him anywhere no matter the size of the prize. In this case, the prize was a car and a way out of the city which was all anyone really wanted at the time. Evan felt guilty, as if he had killed Henry himself, but in a way he did.

As he gathered his wits now outside the room Henry had died in, he went through the stuff in the duffel bag, thinking back on all of his decisions.

He hadn't directly murdered Henry, but surely his actions had caused it to an extent. Right? I mean if Evan didn't encourage Henry to come with then perhaps, he'd still be alive. Maybe if Evan hadn't promised a way out, Henry would've never agreed to follow along. Maybe Evan would be dead if Henry hadn't come with him, maybe he would've been torn to shreds by the pack of dogs. Maybe this and maybe that, none of the questions that were being asked by Evan's internal voice could be answered.

What if this and what if that, you know, asking yourself those questions wastes precious time. You'll spend far more of your days contemplating and overthinking this or that instead of the days you actually spend doing it. Every second in this life we've been given is a gift to two people, that's you and the voice that rationalizes. This voice can be a kind one or a brutal one, mostly it's a brutal one. If only the voice wasn't so strongly attached to us and if only the voice wasn't so damn mean.

Evan beat himself up while taking the family portrait from the smashed frame and stuffing Jade's childhood stuffed animal in the side pockets of his cargo pants. He beat himself harder than Johannsson had beat Henry, and simply with his words.

Words are the worst; I wish language hadn't been invented, (but then of course I, the author wouldn't be able to write this book, and that would suck).

You can regret every little thing you've ever done wrong, but it doesn't change what you've done, sure it makes you feel a little better about yourself, but it certainly doesn't change what you did. Not one bit.

He regretted lying to Jackson and his family about where he was taking them. He regretted throwing the first punch. He regretted even waking up in that mall. He regretted going to such great lengths to find his daughter, which at this point was a lost cause with the bite on his arm. He regretted killing the men on snowmobiles. He regretted killing the dogs, even though they inflicted a self-destructive time limit on his journey. He regretted taking Henry along. He regretted being there.

He stood there, fists solid against the table and teeth clenched. His tired eyelids were closed, and his eyelashes painted his eyebags with shadowed stripes that hung over his lower face. The bite had started to stiffen his arm, he could feel the effects setting in. His head felt like it was swelling and the area around the bite mark felt like it was pulsating.

He tried to fight the thoughts in his head as well as the infection raging in his body. Through all this pain, he still had no clue as to the whereabouts of his daughter. He had no clue how much time he had left, but clearly his time was running out.

~ . ~

The crowd was now especially rowdy, people shouting and gathering close to the Northern seats of the stadium. Jackson began to usher his family and Jade into the center of the crowd. The bullets would have to tear through countless people before reaching them in the center. Jackson's naturally tall stature allowed him to see the front of the crowd, there were several men and women teasing the armed soldiers, trying to make them fire the first shot. They had started throwing things at the gunmen.

Everyone was shoulder to shoulder, packed together like sardines in a tin or rather cattle in a slaughterhouse.

Jade stuck close to the family, the independent part of her wanted to split off and fend for herself, but the nervous part of her chose to stick close to Jackson. She didn't trust him, but she certainly didn't trust anybody else in that huge crowd. Following him was all she could do.

For a split second, the crowd went silent. Jackson didn't know if they had actually gone silent or if it was his ears messing with him, but when the ruckus resumed, it was followed by a spray of gunfire. Nobody knew who fired first, but regardless, the crowd ran forward, climbing the field wall and rushing the nearest soldiers to take their guns.

The men at the front easily overpowered the soldiers and took their rifles, continuing to shoot the surrounding gunmen without a second thought. The combined will of all the men and women in the crowd was too formidable to even try fighting against. They were a tsunami, and the military was a coastal city.

Jackson simply tried to usher his family along with the crowd, he didn't want his loved ones to get trampled in the stampede. Jade grasped Ana's hand as to not get separated. The embrace of a lost daughter and a scared mother.

Snipers above took down several men at the front of the crowd, dropping them as if their lives meant nothing. It was much easier to take a human life if you had no prior knowledge of your victim. If the snipers knew each and every person they were shooting, they'd have thought before pulling the trigger, but we do not live in a perfect world, and we for sure cannot know that many people. The struggle to their freedom was a bloody struggle, one that was surely going to be put to an end soon.

Johannsson had been led out to an overlooking platform in the center isle in the middle of the Western overhang. It was enclosed and every wall was glass, the room was clearly meant for high rollers who attended the games. Each table was polished beautifully and the leather sofas that sat on the edges of the room were all pristinely kept. As if this room specifically hadn't experienced the end of the world.

Him and the soldier who'd alerted him stood there, looking below at the crowd breaking the military lines. Johannsson towered over the soldier on his right, letting out a long sigh of disappointment. He was just as tired of the fighting as anyone else. The gunshots were barely audible within the high roller room.

This stadium was Johannsson's final message to Liv, his plan was to capture any and all Revolutionists and extinguish the flame that had started the rebellion in the first place. Without people, there wouldn't be a cause and without a cause, his opposer would fall. Liv would fall and he would have the city to himself. He wanted to send a message to Liv, but now, his message had no meaning. His prisoners had broken through and truly shown their raw determination.

There was nothing anyone could do against a fighting will, the only thing you can do is let them win, or kill them for wanting to fight, but killing a person simply for fighting back isn't especially dignified.

Liv's voice suddenly blared on the radio that hung from Johannsson's vest. Her voice was louder than he could ever imagine.

"Johannsson, this never had to be a fight, nor did this ever have to be drawn out to this extent. You've already committed several war crimes but this above all is your worst yet, Hitler is in hell smiling at you."

Johannsson spun fast, facing opposite of the soldier that had led him to the room. He unlatched the radio from his chest and started speaking.

"This was supposed to be a message—" His index finger and thumb clasped the bridge of his nose.

"A message? You've been playing the wrong game of cards for a while now; I get that you're not afraid to lose a queen or a jack so long as the king stays in your hand."

"This wasn't about me, not one bit, it was about you. This fight started because of you, I tried to keep the peace."

"You're incompetent and you're a fool. You didn't want to keep the peace, you wanted to be at the top and you didn't care about who you squashed under your boot while getting there." Liv paused. She had brought herself and all of her strongest men in tanks to the stadium, she had the upper hand, and she had more firepower. "Listen, Johannsson, come out here and face what's to come. Your time is over, accept it."

She had to stop and take a deep breath. If she didn't, she'd surely overstep her boundaries.

"I am not coming outside, and I certainly won't die today. If you want me so damn bad, come in here and face me yourself. Bitch."

Johannsson whipped his radio against the wall, smashing it to pieces and directing the soldier to go out and help fight. *"Get out there now, help us win."*

The soldier scurried out of the room like a squirrel running from a dinosaur and shut the doors behind him. This soldier would take the stairs down and arrive a moment too late to catch the crowd. Instead, he ended up in the midst of something else.

Johannsson stood and watched the madness ensue below. He watched his men crumble and fall beneath the stampede of the crowd. There was no stopping them now.

One man had brought the entirety of Minneapolis to the brink of annihilation. Never once did he imagine losing, he figured that it would never become a reality. Yet here Johannsson stood, watching his throne crumble beneath him.

It was all over, and he knew it. He didn't intervene with the fight below, he simply watched it unfold. This was it.

He was quiet while he watched it all fall apart.

~ . ~

Evan lifted his head from its hung position at the sound of gunfire, what possibly could've caused it?

He snatched his big gray coat and threw it over his shoulders, slipping it on and basking in the warmth it provided. The once blue plaid interior was now stained with blood and dirt, the outside of the coat was now scraped up and had multiple tears all around. He had no weapon, not even a blade, the only defense that Evan had was his fists and outwitting nature.

Before exiting the main door, he looked at the room where Henry had made his final resting place. Looking at the door before twisting the knob slowly and leaving the room.

He entered a long winding hallway, stone walls, and bland architecture. The gunfire sounded far above and faint from where he stood. He must've been underground he realized; the audibility combined with the absence of windows led him to that conclusion.

He had to go up, now he just had to find a stairway or a ladder or something.

Evan didn't know what he would face when ascending, but he was ill equipped to deal with whatever would stand in his way. His shoes were still damp from the snow that had melted over them. His skin still felt frozen, but the clothing helped. His right arm was swollen and stiff, and his chest begun to feel rock hard.

The wide hallways made Evan feel insignificant and small, like an ant walking through the vents of a house. The air was still quiet, the place obviously hadn't been heated in months, the place was so innately cold that you could eat ice cream without having to worry about it melting.

After a few minutes of continued gunfire, Evan had finally reached the staircase, situated right next to the trio of elevators. Gripping the handle was like holding dry ice, it was truly painful. The door finally came open and Evan slipped on in.

His sloppy footsteps echoed up the stairs and the sound of gunfire became even louder with Evan's ascension upwards. On his way up, his chest started spazzing, he felt an uncontrollable choking sensation deep in his lungs, like someone had made him eat glass while he was unconscious. It felt like his throat was going to explode.

Evan coughed, spraying red mist onto the railing. As he begun staggering down, he gripped the same bloodied railing to stop himself from falling. He shook up and down, regurgitating the snot and puss from his lungs, puking the blood caked mixture as it left his mouth. His hands trembled and struggled to keep hold of the railing.

Each cough felt like it was ripping his throat to shreds. His lungs felt like a shredded pair of balloons. He was dying, and now his body was making it obnoxiously obvious. The virus was raging through his body, ripping through blood vessels, and slowly making its way to the brain and heart, preparing to take Evan as prisoner to burn in an eternal hell. Soon, the virus would take over Evan's body and disable control over all of his movement, making him melt away into a shell of a person.

He tried to continue up the stairs when his coughing finally started to become less sporadic. He would spit blood globs onto the floor, trying to clear his throat and soothe his burning lungs.

A sign indicated that the first level was ahead when Evan finally reached ground level. Instead of ugly stone walls, there were now vender shops set up everywhere. The amount of advertising was almost suffocating.

The gunfire was so loud now, it seemed to echo around the entire stadium, amplifying its volume. Evan ran out to the first set of seats that he could see, observing the complete and utter chaos. At least a few hundred people were storming up the Northern side of the stadium. Charging the military lines and winning. Several groups of soldiers were descending upon the crowd, ready to kill. Evan was too weak to do anything, even if he wanted to intervene.

People were screaming, either from pain or as a show of might. So many horrific noises were audible, even at Evan's distance. He stood there, leaning on the seat, and watching the fight, same as Johannsson.

The crowd was now progressing upward and into the looping hallway behind the seating. Evan and the crowd of freedom fighters were now a part of the same hallway, just on different ends. From Evan's right, opposite of the direction the crowd had entered, he heard bellowing footsteps, at least half a dozen men were coming his way.

Evan ran and dove behind a tiki themed kiosk that at one point served smoothies to the smoothie loving masses. All the shops were very reminiscent of the mall that Evan had woken up in all those days ago.

The clamor of boots hitting the concrete sped past the kiosk, clearly headed to further distinguish the fight. Evan waited for them to pass before peaking his head out. Even lifting his head was far too much effort for his body to handle. The soldiers had now jogged halfway down the hall and the sound of gunfire had erupted, sounding louder than anything Evan had experienced thus far. It echoed horrifically through the winding hallway and tall stadium walls.

Evan stood up, wanting to head toward the gunfire and see what was going on, he resisted. Standing there, one man in a huge city *split* between two groups. This was the stuff that people prophesized about.

Soon the gunfire had stopped, either all the civilians had been shot or all the soldiers had been defeated.

Either way, Evan started to head down the hallway, toward the previously heard ruckus.

~ . ~

Jackson held his family close, while Ana still maintained Jade's trusting handhold. They were not going to lose Evan's daughter in the crowd, and Jackson certainly wasn't going to lose his family amidst the chaos.

Still maintaining their middle place within the packed crowd, they moved with it, attempting to not get trampled. Gunfire near the front told them that the bravest put themselves on the front lines while the ones who needed protection, hid within. Jackson would try to look around and keep view of the situation. Both sides were losing, but the military was losing way quicker.

As soon as someone at the front was put down, another would grab his firearm and start shooting. Nobody was backing down and nobody was giving up. They had will to fight for and fight for it they will.

Soon they had entered the winding hallway, somewhat out of the cold but still freezing. The crowd barely fit within the hallway, but this meant that the snipers above no longer had a good shot. They used the architecture to their advantage, taking cover behind pillars and shooting from kiosks. They were winning and the soldiers simply didn't have much to fight for compared to their opponents.

They pushed forward, fast, and steady, but the crowd was being thinned out just as quick with people hiding and dispersing amongst cover to hide from the bullets.

Jackson scrambled to decide where to go, ultimately taking his family and Jade to the inside of a hotdog themed fast-food place adjacent from the seating. He leapt through the door and made everyone duck behind the front counter.

Through the gunfire, Ana tried speaking to her husband. "You promised me breakfast in bed!"

Jackson looked down at her, letting out a momentarily blissful smile. "If you can find the eggs... I'll cook them for you," he joked around, trying to make the deadly situation somewhat lighthearted, though just for a moment.

Jade ducked down, close to Matt. They all were simply trying to wait out the violence.

Jade spoke to Matt, an offer to start a friendship despite the current situation. "Did you guys really know my Dad?"

Matt looked at her, almost shocked that she had even spoken to him. He was always timid around girls, so his response was awkward, "Well, yeah."

"Well yeah?" Jade mocked, making fun of his soft voice.

"Yeah," Matt nearly laughed, "Yeah, yeah."

"Yeah, yeah yeah?"

"Yeah yeah," Matt concluded, mocking her back playfully.

This confirmation lifted Jade's spirits. She had it on three accounts now that her Dad was alive. He was somewhere, and she was going to find him. Matt was somewhat shocked that Jade had spoken to him, he hadn't really had a conversation with anyone outside of his immediate family in a long time.

The crowd was now moving forward when the gunfire ceased, people were running to get out.

Jackson ushered his family out, trying to keep up with the fast-paced nature of the mob of freedom fighters. They ran to get back within the crowd but simply couldn't. Suddenly another fight broke out, people at the front shot the new set of soldiers and the people in the back hid and cowered. The people at the front were the true heroes of this battle. Jackson tried to peer above the now dispersed horde, looking upon nearly half a dozen opposed streams of fire, watching the men and women at the front take the soldiers down.

The fight was nearing its end.

When the gunfire stopped once more, the screaming did not. The consistent painful moans of those who had been injured were the only sound left after every soldier had been killed. The mob continued, dragging the injured and heading for the exit of the stadium where Liv was waiting for them.

~ . ~

Evan walked toward where the screaming emanated. Steadily tiptoeing to avoid being mistaken as a soldier. He was a lone man in a huge hallway, nearing a crowd that had fought their way through impossible circumstances.

He felt like a lost boy trying to find his way back home past sundown, walking in the right direction.

Home was ahead. Home was Jade.

With each step, he bogged side to side. Finally, he had reached an intersection that connected the winding hallways to an entry way, or rather an exit way depending on which way you looked at it. The crowd was headed his direction, to freedom. He could feel the walls and floor shaking from the pure number of men and women who had been gathered in the crowd.

He didn't know what was going to happen after he went with the crowd, but he figured that it would be the right move.

Finally, he saw the crowd.

~ . ~

Jackson's family and Jade were barely able to keep pace with the crowd, especially since they'd been hiding far behind and away from the gunfire. For a split second, all was quiet as everyone ran to the exit. This was their way out.

Everyone bolted out of the exit, rushing out and making sure the injured were making their way out all the same.

Through the panic and struggle, Jackson was the first to see him. Then Ana and Matt. They all stopped dead in their tracks as if they had seen a ghost. As if Evan was a phantom haunting them all simultaneously experienced as a conjoined psychosis.

Evan made the same eye contact with all three of them, he had the same look on his face. Like he was staring at a trio of ghosts, but when he saw the face of his daughter, his expression changed from shock to disbelief. She was alive. His journey wasn't for nothing. Henry didn't die for nothing.

Jade was alive and he was looking at *her*.

When Jade's eyes connected with her father's, they made the same expression.

Disbelief.

They couldn't believe that they were looking at one another. It felt fake, like an illusion set up by Evan's ever sick growing brain. His daughter stood just meters from him, and all the pain he'd been through was worth it. Finally, Evan was home.

The crowd had mostly cleared when Evan had taken a step toward his daughter, trying to slowly close the gap that had been made by the outbreak and chaos in the city.

Jade noticed that her Dad looked different, uncut, and far thinner than she remembered him to be.

Jackson and his wife stared at the two of them, who hadn't broken eye contact since they'd connected. Matt had his jaw drop to the floor. It was like seeing an extinct animal in the wild flourishing amongst the nature that surrounded it.

Finally, since leaving for deployment out West, Evan had gotten to see his daughter, the same one he's struggled so hard to find. The same one he loved unconditionally to the end of time. The same one he'd done countless things to find. This was it, he found her.

She looked different than he remembered, her eyes especially. He didn't remember them looking so dim. The Winter had changed her same as it had changed him and all the other souls in the world.

Jackson wanted to hug Evan, after everything that had happened since they *split* on the highway. Not a single bit of hatred or distain was felt toward Evan, not one bit. Ana rejoiced her faith in humanity by seeing the two converge on one another, opening their arms for a hug when suddenly from behind Evan, a stairwell door flung open.

A lone soldier scurried out, expecting to see the crowd but only seeing Evan and the rest. None of them were armed and the soldier was given direct orders to open fire on any and all civilians if the chance was open. It was the same soldier that Johannsson had directed to go and help.

This soldier had no specific hatred toward the Revolutionists or any civilian, he simply did what he was told. The reason he didn't even stop and think about pulling the trigger was the promise of reward for murder. Johannsson had set out a reward system for Revolutionists killed. This soldier simply wanted to be rewarded. For no reason other than coincidence, the soldier descended the very stairway that Evan and the rest were standing close to. He had never seen the family or the father and daughter before in his life, he simply was directed to head down and handle the situation. He didn't stop for a second to rethink his course of action regardless of who he would hurt.

Evan heard the door open and briefly saw the expression on Ana's face, indicating danger. He spun around to face the suspected danger. The soldier stood there momentarily, not necessarily doing anything, just analyzing the situation. He held his gun like a kid holds a stick pretending to be a gun.

The powerful and unstoppable river of time briefly flowed to a stop, offering Evan a chance to run through his options. He didn't utilize this chance at all, he knew what needed to be done so he acted as fast as he could.

Evan bolted to disarm this soldier. Fearing for a bullet to strike either his daughter or any member of Jackson's family. Evan moved quicker than he ever had, like a spider striking its prey.

Evan's sore and brutalized body ached as he headed toward the soldier. If the soldier didn't shoot the man bolting toward him, he would surely die. If Evan didn't attempt to disarm the soldier, then surely, he and the people behind him would be shot to death. It was truly a duel between two men who both didn't want to die. The catch was: one man had more to lose.

Before Evan had reached the soldier, gunshots had sounded, a barrage too quick to count; and nobody saw where the bullets had hit. From Jackson's view, the rifle produced a bright flash, and the loud sound caused his eyes to flinch, simply seeing the flash and then the takedown.

Evan gripped the barrel cage with his left hand and pushed the body of the rifle away from the soldier. He had easily pulled it away, ripping the firearm away from the soldier and tossing it several meters away.

A tense Evan managed to stuff his hand into the soldier's stomach, knocking the wind from him. Evan blocked an attempted counterattack and then struck his opponent once more, making him stagger back and deciding to finally run down the hallway and scurry away like a coward.

After making the soldier run off, Evan stood there, like a statue of a once great leader. He slowly turned around after watching his opponent run down the curved corridor. From behind, Evan didn't look scathed at all, he looked rather clean actually, but when he turned around, presenting his front, everyone gasped.

His shirt was tattered with bullet holes, Jade counted five of them. The wounds had already spouted blood onto Evan's once clean white t-shirt. The bullets clearly hadn't gone through, evident by the unscathed jacket that Evan wore. Nobody had even started crying, they were all simply in shock for the time being. He hadn't even realized that he'd been shot.

He saw the family and his daughter both looking down at his torso region, this made him look too. The sight of his bloodied shirt coupled with the holes in his shirt told him everything he needed to know. Suddenly he went to cough but couldn't. A large bubble made its way up Evan's throat and when it reached the threshold of his mouth, it popped, launching blood from his mouth, and staining his lips red. His original stubble now had droplets of his own blood caught amongst the hairs.

Evan staggered back, seeing things in slow motion as he fell to his butt, leant up against the wall. He tried to stay off the floor but was simply too weak. He was dying.

The group yonder observed Evan struggling to breathe and struggling to stand. They ran to him.

Jade was the first, followed by Jackson who helped hold Evan up.

Jade was silent, still trying to even make sense of what had happened. She did *not* want to experience her father's death a second time. Jackson didn't speak a word; he knew what needed to be done. He slung Evan's arm around his shoulder, trying to move him out of the stadium and out to one of the trucks to be brought to Longfellow. If Jackson were honest, he didn't know why he was trying so damn hard to get Evan out of there. He knew that he wouldn't make it far, of course he knew that, but some deep obligation to Evan and his daughter kept him hoping.

Jade followed along, trying to help Jackson as much as she could while Ana and Matt were there, hands over their mouth shocked. Ana looked like she was going to cry, Matt looked like he was going to lose it.

Even though she tried desperately, Jade made no difference in how much of a struggle it was to try and carry another man. Jackson simply tried speaking to Jade, "Listen, run up and make sure it's clear up there."

Jackson held his friend, trying just as desperately as Jade to help. He wanted his friend to have a happy ending and he wanted his friend to make it. He wanted him and his daughter to *make it*.

Nothing hurt more than seeing a man finally rejoice after so long of suffering, then seeing everything he fought so hard for tarnished by a completely random act of violence. He would not let Evan die there, and certainly not like that.

Ana and Matt followed like angels coming to take Evan away to the clouds above, but angels probably don't exist, and if they did, nobody would've died that day.

Evan knew he wasn't going to make it, that much was clear. He didn't know why they were trying so hard to help him. He tried to move his feet but was only able to drunkenly shuffle them along the floor. He watched as Jade ran ahead to make sure the coast was clear, though Evan knew he wouldn't see the outside of the stadium, he tried to hold on as long as he could, just keeping his eyes open.

Carrying Evan soon became too much of a struggle to keep up with, Jackson started to stagger.

They hadn't even made it to the security gates before Jackson had to let Evan down, laying him against one of the pillars in between the winding hallway and the exit to the outside. They had a clear view onto the baseball field surrounded by the seating and a clouded view out to the triplet of tanks that sat outside that posed as a middle finger in Johannsson's face.

Gunfire was still somewhat erratic, but the only audible thing was Evan's voice. He was telling them to stop and to get out of there, "Get out of here, you guys need to--."

"I know, just stay man," Jackson pleaded.

Jade circled back to her Dad, seeing him leaned up against the pillar with a blood-stained shirt. There was so much she wanted to say to him, so much she wanted to tell him. so many things she wished she could express to him but unfortunately, she was constrained by the ever-flowing river of time. A brutal and unforgiving river that never stopped, not even for your dying father.

He looked up at his daughter, the person he'd put everything on the line for. His eyes winced in the pre-wrinkle fashion, folding the skin on the outer eyelid. His tried to hold a smile when she dropped to her knees to get on the same level as him.

Jackson backed away, letting go of Evan once and for all. Nothing he could do would save his friend. Nothing he could do would lift Evan up and away from that place. Nothing was going to fix the situation.

"Dad…?"

"Yeah?" Evan replied as if no time had passed since he'd last seen her, as if he simply wanted to save the hellos for a later date and simply tell her how much he loved her.

"You know…" she stopped to hold back her reservoir of tears. "I never thought I'd see you again," she wiped her eyes. "I miss your clean-shaven face," she smiled, remembering how goofy his neck looked without the usual stubble that was almost an icon of her father.

"Me too," he smiled with his eyes. "Your hair needs to be brushed out," he teased.

She outstretched her hand to her Dad, taking hold of his and holding it firm. Jade couldn't express everything at once, so it all came out in an embarrassing jumbled mess. So many different words were fused into one goliath sized monstrosity that ended with an extremely fast, "I love you."

"I know, I know," he tried to calm her down, "Sweetie, I know. It's okay, it'll be okay. I found you, that's what matters."

"But Dad... you're... you were shot."

Evan stopped to exhale the hot air that had been cooked in his lungs, "This means I'll always be with you. No matter where you go." He couldn't hold his daughter's hand for long, the firmness in his grip was fading.

Jade didn't think much of the Bible nor the things within it, but she did believe in guardian angels. She believed that each family member who died would become a watchful dove from a powerline, exuding love and clearing a path of safety for her. Evan knew this of course.

"We won't ever lose each other again," he spoke, trying to last long enough to see her smile again.

He tried to cook something up, wanting to see his little girl's trademark smile, the same smile that was like cocaine to him.

"Do you remember that day me, you and Mom went to that trampoline park?"

Jade was initially confused. "Yeah...?" she said, briefly distracted by the tragedy before her eyes.

"I don't think I've ever seen Mom so entertained..." he spoke, recounting an old memory. "God, she would laugh like she was in an asylum."

Jade giggled briefly while Evan reached up to wipe her wet eyes, sliding his thumb across the bottom of her eyelids, clearing the wet skin. "She loved it."

Jade started telling her side of this specific memory, "You remember how she'd almost pee herself when she laughed like that." Jade giggled, thinking it was hilarious, same as her Dad.

The two giggled, thinking of the same memory. Evan did as Henry had told him, remembering the good times. Jade chirped in, now almost forgetting to cry, "I know you remember that time on that lagoon—" before even finishing, Evan knew what she was going to say.

"When I got a leech on my nose?" he calmly chuckled.

"Yeah!" She said, "Then you flipped out like it was a snake or something." Jade hadn't realized how much she missed her Dad during his absence.

"I had no clue what the heck it was—" Evan smiled, despite facing his end. He smiled because he got to see her before checking out, because he got to see her smile one last time. The two reminisced about the time before everything got so complicated, before they were taken from each other by circumstances out of their control. Before the end of their world.

Before the split.

Jackson had looped around and stood between his wife and son, hoping that the two of them knew how much he loved them. You truly never get to tell people how much they really mean to you until you run out of time to do so. Ana loved the man she married, even though he wasn't the strongest knight in the kingdom, he was gentle and caring in ways that were as transparent as the air that cycled through their lungs. Matt loved his father, though they often fought over sour cream and onion chips, he knew that his father would do anything for him, like giving him leftover sour cream and onion chips.

The family observed the last moments between a father and his daughter.

For a few seconds, the world revolved around Evan and Jade. Encapsulating and recapping every single memory they'd ever made. Things were coming to an end, Evan knew that he couldn't hold on much longer, he found himself struggling to keep his eyes open. His weak heart was having trouble maintaining the flow of blood. While Jade was reminding him of every unimaginably wholesome memory, Evan reached into his pocket, pulling the folded family portrait, and offering it to Jade.

"Listen, you need to keep this... I need you to remember what me and Mom look like."

Jade had paused her story about something or other and glanced at the family portrait. Her Dad spoke again, "I won't need it where I'm going."

Evan handed it to her while looking at his wife in the picture, seeing her face one last time before leaving this world. His beautiful wife and her long black hair, the pale skin and vampire eyes. He loved her and he missed her deeply.

Jade took the picture, seeing her Dad's clean-shaven face and her Mom's ever so pretty smile. Then, Jade looked at herself in the photo, her happy face was almost enough to start up the tear factory once again. She never thought she'd be happy again but being able to talk to her Dad one last time and sharing all their best memories was enough to make her feel the way she did when that picture was taken.

Evan reached down again to his cargo pants pocket, pulling a battered and old stuffed animal. It was the same stuffed bunny rabbit that Jade would take with her to sleep, the same one that she couldn't leave the house without when she was a kid. Bunny-FuFu, her childhood stuffed animal, her only true best friend. She now held the photo and her stuffed animal, looking at both at the same time. Her Dad obviously took these from their home in Elba and brought them all this way.

Jade looked back at her Dad, telling him everything she needed to tell him simply with how her eyes connected with his. He understood what she had to say and understood that there simply wasn't enough time to tell him everything she needed to say.

He nodded with his now pale face, "Sweetie?"

She looked at him the same way a dog looks at someone holding a treat.

"Yeah Dad?"

"I want you to go with Jackson and his family... he's a good man and his family are good people. I want you to go with them, they're the only decent people left that I trust."

She looked at the family then back her Dad, afraid but understanding. Evan called Jackson over with his ever-quieter voice. He walked over to see what he had to say.

He reached his right hand out for a handshake, Jackson met the same energy, but Evan pulled him close. "You're a good guy,

Jackson. I shouldn't have brought your family here—" before Evan could finished, Jackson argued.

"It's okay, Evan. I understand."

Evan stopped, almost like he was at a loss of words. Like his train of thought was derailed. Jackson understood why Evan did what he did.

Evan handed Jackson a small piece of paper, carrying on what Henry had given him. "Take this, make it someday."

Jackson smiled at the tattered sheet, swiftly reading through it, and recognizing it as a tattered pizza sauce recipe.

"Take care of her, I know you will. Thanks for everything Jackson."

These words would stick with Jackson for the rest of his life.

Ana and Matt stood there, ready to embrace Jade into their family and care for her just like Evan wished he could.

Jackson shook Evan's hand. The two were brothers.

Jade returned to her father, seeing his dry lips and pale face, she leaned down for a hug, wishing that she didn't have to say goodbye but knowing that she had to. She wrapped her arms around her Dad one final time. Evan could barely raise either of his arms, but he tried, he was barely able to fold his arms around her, but luckily was able to embrace her.

"Now, you be good for Jackson, okay?" Evan said, hoping to lighten the mood. He didn't want to see his daughter cry, so he asked her not to. "Don't cry, just think of all the good." It was something that Evan's grandma used to say to him when she'd have to go back home after the Holidays. Now those words found themselves being used through a different way. Telling his daughter not to cry, to simply remember the good times.

"You're my girl…" he said as he moved his hand from her back to her head, trying to calm her tears. She wanted to respond in so many different ways but not a single word fit how she was feeling.

"I love you Dad," her shaking voice muttered to him.

"I love you too."

Love above all was the most powerful thing. It is the only emotion known that can make you exhibit all the rest, joy, generosity, jealousy, hatred, bliss, pleasure. The only emotion that Evan felt however, was security. He felt secure knowing that his daughter was safe with Jackson and in the end, he found his little girl. That was all that mattered.

Jade experienced the other side of love, the somber side. She felt loss, she felt tragedy, she felt alone again.

It felt like Jade would never let go but then, she did. Her arms released and she pulled away. Evan's arms released next, slowly falling to the spot where he sat. That hug was the final embrace between a father and his daughter. The final event in the life that they had shared.

Evan knew that this was it. He went to speak one last time, one final message to the most special girl in his world.

"I'll always be up there, watching over you."

He gestured to the sky and finally set his eyes on Jade.

"Always," he concluded.

She didn't say anything after that, she simply gave him the daughterly look as to let him know that he'd done a good job. That he did his part in raising her. She knew that he wouldn't be able to go on, but she understood that if he could stand, they'd already be halfway back to Longfellow by now.

Evan smiled back at his daughter, presenting his developing wrinkles under the shade of overcast daylight.

Ana offered her hand to Jade, which she took. The family began to walk away, Jackson and Jade were the only two people looking back at Evan as they approached the exit. Though far away now, they could tell that he was looking back at them.

His blue eyes spoke a lullaby.

Safety and tranquility. The orgasm of death was upon him, and he was ready for it. A man who had been fighting since this story started had finally achieved his goal. He was happy with that. He accepted his fate and soon, his daughter nor the family could be seen from where he lay. He found peace in the end.

They all found peace in knowing that Evan got to speak to his daughter before facing his end. Jade found peace in knowing that her Dad would now join her Mom in the task of being her guardian angels.

Evan closed his eyes as he thought back on every single second since Jade was born. Every joyous memory from before the apocalypse. He smiled as he took his last breath.

Evan was finally free of any burden or pain he'd experienced along his journey. He was free, knowing that his daughter was safe, and he was free knowing that she knew how much he loved her.

He could finally rest.

Epilogue

The city remained in a state of disarray.

Much didn't change after everyone was evacuated from the stadium. There was still violence, and the military was still present. Liv eventually rushed into the stadium to look for Johannsson after the crowd had left, but nobody ever heard if she'd found him or not. He could've died or he could very well still be alive, people were too scared to ask her of course.

There were rumors about whether or not she found him, but all died quickly or were simply too farfetched to be believed by anyone. Life never resumed as usual in Minneapolis. Even though the Revolutionists had won in the end and the military had no Leader, people still fought. Whether it be over resources or territory, none of the two factions ever reached a state of peace. People like Liv never left and people like Jackson fled out of the city as soon as he could, bringing his family and the daughter of his friend.

The entire rest of the country was just as divided as Minneapolis was, if not more. The coasts were hit the hardest by the virus and the military was deployed to the places that needed it the most, but of course, those are stories for another day.

The Spring was worse than the Winter had been. Mud made travel near impossible, and food was about as scarce as seeing new people. Matt and Jackson hadn't had sour cream and onion chips in months. Though it was getting warmer, Jackson noticed that in the warmth, those creatures became more agile than before. Almost like the cold had limited their true ferocity.

All four of them made it through the Spring and now had to reduce their snow gear to t-shirts and shorts for the humid Minnesotan summer that was to come. Jackson and Jade would often speak about Evan while Ana and Matt would listen. Jade blended rather nicely with the family despite never meeting them before.

Tragedy often times bring people closer than they'd ever think was possible.

The group didn't find a permanent place to stay until about mid-Summer when they stumbled upon a ranch far North of the city, secluded from all the evil in the world. The ranch was nice and open with the sky above them cascading the crisp blue for miles. The tall pines surrounded the property like buildings surround city streets. The forest around the farm was dense and lush with wildlife and flora.

The house had enough rooms for everyone to have their own personal space and down the road was a small town, big enough to last them years down the line. A town with enough resources to provide sustainability.

Jackson found himself learning to play the harmonica in his free time while Jade picked up the ability to play guitar. The instruments were just lying around of course, so how could they resist? Matt learned to hunt while Ana learned to knit. However, they all learned how to communicate, despite only knowing each other for a few months.

They tried to grow a small garden, but it proved to be more challenging than algebra in high school. Because you can obviously cheat a math test, but you cannot cheat nature.

Soon, another Fall began with the pines remained a natural rich green while the oaks were being painted fire orange and blood red with their magnificent vibrancy. The Fall was quick, and the Winter came around just as fast as it had last year. The first blizzard snowed them in for about a week, but in their boredom, they attempted to recreate the pizza sauce recipe that Evan had given Jackson.

They didn't have all the ingredients, but they came close enough. Soon they all found themselves drooling over the most perfectly put together pizza they had ever eaten. It was near incomparable to anything they'd had before.

At times, they even managed to enjoy some hot cocoa.

Occasionally, the weather became tolerable enough for Jackson to sit outside and play the harmonica in rhythm with Jade's guitar. Sometimes the two would try to make a song. They could never find the right keys or the right chords to make their vision complete, so they settled on simply playing what felt right when it felt right.

When the next Spring came around, Matt and Jade had spent quite a lot of time getting to know each other during the Winter. You know where it went from there of course. The two were good for one another and Evan would've thought highly of Matt if he were there.

Things were looking up despite the previous Winter.

Ana would manage to scribble down a few unorganized sentences regarding each day that passed, also doodling whatever shy and lanky image that would come to mind. It was the only record the family kept.

The situation was comfortable for all of them.

~ . ~

Every day, Jade would try to go outside and see a bird. Whether it was a raven or a cardinal, she would find one… and when she did, she would follow it.

Almost like a lost dog.

These birds that she would find reminded her of her Dad, but one instance in particular stood out among this daily ritual of hers. One day she found herself face to face with an eagle. Not a normal eagle either, one that had been through hell and one that was old. It seemed as if it stood in the same place for too long it might become a statue. She followed this eagle for at least a few miles where it lead her to a hill that overlooked the Mississippi River.

She saw the river stretch from one end of the planet to the other, connecting the Northern horizon with the Southern one. Long enough to fit every single person on the planet. Mighty pines stood atop distant hills and offered shelter from the sun who never took a day off.

That hill overlooked everything. The eagle often retired from a long day's work to sit atop a dead tree's skeleton and gaze at the view. Though Jade enjoyed the view, she started stacking rocks, dozens of them until it was piled to her knees. The pile would be there until it was eroded away but that would be long after the hill was no longer a hill anymore. She knew that this pile would sit there and experience the same view every day until the end of time.

At the end of the day, just before the sun sunk below the West horizon, the eagle fell from its resting place and onto the pile of rocks. Jade stared at the eagle as if she had seen her Dad die for a third time. The bird was with her all day, watching her stack rocks. The eagle hadn't moved an inch, it was watching over her.

When it fell from its perch, Jade didn't know what to do. It almost made tears appear. So, she picked up the once ferocious and noble bird that symbolized freedom and placed it against the rock pile, facing West toward the sunset and toward the river.

The river of time that never stopped flowing.

Jade sat there for a moment, dirtying her pair of jeans as she did so. She stared out at the entire world and finally, she could rest knowing her Dad was always with her.

It had been a long time since she'd felt that kind of warmth in her chest, the kind that makes tears build up in your eyes and goosebumps appear on every inch of your skin. The kind of warmth that's present only when you and a loved one depart for some time, only being reunited at last.

Every waking second since the *split* was spent hoping for change, hoping for a better way to live.

Finally, Jade had found it.

A word.

Here I sit, in the coffee shop on Main, having one of the most kick-ass mochas in the world.

Finally putting an end to years of work.

It's sad honestly, saying goodbye to the characters I've known for so long and passing on a story that until this point, has been known only by me and a couple of select friends and family members. Passing my story on and publishing this book has brought tears to my eyes, warmth to my heart, and gratitude to those who've been there for me while working on this project.

I love all who've encouraged me to keep writing and all who've told me they can't wait to read this thing. All who helped me revise and edit my messy grammar. You guys are awesome, and I couldn't describe the emotion I feel while writing this final statement.

I'm already working on a new project to someday publish, and I cannot wait to pass that story on as my own in the next couple years. Though it won't be about any of the characters you've just read about, or the world I stitched them into, you can bet that it'll be just as thrilling as this book (if not more).

The only sneak-peek I will offer here is this: The next story deals with how the characters influence the story, instead of the story influencing the characters. Oh, and it will be about hobos.

I want to thank you (the reader) one last time. It means the world to me that you picked this up and read through my work.

Thank You. You're Cool.

-Kyle

Take it easy.

ISBN: 979-8-9863474-1-7

Paperback edition #2

Made in the USA
Columbia, SC
29 July 2022